HEAD COUNT

HEAD COUNT

BRIAN DUFFY

G. P. PUTNAM'S SONS
New York

G. P. Putnam's Sons
Publishers Since 1838
200 Madison Avenue
New York, NY 10016

Library of Congress Cataloging-in-Publication Data

Duffy, Brian.
Head count / Brian Duffy.
p.   cm.
ISBN 0-399-13669-X
I. Title.
PS3554.U31916H43   1991   91-13024 CIP
813'.54 — dc20

Printed in the United States of America
1   2   3   4   5   6   7   8   9   10

For Jo

To Esther Newberg, who makes things happen,
and to Neil Nyren, who makes things better. Much better.

HEAD COUNT

ONE

AFTERWARDS, evidencing a fine if unusual sense of precision, nearly everyone in Fado referred to it as the head of Vladimir Lenin. Someone had liberated it from the rest of the body and left it under a mopani tree on a busy stretch of Avenida Vladimir Lenin. Hence the eponym.

The rest was not quite so straightforward.

"Filthy," Cecelie said to the head. She was the first of the coconut ladies to arrive that morning. It was just past five. "Filthy goddamn thing."

The mopani marked the coconut ladies' regular place of business, a dirt strip between one of the city's last good curbstones and a disintegrating sidewalk that had long since ceded victory to the tree's shallow killer roots. It was that way everywhere in Fado, the capital in pretty much name only. In this particular turf war, the mopani had been a formidable avant-garde. Behind it, in an endless web of splintered sidewalk, bright and hardy flora had learned to thrive, transforming Fado's once-handsome walkways into a kind of furry mosaic. Unplanned, like nearly everything else in the country, the sidewalks were among Fado's most charming features. Some people thought so, anyway.

Gub didn't especially agree with the view. Tall and fair-haired, with a spreading paunch, Humberto Gub III was a hard man to miss in Fado, his loping gait distinguishable a half-block away. He carried the extra weight with an athlete's grace, but at 220 he was an easy 40 pounds over his playing weight. At six two he had been a short forward on the Cape Town club team. In the style of Bill Bradley, Gub told himself, though he had never actually seen Bradley play. That was all ancient history, however.

A long time ago.

There were more than a few people in Fado who had learned the hard way that the detective's long silences were at least a little misleading. He was a decent man, honest, and a fair police officer: that was the generally held view. His own was somewhat less charitable. He was usually inclined to do the right thing, he thought, but only because it kept the number of possible complications to a minimum. What he lacked, he thought, was constancy. And most evenings he pretty much left it at that.

In the recounting of the discovery of the head of Vladimir Lenin, Cecelie had left nothing out. "Focking head," she had said, over and over again. Giggling.

"Take it from the top," Gub had told her. "Nice and slow."

It turned out the head of Vladimir Lenin was sitting upright on a piece of sidewalk shaped more or less like a parallelogram, the asphalt reduced to fine dust in one corner where tufts of yellowweed blazed. By the time Gub had gotten there, the tips of the shoots were still plastered with dew against the pebbled concrete. Blood from the head had leaked onto several, staining them ocher. Red ants in column formation had begun an ascent of the neck. Cecelie said she had stared at the head for a while. Weird the way it seemed to stare back, she said. One lid, the left, had drooped closed. The right one was wide open, though, and the head of Vladimir Lenin, as Cecelie recalled it, seemed to be winking at her. A bit presumptuously, she thought.

Cecelie was the oldest of the three women who earned what passed for a living cracking coconuts against the curbstone and selling the sweet meat to city children and passing motorists. There were no tourists in Fado anymore.

With its broad beaches reaching north from Fado, a wide white band separating the deep blue of the Indian Ocean to the east and the bottle green that spread west into the interior, the country should have been more prosperous. Before the troubles that had convulsed so much of the sub-Sahara, it had been a place of some hope. For a few years, it had shined, a beacon, a way out from the cramped lanes and crooked alleys of Europe. An empty corner of a continent on a glittering and abundant ocean, it had gleamed, a chance. Disenfranchised, so many had left Europe in those early years before World War II, not so much because they had known that the war was coming, but because they could anticipate only the painful constraints of the *rentier* or the specter of starvation-wage poverty. The lucky ones, those who had left in time, refused to forget the Old World, however. In the cut curbstones and fancy city plans of Fado, in the aped designs of architects from Lisbon, Barcelona and Paris, was a fierce allegiance to a boiling continent that no longer had room or use for them. If it was sentimentality, Gub thought, it was strange, and more than a little bit schizophrenic.

By the time he got to the coconut ladies' place on Vladimir Lenin, the traffic was already building, drivers navigating without headlights. Replacements were nearly impossible to come by, and car owners, the few who ventured out after dark, saved the headlamps for Fado's back streets where potholes like craters regularly shattered the suspensions of Land-Rovers and the big four-wheel-drive Mitsubishis.

"Who is it?" Elena asked Gub. Younger and prettier than Cecelie and Maria-Louisa, she was the last of the coconut ladies to arrive each morning. Elena came from north up the beach a few miles south of the Costa do Sol, where she lived in a tin hut fashioned from part of a construction trailer—before construction of the big new beach hotel had been abandoned. Elena pleaded the long trip, walking and hitching rides down the ocean road from the far outskirts of the capital. The coconut ladies blamed a worthless husband none had ever met.

"Too long in the bed again, sweet Elena."

She ignored Cecelie's gibe. "Who is it?" she asked again.

Gub said nothing, examining the head. Someone had taken great pains to shave it, an expert's job; even the eyebrows were gone. The nose was broad, flattened in the middle and tipped down at the end, as if its owner had once taken a bad fall. The lips were unremarkable, but a few shiny white teeth poked out of the left side of the mouth. The right eye, brown and clear, stared straight ahead.

Gub studied the head. "Focking head." The coconut ladies had nothing useful to tell him about the head of Vladimir Lenin, Gub was sure of that. He wasn't quite so sure about Matthias, though.

Shortly after finding the head on the sidewalk, Cecelie told Gub, she had discovered Matthias standing in the gloom under the mopani and sent him hustling to Gub's house. "Ma-tee-us," she had ordered, "go, run find Gub." She had had no doubt he knew the way; everyone knew where the detective's place was.

Gub had greeted the boy, rubbing his eyes and standing in the open doorway of his ground-floor flat, in his glen-plaid pajama bottoms and the Celtics T-shirt he had picked up with Mireles in Boston. Like nearly everyone else in Fado, Gub knew Matthias wouldn't open his mouth and form words like normal people. The kid didn't talk.

Gub had learned that three months before. He even remembered the date. It had been October 4, four years to the day after Teresa's death, almost fifteen since Mireles had left Fado for good. Gub and Mireles had been best friends since childhood; Teresa he had known for just slightly more than the three years they had been married. Now she was dead, and that, Gub thought, brushing the lead ants from the column on the side of Vladimir Lenin's face and letting his mind run lazily from the head on the broken sidewalk to Matthias to Mireles to Teresa and back to the head again, was pretty much that.

Using one of his good handkerchiefs to grab the head, Gub wondered briefly what Mireles would think of Matthias. No doubt the FBI instructors at Quantico would have frowned on roping a seven-year-old orphan into an investigation of a shaved and severed head, but then, Gub thought, picking the head up carefully with both hands, the FBI never worked in a place like Fado. Work with what you got, Gub thought. Setting the head carefully in a cardboard box that usually held jumper cables and a jumble of tools, Gub climbed slowly into the high-sprung Toyota jeep, waving goodbye to Cecelie and the other coconut ladies.

"Well," the detective said, buckling Matthias into the passenger seat next to him, "you know about this focking head?"

Matthias smiled gnomishly and fiddled with the radio.

"Some help you are." Easing the Land Cruiser onto Vladimir Lenin, Gub headed west across the center of Fado, to the new embassy district and Betty Abell's flat. It was too early to go to the department, and besides, Gub thought, his mind still idling, recalling the first time he had met Matthias, Betty had a way with the boy.

In a way, in fact, if it hadn't been for Matthias and his strange silence, Gub and Betty Abell would probably have never gotten together.

On the morning of October 4, Gub had planned to go out to the cemetery near the port to put flowers on Teresa's grave, but instead he had found himself in a cluttered alley behind the Okavango, the ugly state-owned hotel across from the cathedral, trying to make conversation with Matthias. The Okavango's day manager had called Gub at home an hour before to report that one of the hotel's "guests"—the way the deskman said it indicated the man had not enjoyed the highest esteem of management—had had an unfortunate accident the night before. The victim, Gub discovered, was a Danish seaman who, having consumed more of the Okavango's bad beer than was good for anyone, had wound up insulting a hotel employee, the employee's mother or the charms of the employee's latest girlfriend; the details were not clear. Gub, as usual, had had very little to go on. No one had seen or heard anything, it seemed, despite the fact that the sailor had been stabbed repeatedly with what must have been a very dull blade.

"You see anything around here last night?" Gub had asked Matthias.

Accelerating as he turned north onto the four-lane coast road, Gub remembered that the boy had been wearing the same clothes then as now, black shorts with no belt and an outsized Shell service station attendant's shirt with the name "Angelo" stenciled on the breast, red against a white oval. Cecelie, always a useful source of gossip in the capital, had told Gub about Matthias months before, and Betty had filled him in on what few other details there were to be had. Somehow, though, for as much time as he spent on the streets of what was, after all, a pretty small city, Gub had never met the boy before.

Having tried and failed to get word one out of Matthias behind the hotel, Gub had been completing his inspection of the alley when he'd noticed the boy standing near a double row of gray plastic laundry carts tapping one of them with a stick that was just about as long as he was tall. He had wandered over. "What's here, Matthias?"

With his stick, the boy had hit the third cart in the row of five. Gub had pulled it out.

Matthias had then poked the cart against the hotel wall behind it.

Gub had pulled that out, too, and against the base of the wall, protected from the morning sun by the heavy gray cart, the gravel pavement had still been wet where it had been sluiced with what looked like soapy water. It was loose gravel, and there were several uneven patches stained darker than the rest. It could have been oil or some other automobile fluid, Gub thought.

Or it could have been blood.

With Betty's help later that morning in the Save the Children office on Vladimir Lenin, Gub had pulled the story slowly out of Matthias. Actually, as he recalled it now, swinging the Toyota Land Cruiser into a spot at the curb next to her building, Gub had done very little at all. Betty had given Matthias crayons and a stack of drawing paper, and after a while, with Betty asking the questions, Matthias had begun drawing, slowly and clumsily, it was true, but very deliberately.

It had taken nearly thirty minutes before he finally stopped, and Gub remembered there were seven sheets in all. He had been unable to make heads or tails out of any of them.

Gub had given Betty some background on the dead Dane, most of the little he knew. He had given the boy's drawings to her, and she had looked at them for at least a full minute. He still remembered the green eyes welling with tears. "Fuck," she had said, low and angry.

Even now he was stunned by it, not the word so much but the force behind it. To look at Betty Abell, a slender chestnut brunette with perfect teeth and quick emerald eyes, Gub wouldn't have figured her for the swearing type. Twenty-eight, the owner of a newly minted master's degree in child psychology from the University of Chicago, she had been in Fado all of six months, and she was ferocious in her dedication to the kids she worked with at Save the Children, and driven nearly to distraction by the long odds they had to beat just to survive. For sure, Gub thought, she did not look like the kind of girl who had grown up using swear words around the club pool in East Grand Rapids. But then what did he know?

"What's the matter?" he had asked, the scene playing out in his head again, sitting back in the Toyota as Matthias slid a Rolling Stones cassette into the tape deck, Gub wondering whether it was still too early to try Betty's bell. It was not yet six.

The little cameraman in his head rolled the tape for maybe the thousandth time, Gub thinking how much better he liked Mick's version of "Just My Imagination" than the Temps, gears slipping and missing somewhere inside him, reels running as the little cameraman reversed and fast-forwarded at Gub's unspoken commands. In the Save the Children office, with Matthias's stick-figure drawings on the table and Betty Abell's plosive anger like a punch, Gub had felt ... what? Energy, desire? Whatever it was, it had felt good, strange muscles unlimbering after long years of disuse.

"Roll tape, little man," Gub said to himself, the Stones' jive Motown far away, the slow dissolve ending finally in a long exterior shot of the little office on Vladimir Lenin, Matthias, Betty and himself to one side of the room near a desk.

"This is a fucking six-year-old boy, a six-year-old boy!" The words hissed, Gub remembered that. "Do you know what kind of life he's living out there?"

"The same kind they're all leading. Besides, he's seven. What about the drawings?"

A tear squeezed out of one eye, and Betty rubbed it away. "What time did you say this murder, or whatever, happened?"

"I didn't. But if I had to guess, I'd say it was sometime after ten. That's when the bar at the hotel shuts down."

Matthias, ignoring them both, had lined up the crayons end-to-end on the little desk: yellow, purple, blue, red, black.

Waving the sheaf of drawings vaguely at Gub, Betty had explained, or tried to. "What these mean is that Matthias—this six-year-old boy, or seven or whatever—was roaming the streets sometime last night, presumably after ten. God knows what he was doing. Looking for a place to sleep or for something to eat, probably. And somehow this six-year-old boy found himself behind the hotel in the dark, where he watched as a man was stabbed to death. That is what these fucking drawings mean."

Mick and the boys were easing into "Wild Horses" when the little man let the tape flicker black to gray as Gub rubbed his eyes, staring vacantly out the jeep's dirty windshield. He knew well enough how it had ended. Unbuckling Matthias from the passenger seat and locking the door, Gub remembered how Betty had coached the boy into working up some more stick-figure drawings, thirteen in all.

The second batch, under Betty's sharper questions, had been better than the first. Betty had deciphered for Gub. Behind the hotel, someone had left a jumble of clothing in one of the gray plastic carts. The shirts and pants were all big—Matthias had tried some of them on. Then he had turned a cart on its side against the hotel wall, covered himself up with the clothes and gone to sleep. Betty guessed the noise must have woken him up sometime later.

One drawing showed what had happened to the luckless Dane. It had what looked to Gub like a lot of intersecting lines in a shade the Crayola people called ultra yellow. Gub still had it tacked to the living room wall in his apartment. He didn't follow it exactly, but according to Betty, the drawing showed two men dressed alike—the row of vertical purple X's along the two longer yellow lines indicated a uniform of some type. One had had a knife—that was the long blue thing protruding from one of the yellow sticks with the purple X's. The black stick on the ground, Gub remembered Betty saying, was the Danish guy getting the business end of the yellow sticks' blue knife.

Pressing the buzzer to Betty's fourth-floor apartment and holding Matthias by the hand, Gub thought the rest of the investigation had taken longer than it should have; Mireles would have had it nailed much faster. Bluffing and intimidating, though, Gub had persuaded one Okavango busboy to finger another. The bloodstains in the gravel had matched up perfectly with the Danish seaman. That had helped. Confronted, the second busboy had accused his accuser, and when all was said and done, the bullshit and gunsmoke cleared away, the first busboy had agreed to plead guilty to a charge of manslaughter. The second was convicted by a magistrate of second-degree murder. Gub never did get a good fix on the motive; the two busboys had told wildly conflicting stories. But who cared? he thought. It was just like the old days. Or almost anyway. The fact was that nowadays, even when he was lucky enough to come up with what he thought was enough evidence for a conviction, almost none of Fado's murder investigations resulted in trials, let alone prison terms. Murder and mayhem were too commonplace in the country, and there was little will among the few honest magistrates left in the capital for trying and jailing violent spouses, jealous lovers, barroom brawlers or the odd highwayman who got a bit carried away. Gub investigated, then filed a report. And for longer than he had cared to admit, that had pretty much been fine with him. Old Gub, he thought, go along, get along.

Until the day in the Save the Children office.

"Who is it?" Betty's voice was sleep-fogged over the intercom.

"It's me," Gub said. "And my silent partner."

"Christ." Betty Abell punched the buzzer that unlocked the elevator gate. "What time is it?"

As the elevator bumped its way the four floors, Gub wondered how even the good neighborhoods in Fado had turned into such dumps. When he was a kid, it all used to be much nicer, even the downtown parts. Betty's building housed mainly ex-pats now. With the ridiculous exchange rate, they could afford the best places in Fado. But why couldn't anyone keep them painted anymore, keep the pool cleaned? Outside hallways ran the length of Betty's building, and Gub noted the mildew blotches blooming in batik swirls from the rough-troweled concrete. He had no doubt the cement had been mixed with salt water, fresh being harder to come by and therefore more expensive. He gave the building another five years before serious structural problems developed, seven by the time the rich folks left and the squatters moved in. Seven years, Gub thought. A hell of a lot could happen in that time.

Matthias was humming when Betty poked her head out of 4H. She had run a brush through her shoulder-length hair, Gub saw, and splashed some water on her face. But she hadn't had time to dress. She was wearing a long tank top with a logo advertising expensive French sunglasses, and Gub noticed as they followed her into the apartment's living room, gray dawn slanting through dirty glass doors, that that was all she was wearing.

"Nice jammies," he said.

"You want coffee or you want to make jokes?"

"Coffee'd be good," Gub said. "For my partner, too, if you don't mind. He loves a good cup first thing in the morning."

Betty ignored him, spilling Folgers crystals into three cups while the kettle on the gas range sputtered to life. "Matthias," Betty said, kneeling to look at him and squeezing his skinny shoulders, "we're going to give you some breakfast and a bath today, so you start the day off right for once."

Matthias squirmed away, Gub winking at him.

Fishing a box of Special K from a cupboard, and a banana from a bowl on the counter on the other side of the galley kitchen, Betty fixed two bowls, slicing the banana on top and adding milk. "I know you don't want any or I would have asked," Betty said. "What's he humming anyway?"

"The Stones, I think. We had 'em on in the car."

Betty hoisted Matthias into one of three tall chairs at the counter, Gub admiring what he thought of as her country-club thighs as they disappeared into the T-shirt. On the back it said "Mad for the Maldives." Taking the chair next to Matthias, Betty ate hungrily as the water boiled and Gub watched. "Nutrition," she said after about a minute, around a mouthful of cereal and banana. "Something you wouldn't know about. What are you up to with Matthias anyway?"

"Heads," Gub said. "Cecelie found one when she came to work this morning. Severed at the neck. Matthias came to get me, and we were driving around with the head in the truck and thought we'd stop by."

"Nice," Betty said, around some more Special K. "Did Matthias have to look at it, the head?"

"I think he saw it, yeah."

"Shit. Who was it?"

"Cecelie calls it Vladimir Lenin. Which reminds me, can I use your phone?"

In the American police shows he was so fond of, Gub marveled at the seeming efficiency of things. A starched sergeant behind a big desk directed traffic from jail cells to interrogation rooms, detectives broke cases with winking green computer screens, and a pretty dispatcher kept patrolmen in radio cars on the tails of fleeing suspects, enabling them to make screaming, heart-stopping arrests just before the commercial breaks. On the local channel in Fado, which still worked most of the time, Gub got *Kojak* and *Hawaii Five-O* two nights a week. From the small satellite dish he and three neighbors had gone in on, each stealing a piece of the signal by splicing into the coaxial-band cable at the base, he got a bunch of other shows from Johannesburg. *Hill Street Blues* was his favorite.

The capital police department Gub worked for had no starched sergeants, no winking computers and certainly no pretty dispatchers deploying fleets of sleek radio cars. What it had was Gub, the chief of detectives and, for all intents and purposes nowadays, the only detective. He got more calls on the answering machine next to his bed at home than he did at the office, and he was curious to see whether anyone had called yet about the head of Vladimir Lenin. Leaving a severed head on Fado's main thoroughfare where the coconut ladies set up shop each day could mean one thing only: whoever did it wanted to make sure the word spread far and wide, and quickly.

Gub wondered if Carlos had heard about the head and hoped that he hadn't. A thin-lipped consumptive whose nylon shirts were damp at the armpits at all times of the day, the better parts of which he spent in the air-conditioned bar of the Okavango, Carlos was Fado's police chief. Beer and A.C. were provided to the chief courtesy of the hotel management, which figured, Gub thought. The government

owned and ran the place, and it was the government, or more specifically, Carlos's uncle, the works minister, Mr. Eduardo Abulbacar
Sultan, who had gotten Carlos the job as chief of the tiny police
force. As sinecures went, it wasn't much. But it wasn't too bad either,
Gub thought, punching his number into the Touch-Tone in Betty's
bedroom, considering Carlos didn't know shit about police work.

As if confirming a bad dream, Carlos's voice came across the line
into Gub's ear. "Where the hell are you? Call me. It's Calamidades."

That, too, figured. Murder or rape of an ordinary citizen wouldn't
have been enough to disturb Carlos this early. It had to be official,
and Calamidades, as the Department for the Prevention and Combat
of Natural Calamities was known, carried about as much official
clout as any agency of the government. More, probably. Certainly,
Gub thought, it was the only part of the government that ever
seemed actually to accomplish anything.

Gub dialed Carlos at home.

"Where the hell have you been?" Carlos began, interrupting himself almost immediately. "Never mind, listen. Calamidades," Carlos
said, working his way into things, "has a head in the front entranceway. On a piece of fucking waxed paper, if you can believe that. So it
wouldn't drip all over the new tile, I guess. Thoughtful, right?"

Gub said nothing. It was useless talking to Carlos most any time
of day; this early made no sense whatsoever. Gub wondered whether
Carlos had started drinking yet.

"There are people already outside the building," Carlos continued,
"just standing outside the fucking building. A janitor finally went in
a while ago and got on the elevator. You know what happened?"

Gub said that he didn't.

"There was another fucking head in the elevator."

Three heads and counting, Gub thought, scribbling on a notepad
on Betty's night table, not missing Emerson Allsworth's name and
home number in the upper left-hand corner. Gub decided not to tell
Carlos yet about the head on Vladimir Lenin. It would only upset
him.

"I want you to get over there now," Carlos was saying. He was
calming down a little. "Make a show of collecting evidence, talk to
all the Calamidades people you can find, have someone from the
department taking notes and make sure they're typed up afterwards.
I want a report for the minister by this afternoon. And Gub," Carlos
said, "no typos this time."

"No typos," Gub agreed.

"Well," Carlos said finally, "whaddya think?"

"You know what I think." The government had been fighting a seesaw battle for years with a loosely organized but apparently well-financed insurgency. With slash-and-burn terror tactics, they gained, then lost, huge parts of the interior. But they had never managed to make serious trouble in Fado. At least not yet.

"Yeah," Carlos sighed. "Bandits, shit."

Ringing off, Gub took a second to copy Allsworth's number. The deputy chief of mission at the American embassy, he had taken Betty for a weekend of scuba diving before she and Gub had met. Gub hadn't known she was still seeing him.

"Coffee's ready," Betty called from the kitchen. "What's going on?"

"Can you take care of Matthias? I've gotta run."

"What's the matter?"

"Nothing," Gub said, "I've gotta go pick up some more heads. I've got Lenin already. Now it looks like some of his buddies, maybe Marx and Engels, are over at Calamidades."

Betty handed him a mug of black coffee, and he took a long gulp before setting it down on the counter and giving her a quick kiss and trotting out the door. Bumping down the four floors in the scarred elevator, Gub wondered what Mireles would have done about the heads. Probably convene a task force or something, he figured. Something clever like that.

TWO

THE Motorola unit burped just as he was about to get on the expressway to Long Island.

"Damn," Mireles said. They had an especially important surveillance going, but it was in the hands of a good supervisor, and Mireles had felt just comfortable enough leaving it there. Hoping the traffic would cooperate this once, he had left the office on lower Broadway at eight sharp, hit a brief tie-up on the Manhattan Bridge, where there seemed to be an endless repair job in progress, and made good time on the Brooklyn-Queens Expressway until he hit the backup about a half mile from the turnoff to the Grand Central. For at least three weeks, with the exception of the past two Sundays, when he had put in a couple of half-days at home, the twins had gone to sleep long before he had trudged in the door, some nights damn close to midnight. It was getting so he never saw the girls anymore, Mireles thought. Just before he locked his corner office on the twenty-sixth floor of the Javits Building, he had phoned Amy to tell her he was running on time, at least this once. She had told him not to worry, she would let the girls stay up a little past nine, and if he made it by then, he made it. If not, she reminded him, he had promised to take next weekend off, all of it: the twins could see him then. Well,

Mireles thought, reaching for the black handset, it looked like he wouldn't get to see the girls tonight after all. "A-SAC, FCI."

"We're sitting on the location," Wasick said, "but no sign of our lad, Tom. My guess is he won't show. I thought you'd want to know."

That was Wasick, Mireles thought, thorough as hell. A better supervisor you would not find anywhere in the Bureau. Without Wasick, Mireles knew, he would be out there running the surveillance himself, sitting in the fogged-up car, smoking cigarettes and drinking coffee till God knew when. Mireles was beat, and when John had offered to run the surveillance, he had hesitated less than a minute before agreeing. Ever since the tired weave of communism had begun pulling apart in Eastern Europe, Mireles had been busier than ever. He was as glad as anyone that the old regimes had begun toppling like dominoes, but he didn't buy for a minute the crap about the end of history and how the West had won. Where did everyone think the spies had gone, for Christ's sake?

The surveillance they were running tonight was designed to help answer that question, but Mireles was not at all sure his bosses would like the answer when he gave it to them. At the highest levels in the U.S. intelligence community, the only question of greater interest than the old regimes' spies was the likely fate of the man who had let the East Bloc go, and there again, Mireles thought, the conventional wisdom was probably sadly mistaken. Mikhail Gorbachev may have started out a reformer, as the judges in Oslo evidently believed, but weren't they just a bit embarrassed now that his troops had begun murdering people in the breakaway Baltics? The boys at Langley were split on the question, Mireles knew, some hailing Gorby as a once-and-future savior now just another victim of the law of unintended consequences; Mireles was no expert, but he figured the old communist had simply made a virtue out of necessity and let Eastern Europe go. Anyway it was none of his business.

Mireles's job was the spies from the bloc services and finding out what they were up to. The surveillance Wasick was running was on a commercial attaché at the Czech embassy, which, if it panned out, could shed some light on things. Mireles's agents had been watching the guy for over a year, well before anyone had any idea that a "velvet revolution" would sweep a brave playwright into the president's office in Hradčany Castle in Prague. But even the new playwright-president probably had no idea what Prague's spymasters were up to, Mireles guessed.

Mireles had to know. The head of the FBI's foreign-counterintelligence section in New York, he was among the handful of senior C.I. officials assigned to sort out the players in the new post–Cold War world. The attorney general had instructed his bosses at the Bureau to deliver a report on the issue in a couple of months, and there was scarcely an hour in any day when Mireles didn't worry about what the report would say. That was understandable, of course: he would have to write most of it.

"Okay, John, thanks. Give it another couple of hours, and if he doesn't show, let the guys go home." Screw it, Mireles thought, there'll be another shot in a few days, and he could handle it himself then.

"Ten-four," Wasick said. "Safe home."

"You bet, thanks. I'm going ten-seven."

It was no big deal, Mireles thought, turning the car phone off and swinging the LTD Crown Victoria onto the eastbound Long Island Expressway. With luck, he'd be at the house in forty-five minutes, and if anything came up, Wasick could reach him there. Besides, it was safer than talking car-to-car.

Normally, Tom Mireles would have taken the Northern State Parkway to avoid the truck traffic on the expressway, but at this time of night, he figured, the L.I.E. was probably a safe bet. Separated by a thin strip of greenbelt, the expressway ran side by side with the Northern State up the spine of the world's most populous bedroom community. Like twin stripes, Mireles often thought, up the back of a big skunk. Truth be told, he didn't think all that much of New York. In the six years he had lived on Long Island, he had heard all the theories about the best shortcuts into the city, the tricks to shave a few minutes here, beat a few lights there. As far as Mireles could tell, they were all bullshit, but that still didn't keep him from playing out the commute's different permutations in his head each time he got in the car. Some people sing along with the radio, Mireles thought; he memorized maps and street grids.

When he had first arrived in New York from Boston, after yet another brief stint at headquarters, the Bureau's relocation office had had a nice house in Garden City to show him and Amy. Another assistant special-agent-in-charge had been promoted to the top job in the Kansas City field office and sold the place to the Bureau. It was standard procedure, given the way headquarters was always shuffling people around. Amy had loved the place in Garden City, a big brick center-hall colonial with four bedrooms on an oversized lot. And it had only been thirty-two miles door-to-door to the office, Mireles had thought at the time, instead of the forty-one miles from the place they had finally settled on in Locust Valley. Every night, passing the Willis Avenue exit to Garden City, Mireles thought about the extra nine miles home. Still, he didn't really mind it.

He and Amy had known no one on Long Island when they had first moved there, but Mireles had known he wanted good schools for the twins, and to be as close to the water as possible. Garden City certainly had excellent schools; Mireles had checked. For all its other charms, though, it was almost smack-dab between the North Shore and the South Shore. Of the two, the North Shore had far more appeal for Mireles. His thirteen-foot Boston Whaler, perfect for the Sound, would have been downright perilous in the ocean. But Mireles had had other reasons for the choice. Typically, he had researched the demographics and just about everything else about the place. He knew there was plenty of old money in Locust Valley, but there were also a few areas close to the center of town where you could still get a nice house on a quarter acre for $150,000. More to the point, the old money had financed and maintained one of the nation's best school systems, a system that now had a number of tried and tested teachers and a shrinking student base. Mireles liked the sound of that. Amy, too, had come to appreciate the move. Every day, on her way to the small special-needs school in Glen Cove where she had been made principal three years before, she dropped the twins at the grade school just off Birch Hill Road. Most days she got out early enough to pick them up on the way home. Some people hated routines like that, Mireles thought; his wife, God bless her, she loved it.

Wheeling the LTD into the banked exit from the expressway, 39N onto Glen Cove Road, Mireles turned the car phone back on, just in case. If he hit the lights just right, he knew, he'd be home in twenty minutes. But twenty minutes was a long time. No doubt about it, Tom Mireles was a worrier.

Which made it all the more amazing to him how well life had worked out. He and Amy had already decided that even if headquarters came up with another must-do move, they would turn it down. Mireles was grateful to the Bureau, more than he could ever say. Fifteen years ago, he had been the chief of detectives in Fado, a dipshit place most people had never even heard of. And now? It was almost too good to believe, he thought, pressing the accelerator a little closer to the floor.

The end in Fado had been ugly; even now Mireles couldn't talk about it much. After the kidnapping, and nearly three weeks as a hostage with the bandits before Gub had shot his way into the place and rescued him, Mireles had felt like his guts had been hollowed out, like a part of him had shriveled up and died. He had resigned from the department immediately, recommending Gub as his replacement. Then he had left. His mother had passed away when he was still in high school; his father, with whom he had been close, had died a year before. An only child, Mireles had aunts, uncles and cousins all over Fado, but that hadn't been enough to keep him there. With the economy a shambles and the bandits making more inroads in the countryside every week, he had seen no future for the country. But probably more to the point, he confessed, the abuse by the bandits, who had beat him and held him naked in a hole for most of the three weeks they had had him, had shamed and embarrassed him. As long as he remained in Fado, he thought, he'd never shake the feelings.

That was the real reason he'd wanted out. It had taken him a couple of months to arrange it, but finally he had left for the States. He had never been to America before, but he had an uncle in Providence, Rhode Island, who was a city councilman. Mireles had written him, then called and finally flown over for a visit. Mireles had felt embarrassed, pleading like that for help. But as he looked back on it, he realized he really hadn't been himself then. Gub had called him a zombie, told him to snap out of it.

It had taken years, and Mireles still believed it would never have happened if he had remained in Fado. Rhode Island was a small place, and his uncle had known someone who had known someone else in Immigration and Naturalization. The green card had come almost instantly after he had landed in Providence; full citizenship had taken nearly a year, and Mireles didn't want to know how that had been arranged. In any case, thanks to his uncle again, he had gotten a job as a probationary patrolman with the Providence P.D.; and about six months after he had gotten his citizenship papers, they had jumped him up to detective in robbery. Mireles figured his background in Fado had helped, but it was also his no-nonsense approach to the job. Withdrawn, he was never one of the boys. "Icebox," they had called him around the department. Or "Mr. Paco," making fun of his heavily accented English. Mireles didn't give a shit. He was out of Fado, making a decent wage, and that was all that mattered.

When he wasn't working or sleeping in his $325-a-month walkup on Atwells Avenue, Mireles had been in the department gym, lifting weights. At 155 pounds, he could bench-press 210. Five foot ten, with his dark eyes and olive complexion, Mireles was more than usually good-looking. Whether it was because, or in spite, of his chilly relations with the other detectives, he didn't know, but he had been the subject of endless gossip by the department's secretaries. Mireles had said barely a word to them, though, preferring to type his own reports and file them himself. Except for his landlady, Mrs. Fortunato, Mireles had spoken with almost no one outside the department, slipping through the routine of days and months with polite thank-yous to the dry cleaner's, where he had his suits and uniforms done, and the deli, where he picked up his salami-and-cheese grinder on the way home from work each night. His uncle, the city councilman, he'd seen on holidays. But in spite of all he had done for him, it was just obligation, Mireles's awkward silences making the small talk painful for everyone. After a while, they had stopped asking him, except for the big ones, Christmas and Easter. "Ungrateful bastard," the councilman had called his nephew the detective. But he had never said it so that Mireles could hear.

Approaching the turnoff to Birch Hill Road, Mireles thought it was one of the many things he had to make up for, the lack of gratitude, the long silences. Amy said it was PTSD, what a lot of the guys from Vietnam got, post-traumatic stress disorder. Whatever it was, it had taken a double jolt to knock Mireles out of it. The first had been the offer from the Bureau, working on an organized-crime task force for the FBI in Boston.

The second had been Amy Marshall. Coming back to Providence one night in mid-December, after another long day at the task force, Mireles had nearly plowed head-on into a car in the far right lane of I-95. The car had been facing north, the wrong direction, and another had spun sideways in the breakdown lane. Rain had turned to sleet, and Mireles quickly pulled off the highway to see if anyone was hurt. The state police hadn't arrived yet, and it was before they had installed those emergency phone boxes every mile or so on the interstate.

Miraculously, no one had been injured, but the redhead in the little Datsun wagon had been badly shaken as Mireles helped her out the passenger-side door, the driver's side jammed shut from the accident.

Since the car couldn't be driven, Mireles had offered to take her back to Newton after the state police arrived, and on the way, sleet lashing the windows, she had gradually relaxed, the knot of fear dissolving finally, replaced by a stream of chatter. Twenty-three, just two years out of Boston College, where she had been one of the few commuter students, Amy Marshall had luminous blue eyes, pale freckles scattered like stars around them and a smart pageboy haircut. Even with her heavy winter coat, Mireles could tell she had a delicate, slender grace. Mireles reflected that he had never known anyone with freckles before, and Amy Marshall seemed barely to notice that he said hardly a word during the twenty minutes in the car. In response to a question, he had said he didn't know what he was doing for Christmas, he was new in the States. It was at least half a lie—he'd been there over two years. He still didn't know why he had told it, but Amy had promptly invited him for Christmas dinner. "It'll be clan there," she said. "They love cops."

Mireles had begged off with his uncle, and suspected, quite correctly, that no one was really heartbroken about it.

It wasn't long after that Christmas that Mireles had woken up one night thinking his blind flight from Fado had maybe saved his life. Two years after that, he and Amy Marshall were married quietly, and when she delivered twins less than a year later, Tom Mireles was absolutely convinced that he had somehow been marked for salvation.

It was dizzying, he thought. He had been chosen for the task force not because he had been deemed a particularly good detective by the FBI, but because of his language skills. In his father's small import-export business back in Fado, he had learned Italian, Spanish, French and English. Except for English, the most different from his native Portuguese, Mireles spoke them all flawlessly, and had even picked up several dialects. There was no doubt he had a gift for it. Because the Bureau needed an Italian speaker for the task force, agents with similar language skills being tied up on other cases, Mireles had been asked, and for seven nerve-jangling months after that, he had gone undercover, moving out of the flat on Atwells Avenue and into a secluded three-bedroom bungalow on Green Hill. The neighbors had known him as Mr. Bondanza, and he'd waved shyly from the big Chrysler LeBaron each morning as he passed, heading for the interstate and back up to Boston. He had been scared shitless the whole time.

One of the mob's old Moustache Petes, Alberto Spavento, had

vouched for Mireles. Spavento had been seventy-one and looking at a long prison stretch from a racketeering indictment, the result of a big heroin-importation scheme the Bureau had broken up six months earlier. The RICO charge carried a mandatory minimum of twenty-five years, a prospect with which Spavento had not at all been thrilled. So after some conversations with the assistant U.S. attorney for the Eastern District of New York, he'd agreed to introduce Mireles to the right people in Boston. At sentencing, Assistant U.S. Attorney Myles McGovern had told the judges that in consideration of Mr. Spavento's questionable health, the government was willing to accept a plea to several lesser charges and that it would drop the RICO count. Unstated in any of the court papers was Mr. Spavento's assistance to the Boston field office of the FBI in getting Tom Mireles into the very heart of the Patriarca organized-crime family.

Intro or no, there had been some hairy moments. At one point early on, his backup team had lost Mireles completely, and he had found himself squeezed into the front seat of the LeBaron between two muscle guys, both of them packing. For three hours they had cruised aimlessly through the Berkshires, the perspiration causing Mireles's electronic body bug to itch something fierce. It'd turned out the two pistols were just killing time, and they'd left Mireles and the LeBaron near Faneuil Hall late that night. The backup team had caught hell, but Mireles, shaken, had never uttered a word of complaint. Eighteen months after that, the case had finally come to trial, the first in a long string the task force would bring against the Patriarca family. Mireles, as the government's star witness, had come under a withering cross-examination by Thomas Flannagan, one of the brightest stars of Boston's criminal-defense bar. For a day and a half, it had gone on, the packed courtroom spellbound. Through it all, Mireles had answered the lawyer's questions politely and precisely, and as good as Flannagan was, Mireles had been better. When Flannagan had misconstrued an important conversation between Mireles and Flannagan's client, a dapper businessman with no prior record to speak of, Mireles had quietly corrected him, directing the attorney, without referring to notes, to the precise page and line number in the eighty-eight-page wiretap transcript. When it was all over, even Flannagan congratulated the FBI part-timer, and Jack Fox, the Boston SAC, wasted no time, after conferring with Washington, in changing Mireles's part-time status to full-time.

Fox had been his rabbi, but it had still taken years for Mireles's career to catch fire. Like so many Hispanic agents in the Bureau, Mireles had initially been consigned to the "Taco Circuit," spending weeks on end "on the muffs," usually sitting in a hotel room jammed with eavesdropping equipment listening to a couple of mopes talking in Spanish about how to move a load of coke or marijuana from one place to another. It had been mind-numbing work, and when he had complained, after nearly a year on one such case, Mireles had been dispatched first to Tampa, and then Miami. Along with El Paso and San Antonio, these were the worst outposts on the Taco Circuit, the Bureau higher-ups confident that one Hispanic agent, no matter what his background, was pretty much interchangeable with the next and could therefore work undercover against Cubans, Mexicans, Colombians. A wetback was a wetback was a wetback.

Bullshit, Mireles had told Fox. But Fox, a fast-tracker then running the FBI Academy in Quantico, couldn't block the move, and that's how Mireles had found himself one bright spring morning sipping a *café con leche* in a bar on Miami's Calle Ocho, trying to get a line on a couple of slick Cubans. For some reason Mireles had never been privileged to learn, Washington figured the pair for a couple of Fidel's paid agents.

It had been his third meeting with the Cubans, and Mireles had told his supervisor after the first that these guys weren't buying. The supervisor, one of the Bureau's Mormon Mafia, hadn't given a shit, and Mireles had been instructed to stay on the case, to keep meeting with them. The only problem was, nothing from Mireles's background in Fado, with the possible exception of the heat and humidity, correlated with the Cubans' background in Havana. Mireles knew they knew he was an imposter, and when one of them waved an ugly little pistol at him across the table of the bar on Calle Ocho, that was it entirely. Shit, they hadn't even taken him outside, "*Vendido*," the older man spat. "Sellout." And the younger man had shot him once in the chest, the .22-caliber slug ripping into him just above the heart, missing the aorta, the doctors said afterwards, by the slimmest of margins, a couple of centimeters. When he had come to in the hospital several hours later, Amy had been there, weeping and cursing. They never had found the two Cubans, and when Fox had heard about it, he'd gone immediately to the Director, reminding the Judge about the Boston case, Mireles's language skills and his background in Fado. Leaving the Director's office, Fox had flown to

Miami to give Mireles the news: he was coming to Quantico as his personal assistant. Finally, Tom Mireles's days on the Taco Circuit were over.

Whether it was because of Fox, the Judge's intervention (which everyone in the Bureau soon heard about) or Mireles's intensity on the job, he had been tagged as a comer. After Quantico, he had his ticket punched at headquarters before returning to Boston as a supervisor of organized-crime investigations. Fox, now an A-DIC, an assistant director-in-charge, in Washington, said Mireles was destined for an SAC job of his own one day, a special agent-in-charge of one of the Bureau's fifty-nine field offices. It was a hell of a long way from his days in Fado, Mireles thought, as he pulled the LTD into the gravel drive, fishing the garage-door opener from the glove compartment and pressing the Up button.

Before he was even out of the car, the twins were in his arms.

Tucking one under each arm like squirming fish, Mireles knew for sure he would never take the SAC job if and when it was finally offered. It was one thing for him and Amy to discuss it rationally over a beer, but with the twins in his arms, teasing and laughing, Mireles knew it was so. There was college to worry about for one thing, and with the 25 percent supplemental salary increase Congress had authorized the year before for agents in the New York field office, Mireles couldn't make any more money than if he was the Director of the FBI. In fact, if he moved, he would suddenly be making much less.

Besides, he loved what he did. He had started out with the Bureau chasing the Mafia. LCN cases, they called them, short for La Cosa Nostra. Now it was FCI, foreign counterintelligence, and Mireles thought that he had never found his work so absorbing. He had had to learn all the arcana, and he loved it. The Bureau had sent him for the long course at "Blue U.," the spooks' secret finishing school in Arlington, Virginia, just outside of Washington. There he had learned well, watching how our guys did it, so he could defend against theirs. Flaps and seals, secret commo plans, onetime pads: he had seen and done it all. And now he was putting it to work in New York. Chasing spies was different from any other kind of police work. In most investigations, the object was to identify the guy who committed the crime. In FCI cases, it worked just the reverse: you identify the guys who will commit the crime before they can do it. Whether it's stealing secrets from defense contractors or co-opting weak-willed diplomats, you can only stop it if you know who's going to try it. Among the many FCI jobs in the Bureau, the New York job was the best, the "show," with their best guys working against our best guys. And the reason for that was simple: the United Nations. Mireles called it "the womb."

Anyway, he thought, kissing Amy on the lips, it was a hell of a long way from Fado. Like a goddamn movie.

THREE

VIKTOR Alleja was also a long way from Fado, though not as far as Tom Mireles. He was in Lisbon. Of the many differences between the two men, there was this: where Mireles hoped never to see Fado again, Viktor Alleja wanted nothing more.

He was not handsome in any ordinary sense of the word. At five foot five and something close to 200 pounds, Viktor Alleja occupied space the way a low hill clung to a flat landscape: he could be moved, but only with a quantity of dynamite or some considerable bulldozing. The man had some kind of specific gravity. His ruddy complexion and his heavy, well-barbered jowls advertised a diet of fine wines and heavy sauces. Let others worry about cholesterol; Viktor Alleja wore his high coloring like a badge. It bespoke a life of luxury, Viktor Alleja thought, proclaimed that its owner had arrived, and damn the consequences in having gotten there.

Say what they did about him, Viktor Alleja also had style. His salt-and-pepper hair was full but close-cropped so it stood straight up like a fine brush. In the closet of his new apartment in Lisbon's Alfama quarter, twelve starched white-on-white Bijan shirts hung side by side on carved cedar hangers, all long-staple Egyptian cotton, all single-needle-stitched. The crisp white shirtfronts set off the soft

Jacquard weaves and the impenetrable paisleys Viktor Alleja had come to favor with the dark Aquascutum suits he special-ordered twice a year from the shop in Regent Street. At something like $200 a shot, the shirts—never mind the shoes, the suits and the engraved Gurkha luggage—certainly had no business in a place like this, Alleja told himself, glancing absently around the apartment.

Most would have considered the place a steal. With its hand-molded fourteen-foot ceilings and heavy, lead-mullioned windows, its two trellised balconies giving onto the narrow street below, the two-bedroom flat was among the most handsome in Lisbon. It rented for $2,300 a month, utilities included, and that had put only a small dent in the $162,000 Viktor Alleja had managed to spirit out of Fado when he'd left. There were some things about the place Viktor Alleja liked. The Arraiolos rugs, for one thing. There was a beautiful ten-by-twelve in the parlor and a rare four-by-twelve in the narrow sitting room. Embroidered by hand and naturally dyed, they were made only in the Arraiolos region of the Algarve, and they cost plenty. Viktor Alleja knew. He had admired them many years ago in the big houses of Cape Town and Johannesburg, the places he had been invited as a guest but could never afford himself. In Fado, he finally had the money to buy them for the big new house he had bought, but at something like $650 a square meter, it was more than he'd been willing to part with, and he had settled for some second-hand Persians instead. Viktor Alleja liked to live well, but he was no fool when it came to money. He would have preferred a bigger place in Lisbon, for instance, but for now the flat in the Alfama would have to do. God, how he missed the place in Fado.

It wasn't just the house either, but everything about the place, the sense of possibility most of all. It blew through Fado, Viktor Alleja thought, like a breeze come from a long way over the water.

Viktor Alleja knew the country's history and, he had thought, pacing up and down the paneled sitting room, its future. It was nearly 1950, Viktor Alleja recalled, when the first shipments of stone for Fado's broad boulevards and high curbs were sent from Europe. It had been quarried less than thirty miles from Lisbon and shipped south, at considerable expense, by barge. Wicked seas off the Cape Verde Islands had capsized several of the vessels, driving the unit cost of the stones that would be cut into curbstones higher still. But no one had grumbled at the expense. It had all seemed worth it at the time. The curbs and the boulevards—two lanes on one side of a manicured hedgerow median, two lanes on the other—were testaments, Viktor Alleja thought, to a touching if confused sense of optimism, talismans of dreamers.

The dreams, however, like the country itself, were jumbled and incoherent. Still, Viktor Alleja believed that dreams ought to count for something. Though his own had lately crumbled like the curbstones of Fado, he was determined to fashion a new and more splendid dream from the wreckage of the old, his small quarters in the Alfama be damned.

How had it all gone so wrong?

Viktor Alleja turned the question over and over again in his mind. Having been driven in disgrace years before from his big office in Johannesburg, he had landed, through his own cunning and the kindness of influential friends, in Fado, a city with promise, a man of some means and with the chance to make more money than he had ever dreamed possible. By training, he was a policeman, although his had been a rather specialized corner of the profession, one the Directorate euphemistically labeled "intelligence." That had covered a multitude of sins, none of which Viktor Alleja particularly regretted, even now. Even the sin of getting caught wouldn't have been so bad, Viktor Alleja thought, except his masters had suddenly changed the rules, going public on him and showing him the door after the indignity of a long public inquiry and a drumbeat of newspaper headlines.

Politicians, Viktor Alleja thought, the absolute lowest form of life. Thank God for his friends, though. For years, Viktor Alleja had taken pains to ingratiate himself with the right people in Cape Town, Pietermaritzburg and Johannesburg. An industrialist's daughter needed an abortion? Viktor Alleja arranged it quietly; no hospitals necessary, no publicity. A barrister's son crippled some kids in the townships while driving drunk? Viktor Alleja swept the case away with a handful of cash, a muttered threat and a passing comment to a pliable magistrate.

In his eighteen years with the Directorate, Viktor Alleja had done hundreds of favors like those. Except he thought of them as chits. He never cashed them, but he never forgot them either. And if his friends thought they had paid him back with the gaily wrapped cases of estate-bottled Bordeaux and single-malt Scotch that swamped his big corner office each Christmas, well, they had thought wrong, that's all. Fortunately, not many had, and even before the end came, his friends had arranged for the new job not too far away in Fado, just across the border. Viktor Alleja knew next to nothing about business, but in the new capital, thanks to his friends, he had been established as a businessman. It was a matter of discipline, Viktor Alleja had told himself at the time, and none was more disciplined than he.

Some things are beyond the reach of even the most disciplined men, however. And when the end came so soon after his arrival in Fado, Viktor Alleja lost not just his grand home and his promising business, but the best chance he was likely to have of rescuing an old man's dreams from the ash heap of unfilled promises. Just as the old stonemason would have been sickened to see Cecelie and the others cracking their coconuts on his carefully set curbstones, Viktor Alleja was sick at the waste. The only difference, he thought, wearing a path on the Arraiolos in the sitting room and glaring at the phone on the polished end table, was that he intended to do something about it. Where the hell was Sturua, anyway?

The Securitate man should have been in touch a day ago. The flight from Lisbon had left four days before, and Viktor Alleja had not heard a word from Nicholas Sturua since. The two men had agreed to communicate at least once by phone until other arrangements could be made. So far, though, Viktor Alleja had heard nothing, and he wondered, not for the first time, whether the $5,000 he had given the Securitate man was a wise investment after all. The man was desperate, he knew. Just desperate enough to have taken the $5,000 and vanished.

EVEN before the demonstrations in Timişoara's Opera Square, the thick crowds washing like tide around the clubfeet of the giant statue of Romulus and Remus, Nicholas Sturua had seen the end coming. After the crowds had begun gathering in University Square, in the very heart of Bucharest, Sturua had known it was just a matter of days, weeks at most. The chief of the Inspectorate Division of Romania's loathed Securitate, Nicholas Sturua intended to have no part of it. He had watched on television as Ceauşescu had come out to address the demonstrators, still dreaming he could frighten them into submission, ignoring the riptide of democracy that had roared across Eastern Europe. The old man had looked so feeble, Sturua thought, remembering the look of incredulity on his face as he had stopped in midsentence, interrupted by the ragged chants welling up from the square below him. "Pig fucker," the students had called the dictator to his face, "butcherer, murderer." In that instant, Sturua thought, the old man must have known it was over. A helicopter had swept him and his dreary wife away hours later, and a firing squad had shot them both on Christmas Day.

By that time, though, Nicholas Sturua had been long gone. When he'd heard about the firing squad, late in the afternoon on Christmas, he had been in the bar of the Atlantis Vilamoura on the deserted Algarve, watching as sheets of freezing rain lashed the empty Vilamoura yacht basin and wondering whether he should keep his appointment the following afternoon with Viktor Alleja. The two had met years before during a seminar in Algeria, and the older man had taken a liking to the Romanian. They had stayed in touch ever since, meeting occasionally in Europe or Africa and talking every few months on the phone. Viktor Alleja had phoned several times from Fado. "You should come down," he had told Sturua, only half jokingly; in truth, he could have used an assistant. "A young man like you could make a fortune here. And the weather's incredible."

Sturua didn't give a shit about the weather. He had lived under the Ceaușescus long enough to think that rain-smeared smog was fine for most any kind of human endeavor. What he had been concerned about at the time of Viktor Alleja's last call had been his skin. Besides the Ceaușescus themselves, Sturua knew, he was probably the most wanted man in Romania. Though ordinary Romanians knew nothing about him, the entire Securitate knew who he was, and they hated him with something very nearly approximating passion. It wasn't the regular travel abroad and the enormous rent-free apartment in the Strasse Ploscaru that angered them. It wasn't even the fact that Sturua, an outsider from the sticks of Timișoara, had been handpicked by Ceaușescu and vaulted over the heads of dozens of older Securitate men in Bucharest. What it was, was the job itself, and Sturua had to admit that he had been quite good at it. As chief of the Inspectorate Division, Sturua had had virtual autonomy over hirings, firings and all internal investigations and disciplinary actions. It was the latter, he mused, that had engendered so much hate among his Securitate brethren. Before that, he had been just another Securitate grunt, though far better than most, he liked to think. Before coming back to Bucharest to take the inspectorate job, Sturua had had nearly ten years with the Securitate abroad, mainly in the other bloc countries, with whom the Ceauşescus enjoyed mainly lousy relations.

Primarily, it had been an intelligence-gathering job, bribing members of the other bloc services for a reasonably steady stream of information. It had also involved some "wet work," eliminating the stray agent or defector when he was so instructed. That had been the exception rather than the rule, however, and in any case, his track record wasn't particularly why Ceauşescu had picked him for the inspectorate job. Sturua had gotten the nod, he figured, as much because of his effectiveness in the field as because of the fact he was an outsider who didn't particularly care if he made a few enemies.

Thus, when the phone call had come from Viktor Alleja a few weeks earlier, it had seemed too good to be true. Sturua had known since the early rumblings in Timişoara that he would have to leave, but he had had no idea where to go. Viktor Alleja, as if it had somehow been preordained, had given him an answer. But on the wind-whipped Algarve, as he'd ordered another brandy and soda from the pretty bartender, tearing her away from her copy of *Vogue*, Sturua had had second thoughts, wondering whether the offer from Viktor Alleja was some kind of trap. Contemplating the brandy, and then the shapely ass of the bartender in her black bolero pants, Nicholas Sturua had decided that it probably was not. If they had wanted to lure him somewhere to kill him, Sturua thought, far easier for the Securitate brass or their successors to have done it back in Romania. But perhaps Viktor Alleja was in league with Interpol. Sturua knew he had to be on their watch list by now. Trap or not?

Driving north the next day in the rented Mercedes, Sturua had run all the possibilities through his mind once again and considered finally that he had no options, at least no good long-term ones. With his pocketful of passports and the few thousand dollars he had taken from his office safe, he could have gone just about anywhere with little or no trouble. But what would he do when he got there? As the traffic had thickened just outside Lisbon, Sturua had fought one last impulse to take the cloverleaf turnoff for the international airport. Viktor Alleja had always liked him, he thought. The odds were it wasn't a trap. And if he was right, Sturua thought, and Viktor Alleja had a line on a deal of some kind down in Fado, well, there were plenty worse things than taking it easy somewhere in the sun.

In Lisbon, Sturua had confessed his doubts laughingly to Viktor Alleja, who had pumped him for details on his escape from

Bucharest. It had been remarkably easy, Sturua had said. He had driven across to Bulgaria, where he had spent three years for the Securitate. He had friends in useful places there and knew every border crossing. From there, he had driven into northern Greece to Salonika on his Bulgarian passport, then on to Athens, where he had taken the short flight to Rabat in Morocco, crossing at Gibraltar, where he had picked up the Mercedes, driving it from there across the border to the Algarve.

Viktor Alleja had listened politely, filing the details away. Then he had told Sturua about the situation in Fado, taking his time over dinner at an Italian place he had come to like. Over veal piccata and a bottle of Chianti, the two men had reached an agreement. Sturua would go to Fado, get things lined up quickly and report to Viktor Alleja at least once every three or four days. Viktor Alleja would manage the money end of things from Lisbon, but he had emphasized that there wasn't much money just yet and that Sturua would have to work fast.

VIKTOR Alleja cursed the Securitate man one final time, then pulled on a navy blazer over his starched white shirt. It was time to get some dinner. He would give Sturua one more day, he thought, already salivating at the linguini with clams he had been contemplating since lunch. Besides, in another day Hagen would be here, and they could talk things over. Sturua might think he'd be working alone in Fado, but Nicholas Sturua would find out that he was wrong. Why use one desperate man when desperate men could be found now all over Europe? In that sense, the collapse of communism in the East Bloc was a great unlooked-for benison, Viktor Alleja thought, smiling as he contemplated its myriad possibilities. He was becoming, he thought, something of a connoisseur of chaos, or at least of sudden, and occasionally violent, change.

FOUR

Driving back across town with the head of Vladimir Lenin in the rear of the Land Cruiser and all the windows open, Gub figured he'd better put the thing on ice. It was already beginning to stink. Might as well put it in the refrigerator for now, he thought, parking in the space in front of his flat. When Teresa'd been alive, the place had been nice. It wasn't much, three railroad-style rooms one after the other—living room, kitchen and bedroom way in the back, all done up in dreary landlord white. After the wedding, Teresa had bought some expensive new furniture for the place and put new slipcovers on Gub's old sofa and reading chair. Since her death, Gub admitted, dustballs flying as he hurried across the living room to the kitchen, he had done a lousy job of keeping the place up. He promised himself he'd do better, but somehow he never did.

To make room in the refrigerator for the head, Gub had to take a couple of six-packs from the first shelf. This was really playing hell with the chain-of-evidence rules, Gub knew, but it saved time, and besides, he thought, who the hell cared about things like chain of evidence anymore?

Fucking Carlos probably didn't even know what the term meant.

In the bedroom, Gub figured he might as well follow orders

anyway and rang the office. It was too early for anyone to be there yet, but he could leave a message. The capital police department couldn't afford an overnight shift, couldn't even afford patrolmen anymore, Gub mused. But since most sensible people in Fado didn't venture out after dark, there had been no hue and cry for greater police protection after hours and little expectation that things would be much better during the day. Gub had two explanations for the tiny department's continued existence. The first was that Carlos's uncle, the works minister, had considerable sway with the president and the cabinet, was a believer in good law enforcement and so put in a good word for old Carlos every so often; then again, maybe old Carlos had some interesting and perhaps even useful photographs of the works minister, who knew? Gub's second theory was straight CYA. For as long as he'd been with the department the president and his yes-men had been gutting the place, the rooms of empty desks in the barracks-like headquarters depressing as hell each day. Because a lot of the government's foreign aid was tied to things like human rights and whatever the annual Amnesty International report said, the government had to be able to point to an agency of its own that investigated murder and mayhem and, theoretically at least, brought those responsible to justice. Thanks to the president, the department was now able to perform its functions largely only in the realm of theory, but its existence kept the aid spigot wide open, at least for the moment. Gub liked his first theory better, especially the blackmail part, but he conceded that the second made marginally more sense.

On the department's answering machine, which had been paid for, along with three electric typewriters, a Dictaphone and a portable Sony tape recorder, with either British or Italian aid money—there was a certificate somewhere—Gub left a message for Ellis.

Like most government-job holders in Fado, Ellis was young, black and very sure of himself. Gub, being none of those things, liked Ellis anyway. He took the job seriously, believed earnestly that government officials were servants of the public (Carlos had already cut some deep nicks in that fine notion), and he was always asking Gub if there was something more he could do to "improve my skills." Gub tried to help him out. He liked Ellis. And besides, it was in his interest: there wasn't anyone else in the department he could really trust.

On the tape, Gub told Ellis to send one of the department's three working cars for Anna-Marie. Overweight and inattentive, she was the department's only stenographer, and she was the exact opposite of Ellis. Her transcriptions were riddled with errors. In his reports, transcribed by Anna-Marie, Gub often found "perpetrator" rendered as "perpetuator," or something equally bizarre. In a particularly ugly domestic one time, he had listed the cause of death as "asphyxiation," which had subsequently been rendered "aspiration." Gub wasn't sure Anna-Marie had too many of those, aside from her one and abiding concern. In her late twenties, Anna-Marie wanted a man, plain and simple. Gub bet that pretty much any man might have done; that it would have convinced Anna-Marie entirely that there was a God in the heavens, and that he was a pretty good guy at that. But no man ever materialized, and the department's reports were much the worse as a result. Anyway, Gub thought, if he waited for Anna-Marie to show up at the office, the heads at Calamidades would be doing a fine bake by eleven or so. The car would flatter her, and at least get her to Calamidades by nine.

While he was trying to think if there was anything else he should do, the phone rang again. This time it was the Lisboa.

The Lisboa was hardly what anyone would call fancy, but compared to the Okavango, it was heaven. The beds were reasonably comfortable, the service was polite if not quite prompt, and more than half the rooms gave onto a splendid view of either the ocean to the east or the shipping channel and the port beyond to the south. On the top floor of the hotel, enclosed by glass on three sides, was a reasonably good restaurant that did astonishing things with prawns. Miraculously, Gub thought, it also maintained a pretty fair wine list. The international press, the few who ever bothered to come to Fado, usually stayed at the Lisboa. So did the foreign-aid types on their expense-account budgets.

"Gub, I'm sorry to bother you at home. I apologize."

Eduardo Antonio Sebastião, Tony to his friends, had the best manners of anyone in Fado. Though his dark tropical suits had long since acquired a bit of a shine and he was forced nowadays to make do with barbering himself, the diplomats' wives still cooed over his polished manners, his ready wit in five languages and his mysterious facility for acquiring thick shell steaks in summer, American Butterball turkeys at Thanksgiving and fresh Bresse chickens at least every three or four weeks.

The Sebastião family had owned and operated the Lisboa for more than seventy years, and when the revolution came, Tony, anticipating confiscation by the new government, still could not bring himself to leave. A friend had arranged a meeting with one of the new ministers, an older man who had lived abroad some years, and Tony had spoken at length of the many important people who had stayed at the Lisboa over the years. These were not movie stars or foreign millionaires, Tony had said, no stranger to the new government's favorite *bêtes noires;* they were executives of aid organizations like Oxfam and the Red Cross, people, Tony pointed out, who had access to large sums of money who could, if they were so inclined, make some of that money available to the new government. But that would mean they would have to have a place to stay in the capital so they could come to check up on how their money was being spent. And that, Tony said, meant the new government should see that it was in its interest to keep the Lisboa open and operating. Even the old minister, he guessed, probably mistrusted the doubtful charms of the Okavango, which the new government had already claimed among its first and most dubious prizes.

It may not have been the most seamless pitch, but it worked. Somehow—perhaps the minister had developed a fondness for fine dining in his years abroad—the Lisboa and the new government had arrived at what Tony described, with studied vagueness, as "an arrangement." Its terms were one of the most closely kept secrets in the capital, though Tony allowed as how, in apologizing for the occasional price increase on the restaurant's menu, he now had "masters to please." The exact size of the new masters' cut was never discussed, but Gub figured it had to be pretty hefty.

"What can I do for you, Tony?"

"Gub, I just got in, the girl on the desk didn't know what to do. She's beside herself. The waiters will not come out of the kitchen. Fortunately, most of the guests have not come down yet. I just threw a towel over the thing, but I don't know what to do."

"What is it, Tony?"

"I don't even know how to say it. Maybe you see things like this in your work all the time, but I . . ."

"You've got a disembodied head, is that it, Tony?" Gub was guessing.

"How did you know?"

"Where is it?"

"On the diving board," Tony said. "I'm afraid it's going to fall in."

Gub showered quickly. Four heads and counting. There was Vladimir Lenin, now sitting next to a head of lettuce and the six-pack of Carta Blanca in his refrigerator, the two at Calamidades and now the one on Tony Sebastião's diving board at the Lisboa. There had been other heads before. And arms and legs and unspeakably mutilated torsos. Someone out there, Gub thought as he toweled himself off, had a very evil mind and a more than usually sharp set of knives. But for most of the people in the capital, black and white alike, that was precisely the point. Whoever had the knives was Out There and, at least until this morning, he had seemed content to stay there.

In the capital, most people referred to this state of affairs as "the situation." Not a war, Gub thought, or an insurrection or even a campaign of terror whose only analogue in the late twentieth century was the madness of the Khmer Rouge in Cambodia. No, as long as the murder and the mutilation were happening in the thorn-scrub savanna of the interior of the loam-rich bottomlands that curled west from the ocean between twin ribs of high dunes, it was simply a "situation," of some concern and inconvenience to be sure, but not much more than that.

It was impossible to say exactly when the situation had begun. Long before the Armed Forces Movement had driven Marcello Caetano from Lisbon in April 1974, Portuguese troops had been rampaging through the colonies committing unspeakable atrocities as they skirmished with rebel movements. Spanish missionaries had told a United Nations commission in 1972 of "a whole series of massacres rivaling that of My Lai," and for an instant, the world had taken notice. Then the story had faded quickly from the front pages, and the killing had resumed in earnest.

In each of the colonies, the rebels had been emboldened by the turmoil in Lisbon, and it had spurred them on to feats of ever greater boldness and depravity. In Fado, a charismatic leader named Michel Baptiste had rallied thousands with his hot Marxist rhetoric, and by the time the new government in Lisbon had announced in July of 1974 that it would begin transferring power to the colonies, Baptiste and his young ideologues had already been moving into their handsome government offices in Fado. One of the first things they did, after renaming all the streets in the capital and even some of the towns in the countryside, was nationalize just about every profitable business and industry; Tony Sebastião's Lisboa was a rare exception.

There had been two problems with Baptiste's program, however. The first was that he never paid anything near what the businesses were worth: some "offers" were damn close to outright theft. That pissed off a lot of people, including quite a few who actually wished the new government well. The second problem was that Baptiste and his yes-men didn't know jack-shit about business, and wound up sending a mess of them down the tubes through sheer mismanagement and stupidity.

The upshot in any case was that some of the old Portuguese were invited back after a while to clean things up. It wasn't too long after that the killings began again in earnest. A combination of demobbed Portuguese troops, jobless workers and even a few paid killers for hire, they had no political agenda and made no bones about the fact. The locals called them bandits, or matsangas, and they got money from all kinds of places. A Baton Rouge businessman gave $200,000 to "fight the communists," people in Johannesburg gave more still, and trogs to the right of the apartheid government gave more still, concerned, they said, by the prospect of so many unstable—read "black"—governments on its borders. The bandits also got plenty of money from Lisbon, from rich guys mainly, who paid for the campaign out of a combination of pure cussedness and revenge.

Gub figured that if you had to date the beginning of the situation, pick '75. That meant more than a decade and a half of terrorism, who knew how many dead? Some human-rights groups said a quarter of a million. It was a nice round number.

To his chagrin, Gub realized he had felt pretty much the same as everyone else in Fado. Severed heads in the countryside were one thing. But in the capital now, they were serious goddamn business. Perhaps, Gub thought, slipping into his good navy trousers, it was because finally the heads without owners were not showing up in the tiny villages and empty dirt tracks of the interior. Now they were within the city limits of Fado. And that meant they were his responsibility.

Guessing it would be a long day, and not knowing which government office events might take him to, Gub selected a blue oxford shirt and, just for the hell of it, a dark silk tie. Tony will appreciate that, he thought. Maybe it'll make him feel a little better.

Somehow Gub doubted it, though.

Tony Sebastião was one of Gub's oldest friends. Their fathers and grandfathers had known each other, and, with Mireles, Gub and

Tony had gone to Francis Xavier High School together, Tony and Mireles a year ahead of Gub. Because Maria wouldn't get to Calamidades for at least another hour and a half, Gub figured he had time to swing by the Lisboa first and help his friend Tony do something about the head on his diving board.

Before it fell in, that is. If it went into the pool, Gub muttered, locking the front door behind him, his old pal Tony was on his own.

Gub had seen Tony handle all sorts of situations with an easy manner that, frankly, he envied. The most unusual, he thought, pulling the Land Cruiser into the circular lot in front and casting his eye about for a spot in the shade, had been a New Year's Eve a few years before the revolution. Tony had hosted a small dinner for his best customers in the upstairs restaurant. Gub, being an enthusiastic and frequent diner at the Lisboa, not to mention one of Tony's dearest friends and a generally useful person to know in the department, had been invited. There had been some military types, a clutch of businessmen and the usual assortment of ex-pats, mostly diplomats and aid executives.

It had started out a splendid time. Somehow one of Tony's mysterious suppliers had laid hands on a half dozen cases of Cristal Roederer, and Tony had thought nothing of uncorking it all to help his friends ring in the New Year. His three best waiters, a matched set of silver-haired gents with probably seventy years' serving experience among them, had been given standing instructions to put a bottle each aside for themselves, but otherwise to keep the champagne flowing as long as there was more to drink and those inclined to drink it.

Building goodwill, Tony had called it.

Sometime either before or after the ceviche, Gub couldn't remember and neither, apparently, could anyone else, the wife of the Spanish ambassador, a dour, pear-shaped woman with an insincere chirping laugh, had picked up a beautifully carved ironwood figurine from an unused serving table and, without saying a word, delivered a surprisingly good forehand smash to the back of her husband's head. The ambassador had gone out cold, drinks and dishes had clattered to the floor, and the ambassador's wife, without looking at anyone in particular, had excused herself in flawless Spanish, French and Portuguese. Then she had stridden to the elevator in the foyer and, when it came, pressed the button for the lobby. None of those in the room ever saw her again.

In an instant, Tony and his waiters had removed the stricken

ambassador to a suite on the floor below. A doctor had been summoned, dishes were cleared and tablecloths changed. Tony had in-
formed his guests calmly that the "ambassador is being attended to,"
implying with a sharp look that no official note need be taken of the
incident. Within minutes, Gub remembered, parking and locking
the Toyota, fresh bottles of Cristal had begun making the rounds,
and without missing a beat the matched set of waiters had served the
next course, a chilled cucumber soup with sprigs of fresh mint and a
splash of cream.

Gub could almost taste it still. He loved to eat, and he was endlessly amazed at the inventiveness of the Lisboa kitchen.

As Tony Sebastião hurried towards him across the parking lot,
Gub tried to recall whether he had ever heard the reason for the
spousal attack on the Spanish ambassador and decided he had not.
He did remember that, after initial fears of brain damage, the ambassador had spent a couple of months recuperating in a sixth-floor suite
at the hotel while Tony had gently fended off the importunings of an
overzealous deputy chief of mission, using the Lisboa's ancient telex
to communicate directly with Madrid on the few pressing matters
that arose. For all intents and purposes, while the ambassador had
been on the mend, Tony had run the embassy out of his cramped
office behind the Lisboa's polished mahogany reception desk. And
according to those who claimed to know, mostly others in Fado's
incestuously small diplomatic community, Tony had deflected what
could have been a rather embarrassing official inquiry into the matter from Madrid. Less than a year later, the ambassador had been
posted to Oslo, considered a big step up among the striped-pants set.
And on every New Year's Eve since, Tony Sebastião's closest friends
had feasted on fresh Norwegian salmon, sent by overnight airfreight
from Oslo in a shrink-wrapped crate of dry ice. Tony always made a
point of showing everyone the note. Bearing an expensive water-
mark, it said simply: "Por un amigo verdadero."

If the owner and operator of the Hotel Lisboa ever had any idea
what had caused the pear-shaped wife with the chirping laugh to
try to murder her husband among friends on a long-ago New Year's
Eve, he never said. And none of his friends were ever foolish enough
to ask.

"Thank you for coming, Gub." As always, Tony was impeccably
dressed. This morning, it was a tan linen sports coat with gray twill
slacks and a pressed yellow tunic open at the neck. A blue silk

handkerchief peeked from the breast pocket. "I just didn't know who else to call."

"No problem, Tony. Let's have a look." Following Tony past the hotel kitchen's double doors out to the pool area, he spied a pair of waiters chattering excitedly inside.

"I had to send the girl on the desk home, she was hysterical. I feel like going home myself. Fortunately, the guests don't know. I think I covered it up in time, but the staff is bound to talk. At least I think the guests don't know, but I'm not sure."

Gub had never seen Tony so flustered, but he guessed a severed head on one's diving board could throw even the most impeccable manners temporarily into the tank. Gub doubted that there had been any instruction on the point at the famous hotel school Tony had gone to in Lausanne. ("Heads, severed: care and handling.") Certainly nothing in the Lisboa manager's vast store of skill and polish had prepared him for such a problem.

It looked like the Lisboa's pool hadn't been painted in quite a few years, and Gub guessed the filtration system could probably use a good overhaul as well. But the water was still as clear and blue as Gub remembered it as a kid, and not a stray leaf or water bug defiled the wind-riffled surface.

"I hope I didn't do anything wrong," Tony said. "I just wanted to cover it up as quickly as I could."

At the end of the diving board, a beige beach towel with the Lisboa's faded logo, the letters "HL" over the Sebastião family seal, concealed a basketball-sized object. A corner of the towel dangled just above the water. Carefully, Gub made his way to the end of the board, lifted a corner of the towel and stared. Ridiculously, the first thing that came to his mind was Yul Brynner. Gub's father had bought the sound track of *The King and I* when Gub was a teenager, and for some reason, he had never forgotten the photo on the album cover with Deborah Kerr. Strange, the things one remembered. Beneath the towel, the head was abnormally large, but carefully, even expertly, shaved. Just like Vladimir Lenin, Gub thought.

"Please, Gub, you can look at it all you like later, if that's what you have to do. But could you just get it out of here now?"

Gub appreciated Tony's concern, but he wanted to do this right. He noticed the cut at the neck was clean and exact. Whoever had left the head had placed it carefully on a small square of waxed paper, so as not to mar the diving board's white stippled surface.

"Hurry, please, Gub."

Reluctantly, he reached down and grabbed the corner of the towel dangling above the water, gathered it with another corner in his left hand and tipped the head gently sideways into the scooped folds of the fabric, taking care to cover the head completely as he turned it upside down and eased it into the crook of his right arm. This way, Gub figured, the thing wouldn't leak onto his shirt or trousers. With his left hand he picked the piece of waxed paper up by a corner, folded it carefully between his thumb and forefinger and placed it in his breast pocket. It was almost certainly a waste of time, Gub thought, but they might as well dust it for fingerprints anyway.

"Gub, I don't know how to thank you." They were in the parking lot, and Gub had already placed the head in the towel in the back of the Land Cruiser. He didn't have another box to put it in, so he wedged the head in the towel between the heavy-duty jack and the spare he had still not gotten around to having repaired.

Tony was hovering by the car, but the look in his eye said he wanted to do nothing so much as to go back and begin the damage-control campaign from his command post behind the front desk.

"I'm grateful you came, Gub," Tony said, as the detective slammed the rear hatch of the Toyota, hoping the head wouldn't roll around on the way to Calamidades. "Why don't you come by later in the week, say Thursday, and we'll have dinner? Just the two of us? A couple of bottles of Muscadet, some grilled fish? It'll be just like old times."

"I'd like that, Tony. I'll give you a call." Back in the Toyota, Gub eased out of the Lisboa parking lot. The heads were adding up, he thought. How many more?

FIVE

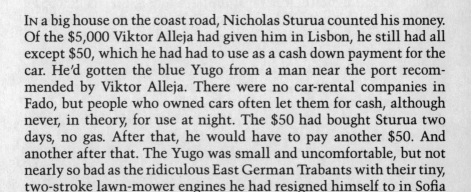

IN a big house on the coast road, Nicholas Sturua counted his money. Of the $5,000 Viktor Alleja had given him in Lisbon, he still had all except $50, which he had had to use as a cash down payment for the car. He'd gotten the blue Yugo from a man near the port recommended by Viktor Alleja. There were no car-rental companies in Fado, but people who owned cars often let them for cash, although never, in theory, for use at night. The $50 had bought Sturua two days, no gas. After that, he would have to pay another $50. And another after that. The Yugo was small and uncomfortable, but not nearly so bad as the ridiculous East German Trabants with their tiny, two-stroke lawn-mower engines he had resigned himself to in Sofia and Bucharest. Small and anonymous, the blue Yugo would do just fine.

Viktor Alleja had arranged for the house, so there was no expense on that score, either. The place belonged to a man named Paul Achebe, Fado's in-town *curandeiro*, as Viktor Alleja had described him. Sturua had seen plenty of strange things during his years with the Securitate and the mind games they had played with new recruits. But that was no preparation for dealing with a medicine man, which is what Viktor Alleja had said a *curandeiro* was. Achebe must have been no ordinary medicine man, Sturua thought, opening and shutting cupboards in the big center-island kitchen with the built-in G.E. refrigerator-freezer. Sturua had never seen anything like it or, despite his privileged status as a Securitate shopper back in Bucharest, the stuff inside of it. In the freezer were a half dozen frozen racks of lamb dressed out with the fat already trimmed from the ends of the ribs. There were a dozen frozen sea bass, something that looked like frozen marinara sauce in a big Tupperware container and about two dozen steaks of several different cuts. The refrigerator part had even more goodies. There were boiled spiced prawns in a ceramic dish covered with plastic wrap, two boiled spiny lobsters on a white platter, uncovered, and a cold three-bean salad of the type Sturua had had during a brief summer stopover in Geneva a few years back. Where the vegetable drawers should have been at the bottom of the fridge, there was a modified rack of sorts. The medicine man must also be a big beer drinker, Sturua thought. The aluminum rack held what Sturua guessed must be about a case and a half of beer, and since it sat directly over the G.E.'s powerful refrigeration unit, the beer was very cold indeed, rows of green and brown bottles perspiring in their little aluminum tombs. Sturua grabbed a Pilsen Urquell, opened it on the Coca-Cola opener screwed into the doorjamb and climbed up on a tall cane-backed chair at the kitchen's center island while he decided what he wanted to eat.

Opting for the prawns and some of the bean salad, Sturua grabbed another Pilsen Urquell and considered his options. Viktor Alleja's $5,000 wasn't much, he knew, but he would have few expenses here. And the job seemed easy. From what he had been told in Lisbon, the bandits already had control of the countryside; it would take only a brief, intensive assault on the capital to send the government packing.

It could not be a conventional military attack, however. Viktor Alleja had stressed that in Lisbon, and in just three days in the capital, Sturua had seen the reasons why for himself. The country's army was pathetic. Some troops, as he had seen on his way in from the airport, didn't even have shoes. But they were bivouacked around the outskirts of the capital, and they did have guns, at least more than the bandits probably had, as well as a sizable numerical advantage. No, Viktor Alleja had said, and Sturua agreed with him, the assault would have to be such that it would give those in the capital such a bad case of the shakes that the government would be totally discredited, ripe for plucking by a tough law-and-order alternative that Viktor Alleja would doubtless provide.

The government in Fado was hanging on by just a thread, Viktor Alleja insisted. If that was so, Sturua figured, this would be a reasonably quick job indeed. All it would take was a little shove, and the best way of delivering that was with some good old-fashioned terrorism.

The heads alone would probably be enough to do it, Sturua thought, helping himself to some more prawns and the bean salad. Hell, the heads would probably be all he'd need.

LESS than twenty miles to the north of the medicine man's place on the coast road, Padre Francisco also had heads on his mind. For twenty-three years the funereal Franciscan with the somber gray eyes had served the village of Plumtree, and he had seen plenty in that time. Still, the five headless torsos littered like ragdolls outside the cashew plant down the road from his little house were a first. All had come from the village. Their families had had to identify them by their clothing and by birthmarks. Padre Francisco had buried them all that morning.

It made him wonder. Until now, he thought, the bandits had been interested only in knocking out the cashew-shelling plant. It was less than a quarter mile from his place, and it had been hit before—twice, in fact. Still, despite the entreaties of his parishioners in the village, Padre Francisco refused to move. He liked it here. He liked just about everything about it, in fact. Where many others complained of the searing heat, Padre Francisco perspired along with them, but he relished the feel of the sun on his thin hair. He had read about the greenhouse effect and didn't believe a word of it. Still, after his morning shower, he'd spray under each arm, then give an extra blast of Arrid out the bathroom window. "For you," he said. "God bless."

The priest especially liked his little place just outside of Plumtree. Beyond his small patio outside the sliding glass doors, a craggy hill rose gently to the sky, obscuring his neighbor's farm a quarter mile away in the other direction from the cashew plant. A few goats sometimes wandered through, browsing in the dry grass, but they did little to disturb the solitude that allowed Padre Francisco to daydream uninterrupted for hours. Sometimes, in the deep shade of the roundwood tree that kept the patio bearable even in the heat of the day, Padre Francisco dreamed that he was the last man on earth. Then a thin breeze carried the noise of the metal machines shelling the cashews, and Padre Francisco began to stir.

On one such day two weeks before, the priest had awakened to the sight of a bandit on the hill. He had been a small man, maybe two hundred yards away, and he'd had a rifle and some kind of heavy backpack. Padre Francisco was sixty-eight, but his eyes were as sharp as ever. In his brown robes in the deep shade of the roundwood, the priest had apparently been invisible to the man on the hill.

"Son of a gun," Padre Francisco had sworn to himself.

For more than an hour, he had watched through hooded lids as the bandit ate some food, drank briefly from a canteen, then urinated against a long-dead Senegal khaya. Finished, the man had looped one of the backpack's shoulder straps over the tree's lowest branch, so that it hung in front of him, about chest-high. Then he had uncoiled a short cable and a gray conelike dish from the pack's wide side pouch. The bandit had done some other things with the backpack device that Padre Francisco hadn't quite understood, then he'd spoken briefly into a kind of microphone, which he'd held in his right hand. And after that he had listened for nearly three minutes, by Padre Francisco's watch, every so often scribbling rapidly into a notebook he kept in the breast pocket of a sweat-stained green T-shirt. When he was finally done, the bandit folded everything back up, looked around once in a sort of careless way, then marched off east around the hill.

The second attack on the cashew factory had come exactly two days later.

The thing about the bandits, Padre Francisco told people, was they were amateurs. Ruthless amateurs, it was true, but amateurs all the same. The first attack on the cashew factory, for instance, had been an absolute botch, a complete miss, and then the attackers had scattered like Fonseca's barnyard hens. The second had been a little better. At least they'd hit the building that time. A rocket-propelled grenade had knocked down a section of corrugated tin wall, but the angle had been such that it had merely glanced off it and skidded away harmlessly into the woods. A few factory workers had simply propped up the wall with wood struts, and the factory had lost less than four hours of operating time.

The headless torsos, though, didn't square with Padre Francisco's other thoughts about the bandits. Sipping a Campari and soda as the shadows fell slantwise in the grass and the sun dipped to the slope of his hill, the priest could understand the attacks on the cashew plant. Clearly, the bandits intended to destroy what little remained of the country's shattered economy, and cashews, amazing as it seemed, were now the country's principal source of export revenue.

Not that the country was poor. Coal reserves were estimated at about 700 million tons, iron ore about half that, and there were sizable deposits of natural gas, manganese, uranium and diamonds. Before the revolution, Padre Francisco knew, there had also been a nascent but highly promising effort to extract and export tantalite. The country had what was believed to be the world's largest deposit of the stuff, and because of its terrific anticorrosive qualities, it was becoming highly prized in the production of chemical fittings and electrolytic capacitors.

Someday, Padre Francisco told his parishioners, such riches will make your country great and prosperous. But for now, he thought, returning to his patio chair with another Campari, they would have to rely on the cashews.

But what if the killings continued? What then?

The shadows fell long and purple against the black hill beyond his patio, the limbs of the dead khaya splayed against the empty sky, and Padre Francisco thought sadly about the five men he had buried. All had been parishioners, but he had known none of them well; he knew none of his parishioners well, even after all this time in the village. Outside the little cemetery, he had mouthed the words of condolence to the grieving wives and children, feeling like a fool even as he did so. Not because he didn't mean them, but because they seemed so inadequate. The knot of family members had continued sobbing, unhearing. A lousy priest, Padre Francisco thought, swirling the Campari and soda water in his glass; he was truly a lousy priest.

He dozed briefly, and when he woke it was nearly dark; the last faint rays of sun limning the lip of the hill and the figure of a small man moving quickly around it.

The bandit with the backpack, the priest thought. He rubbed his eyes.

Padre Francisco had few steady habits. Since he had come to the country twenty-three years before, a middle-aged missionary dispatched by Rome to this distant backwater, he had kept up with two things only. The first was his bird-watching. As a boy in the Ticino, he had been a keen hiker and avid birder. On his eleventh birthday, his parents, well-to-do by local Swiss-Italian standards, had given him a pair of small but powerful Ernst Leitz binoculars, and the glasses had rewarded him on countless occasions since with a better look at a rare finch or wood thrush. Fifty-seven years later, he still had the binoculars, hanging from a frayed leather band on the kitchen doorknob near the window above the sink. The second thing was his office. Padre Francisco still read it every day without fail. He read lots of other things, too, but he always returned to the office, sometimes supplementing it with something from the King James. Just for the sake of variety, he told himself. The priest would gladly have given up Sunday mass, as he had the daily mass years before. But there was something special still about the office. Perhaps it was that it reminded him of when he was young, still filled with Franciscan zeal to go out and save the world.

Padre Francisco no longer wanted to save the world. And the world, to judge from all the available evidence, felt just about the same about him. In fact, as far as the rest of the world was concerned, Padre Francisco officially did not exist. He was, according to the official paperwork, quite dead.

In the first days of the fighting that had led to the revolution, Padre Francisco had been reported mortally wounded in an attack by bandits on Plumtree. By the time the foreign-aid workers had reached the place seven months later, Padre Francisco had been disinclined to correct the error. Rome had written him off, he figured; the hell with them. He had his parents' small inheritance to live on, and his wants were few. In the village it would be more than enough. In fact, Padre Francisco had been grazed by a bullet fired by one side or the other during the attack on the village, but the shoulder had long since healed. On his irregular ambles around the outside of his small house now, the priest swung an old three-iron that had been left behind by the French physician, one of the idealist young doctors from Médecins sans Frontières, who had rented the place before him. The priest didn't know the first thing about golf, but he liked the way the club whirred through the dry grass, kicking up a flutter of brown blades behind its arc. Swinging it, he found, also did wonders for his back.

On the hill, the shadows deepened, but Padre Francisco could still make out the form of the bandit at the base of the dead khaya. The priest would have dearly loved to have the Leitz glasses now, but he was too scared to move.

"Stupid bastard," the priest swore.

As if to confirm the thought, the shadow lit up a cigarette. The priest leaned back to wait. The man must have been tired, he thought, to be so careless. If they had known he was there, any number of people in the village wouldn't have thought twice about killing the man. Since the murders at the cashew plant two days before, the men of Plumtree had beefed up their nightly patrols around the village. Padre Francisco thought it must be exhaustion that made the bandit so careless.

In less than ten minutes, according to the luminous dial on the priest's watch, the shadow stubbed the butt out, urinated against the dead khaya and lay down on the dry grass to sleep.

The priest gave it another hour before he moved. He wasn't sure what he intended to do, but the longer he waited, the angrier he got. Twenty-three years in this country, he thought. He no longer gave much of a damn about the rest of the world, but in a strange way he had come to love this far corner of it. He thought of the progress that had been made, the strides against the infant-killing diseases, the improvement in literacy, in farming techniques. Now, he thought, nearly everything had been undone in just a few years of war, and for what? These bandits, the priest thought, they were no more than thieves and murderers.

"Even so, faith, if it hath not works, is dead, being alone."

The priest recited the words to himself. James 2:17. It wasn't part of his office, but then, he thought, hefting the three-iron and rising quietly from his chair, neither were so many of the things he read these days.

On the hill where the shadow was, there was no sign of movement.

Enough, the priest thought.

Padre Francisco was not a man ordinarily given to anger. Small as a boy, he had watched birds while others chased balls on fields. As it was then, solitude now was really something he cherished, he realized, to an inordinate and unhealthy degree. He had never really been cut out to be a priest, he said to himself, not for the first time. Though he had wanted to help people—thus the Franciscans and the missionary life—the real draw had been the sanctified loneliness.

Well, he certainly had that now, even if it had all become a bit unsanctified.

With the bandit sleeping so close by on the hill, Padre Francisco realized how very little he really understood himself. What had it all been worth, nearly a quarter century here, retreating to his own quiet place at night, not really knowing the people he was supposed to be helping? He couldn't bear visits to strangers' homes. And he had done everything he could to discourage calls at his own home from the people in the village, pleading age or fatigue or the occasional stomach disorder. So the people, after a while, had taken the hints and stayed away.

And whether that made the priest more lonely still, he couldn't have said. But he had no doubt now that he cared for the people of the village and had, in his own way, done them a fair bit of good. Who else would have come and stayed, as he had, after all these years?

Walking across the dry grass up the gentle incline of the hill, Padre Francisco thought the voices in his head would never stop. But it was not something he had much control over anymore, the afternoon's patio daydreams slipping seamlessly into the long twilight cocktail hour; no difference, it seemed, between waking and sleeping.

Giving the three-iron a soft half-swing, the priest approached the bandit from uphill. The man had hung the backpack, just as he had the last time, from the lowest branch of the khaya. From twenty-five yards away, his sandals in his hand, the priest could see the pack's silhouette against the sky clearly. The bandit had probably hung it up to protect it from the early dew, Padre Francisco thought. That meant he wouldn't be leaving for several hours at least.

Crossing the last stretch of grass swiftly, swinging the golf club, the priest had several thoughts. Perhaps the bandit would awake and struggle. Maybe he would have to hit him, use the golf club on the man. The thought made Padre Francisco weak. Standing over the bandit—he was no more than a boy, really, sixteen or seventeen at the outside—the priest suddenly lost his taste for any such adventure. Quickly, he lifted the backpack radio from its tree hook, looped a strap over his shoulder and marched away in his bare feet, downhill towards the patio and the deeper shadows under the ancient roundwood.

It was only after he made it, standing barefoot on the cool gray slate, that Padre Francisco realized he was humming. For a moment, he couldn't imagine why.

SIX

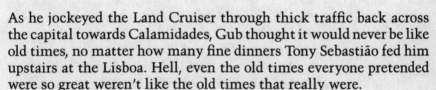

As he jockeyed the Land Cruiser through thick traffic back across the capital towards Calamidades, Gub thought it would never be like old times, no matter how many fine dinners Tony Sebastião fed him upstairs at the Lisboa. Hell, even the old times everyone pretended were so great weren't like the old times that really were.

Everything about the country, Gub thought, seemed to be associated with some strange disconnect. The traffic, for example. The conventional wisdom in Fado had it that, because of the "situation," so many people had fled to the city in cars and on motorbikes that the streets had simply become too congested.

That was nonsense.

The truth of the matter, Gub reflected as the high-sprung Toyota jounced through a deep rut, was that the streets were in such lousy shape simply because it was suicidal to drive on them above fifteen or twenty miles an hour. They had just been let go, the streets. There was no money, and so, no maintenance. In some places, yawning holes and junked cars reduced passage to less than half a lane of roadway and some of the crumbling sidewalk.

The business about the good old days was so much like that, Gub thought. The British, the Spanish and the Portuguese had all had their crack at the country, and each at the time had professed to have imposed its will on it.

More nonsense.

Outside the capital and the few larger cities in the interior, the people lived as they had always lived. Family and village were what mattered, and if outsiders came along and made their lives hell, the families and villages soon disappeared, vanishing into the night and finding new fields to till still further from the rich bottomlands close to the coast.

Not all the newcomers to the country had been bad men. Gub knew that. But he also knew that therein lay the germ of the elaborate mythology about the good old days. Of this, in fact, Gub had direct and personal knowledge. The best kind.

Even now, years later, he could still recall the sweet kitchen smells from the big farmhouse near the river and see his grandfather's handsome waistcoats at Sunday dinner. Dark wool, in spite of the bright heat and the clouds of humidity that rolled off the big river a half mile away. The whole family dressed for dinner, and even at age six, Gub knew what the small fork was used for and the penalty for using the big one first.

"Manners and breeding," Humberto Gub, Sr., had instructed his small clan on the river. "These are the mark of the gentleman."

Until very lately upon his arrival in Fado, however, the old man's claim on the title had been of the utmost dubiety. With little means and even less good fortune, he had been, until the very final quarter of his life, a brutal and incurious man, convinced of his own victimization in some great, inexplicable and cosmic wrong. In fact, he was luckier than most. The son of a self-educated Lisbon lawyer, Humberto Gub, Sr., had inherited the modest practice that catered to small businessmen, export shippers and property owners. It wasn't that he had run it into the ground precisely; the Depression had seen to that. But he had done very little to salvage the parts of the practice that might have been saved. An attorney whose big-knuckled hands seemed somehow less well suited for drafting contracts than for hard manual labor, Humberto Gub, Sr., had not owned his home, and unlike his father before him, he'd no prospect of doing so. Indeed, he had been beset by a growing mountain of debts that threatened to come crashing down on him and his still-growing family.

Not that Humberto Gub, Sr., had cared a whole hell of a lot about the family. What little interest he took in his wife and five children seemed, between fits of depression and the nightly bottle of port, to be expressed mainly in terms of general invective and vague but energetic criticism. Humor, Gub remembered, wrestling the Land Cruiser around an ancient Chevy Impala long since cannibalized for parts, was not among his grandfather's more endearing qualities.

The old man had been a piece of work, Gub thought. He had passed away when Gub had been just seven, but the stories about him were as fresh as yesterday. Mainly they had come from Gub's father, a more ethereal soul who had loved books and the law the way the old man somehow never could. As he had told it, Humberto Gub, Sr., had come home from the office in the Bairro Alto, the upper city of Lisbon, one unusually warm spring evening. Gub's own father had been just sixteen at the time, the oldest of the five children. Instead of the usual grumbling that night, before settling his bulk onto one of the six hard chairs around the oval kitchen table, Humberto Gub, Sr., had hefted one daughter onto a shoulder and given his tiny wife a kiss. "Humberto," Maria Gub had complained, "you've been drinking."

The lawyer, forty-one at the time, ignored the remark. "Maria," he said, easing his daughter to the floor and fishing a crumpled map from a pocket, "we are going to Africa." The year: 1931.

The rest was history. The Gubs had gone, all right, subsidized by a Lisbon investor who had acquired a vast stretch of land north of Fado for next to nothing. Humberto Gub, Sr., didn't know the details. All he knew was that the man had offered to assume his debts, which then amounted to some $2,840, and pay for the family's passage by ship. In return, Humberto Gub, Sr., would serve as the investor's eyes and ears in Fado, securing the necessary documents for the property and seeing about what good use the land might be put to.

The Gub family, in tears except for their impatient patriarch, had set sail on a broiling July day. It had been a hideous journey. Off the Cape of Good Hope, one Gub daughter, Antonia, had died of dysentery, and another very nearly perished. After nearly two months recuperating in Fado, the journey by flatboat up the big river had inflicted only slightly less trauma. At the first crocodiles she had seen slithering down the mud banks of the big river, Maria Gub had fainted. When she had been revived with smelling salts and brackish river water, Maria Gub had sworn up and down at Humberto Gub, Sr. Then she had fainted again.

Yet somehow the family survived, and even prospered.

The lawyer's big hands, so clumsy around desks and documents, were gifted in the tilling of soil, the mending of machinery and the construction of shelter. Within just a year, a skeleton of the handsome farmhouse had taken shape, and women of the Tsonga tribe were pushing Humberto Gub's leased fields further and further towards the horizon, while their spouses tended their own cattle, having agreed to breed them the following year with a bull already purchased by the new white man on the big river.

Humberto Gub, Sr., had written a long letter to his benefactor explaining that his newly acquired land, some one thousand acres, was wild. In truth it was. What Humberto Gub, Sr., was clever enough not to mention, however, was its enormous potential. Pleading necessity and the cost of the long journey back, Humberto Gub, Sr., had offered to lease the land from the investor, with a provision to buy sections of it at future dates, to be specified later. Presumably, the investor was satisfied with the arrangement. After all, thanks to his faith in the failed Lisbon lawyer, at least he now had proper title to his property. And if his first payment on the lease was a properly executed but likely worthless IOU, so what? He had no immediate plans for the land, and besides, in his heart of hearts, he didn't know whether his meager investment would ever be worthwhile and so didn't mind selling part of the property off.

On the new homestead of the Gub family, evidence of abundance was everywhere. The children harvested groundnuts with ease, fat cashews virtually fell from the squat, broad-leaved trees and both yielded ready cash to the sweating traders who plied the big river in their long low boats.

Though he would later claim, over Sunday dinners in the big house, that he had had it all planned, Humberto Gub, Sr., was no visionary. Bored and frustrated late in life, he had grasped blindly at the only chance fate seemed likely to extend his way, and his bet had turned out a bigger winner than anyone could have imagined. Just a year after the Gub family embarked on the schooner *Fair Wind*, Portugal's new dictator, Antonio Salazar, offered reduced passage, land and other incentives to boost emigration to his colonies in Africa. The promise of land was key. Thousands of peasants and laborers, with little or no chance of owning anything, rushed to Fado. Bewildered in their strange new home, many soon found themselves in the fast and capacious embrace of Humberto Gub, Sr.

The lawyer charged them only a modest fee for the privilege.

The elder Gub flourished as never before. The big farmhouse sprouted room after room to accommodate new arrivals of would-be land barons like himself. Land was virtually free for the taking, and Humberto Gub, Sr., had already laid claim to sizable pieces of the Lisbon investor's vast tract, paying cash when he could, signing IOUs when he couldn't.

The investor was simply pleased to see the first profits from the venture.

Humberto Gub, Sr., was also pleased. As pleased as punch, in fact. At midday, the wide veranda sheltered the extended Gub clan as it took its meal before returning to the fields. The house was his. And before too long, he thought, casting his eye to the horizon, all the land he saw would be his, as well.

Stranger than strange, Humberto Gub, Sr., the incurious Lisbon lawyer, also began to develop into something like a man of learning. At nights in the farmhouse near the big river, he began reading history and philosophy.

He even became something of a philosopher himself, Gub recalled, swinging the Toyota into the parking lot at Calamidades. Just as he had learned to build a comfortable home from tough ironwood and baobab trees, Humberto Gub, Sr., had used his reading to construct a theory of his own presence on the continent. It had had a huge effect on Gub's father, the lectures to new refugees before a flickering fire in the big farmhouse's great room. The elder Gub had held forth, dishing up all sorts of arcana for his captive audience. Magellan's pioneering journey down the African coast in 1498 was a favorite. So was the Berlin Conference of 1885, when the powers of Europe conveniently carved up the Dark Continent among themselves.

Humberto Gub, Sr., found the subject endlessly fascinating. The Portuguese had been a great people, world-beaters, he had lectured. In 1542, they had been the first Europeans to discover Japan, where they had introduced Christianity and gunpowder, a neat study in contrasts. But it was here on these fertile plains, Humberto Gub, Sr., had said, gesturing with both arms out across the veranda of the big farmhouse, that the future lay.

Long after, when he was a teenager, Gub's father told him how the lectures were wrong on a lot of counts. Magellan, for instance, was hardly the swashbuckling figure Humberto Gub, Sr., painted him as. Lame, short and inarticulate, a figure "without much personality," as one of his contemporaries recorded, he had nevertheless been a splendid navigator. The problem was, as Gub's father pointed out, Magellan had done his navigating for the Spanish, not the Portuguese; in fact, the Portuguese had been so concerned about Magellan's threat to their holdings in Asia they had contemplated assassinating the bandy-legged sailor. As for another of his grandfather's heroes, Prince Henry the Navigator, alas, he hadn't gotten that story quite right, either. True, the prince had established Europe's first maritime academy, assembling navigators, mapmakers and ship captains at a gloomy, storm-racked battlement on the Portuguese coast. But as his father pointed out gently, the prince had never actually gone anywhere; an ascetic recluse vowed to chastity, he just liked to plan trips and voyages. A small boy, Gub could recall his grandfather's flashing eyes and querulous tone. When he learned about the dubious historiography years later, he wondered why no one had ever challenged the old man on it.

Of course no one ever did.

As he locked the Toyota and headed into the mob of people outside Calamidades, Gub thought that they might have been doing the old man a great kindness. But then again maybe not.

It was nearly 8 A.M. by the time Betty and Matthias had each had a shower. Matthias hadn't liked the flat, hard spray at first, but after Betty adjusted it, he spent nearly twenty-five minutes in there, Betty dragging him out in the end and shoving a towel at him.

It was just twelve miles to the office on Vladimir Lenin, but with the traffic and the endless stream of people pushing and hauling carts of furniture and bundles of rice, firewood and maize on both sides of the road, it had taken more than half an hour, flies and dust scuttling through the open windows, because Save the Children still hadn't gotten the air-conditioning in the two-year-old British Land-Rover fixed. By the time they arrived, Betty had perspired through the back of her drip-dry summer dress with the blue cornflowers on it, and Matthias, having had no tape deck to play with the whole way, had bolted before Betty could even say goodbye. By the time she got to the orphanage, which was another five miles from the office on Vladimir Lenin, it was 9:15, and the place was bedlam. It had taken her twenty minutes to corral the boys into the classroom, and now, finally, silence reigned.

It never failed to strike Betty Abell how quiet twenty-seven boys in one room could be.

They ranged in age from six to fourteen, and about the only thing they had in common was that they had all been captured by the bandits at some point in time and pressed into service as porters, animal tenders or, in a few cases, killers.

The sun was hot and bright outside, but a soft breeze blew through the classroom's big windows, carrying the chatter of insects and the bleating of sheep from the field next door. Though the spelling and arithmetic exercises were plenty worthwhile in their own right, Betty knew their real value was in taking the boys' minds off the black, bat-winged fears she glimpsed from time to time flitting like shadows in the corners of their eyes.

Nighttimes in the orphanage were the worst. Some nights Betty wouldn't leave till well past midnight, her hands still damp from toweling off fevered foreheads. Some of the kids—she thought of Matthias and what the textbooks called his elective mutism—would probably never recover from their trauma. Nearly all manifested some kind of psychophysiologic disorder, though most were not as severe as Matthias's. In her six months in Fado, however, nearly all the boys had begun to show signs of progress. Some had broken her heart, not just with the stories of their abuse at the hands of the bandits, but with their shy kindness towards each other. Philippe was among the oldest in the group, a tough kid of eleven. In seven months with the bandits, he told Betty, he had killed five or six people. He couldn't remember exactly, but he had used a knife on each one. He remembered that much. With a stack of chewed-up Crayolas, he had even re-created three of the murders for Betty. Philippe had escaped finally during a brief skirmish between the bandits and some government troops, and the soldiers had brought him to the capital. Philippe didn't know where any of his family was, and he had nightmares about the people he had killed, even though he couldn't quite explain it.

Betty knew from her studies, but more from the months of work with kids like Philippe, that there was something about murder that defiled some special part of a child's insides. Some adults might kill without remorse, Betty knew, but children simply could not. In most cases, nightmares and low self-esteem were typical reactions, but so was an impulse to try and make up for things in some way. The way Philippe chose was to look out for Fernando. He was the smallest of the boys in the orphanage, either six or seven years old. Though neither Philippe nor Fernando was very voluble, Betty had watched in amazement over the past months as they had become best friends, the difference in their ages notwithstanding. Fernando had lost his entire family, murdered by the bandits about thirty miles from Fado. When the dreams got too bad at night and Fernando couldn't sleep, Betty had listened quietly as he woke Philippe, and then she listened some more as Philippe sang to him, soft and low, for hours, quietly, so as not to wake the other boys.

In the darkened dorm room, punctuated by the sound of small boys' snores and the odd cough, Betty Abell thought she had never heard a more beautiful sound in the world. That alone, she thought, made the rest of the work worthwhile.

The money for the orphanage, like her $22,000-a-year salary and the office Land-Rover, came from the U.S. State Department. But had it not been for the persistence of Ambassador Hills, who had forced the money to be disbursed, there would have been no orphanage, and Betty Abell would probably still be back in East Grand Rapids, living with her parents and brothers in the rambling old mansion on Cambridge Street, commuting to the other side of town to work with the Mexican farmworkers' kids.

It would have been a good life, Betty thought often, but nothing like this, nothing so meaningful. The Abells had a cabin in the Upper Peninsula, where Betty's grandfather had taught her to fish and swim. Elliott Abell, a founding partner of Abell and Plimpton, had bought the place in Tranquility nearly fifty years ago, and Abells had been going there ever since. Thinking about it as she traversed the ruined streets of the capital on her way to the orphanage each day, Betty never failed to wonder at how fortunate she had been. Thanks to the A&P, as she and her brothers called the firm where her father was now the senior partner, they had swum in Tranquility's clear waters as children, roamed around Europe as teenage summer tourists and gone on to good colleges and promising careers. Bob, the oldest, was in his last year of law school and would join the A&P when he finished. David was already earning good money as an architect in Chicago. And when Betty had completed her master's there, it had been assumed that she would either take a job near the university or come back to work in Grand Rapids. No one, including Betty, had counted on the bulletin-board notice of the job in the orphanage on the other side of the world. Once she'd seen it, though, Betty Abell had known it was for her.

In the stillness of the morning classroom, as she thought of Philippe's soft nighttime singing and watched the rows of dark heads bowed over their books, she knew she had never made a better decision. Thank you, Ambassador Hills, she thought, thanks, State Department.

"This," Gub told Ellis, shaking him by the shoulders, a full head taller than the younger man, "is a clusterfuck."

Calamidades was even worse than he had expected. Miraculously, Anna-Marie had arrived just before nine, about a half hour after Gub got there. But as he had feared, word of the head on Vladimir Lenin had spread fast, and the two heads at Calamidades had caused a panic among the people packing the dusty courtyard. "Bandits, bandits." The words seemed to fill the air, the susurrus a pregnant cloud in the gathering heat. Everywhere Gub turned, someone demanded information. Was an attack imminent? How many dead?

With Ellis's help, Gub sorted the crowd into two groups, one of which seemed to know very little, the other nothing at all. Of course that didn't prevent members of both from offering theories, guesses and outright lies about what they had seen or thought they had seen. No one challenged the obvious, that the bandits were behind it all, and as people spilled off the stairway leading to the Calamidades offices and across the sidewalk and out into the street, the buzz grew louder still: "bandits, bandits, bandits."

Gub had collected the two heads, the one from the entranceway and the other from the elevator, and put them in a storage closet. Some way to handle evidence, he thought, not for the first time that morning, shooing some more people out the heavy steel front door.

"Clusterfuck," Ellis said to no one in particular. "I see."

With the younger man, Gub herded a half dozen people into a waiting room off the Calamidades lobby. Next he escorted Anna-Marie inside and installed her at a table, getting a straight-backed chair from the other side of the room.

"Names and addresses first," he snapped. "I'll be right back."

Grabbing Ellis by the elbow, Gub went back outside, gave him a notebook from the Toyota and told him to get names and addresses of those people still milling around. "Tell them we'll get back to them in a day or two," Gub said. "Tell them anything, but get them the hell out of here."

"Clusterfuck," Ellis muttered, wading into the crowd. "Okay!"

Gub's report to the minister later that day was a model of economy. In the early morning hours of the eighth of January, between 6:05 and 7:35, four severed heads had been found within the jurisdiction of the capital police, Chief Detective Humberto Gub III investigating. No positive identification had been made on any of the heads, and no suspects had been identified as having placed the severed heads in their respective said locations.

That was pretty much the gist of it. The investigation, the report said, was continuing under the highest-priority status.

That last had been added at the instruction of Carlos, who intended to deliver it by hand to the justice minister later in the day. Gub had made no objection, it being the truth. His only real objection was the one he always raised with Carlos on the official reports: having to sign his full name.

Gub detested the name Humberto.

The only good news was that the report, after several attempts by a distracted Anna-Marie, now contained not a single typo.

After leaving the report with Carlos, Gub went in search of information. Just as the department had no pretty dispatchers and no winking green computers, it also had no coroner to rely on. For an exceedingly modest retainer, however, Dr. Pran, the Indian surgeon at the government hospital, was on call for the few cases where they decided to go ahead with an autopsy. Usually, they didn't bother. If it was clear that someone like the Danish seaman had been stabbed, for instance, the cause of death on the single-page homicide report would simply say: "stabbing."

Mireles wouldn't have stood for that, Gub mused, waiting for Dr. Pran in his tiny office at the hospital, which, when the government junked most of its socialist programs the year before, had been renamed Our Lady of Fatima Municipal and Regional Center for Medical Emergencies. The government had a way with titles, Gub thought. Now if only they'd get around to renaming streets and boulevards; they probably wouldn't even be able to fit the new ones on the narrow signs, he thought, as the wraithlike Dr. Pran made his entrance, heralded by the dueling aromas of curry and stale tobacco.

"I'm afraid there's not much I can tell you, Detective," the surgeon said, slipping into the chair behind his paper-strewn desk. The place was thick with ashes and old cigarette smoke. The Indian was a good foot shorter than the detective, about five two, with a terrible overbite. "There's no evidence all the heads were severed from the bodies with the same knife," he said. "Knives don't leave much of a signature anyway, as you know, and in this instance, there is no indication that the blade or blades used had an identifying nick or a chip of any kind. It is clear, as you noted, that the blade must have been unusually sharp. The cuts are remarkably clean and even."

"So what's your guess?"

"I would not be uncomfortable with the proposition that the heads were severed sometime after death," Dr. Pran said, lighting an unfiltered Camel with a clear plastic lighter. "Obviously, we have no indications of recent bleeding, so I am basing that almost purely on the nature of the cuts, but I feel decapitation was definitely not the cause of death."

"What about the kind of knife used?"

"Well," Pran said, rising by way of indication that the department's modest retainer had just bought about all of the surgeon's time Gub would get, "have you considered a guillotine?"

SEVEN

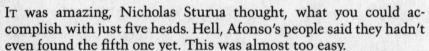

IT was amazing, Nicholas Sturua thought, what you could accomplish with just five heads. Hell, Afonso's people said they hadn't even found the fifth one yet. This was almost too easy.

Putting the second head in the elevator at Calamidades had been his idea. Notch up the tension, Sturua thought. Let them know we can get in and out of their buildings anytime we like. The head on the diving board had also been his idea. Unfortunately, that one hadn't had much effect because the police detective had removed it before the Lisboa's guests had had a chance to see it. The waiters would certainly spread the word, however, as well as some of the other hotel employees. But how much better if a few dozen hotel guests had to stare at the thing as they ordered their breakfast?

Next time, Sturua thought. Afonso said there would be no problem getting more heads.

Afonso: now, there was a piece of work. For all the hardcase sociopaths he had had to deal with in the Securitate, Sturua had never known anyone quite like Afonso. Perhaps, he thought, he was simply so frightening because he was so dumb. It had nothing to do with the fact that the man had never made it past the fourth grade; that meant nothing here. It was more the total lack of any kind of judgment at all, no matter how debased. Sturua had no illusions about his own values, but at least, he thought, there was a certain logic to them: to survive, to get ahead in a brutalizing place like Bucharest, he had had to do what was necessary. If that meant providing terrorists with weapons and money or using a bit of brutality in the course of an interrogation, so be it. It was part of the job, all of a piece with the rest of the baroque furniture in the Ceauşescus' bizarre Stalinist museum. What a place, Sturua thought, the oddball edicts on child-rearing, Ceauşescu's own unreadable philosophical tracts, the government warehouses for the unfit. Homes for the Deficient and Unsalvageable, they were called, Sturua remembered. That's what a truly twisted social order will do for your values, he thought. But Afonso? Shit, Afonso was world-class weird.

He killed, Sturua thought, because he enjoyed it. Sturua was convinced it was no more complicated than that, or at least not much more, anyway. Afonso had murdered his own bandits simply to keep the level of fear at a constant low boil. He had even bombed one of his own camps, Sturua had been told, using an old Dakota from across the border to drop a small, crude but very effective mustard-gas bomb; at least thirty of his men had died. Afonso still laughed when he told the story, Sturua was told, though he had not actually heard the story from Afonso himself. He'd have to ask him about it one day.

The accounts of Afonso's brutality were legion, but Sturua wasn't sure just yet what percentage to discount as bullshit and bluster. Whatever the case, it was clear that the bandits' failure to dislodge the government in Fado was due less to the defensive efforts of the army and Calamidades and more to Afonso's utter inability to think strategically, or even logically, about a plan of attack. Still, it had been Afonso's idea to leave the head near the coconut ladies' patch of sidewalk on Vladimir Lenin, and all the reports from his people in Fado said that was the one that had gotten people going. Of course he had also suggested leaving the fifth head in the airport's international-arrivals lounge, and so far no one seemed to know what had happened to that one. Well, Sturua thought, one out of two wasn't bad. Maybe Afonso would be all right after all.

Dialing the long-distance number from the *curandeiro*'s big study with the floor-to-ceiling windows that gave onto a view of the coast road on one side and the beach on the other, Sturua wondered how Viktor Alleja had ever hooked up with Afonso. Time enough for that later, he thought as the phone rang in the paneled sitting room in the

Alfama. He might as well check in and give the old man a progress report, let him know how things were going.

Viktor Alleja reached for the phone midway through the first ring, interrupting Sturua immediately. "This is not how we agreed to proceed. This is not how we agreed to proceed at all."

Sturua was confident he could pull off the job Viktor Alleja had given him, but he was still exhausted from the long flight a few days before and from delivering the five heads with Afonso during the middle of the night the night before. "We've been busy, Viktor. We made our first delivery last night, and it went well, Afonso's people say. The city is really buzzing. It's just taken more time than I thought to get the lay of the land, that's all. And Afonso, by the way, is not what I would call Mr. Punctuality."

"Never mind about Afonso. He's been very effective so far."

"If he's so goddamned effective, Viktor, what the fuck am I doing here? And why is this piece-of-shit government still standing? In fact, Viktor, if you want to know, it seems to be doing more than standing; it even seems to be working okay. The streets are a mess, but the people are working, and most of the shops seem to be open. If Afonso is your idea of effective, you can count me out, okay? He doesn't have the first idea about how to make this thing work. He's fine up-country, I'm sure. But this, Viktor, this needs a lot of thought."

"And that, Sturua, is why you're there. But we don't have much time, I told you that. It's been several days already now."

"We're working now, Viktor, and we'll keep working it according to the plan. We'll be fine, you'll see."

"I'm worried about the time. How long will it take at this rate? We need to know more about how the government's reacting, what the people are doing."

"I'll get Afonso's people on that and get back to you. That's no problem."

Viktor Alleja grunted, then changed the subject. "How are the accommodations?"

"Great," Sturua said, glad to be off the hook. "I never stayed in a medicine man's place before."

"I thought you'd like it."

"I'll talk to Afonso and get back to you tomorrow, Viktor, but I think we're going to be okay here. I mean it." Sturua minded his words over the phone. You never knew who was listening in on the long-distance lines. It amazed Sturua that any signal came through at all from places like Fado, with so many different parties grabbing bits and snatches of the transmission. "Where is this medicine man, anyway? I can't wait to meet him."

"In due time, Sturua. He's a busy man. So we'll talk tomorrow. I may have some ideas myself to speed things up."

"You can count on it, Viktor, don't worry. Oh, and one more thing, about the family?"

"Done."

"Thank you, Viktor." Among the many things Nicholas Sturua had left behind in the apartment in the Strasse Ploscaru were his wife and the two kids, ages three and five. Sturua wondered if they were still alive and thought not. If they were, Viktor Alleja's cable would inform them of his own untimely death. A pity, that.

THE TAP flight from Lisbon to Rome's Leonardo da Vinci Airport was twenty minutes late, but unless the Air Malta connection to Valletta was in a completely different concourse or he got hung up at immigration, Hagen figured he'd have no trouble making it. He had a brand-new passport, and after three months on the run, things seemed to be breaking his way.

He had spent just a couple of hours with Viktor Alleja in Lisbon. It hadn't taken long for the two men to agree on terms: $15,000 for two weeks of work, plus expenses. Viktor Alleja had phoned in the reservation for The Airline of Portugal flight to Rome, with the connection to Valletta.

Finally, Hagen thought, his luck was changing.

He would never forget the exact moment things had gone south. He had watched it on the nineteen-inch Sony in his apartment in Sandweg Strasse not far from the Frankfurt zoo. Though he was employed by the Stasi, the East German spy service, Hagen had lived in West Germany for years. It was a far more convenient base of operations, but it was also a much better place to live. Hagen loathed East Germany.

The real beginning of the end had come, of course, on November 9, when the Wall had been breached. Hagen still couldn't forget the crowds of Germans dancing long into the night, the East German border guards blasting them with water cannon, the young hooligans on top dripping and oblivious. Still, Hagen had thought at the time, things could somehow be salvaged, no need for him to leave, at least not yet.

A few days later, the real end had come, and he had known it was time to go. The Sony had showed crowds of hoodlums smashing the gates to the Stasi headquarters in the Friedrichstrasse in East Berlin. Hagen had watched dumbstruck as the youths began tossing Top Secret and Classified papers out the building's upper windows, the stiff November winds scattering them to the four corners of the city.

Watching the night sky on the TV whiten with secret Stasi documents, Hagen had thought, my name, everything about me, is in those papers. With the West German news announcer nattering in the background, Hagen had quickly emptied the contents of the small wall safe and thrown a blazer, a sweater and two pairs of good trousers into the battered Hartmann two-suiter. Grabbing his heavy cashmere overcoat, Hagen had shut the lights to the place, locked the apartment door and run past the elevator and down the three flights to the street. In the butcher shop across the way, Herr Hahn had waved pleasantly, as always, but Hagen had ignored him, cursing as he'd fought his way across the crowded sidewalk, flailing his free arm for a cab.

After leaving Frankfurt, Hagen had bumped around out-of-the-way corners of the continent. He had spent over a month in Yugoslavia, and nearly three weeks in a French woman's too-precious Provence farmhouse, Ralph Lauren shit on the walls and draped-over fancy bentwood chairs. It had looked like the set of a play or something, Hagen thought. He had had no idea who owned the place when he'd broken in through the kitchen window. He had simply waited for someone to come home, and when it turned out to be a handsome forty-year-old brunette, recently divorced from a Lyons banker, Hagan had decided then that his luck had changed. But he had been wrong. Though they had gone to bed a few times, the woman had been tense and usually wound up in tears. The increasingly frequent phone calls from a suspicious sister in Nantes had finally convinced Hagen to leave, but not before he had drowned her in the footed tub, Chanel bath beads giving things a nice soapy smell.

Hagen had taken care to sell each of his three Stasi-supplied passports in a different country, getting rid of them for varying sums, all cash, of course. In Belgrade, he had sold the first to an Iranian for $3,500. The second went to a Sicilian in Marseilles, where he had gone after leaving Aix-en-Provence. That had fetched $8,000. The man was surely Mafia, Hagen thought, probably running from some blown drug transaction. The last of the three passports he had dumped on a long-haired American in Barcelona whose plans he had little interest in. It had fetched an even $2,000. A steal for the American, Hagen thought, if only he didn't get caught with it.

Hagen got rid of the last passport only after he had picked up a new one. In the event, it had proved remarkably easy. Hagen had made his way south to Barcelona from Marseilles, and after two full days staking out the main train station, he'd spotted what he was looking for. The man was almost exactly his height and weight, five ten, 160, and his coloring, hairline and eye color were as close to his own as he was likely to find on such short notice. Hagen had followed the man through the vaulted train station down the long corridor between the waiting area and the place where the trains came in. Near a crowded newsstand, Hagen had closed the distance as the man paid for a *Diario las Américas*. Hagen couldn't believe his luck. The man wasn't even Spanish.

Hagen had already picked the spot where he finally made his move. Beyond the newsstand, the corridor to the trains made a sharp turn to the right and another to the left. The lighting was bad, and Hagen had made it worse still by breaking several light fixtures the day before. At the first turn in the corridor there was a maintenance closet. Hagen had already picked the lock. Wearing the crepe-soled shoes he favored for these kinds of jobs, he came up behind the man quickly and hailed him loudly in Spanish. As the man turned, his heavy winter coat flew open, and Hagen shoved the three-inch blade with the black plastic handle expertly into the soft spot just below the sternum. The man dropped both his briefcase and his suitcase as Hagen hustled him to the maintenance closet, uttering protestations of concern for the benefit of any curious passersby. Fortunately, there were none, and Hagen had the man inside, his wallet, passport and traveler's checks in his own pockets within less than forty seconds. The man was already dead, stabbed through the heart. Hagen paused only to remove the blade from the man's shirtfront before relocking the maintenance closet from the outside. Striding rapidly down the corridor, Hagen flipped through the contents of the wallet and travel documents and saw there was a prepaid one-way ticket on the noon train to Madrid. He had made it with ten minutes to spare, rented a four-door Renault in the Madrid train station and driven across the border to Portugal near Évora. It was late, and no one checked his passport.

Thus, Hagen thought, another benefit of European unity.

Getting to Malta would be something else again, Hagen worried as the small TAP plane banked sharply on its final approach to Leonardo da Vinci. It was just under forty-eight hours since he had left the body of César Ochoa, the Colombian businessman, in the maintenance closet of the Barcelona train station. Hagen had scanned the papers in Lisbon while waiting for the flight to Rome, but he had seen nothing about the murder. With no identifying papers and very little else to go on, maybe the Barcelona police were just waiting until someone called up and asked about the whereabouts of a missing Mr. Ochoa.

As he approached the two *carabinieri* standing alertly next to the passport-control center, Hagen hoped to God Ochoa didn't have a nervous-Nelly wife somewhere back in Bogotá.

Two days was a long time, Hagen worried, but there was nothing he could do about it now. In fact, he thought, he had less reason to worry about his new passport and more that some sharp-eyed immigration officer would recognize him from the rifled Stasi files that had certainly been distributed to European police agencies by now. Hagen had cut his hair crew-cut short and shaved his moustache, but a sharp-eyed cop might still detect the resemblance. Hagen knew that duplicates of every Stasi record had routinely been sent to the headquarters of the KGB in Moscow's Dzerzhinsky Square. With its eye on the Soviet Union's increasingly restive nationalities, the KGB was now so concerned about terrorism that it had even begun seeking assistance from the CIA's counterterrorism people, who surely knew plenty by now about Hagen's bloody background. And then there was Interpol to worry about, though Hagen had been making fools of them since he was nineteen.

As he stepped to the head of the line in front of the immigration officer's bulletproof-glass booth, Hagen thought that he would be of particular interest to any number of police agencies. Terrorism had been his business in thirteen very successful years with the Stasi, working with the fanatics of the Baader-Meinhof Gang first and afterwards the Red Army Faction and an assortment of Libyan agents in West Germany and Italy. There was no earthly reason he could think of why someone with access to the Stasi records might not have alerted the CIA, the KGB, Interpol or the German or Italian federal police.

"Next." The dark-haired woman in the bulletproof-glass booth looked unusually severe.

Hagen said nothing, slipping César Ochoa's passport and his buff-colored customs-declaration form into the pass-through.

"Destination, please?"

"Malta," Hagen said politely. "A brief holiday."

"You are from Bogotá?"

"*Sí, señora*," Hagen said. "A long way from home."

"Nothing to declare?" It was the woman's job to look skeptical, Hagen thought.

"Nothing," he replied, glancing obviously at his watch.

"*Grazie*," the woman said after several seconds, banging the *Italia* stamp loudly into the passport. "You may go. Next."

"*Grazie*," Hagen said, already moving. "I've got a tight connection."

If Hagen's change of planes in Rome was fast, his turnaround in Valletta was even quicker. Libya and Malta have no visa restrictions, and the airport was much smaller than Leonardo da Vinci. Changing from Air Malta, Hagen boarded a Piper Alfa belonging to Syrian-Arab Airlines for the quick hop to Tripoli.

Hagen hated Libya. But he knew no better place to get the kind of stuff he needed to carry out Viktor Alleja's assignment in Fado.

BESIDES the solitary three-iron, the Frenchman from Medecins sans Frontières had also left Padre Francisco a world-class hidey-hole. Government troops had had some success against the bandits in the past year, but the campaign of killing and terror had left the country-side paralyzed with fear, and the *matsangas* were still pulling off slash-and-burn raids on villages within ten miles of Fado, small tongues of flame licking the night as homes and businesses burned madly, the business of murder and dismemberment illuminated by the dying embers. Before the Frenchman had left and Padre Francisco moved in, bandits had broken into the place several times looking for drugs and bandages, booze and clothing. Fortunately, because he spent most of his time crisscrossing the countryside, hopping from village to village in a tiny single-engine Cessna, the young doctor had missed the bandits each time. After the last one, however, the Frenchman had spent the better part of a day with an ice pick and an old scalpel scraping the grouting from around two big stones high up in the kitchen hearth. Behind the hearth was the rear wall of the bedroom closet, which was thoughtfully trimmed out in cedar. The builder, lacking proper insulation, had evidently built in a few extra feet of air space to prevent heat from the hearth from igniting the closet wall. On the day he moved out, the doctor showed the priest how to pull the stones from the hearth, above a normal person's line of sight. A good place for hiding valuables, the doctor had said.

Since Padre Francisco didn't have many of those, he hadn't used the hidey-hole very often. But it turned out to be a perfect spot for the bandit's backpack radio contraption. As he went out for a quick nightcap on the patio, the priest only hoped the young man wouldn't come looking for it.

The angry young man striding deliberately towards his patio disabused Padre Francisco of that idea, though he pretended to sleep, praying he wasn't shaking so that it was obvious. Maybe the kid would go away, he thought. Why bother an old priest?

The rifle butt slamming into his right knee ruined that hope. "Old man," the bandit screamed. "Your Excellency!"

"What do you want?"

The rifle butt slammed into the priest's leg again, just above the kneecap. "I have questions, my Father."

Padre Francisco gasped. "I know nothing. What do you want?"

The bandit hit the priest again with the rifle, this time jabbing him with it in the right thigh. "Answers, my Father. I would like answers to my questions."

Padre Francisco remembered his easy assurances to his parishioners. They are fools, these bandits, he had said. Who was the fool now? he wondered. "I cannot help you. I have food and a little money, and you are welcome to that, but I am an old man, as you say. Who are you, my son? What do you need?"

The boy paused at the mention of food. Besides being filthy from sleeping in the fields for what the priest guessed must have been many days, he was wretchedly thin. "Food and money," he said. "Both."

His leg throbbing, Padre Francisco levered himself out of the patio chair. Why had he taken the damn radio anyway? Limping badly, sweat popping from the pores of his scalp, Padre Francisco barely made it to the kitchen. "Bread and salami, my son. Eat, please." From the small refrigerator, he got the piece of blue cheese he had been saving for after dinner. "Cheese, too. Here, please."

Wolfing the cheese and salami and bread, the bandit laid his rifle against the counter. The priest gave him a bottle of soda water, and the boy continued eating, only more slowly. "Father," he said finally, wedging the last piece of blue cheese onto a crust of bread, "I am in very much trouble."

The priest, still shaking, massaged his damaged knee. "What is it, my son?" His voice was ragged with pain.

"I have lost something very important. Someone stole it, but I will be blamed."

"It is the times," Padre Francisco commiserated, rubbing his knee and wondering if he would need to see a doctor about it. "It seems you just can't trust anyone these days."

"Goddamn right, Padre." The boy reached for his rifle and stared at the priest, rubbing his thumb and forefinger together in the universal gesture.

"But where will you go?" the priest asked, hoping to change the subject. He had already given the boy several dollars' worth of food, and except for his fondness for the Campari and sodas each night, the priest wasn't quick to part with a buck. Cheap, the villagers called him behind his back; he gave his parishioners wine at communion, for instance, only on Easter and Christmas. No way the priest wanted to give the kid any money. He tried changing the subject. "But what will you do, my son?"

"Money," the boy said. "All of it, old man. Whatever you have."

"I have only a little. I am not wealthy, you can see."

The bandit raised his rifle.

"Okay." Padre Francisco limped backwards towards the small bedroom. "Wait. Please." In the bottom of the bedroom closet, the priest had a leather satchel in which he kept his passport, the notice of his death, a copy of the one-paragraph obituary that had run in the *Giornale di Lugano* and what was left of his spending money for the month. There was $43.

"What's the holdup?" The boy had crept into the bedroom and was standing directly behind the priest. "Give it here," he said, grabbing the satchel from the priest. The boy apparently couldn't read. He let the passport and the other papers fall to the floor, turned the worn leather bag inside out, then decided to keep it for himself. "Thank you, my Father," the boy said, going back to the kitchen and shouldering his rifle. It was a very old one, an Enfield, the priest thought. The boy was already out the sliding glass doors and on the patio.

"Go with God," Padre Francisco called, waving to the bandit as he climbed briskly around the base of the hill towards Fonseca's. "You son of a bitch."

EIGHT

THE phone in the secure office rang just as Mireles was trying to decide whether to have a Cherry Coke or a Budweiser with the sandwich Amy had fixed him. It was a tuna and tomato on whole wheat, his favorite. Opting for the Bud—unless he was working, he tried to avoid caffeine late at night—he grabbed the receiver on the third ring. It was Wasick.

"Our lad's arrived, Tom, and it could be a long one."

"Where are you?"

"At a pay phone on Utopia Parkway, about a half-block from the location."

"Who's on him?"

"Reid and Lewinski in front, Capobianco and Hanlon behind. Our boy's not alone, which is why I think this could go awhile."

"Who's the other one?"

"Reid thinks it's the CTK guy, the radio reporter. But it's too dark to get a good look. Anyway, it sounds like they're going to be heading into the city, so I thought I'd catch you now while I could get to a phone."

"Thanks, John." Mireles didn't worry about his own phone. Bureau technicians swept the place once a week for bugs and even for parabolic mikes out in the neighbors' trees. They'd never found a thing. The pay phone offered even better security. "Since you've got the two of them, you'll have to stay with them. If they split up, have Reid and Lewinski take the reporter. Capobianco and Hanlon can stay with Radziewicz. Have them keep track of their hours, and give me a call here if anything comes up. I don't care how late it is, I'll be waiting."

"Ten-four," Wasick said. "Talk to you later."

"What is it, Tom?" Technically, it was a breach of Bureau policy for her to listen in on such conversations, but Amy Mireles didn't give a good goddamn anymore. Her husband was working himself to an early grave, she thought, and lately the phone never seemed to stop ringing.

"The guys picked up the Czech. We thought he wasn't going to show."

"Let them handle it, Tom. You're not going out there, are you?"

"No, Wasick's there. But our guy's with someone else, and we're interested in both of them, so I'm going to wait until John checks in again. Where are the girls?"

"Brushing their teeth. How long till he calls back?"

"Probably not long, hon," he lied, closing the office door and heading back through the living room to the girls' room. "I'll get them to bed, and then you can tell me about your day, huh?"

In the big bathroom down the hall from the bedroom they shared, the girls were just finishing up. Both had their mother's red hair, but Kate had his dark eyes, Alison her mother's luminous baby-blues. They were great kids. Good in school, they were both star forwards on their fifth-grade soccer team, something Mireles had seen to especially. Amazingly enough, they rarely fought. The teen years would doubtless be tough, Mireles thought, but if anyone could handle that business, Amy could.

"Come on, team, what's taking so long?"

Before he tucked them in, each gave Mireles a rundown of the day's events. Basketball was proving hard for Kate; Mireles would have to spend a little time with her on the hoop over the garage, and he made a mental note of it. Alison wanted to know what they were going to do this weekend, and Mireles told her to make a list of her three favorite things. Maybe they'd go into Manhattan, he thought. The Christmas decorations were still up in Rockefeller Center, the new Japanese owners making a point of doing the place up like always. It had been a long time, three years at least, since he'd taken the girls skating there, Mireles thought. Maybe they'd do that.

Shutting the light, Mireles kissed the twins good night. "No reading under the covers, now. Get some sleep."

Back in the kitchen, he spilled the untouched Bud into the sink and grabbed a Cherry Coke from the fridge. There was no telling when Wasick would call, and the caffeine would help keep him awake. Besides, he thought, taking a bite of the tuna-and-tomato sandwich, he could do some paperwork while he waited.

"Girls asleep?" While Mireles was tucking the girls in, Amy had jumped into the shower and then slipped into a long silk dressing gown that matched her eyes.

"Great sandwich. Yeah, they're asleep, I think, or close to it. Hey," he said, looking up from the morning paper he had not found time to read earlier, "don't you look great."

"Every so often," Amy Mireles said, sitting down at the kitchen table. "John called yet?"

"Could be a while," Mireles said, flipping to *Newsday*'s sports section. "You know how these things go."

Amy Mireles grunted.

"Goddamn Patriots," Mireles said. Though they had lived in New York for six years, he still followed the Red Sox and the Patriots; forget about the Mets and the Jets. Mireles had started watching sports in Boston during his days on the task force before he had met Amy. It had helped pass the long nights in the bungalow in Green Hill by himself, and it had given him something to talk about with the guys at work, something to help him fit in better than he had on the force in Providence. "The running game has just collapsed. I can hear your dad right now."

"Lousy front line," Amy said. "Too old, too slow."

"That what Mike said?" Mike Marshall had season tickets to the Patriots and the Red Sox. For a few chilly months after Mireles had asked to marry his daughter, the big Irishman had barely had the time of day for his would-be son-in-law. After a while, though, he had come around, and they had become inseparable companions at Fenway and Foxboro, the old man teaching the new immigrant the arcana of hard sliders and halfback options. Maybe the change in attitude had had something to do with the publicity about Mireles's work on the task force. It had all come out during the trials. Mireles didn't think so, however. He had too high an opinion of his father-in-law for that.

"Yeah, he also said you're working too damn hard, Tom. When was the last time you got up there to see a game with him? Last year?"

Mireles recognized the tone of voice and pushed the paper away.

"He's getting old, Tom, you know. He'd like to see you, the girls would like to see you more and goddammit, I would like to see you once in a while. Look at the girls. You barely made it home in time to see them tonight, but before that, when was the last time you saw them to bed or spent more than a crummy half hour with them?"

"Now, hold on, Ame."

"No, you hold on. Look at what you're doing. It's nearly ten now, you'll be out the door by five again tomorrow, and the next day after that and the next day after that. What kind of life is it? Did you ever stop and ask yourself that? What it all means?"

"It's the job, it's just gotten crazy lately."

"It's not the job either, Tom."

Mireles could see his wife's face was flushed, the way it got when she was really upset.

"It's you and the way you do things, Tom. Why does everything have to be so intense that it inflates one part of your life into this kind of monster that crowds all the other parts into small, dark corners? How do you think I feel? The kids are still too small to notice, but they will after a while. And they'll remember the daddy who loved them so much, the daddy who worked so hard so that they could have a better life, that that daddy was never, ever around."

"Look, you're right . . ."

"Tom, just don't tell me how this is going to change, all right? That once you get the report for the attorney general done, things'll be back to normal? The problem is that this *is* normal for you. The job has always squeezed everything else into miniatures. You're a good husband and a good father, but you are going through your life with blinders on. Except for the kids and their school, you have no interest in the neighborhood. You didn't even put the boat in the water last summer, and the way things are going now you won't put it in this one or next. That's fine. But you have no real friends at work, and the one good friend you had in Boston, my father, you hardly even have time to talk to anymore. And poor Gub, your best friend. If it wasn't for him coming to see us a couple of days every year on his vacation, you wouldn't have that friendship either. These are the things that make a life, Tom: loyalties, family, friendships. When you start letting them go, a lot of other good stuff goes with it, and suddenly you wake up and your life is over and you wonder what the hell was so important all those years."

"Sweetheart, I'm sorry, you're right . . ." Mireles had a lot more to say about how he would do better, take Amy away for a romantic weekend somewhere, spend more time with the kids, go up to see a ball game with his father-in-law and send old Gub a long letter. He was going to say all of that and maybe even some more if he could think of it, but he was interrupted by the phone in the office. He ran to get it.

"I wouldn't have called, Tom, if you hadn't insisted." It was Wasick again.

"Don't remind me."

"Sorry?"

"Never mind, John. What's up?"

"Looks like it'll be a quick night after all. Our dynamic duo is having a burger and a beer at a place on the East Side. Couple of sports. Then they say they're heading home. Reid and Lewinski will stay on them to make sure they don't make any detours, but it looks legit, just another night out in the Big Apple for the embassy hacks. I'll be around till Reid and Lewinski check back in, but this one looks like a dud."

"Nice work, John, thanks. I owe you."

Dousing the light in the office, he locked the door from the outside and went out to the kitchen to rinse off his sandwich plate. Amy was gone. Mireles checked the front and back doors, the door to the garage, and turned on the outside floods. By the time he got to their bedroom, his wife was fast asleep. Or at least she pretended she was.

Mireles decided not to investigate. Instead, he went back to the office, the caffeine from the Coke buzzing in his head. Unlocking his briefcase, he fished out a sheaf of surveillance reports and a draft of the intro he was struggling with for the A.G.'s report. He stared at the words for maybe ten minutes, focusing on them hard, trying to blot out the harder words of his wife. Finally, he shoved the mess of papers back into the briefcase and slammed the lid. All along, Mireles thought he had had things figured out. The kids, his wife, the nice house, the good schools, the job, even his retirement. But after all that, it seemed, he had missed something, something very basic and fundamental. Looking out the darkened window into the trees beyond, Tom Mireles even thought he knew what it was.

NINE

AFTER leaving Dr. Pran, Gub spent the afternoon roaming around Fado looking, he conceded, for he knew not what. Strange faces maybe, a change in the usual static buzz of the city. Something. The capital was bounded on the south by the port and the ship channel and on the east by the ocean. To the west and north it fanned out in a ragged oval, ramshackle shops and apartment buildings giving way to the ever-growing camps of squatters, which petered out finally in worthless scrubland punctuated by a few brave subsistence gardens. From its promontory in the southeast corner of Fado, the Lisboa commanded a spectacular view of the ocean, the channel and the port beyond. From the north, the Lisboa was the last in a line of what had once been majestic homes and embassy buildings marching down the coast, their mansard roofs glinting in the sun. Where the ship channel cut inland just below the hotel, a skinny blacktop road straggled west past dirtyard bungalows, a couple of small farms that spilled chicken and sheep through tumbledown fences and, closer to the port, a gaggle of ship chandlers' warehouses and dry-dock and machine shops.

On foot, Gub prowled the streets and alleys around Tony Sebastião's hotel, looking and listening, but he saw and heard noth-

ing out of the ordinary; broken asphalt baking in the heat, the
ticking of shears from behind a garden wall. Gub knew the city as
well as he knew anything. He knew how it felt and moved. And
except for the accretion of grime and the acceleration of decay, the
neighborhood around the Lisboa felt pretty much the same as it had
when he was a gangly kid at Francis Xavier, cutting afternoon classes
for a swim in the ocean.

Clueless, he returned to the Land Cruiser and checked the jerrican
in back. It was a quarter full, which was probably just about enough
for his purposes. From the Lisboa, Gub swung west past the port,
which was still operating fitfully, and then back north through
downtown and the bustle of shops and pedestrians on Vladimir
Lenin. Past the Grand Salon du Thé and the Save the Children office,
there was a used-appliance shop, a used-clothing shop, a curbside
used-tire stand that advertised "free rotation" and a stall selling used
books and secondhand magazines. A secondhand city, Gub thought,
crawling east towards the ocean among the swarm of handcarts,
private cars and the Tap-taps that served as a surprisingly efficient
substitute for any kind of organized public-transit system. For pen-
nies, anyone could climb onto the gaily painted pickup trucks and
covered vans and ride as far as the driver decided to go. There were no
fixed routes, and the traffic moved so slowly that there were not even
any stops. Gub had seen women many months pregnant clutching
chickens and sacks of vegetables and with a couple of kids in tow
vault into Tap-taps like circus performers. The Tap-taps were done
up in wild colors, and each had a name. Even after a lifetime in Fado,
Gub still found them entertaining. There were the obvious religious
motifs, most advertising the Virgin Mary, though Gub thought virtually all the major biblical themes were represented. The Tap-tap in
front of him on Vladimir Lenin, for instance, had a pretty good
depiction of Moses being given the Ten Commandments. That was
on the driver's side of the little Nissan; the passenger's side was
devoted to a cigarette ad showing a cool-looking camel wearing
sunglasses and a pretty girl in a bathing suit behind him.

Gub liked the weird ones. One of his favorites was "Freddy's
Dead," and it carried most of the lyrics from the movie *Shaft* on the
door panels and the wheel wells. Another was simply called "Love
Machine," and on the hood it had a rather good painting of a woman
with two enormous breasts; the hood ornament, naturally, was a
giant phallus.

Idling past Cecelie and the coconut ladies, Gub rolled the window down. "Any more heads today, Miss Cecelie?"

"No, sah, Detective, just coconuts like usual."

"You see anything unusual, you let me know, okay?"

Cecelie and the others bobbed their heads yes, and Gub eased away from them, shoving a Little Feat cassette into the tape deck. In twenty minutes of bumper-to-bumper on Vladimir Lenin, Gub saw nothing unusual, though he had already made up his mind about the morning's events. No doubt about it, he had told Carlos, this is it, the final push. If the bandits did not actually control the interior and most of the rest of the country, they certainly prevented the government in Fado from doing so, and now, Gub was convinced, they had begun an assault on the capital itself. Not a conventional attack, of course; the bandits didn't work that way. Besides, from what Gub knew, they weren't nearly as well organized as they would have to be to pull off that kind of operation; small villages were one thing, a city the size of Fado something else again.

No, Gub figured, if they were serious about toppling the government, it would have to be through unconventional means. It would be a campaign of terror, eating at the capital from the core out, and if it wasn't stopped, Gub was pretty sure the government eventually would fall. Someone claiming to represent authority would step in to "restore order."

He couldn't prove it, but Gub had a pretty good idea who that someone might be. Viktor Alleja.

Gub hadn't seen the burly Portuguese in years, but barely a week went by that he didn't think of him, sometimes even a bit wistfully. Viktor Alleja had been his last big case, his biggest, in fact. The details often came flooding back, but it wasn't the little man rolling tape. The details came from investigative files, his files mainly, from a time when they still maintained such things as a matter of routine in Fado.

The first time he had ever heard of Viktor Alleja, Gub had just quit the university in Cape Town, returning to bury his father. Among the other businessmen besides his father who had been undone by the new Marxist government, he had heard, was a man with the big house off Avenida 21 July. The man had vanished from Fado. Gub had unearthed the details much later.

The head of the intelligence section of Johannesburg's well-known Directorate, Viktor Alleja had made very few mistakes during a long career, but the one big one he had made turned out to be unforgivable: the political landscape was beginning to shift, and Viktor Alleja had just plain misjudged it.

A Portuguese, he could never be part of the old Boer elite that comprised the upper reaches of the Directorate. Elandslaagte, Glencoe, Rietfontein—the hallowed names of the old Boers meant little to him. They were not part of his history, the old men knew, and since it wasn't his, it didn't mean very much. And that was more or less why they had hung him out to dry, Viktor Alleja said years later; nothing personal. In fact, Viktor Alleja had won notice within the Directorate for his brutal efficiency and not, like so many of the old Boers, for impassioned and fatuous racism. By the early seventies, however, a very faint breeze had begun to blow, and there was pressure to clean up the more egregious practices of the Directorate. The end had come with a series of parcel bombs to several black student leaders. The bombs, unforgivably, had been traced back to one of Viktor Alleja's operatives. There had been an international hue and cry, and after the headlines and the embarrassing public inquiry, Viktor Alleja had been let go.

But not before he had picked up those chits he had been collecting all those years.

Because they thought he might one day be useful again, because it was inconvenient not to, some influential people had set Viktor Alleja up not too far away in Fado. Seven very rich men, all of whom owed him favors, had simply formed a consortium. The idea was to begin the groundwork for a big new hotel at Costa do Sol. Each man had gotten a share, and an eighth had been put up in Viktor Alleja's name. As the only actual working partner in the project, he would be responsible for overseeing some of the construction and any one of a million other details that might come up. If things went their way back home, the seven said, who knew, Viktor Alleja might be able to come back one day.

Fortunately, Gub thought, things hadn't gone their way, and change had convulsed not just the old Boers' lands but the region all around them. In Fado, as elsewhere, the new government had thrown out what it thought of as the old exploiters, and Viktor Alleja had been one of the first to go.

Since he couldn't go home, he had knocked around the so-called front-line states, fomenting trouble and terrorism on a pay-for-hire basis, fetching up finally in Lisbon, where some five years later a letter with a Fado postmark on it had invited him to return, "to join with your countrymen in rebuilding a great nation." Viktor Alleja had known what that was about. The starry-eyed Marxists couldn't run a grocery store, let alone a country; they needed help. Happier than he'd been in years, Viktor Alleja had grabbed the next plane.

Gub, Fado's chief of detectives since the departure of Mireles, had run into him shortly after that. The situation had only just begun to get serious in the interior, but things in the capital had not been greatly affected. At one of Tony Sebastião's informal Sunday-night suppers, Gub had been seated across from a short man in a dark suit. A cold wind had been pushing a blanket of thin mist around outside the glass walls of the Lisboa's rooftop restaurant, and Tony had ordered up a rich beef Stroganoff, heady with red wine. Gub had recognized a fellow trencherman when the man accepted a third plateful from one of Tony's matched set of waiters, and the two had fallen into conversation, Viktor Alleja relating how he had moved back into his old house off Avenida 21 July and rounded up Ruben, his original gardener, and Sylvie, the maid.

What Gub had found out only much later was that Viktor Alleja was serving two masters. Besides his partnership in Costa do Sol Ltd., he was also getting a rather hefty retainer from some of his old friends in the Directorate to funnel money and weapons to the bandits in the interior. Some in the Directorate, it seemed, loathed the Marxists on their border as much as the restive youth in the homelands.

The evidence had been anecdotal at first, picked up from the typical run of police informants and political pimps. But Gub had begun keeping a file. A bill of lading for a container cargo for Costa do Sol Ltd. had turned out on inspection by a customs man at the port to contain rocket-propelled grenades, launchers and two dozen AR-15 assault rifles. Gub had called Viktor Alleja on that, and the man had pleaded ignorance. But suddenly the justice minister had been interested in Costa do Sol and Gub had been asked to dig deeper into the matter. He'd already known a little about Viktor Alleja's background in the Directorate, but there was plenty of gossip that wasn't contained in the official record. A lot of it had to do with Viktor Alleja's chits, and a lot more had to do with his extensive network of hit men and informers. After the president had seen Gub's confidential report, he had authorized a wider investigation into Costa do Sol Ltd., leaving it in Gub's hands.

It had taken nearly two years, the end coming when an alert immigration officer at the airport had stopped a stunning blonde who had a passport but no entry visa. A routine check showed the woman was wanted for questioning in connection with the murder of a government official in Cape Town a few days before, and the case had been bumped to Gub. Further questioning and a few discreet phone calls had revealed that the woman was a $300-a-night hooker who for some reason wanted anything in the world but to go back to Cape Town. The dead man there was very powerful, she said, high up in the Directorate; she had slept with him many times but insisted she knew nothing of his death. She was sure she would never get a fair trial, and Gub was equally sure she was probably right. When she started talking about payments and weapons for the bandits outside Fado, Gub had grabbed Anna-Marie from his outer office. Viktor Alleja's name had surfaced a total of seven times in the forty-one-page typed statement. It was hearsay evidence, Gub knew, but with everything else he had, it had been enough. The justice minister himself had authorized Viktor Alleja's arrest, detaching two soldiers and two armed Calamidades men to the department. But when Gub had gotten to the offices of Costa do Sol Ltd. on Vladimir Lenin, the place had been empty. So was the big house off Avenida 21 July six blocks away. Viktor Alleja, the old intelligence officer, had evidently kept up his network of contacts admirably.

One of them had tipped him off just in time.

Gub never did figure out who it was, and though his report on the financing of the bandits had been excerpted by Amnesty International, Viktor Alleja's name never appeared in the published version. There was only a single reference to "Fado business interests." And that was the last Gub had heard of Viktor Alleja.

The growing head count in Fado told Gub he might soon be hearing a lot more, however. He had no idea what Viktor Alleja had been doing since he'd left Fado, but he did know that the only time the bandits had pulled off anything besides burning defenseless villages in the interior had been in the brief period when Viktor Alleja had been living in Fado. The severed heads, strategically placed around the capital, bore the mark of a professional terrorist. It was either Viktor Alleja himself or one of his trained emissaries. Either way, it was the kind of op typical of the Portuguese, Gub thought, and the head of Vladimir Lenin and the three others now in Dr. Pran's refrigerator were just the opening salvo in the operation.

Actually, he thought, turning onto the four-lane coast road where Vladimir Lenin dead-ended, he was surprised it hadn't come sooner.

Since the situation had worsened in recent years, some of the big embassies along the ocean had been shuttered, smaller staffs moving into flats and offices in newer, air-conditioned buildings further north towards Costa do Sol. Betty lived in one of the newer buildings, but since none of the four heads had been found there, Gub decided to save that section for last, focusing instead for now on the big houses set back from the highway along the water.

Gub couldn't remember just who was responsible, whether it was the original Fado city planner or not, but whoever had designed the coast road had left it with something of an identity crisis. The effect that had been striven for was that of Baron Haussmann, the result something more akin to the first of the big interstates begun in the Eisenhower administration. One early consequence was lots of accidents. After a while, cars from nearly every one of the embassies and houses north of the Lisboa having been sideswiped or rear-ended as they tried to bolt into the pell-mell traffic, a kind of service road had sprung up, a dirt track carved from dozens and dozens of clipped front lawns. A few embassies and homeowners had protested, but not many. The dirt track made it easier to get on and off the coast road, allowing drivers to scoot onto the gravel shoulder and into the right lane whenever they spied a gap in the traffic.

Easing the Land Cruiser off the shoulder and down onto the dirt road about a half mile north of Vladimir Lenin, Gub downshifted into second. Servants who doubled as security guards occupied a lot of the houses temporarily abandoned by their owners for safer quarters. Gub waved as he passed, young skinny guys with rifles across their knees staring back vacantly from camp chairs in driveways. Even without the security, Gub could tell which houses were still lived in by the owners and which weren't. Lawns and gardens were usually the first to go, a tangle of weeds furring the edges of flower beds, the seeds blown from the clay pans and bottomlands of the interior, some for probably hundreds of miles, diving into this last stretch of earth, the few lucky ones that didn't get blown out to sea. So fecund was the land, even in the center of Fado, that just a few days without the attention of a gardener, and shrubs and flowers could be all but strangled by gaudy new flora. At many of the houses Gub passed, the gardens were virtual jungles already.

He wondered about the *curandeiro*'s place. It was newer than most, a big chalet-style job that lacked the self-conscious ponderousness of most of the other houses on the coast road. For that matter, he wondered about the *curandeiro*. Gub had met the man several times at the Lisboa, a big albino Negro, heavier than Gub by a good fifty pounds. Tony had introduced Gub at one of his New Year's Eve gatherings a couple of years ago. "Paul," the man had introduced himself. "Paul Achebe."

Gub had heard plenty of stories afterwards about Achebe, but he had no idea how many of them were true. Achebe himself said that he had started out as a "john-johnny," working in the mines outside Johannesburg. Bigger and stronger than most, he had earned top pay working at the mine face with a rasping gas-fired drill. The conditions were atrocious. In one cave-in, according to a story, Achebe was buried for four days, and after the mine owners had given him and the others up for dead, Paul Achebe had dug himself out with his bare hands and a pickax, pulling a seventeen-year-old boy out with him. His white hair powdered with fine brown dust, he had emerged from the broken mine face, the story said, like a specter, saddened by broken faith but damn well determined to do something about it. It was rumored long afterwards that the mine owners had paid him off, and big.

Where the other miners fought and drank and chased whores, Paul Achebe was an ascetic, a forbidding presence who kept to his own corner of the miners' dormitory. The place was bedlam, but his corner was pin-neat, the medical books he was always reading stacked precisely on the wood crate next to his bed. He had stayed in the mines exactly ten years, Paul Achebe had told Gub. And with the money he had hoarded since his very first day there, he had moved to Fado and set himself up as the capital's in-town *curandeiro*. There the myths and stories about the big albino just seemed to abound and multiply.

It was told that a highwayman, armed, had confronted Paul Achebe one night. The man had demanded money, and the medicine man refused. The man threatened him with a knife, and Achebe, unarmed, grabbed the man's arm and snapped it in two. The man screamed in pain. "I asked you to put the knife away," Paul Achebe said, according to the story. "I asked nice, and now I am not feeling so nice." Methodically, the medicine man broke the highwayman's other arm. Then he rolled him onto the ground and jumped carefully on each of his legs, snapping both neatly midway between the knee and ankle.

There were other stories where Paul Achebe was genuinely nice, however. He had paid out of his own pocket for the treatment of a small girl burned in a fire set by bandits. The girl's mother and father had been killed in the attack on her village, and when soldiers found her afterwards, she was barely alive. Paul Achebe heard about her and not only paid for her treatment over half a year, but when she was well enough to travel, he had taken her himself back to the village. They had flown in his private Cessna, which was piloted by Archie, a weather-beaten Brit who had become Paul Achebe's constant companion. Archie served as pilot, driver and chief factotum, and he kept his distance as the medicine man escorted the small girl back through her parents' burned village. Archie had listened, his head cocked and tears streaming down the creases of his face, as the medicine man explained to the girl what had happened and how her parents were safe now. According to Archie, it had taken a few more weeks for Paul Achebe to find an uncle and aunt in another village even further from the capital, but Paul Achebe had delivered the girl there personally. It was what a *curandeiro* should do, he had said, again according to Archie.

Paul Achebe liked to joke that he was not above making house calls, but in truth his patients—Gub wasn't sure that was exactly the right word—were almost all in the city's sprawling slums. Whenever the situation in the countryside got worse, another village torched, rumors of murder and dismemberment refueled, more people fled from the interior to the squatters' camps at the edge of Fado, and Paul Achebe traipsed through the fetid alleyways nearly every day, laying hands on babies' swollen bellies and saying a few words in exchange for a fee. Tired backs, tardy bowels, women's troubles—the big albino with the weird pink eyes had a cure for them all. At least that's what the denizens of Fado's slums believed, and they paid him handsomely from their meager savings for his ministrations.

With his earnings, Paul Achebe had bought the house on the coast road five years before, a steal in a dying market. The representative of the Swiss pharmaceutical firm that owned the place had been happy to unload it. And since then, the *curandeiro* had poured tons of money into the place. Cruising slowly past it in the Land Cruiser, Gub wondered about the landscaping; everyone did. One of the first things Paul Achebe had done after buying the place was to rip out the bent-grass lawn and the trellised rosebushes, replacing them with scalloped hills of tufted papyrus, imported, the neighbors said, all the way from the Okavango Delta. Probably true, Gub thought. In the warm salt air the papyrus had flourished, and a hippopotamus could hide just as easily on Paul Achebe's front lawn as it did in the thick papyrus of the Okavango. In any case, it yielded not a clue as to whether the big albino was home or traveling. There was no security man, and the medicine man's black Lincoln Town Car was nowhere in sight.

Too bad, Gub thought. No one knew the squatters' camps as well as Achebe, and he had hoped to ask the medicine man if he had heard anything unusual up there in the past few days.

Continuing north, Gub saw little to interest him along the water, and after another mile and a half he swung the Toyota out of the dirt track and back onto the coast road, turning left finally onto Avenida de la Revolución, west away from the ocean and towards the sea of squatters' shacks that rimmed the western edge of Fado like gray penumbrae. The ocean of corrugated tin and cardboard shimmered in the heat, a raised eyebrow over the oval of downtown. Unlike Rome or Lisbon, Fado conveyed no sense of palimpsest, of civilizations superimposed one on another like geological strata. The city was conceived slam-bam, Gub thought, had had too little gestation and was raw still even at its center. Here at the edges in the newest of the new slums, he saw, it was as raw as the sewage that flowed in the open trenches along each side of the narrow road.

Gub got out of the Toyota to shift into four-wheel drive. Then he shut the windows and cranked the air-conditioning to push the shit smell out. In the tape deck, Little Feat was replaced by Bob Marley, Matthias's favorite. Crawling in first gear along roads little wider than paths, huts close on either side, Gub scanned face after face, but he saw nothing out of the ordinary. Unlike downtown, where nearly everyone knew him, Gub knew virtually no one here, and most averted their eyes or ducked behind limp rows of drying laundry as he passed. Gub had had a vague hope of running into Achebe as he made his rounds in the slum, but there was no sign of the big albino anywhere. This was no way to conduct an investigation, Gub thought, but he had to start somewhere.

Just after four, he decided he had had it and got back out of the Land Cruiser and shifted into two-wheel drive again. Emptying the last of the jerrican into the Toyota's main gas tank, Gub made a mental note to stop at the B.P. station the next day to get both the main and the reserve tanks filled. No telling when he might have to move in a hurry.

Accelerating north again onto the coast road, Gub reflected that he was no wiser than he was when he had set out over five hours before. It took him less than five minutes on the empty highway to reach the new embassy district, and Gub took a quick circuit of the neighborhood, then parked in his usual spot near Betty's building, rode the elevator four floors and let himself in with the key she'd given him just six weeks earlier.

They had been seeing each other for maybe twice that long, but things had somehow moved to another level recently, though neither Betty nor Gub had commented on the fact. "Shit happens," she had told him during one of their first nights together.

They nearly always stayed at her place, and Gub had even taken to leaving some of his stuff there, a truly banal indicator, but no less meaningful for all that. In the kitchen, he pulled the quart of Stolichnaya out of the freezer and the Noilly Prat vermouth from the cupboard. There were lots of things you couldn't get in Fado anymore, but thank God booze wasn't one of them, Gub thought. And olives. Thanks to the TAP flights from Lisbon three times a week, there was no shortage of the big green ones he loved, hand-stuffed with pimentos. A martini with the little tiny ones with the holes, Gub thought, wasn't even worth drinking. It was one of his few convictions.

He had just finished mixing his second, his feet propped up on the narrow balcony railing, the dirty glass doors open to the breeze, when Betty banged in through the front door, her arms filled with a bulging canvas shopping bag, her briefcase and a couple of bottles of white wine.

"Goddamn air-conditioning, I've had it."

"Great to see you, too," Gub said, coming in from the balcony and kissing her on the cheek.

"I mean it. I don't know how anyone lives in this place without air-conditioning. They're gonna have to get the thing fixed, or I quit."

"I'll look at it tomorrow," Gub said, helping with the bags. "How about a drink?"

"A shower first," she said, setting the briefcase on the hall floor and handing the canvas shopping bag to Gub, "then a drink. I picked up some bluefish from the guy near the port, that okay?"

"Great," Gub said. He hadn't eaten all day. "I'll fix it, you relax. What's new?"

"What's new?" Betty was already in the bedroom, pulling off the cotton dress and her bra in one fluid motion. "What's new yourself?

The whole goddamn city is talking about all these severed heads.
What the hell is going on?"

Gub loved the way she walked around with nothing on. As self-
conscious as a three-year-old, he thought. Betty was standing in the
entryway to the kitchen as Gub emptied the canvas bag, sliding the
two big fillets wrapped in newspaper into the refrigerator.

"I said what's going on, Detective?" Her arms folded over her
breasts, her white bikini panties setting off the tan of her lean hips,
Betty was staring directly at Gub.

"You know, you'd be perfect for one of those Jockey underwear
ads," he said. "Just the figure for it. You should check it out sometime."

"I'm serious, Gub."

"I am, too. You'd get to work on your tan, prance around in your
underwear all day. They probably even have a car where the air-
conditioning works."

Betty spun on her heel, and Gub admired the taut thighs for the
second time that day. "I don't know about the heads, okay?" The
bathroom door slammed, then the shower came on, and Gub was
pretty sure she hadn't heard him.

He went back to fixing dinner, one of his favorite things in life.
Sometimes Gub thought he ought to have been a chef. The hours
were lousy, but then so were those of a detective; the benefits, on the
other hand, were way better. Working deftly, he threw the two bottles
of Muscadet into the freezer to chill. It was about the only decent
white wine you could get in Fado. From under the range, he took a
cheap bottle of white, spilled a third of it into the big iron skillet,
then added a half stick of butter and turned the burner on low. The
greens he washed in the sink under cold water, then set them in the
colander to dry while he sliced red onions for the salad and added
capers from the jar in the refrigerator to the simmering butter and
wine. It was a simple dish, but it had a nice name: "bluefish à la
grenobloise." The oil from the bluefish married nicely with the
wine, the butter and the capers. With a big enough fillet, he figured, a
salad was all you needed for a first-class meal. Also it was easy as hell
and there was almost nothing to clean up.

He was crumbling feta cheese into the salad when he noticed Betty
in the doorway again. She had on lime-green running shorts and a
tight white T-shirt. Her hair was combed straight back, wet against
her neck. "Sorry . . ." he started.

"Smartass, always the smartass." She came up behind him and wrapped her arms around him. Gub could feel the shower-dampness through his blue oxford shirt. "You better go easy on the butter there, big boy."

"I'm gonna start running again, I swear."

"Yeah, and I'm gonna learn Greek."

"Speaking of which, where are those black olives you got last week? We didn't finish them, did we?"

"In the fridge, in the door part. Are you going to tell me about the heads, Gub? I mean it. And I thought you said something about a drink."

Gub grabbed the black olives from the fridge, a bottle of Muscadet from the freezer and the Swiss Army knife with the corkscrew from the silverware drawer. "Greek salad okay?" Uncorking the Muscadet, he grabbed a cheap stem glass from the rack next to the sink, spilled some of the wine into it, sampled the bouquet for no good reason, then filled the glass and handed it to Betty.

"Salad sounds great. How's the fish look?"

"Real good, nice-size fillets for a change."

"I asked special. Now, what about the heads?"

"I don't know, Betty. I mean, it's obvious, I think, what it means. It's the bandits, pushing into the city, a kind of terror campaign to get people stirred up. I always wondered why they hadn't tried it before. And I think I have an idea who's behind it. There's something about this that's wrong. It's not like their usual clumsiness. This has been thought out, the locations picked specifically for the impact. It's more professional that way. That's what I think anyway, but I don't know what the hell I can do about it."

Betty sipped at her wine. "You think this is it?"

"Could be." Gub slipped the two fillets out of the newspaper and tossed the wadded ball into the trash. "The army's done a good job lately, and the airport and the port are still open, though there's not much going out of either. If they can infiltrate the city like they did last night, getting into Calamidades, which is heavily secured, and the Lisboa, which . . ."

"The Lisboa!"

"Oh, I forgot to tell you. Tony called me at home after I left this morning. He had a head on his diving board."

"Are you kidding me?"

"He says he got it covered up before any of the guests saw it, but the staff was chattering away like monkeys when I got there. They're bound to talk."

"So that makes . . ."

"Four," Gub said, sliding the bluefish fillets into the simmering broth of butter, wine and capers. "Four we know about, anyway."

"What are you going to do?"

"What the hell can I do? I spent the day all over the city looking for God knows what. Didn't learn fuck-all. Anyway, it's not like we got a lot of resources here. We got me, Ellis can help out, and that's about it. Carlos is worthless, and Calamidades is stretched to the limit. The army's got all it can do keeping the bandits clear of the airport, and right or wrong they're probably not going to move troops out of places up-country where they've been making progress. Even if they wanted to, it's not clear they would try to move troops here with the roads the way they are. And besides, for something like this, troops are worthless. This is a straight-ahead investigative thing, but we don't have what you could call a great investigative capability. What we got is me. Whaddya say we eat, huh?"

They said little during dinner, Betty devouring the salad but forking over half her bluefish onto Gub's plate.

"You gotta eat, kid, keep your strength up."

She shot him a look, and he went to grab the second bottle of wine from the freezer. Ice-cold, it went down even better than the first.

While Betty cleaned up the couple of dishes and rinsed the skillet in the sink, Gub went into the bedroom and used the phone to check his messages. Ellis, Carlos and Dr. Pran. Fuck them, he thought, it could wait till morning. Stepping carefully out of his good navy slacks and hanging the limp blue oxford on the bathroom doorknob, Gub climbed into the big tiled shower, turned the water on cold and adjusted the shower head. The pressure was good, way better than in his place, he noted, letting the water beat down on his head and neck, long strands of dirty blond hair hanging in front of his eyes.

By rights, he should be out there tonight, he thought, doing something, anything. He might not learn much that was useful, but he'd learn a hell of a lot more than he would in Betty's shower. What he needed, Gub thought, was a plan. But he knew so little, had so little to go on.

Maybe, he thought, the end was preordained anyway. Things had gone so badly for so long. Still, the country had managed to hang on, and the bandits had proven themselves, until now at least, incapable of sustaining any kind of action inside the capital. Gub toweled himself off, rubbing his gut. Too old for this shit, he said. Too fucking old.

"Are you coming to bed, or you going to use all the water in the city first?"

"Coming, dear."

He was hardly beneath the sheets when she was on top of him. Her breasts were not large, but Betty Abell had lost weight in the six months she had been in Fado. Gub could see each of her ribs clearly, and her thinness emphasized the soft fullness of her breasts. Sweet contrast, he thought. And as he began to move with her, Gub figured it was a more pleasurable notion than any he had had all day. For a great many days, in fact.

He woke once in the night, still having a hard time getting used to the surroundings, the bare white walls, the bureau filled with women's things, the smells of powders and soaps.

It reminded him, as it always did, of Teresa. They had been married just three years, and those three years together had marked him, Gub thought, much more than her death in the plane. Even in death, she had been near perfect, he thought. Hit twice, she had still managed to set the little Cessna down neatly at the edge of a line of dunes. When the army troops got to the plane eight hours later, she was dead.

Listening to Betty's deep, even breathing, Gub wondered how things might have worked out if Teresa had lived. Badly, he guessed. The irony was that he had been attracted to her because of her looks. A hurdler, she had won a full scholarship to Cambridge and had even beaten Jackie Joyner-Kersee once at a big international meet in Munich. The training had given her a drop-dead body, Gub remembered, the little man in his head spinning one of the old reels, Teresa's legs flashing hard and muscular, breasts and buttocks sculpted. Callipygous. He remembered looking the word up, and it rolled around still in his head. It was only after he had dated her a few times that Gub discovered the high-octane brain, and the enormous will that drove her to the limit in everything she did. Teresa Achioli had read history at Cambridge, then gone down to London for a year at the London School of Economics. Despite several handsome offers from investment houses in the City, hardly blind to the P.R. value of an exceedingly bright, beautiful and multilingual black woman on the payroll, Teresa had returned to Fado. She'd told Gub she had never even considered the offers. She intended to come home to run the Oxfam office and, despite the situation, extend the programs into the interior. It was for that reason she had learned to fly, so she could supervise the programs herself.

And that, Gub recalled, was how she had died. On a bright October morning coming back from a village where they had begun an irrigation project up the coast, she had flown low over a farmhouse about eighty kilometers north of Fado. The army said afterwards that the place had been overrun by bandits more than a week earlier, the family murdered, dismembered and fed to the pigs. Teresa evidently had not even circled the big farmhouse once when one of the bandits had opened up from a second-story window with the 50-millimeter.

In the wide bed next to Betty, Gub thought how it all seemed such a long time ago, another life almost. Unable to sleep, he got out of bed and went out on the little balcony to sit. He never had figured out why Teresa married him. He had admired her, loved her even, he thought. But they were on different planes, and there hadn't been much common ground to build a relationship on. With Betty it was different somehow, but he wasn't ready to think it all through just yet.

He looked out at the city instead. It was a clear night, the capital black and quiet, the stars high and far away. There was no moon, and so, little light. Somewhere Gub thought he heard a car engine cough, but like the stars, it, too, seemed far, far away, and he couldn't be sure.

The next morning he was up and showered before Betty was awake. He used the drip coffee maker they usually used only on weekends, and it was the smell that woke her.

"What's the occasion?" she said, coming into the kitchen, wearing the long tank top with the logo of the expensive French sunglasses above her breasts.

"Thought we'd have the real thing today."

"Any special reason?" She kissed him, nestling close.

"Because of you, my dumpling," he said, brushing her hair from her eyes with his fingers. "But I've got to hustle." He handed her a mug and took one for himself. They both drank it black.

"Will you promise you'll be careful?"

"So far, all I've been doing is collecting heads. It's not what I'd call a dangerous job."

"Just be careful."

"Okay, are we dining tonight?"

"Wouldn't miss it. Your turn to get dinner, though. I'm going to be late, so let's make it eightish."

"Let's."

Locking Betty's door on the way out, Gub ran down the four flights of stairs. Who knows, he thought, maybe he would start running, lose some of the extra weight. She was only nine years younger than he; no reason he should get old before his time.

Heading back to his own flat to change, he promised himself he would start jogging. Tomorrow, Gub said, accelerating onto the coast road. Tomorrow for sure.

EVERYTHING was just as he had left it, the white thread on the front-door jamb undisturbed. It was the oldest trick in the book, but it worked, and the thread showed no one had crossed the threshold. So why did the place feel so funny? In the dining room, Gub got his answer, or at least part of it. The six-pack of Carta Blanca was sitting squarely in the middle of the ebony table Teresa had bought right after they were married. Gub picked it up gingerly and saw that the condensation from the chilled bottles had dripped through the cardboard. The rich black wood beneath had a rectangular water mark in the shape of a six-pack, and Gub knew instinctively it would never come out.

Placing the six-pack on the kitchen counter, Gub went to the refrigerator and opened it, and he thought afterwards that he knew exactly what he would find even before he found it. Next to the head of Vladimir Lenin on the upper shelf of his secondhand Westinghouse was a second head, considerably uglier than the first.

"Vladimir Ilych," Gub said out loud, as much to hear his own voice as anything, "what's the fucking deal?"

TEN

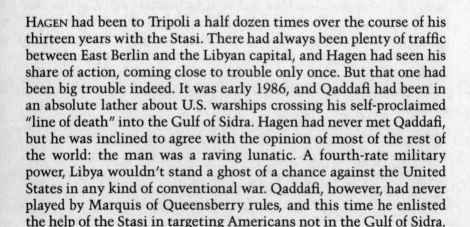

HAGEN had been to Tripoli a half dozen times over the course of his thirteen years with the Stasi. There had always been plenty of traffic between East Berlin and the Libyan capital, and Hagen had seen his share of action, coming close to trouble only once. But that one had been big trouble indeed. It was early 1986, and Qaddafi had been in an absolute lather about U.S. warships crossing his self-proclaimed "line of death" into the Gulf of Sidra. Hagen had never met Qaddafi, but he was inclined to agree with the opinion of most of the rest of the world: the man was a raving lunatic. A fourth-rate military power, Libya wouldn't stand a ghost of a chance against the United States in any kind of conventional war. Qaddafi, however, had never played by Marquis of Queensberry rules, and this time he enlisted the help of the Stasi in targeting Americans not in the Gulf of Sidra, but in the Federal Republic of Germany.

In Frankfurt, Hagen had gotten the call. The job was to help only with targeting and logistics. It was no big deal, and Hagen had taken a couple of weeks to case a number of clubs and discos frequented by the American troops in and around West Berlin. He had passed on the list and a long description of risks and opportunities involved in each, and that was all he had had to do with it. That wasn't the last he had heard about it, however.

From the list of targets supplied by Hagen, Qaddafi had picked a place called the La Belle, and at nearly two o'clock on a Saturday morning in early April, the disco had been packed with American servicemen. When the bomb attached to the urinal in the men's room exploded, one soldier was killed, along with a Turkish woman on the dance floor. That would have been it, Hagen griped afterwards, but the Libyans just couldn't keep their mouths shut. Fucking amateurs. A few hours before the bombing, a British listening post on the continent had picked up a phone call between Tripoli and the Libyan "peoples' bureau" in East Berlin. Ever since Qaddafi had started ranting about the Gulf of Sidra, Western intelligence agencies had been keeping a watchful eye on the peoples' bureaus, as Qaddafi called his embassies; in fact, many were little more than terrorists' drop boxes.

In any case, when the caller from Tripoli referred to "a joyous event," it had set alarm bells ringing—the Libyans were anything but clever with their coded conversations. American M.P.'s had raced to clear the busiest discos, and they were just minutes away from the La Belle when they heard the explosion. Minutes after that, the Brits picked up another call, this one from the peoples' bureau in East Berlin to a Libyan government office in Tripoli. The caller related blandly that the "joyous event" had just taken place. London relayed hard copies of the intel take to Washington, and the Reagan administration used the evidence well, justifying the bombing of Libya a few days later. Hagen swore when he learned the pilots had just missed Qaddafi.

You couldn't trust the Libyans, Hagen thought, as the Piper Alfa taxied towards the squat terminal building on the civilian side of the Tripoli airport. Through the window, he could see the guards in riot gear with Kalashnikovs protecting the military side of the field. It was one of the things Hagen hated about places like East Berlin and Tripoli. They all looked like fucking war zones, guys with guns everywhere.

Hagen didn't like Libya, but it was far and away the easiest place he knew of to get hold of the world's best plastic explosive. The Czechs made it, it was called Semtex and it was highly stable and virtually undetectable by conventional airport-security machines. Qaddafi, it was rumored, had bought two thousand tons of the stuff from Prague several years earlier. If that was true, Hagen thought, the man truly was a maniac. In any case, Hagen knew the Libyans had plenty to spare and usually didn't mind parting with some for a small fee. Since he had a long flight ahead of him to Fado and he didn't want trouble on the way, Hagen figured that only Semtex would do.

Still, he thought, rattling into Tripoli in the back of a wheezing Peugeot taxi, he wished there had been some other place to get it. Fucking Libyans.

Hagen always avoided the big hotels downtown, staying usually at a small boardinghouse about ten blocks from Qaddafi's Azzizzyah barracks. Paying for two nights in advance, he hoped he wouldn't be there anywhere near that long. If he could quickly reach the light-colonel he had dealt with on several occasions a few years earlier, he could be out of Tripoli first thing in the morning.

RECLINING in the big albino's black leather Barcalounger and working on his third Pilsen Urquell, Nicholas Sturua thought this wasn't too shabby at all. Out the big east window of the medicine man's study, the empty beach coiled away to the north, ranks of waves spilling doilies of lace foam onto the sand, crazed fiddler crabs scuttling out to investigate each new arrival for surprises. After rising at noon, Sturua had taken a long walk on the beach, finished with a quick swim and then treated himself to some more of the cold spiced prawns, washing them down with the first of the three Pilsens.

He deserved it, he figured. Slipping the head into the detective's refrigerator had been an inspired piece of work, if he did say so himself. Two of Afonso's guys had cased the place the day before, and when they had radioed the *curandeiro*'s house at nine that night that he had not come home, Sturua had seized the opportunity. Probably with some babe, Sturua thought, remarking to no one in particular that that was the one thing lacking in the otherwise-excellent accommodations Viktor Alleja had laid on for him.

After he and Afonso had distributed the first five heads the night before, they had returned to the *curandeiro*'s place about 3:30 A.M., moving the blue Yugo inside the empty two-car garage. Next to Sturua's door as he got out on the passenger side was a monstrous storage refrigerator, the kind butchers use where the door opens from the top. Afonso, a muscular black man in jeans and a bush jacket but no shirt, had slid around the front of the Yugo. Lifting the top of the refrigerator and beaming like an impresario, he had showed Sturua five more heads, pausing to heft each like a trophy trout.

Sturua knew the heads were coming from Afonso's bandits somewhere outside Fado, and he assumed one of them had a key to the medicine man's place and had dropped the heads off while they were out making their rounds.

"Is beautiful, no?"

"Is beautiful, yes, Afonso," Sturua had replied, letting the door of the giant refrigerator drop shut. "Is fucking beautiful."

Afonso had still been giggling when he had left the *curandeiro*'s place a half hour later, a beer in each hand for the ride home, wherever home was. As the dawn had come up an hour later, even as the coconut ladies were discovering the head of Vladimir Lenin, the first of his five heads, Nicholas Sturua had lain awake in the medicine man's big bed, wondering where he'd put the next five. When he had heard from Afonso's guys later in the day about the police detective's interference with the head at the Lisboa, Sturua had decided immediately that one of the heads should be reserved for him. He never thought he'd get the chance to deliver it so quickly, though.

Like everything else so far, Sturua thought, draining the rest of the Pilsen Urquell and setting the empty bottle on the floor next to the leather reclining chair, it had been ridiculously easy. With Afonso's two guys out front standing watch, Sturua had crept around back of the policeman's flat near the small TV-satellite dish. There had been no light, but he could see well enough. And with the fruit knife he had taken from the medicine man's kitchen, Sturua had scraped the glazing from a pane in one of the two bedroom windows. Removing it gently and standing it on edge against the cinder-block foundation, Sturua had reached his arm through the skinny wood mullions up to the elbow and unfastened the catch inside. It had taken less than a minute to crawl through the window with the head in the plastic bag and make his way to the kitchen, and he had nearly dropped the goddamn thing when he had opened the door to the refrigerator and seen the other head sitting in there next to the beer. Recovering, he had pulled the six-pack out, set it on the big dining room table and then pulled the new head out of the plastic bag, setting it on the shelf of the refrigerator next to the old one.

See what the detective thinks of that, Sturua thought.

Climbing back out the bedroom window, Sturua had replaced the pane in its place and reglazed the window with the putty he had brought especially for the purpose from the medicine man's well-equipped workshop, using the fruit knife to trim off the excess nice and neat. The detective would surely notice it, but Sturua thought it would send the message he intended: the cop wasn't dealing only with crazy bastards like Afonso anymore; this was the fucking big leagues.

THE sun was just beginning to slip towards the top edge of the priest's gentle hill, the dead khaya's shadow creeping towards his patio. In the shade of the roundwood tree, however, the light was already nearly gone, and the dials on the bandit's backpack radio glowed green and orange in the gloom.

The kid with the rifle had disappeared around the hill towards Fonseca's place nearly twenty-four hours earlier, but Padre Francisco had not worked up the energy to remove the radio contraption from its hidey-hole in the kitchen until now. The priest had no idea how the thing worked. He had never owned a radio or any kind of electronic device in his life, and it had taken him nearly twenty minutes just to extract the thing from the nylon webbing of the backpack. Uncoiling the wires and hooking the thickest of them to the cone-elike dish on the grass, the priest began fiddling with the dials, watching number after number float up into the lime-green screen and then disappear as he spun the big knob on the right of the machine slowly back and forth. For the better part of an hour, all he got was static. It reminded him of the cicadas they had had in the village a few years before, only not so loud. Near a couple of the numbers, the priest picked up some other noises, but they sounded more like interruptions, hiccups in the steady background chaff. He couldn't make much of it, and as he limped into the kitchen to fix his first Campari and soda of the cocktail hour, he decided he would leave the radio thing on the number where the background noise was loudest. Maybe the thing would come to life, maybe it wouldn't. All Padre Francisco knew was that his knee was killing him; he imagined he could hear bone chips like broken glass rattling around in there when he moved.

The priest had just settled in with his third Campari and was contemplating how the topmost branch of the khaya had speared the new moon like a big marshmallow. The bandit's radio suddenly stopped spitting chaff and coughed up what sounded very much like human voices. They were indistinct and far away, and as the priest lurched out of his chair towards the radio he banged his bad knee against the small metal table and dumped three quarters of the Campari and soda down the front of his cassock.

"Son of a bitch," he swore, for maybe the fiftieth time since the bandit had left.

Ignoring the pain, he knelt in front of the radio, frantically adjusting the big knob on the right back and forth. For a minute at least, he heard nothing, then, suddenly, a man's voice. That was bell-clear; for a second the priest thought the man must be very close by, and he panicked.

"How long have you been there?" The man had a thick accent the priest couldn't place, and the question was followed by a muffled reply he couldn't follow.

"You're sure it's the place, the detective's?"

Another burst of chatter, but it, too, was indecipherable. Padre Francisco was getting only one side of the conversation.

"Okay, stay there. I'll be there right away."

There was a final explosion of indecipherable noise, and then the radio went back to its one-note cicada symphony again. The priest finally turned it off, wondering whether he had let the thing run too long, whether it had some kind of power supply that would run out or what. He had no idea, just as he had no idea about the significance of what he had just heard. The reference to the detective was clear, he thought. Maybe the bandits were trying to kill a policeman. Padre Francisco thought about it and concluded that that didn't make sense. There was no policeman in his tiny village or any of those nearby as far as he knew. Padre Francisco knew there was a police force in Fado, but he hadn't been there in years, not since before he was declared dead, in fact. Besides, he thought, Fado was over twenty miles away. Impossible.

FORTUNATELY for Hagen, and he supposed unfortunately for his one-time colleague Hassan Tarek, things had not changed much at all since the last time they had seen each other, when Hagen had spent a miserably humid month as a guest instructor at Qaddafi's infamous terrorist-frogman school. Tarek knew nothing about frogman tactics and probably couldn't even swim, Hagen thought, but somehow he had been assigned the school's administrator. He had moved on since then, Hagen noted, but he was still a lieutenant colonel now with a small office in the Azzizzyah barracks and doubtless doing some other factotum-type job. Making small talk as evening fell outside on Tripoli and a bottle-green horsefly hammered itself again and again against a filthy window, Hagen was reassured to see that Tarek still had the same oily way about him.

Women, politics, women, the collapse of communism, women—they talked and talked as the sky turned black outside Tarek's grimy window. Hagen noted that even the fly had given up and gone home. At what he thought was a suitable moment in the conversation, Hagen mentioned that he was somewhat pressed for time and perhaps Tarek, his old friend, might be able to expedite a small transaction for him.

All of a sudden, it was the ornate language of the Arab bazaar. "Everything is possible for friends, especially for old friends of our country," Tarek replied. "How may I help, Hagen?"

"You are kind, as always, Colonel, and I will be brief. I have an assignment in a place quite far away. It requires some discretion, as always, but also some of the Czechs' splendid Semtex. Because of the long journey, only the Semtex will do."

Tarek folded his hands piously on his desk. "Semtex, yes. It is extraordinary stuff, but then you know that far better than I."

"Ordinarily, I would have made such a request through Berlin, but things have changed."

"This, I assume, is not a piece of work commissioned by your former employer, then?"

"That's correct, Colonel. The identity of the employer, and of the job itself, doesn't matter. But I can assure you neither has anything to do with the Libyan people."

Tarek nodded absently. "And how much of the Semtex would you be needing for the Libyan people to release to you?"

"I don't expect anything for free, Tarek." Hagen was getting frustrated, as he always did, when dealing with the Libyans. "I'm prepared to pay whatever you say is fair. In fact, it is the very reason I came to you."

Tarek smiled. "If it were for our old friends in the Stasi, perhaps it would be ordered that there should be no charge. We have done that as a matter of courtesy before. But this, our long acquaintance notwithstanding, Hagen, this cannot be done. It is difficult."

Hagen removed a billfold from the inside pocket of his blazer. With the $15,000 Viktor Alleja had given him, the $8,000 for the passport in Marseilles, the $3,500 from the Iranian in Belgrade, the $2,000 from the American longhair and the $1,200 in traveler's checks he had cashed from César Ochoa's wallet, he had well over $25,000. It was an impressive flash roll, and Hagen smiled as he watched the Libyan's eyes go wide. "How much, Tarek?"

"One thousand dollars a pound," the man said, too quickly. "It is a very good price."

"Fine. But I need it tonight."

Hassan Tarek nodded, Hagen rose soon after, and nearly four hours later, just before midnight, the Libyan lieutenant colonel, wearing baggy black pants, a dirty fisherman's sweater and a beret, met Hagen in a shuttered café roughly ten blocks on the other side of the Azzizzyah barracks. Hagen had specified that the Semtex be rolled into long strips, refusing to pay the $200 extra Tarek demanded. Counting out the $5,000 in hundreds and fifties, he gave it to Tarek, who recounted it carefully. Only then did he remove a green nylon gym bag from beneath the café counter and hand it to Hagen, who hefted it, nodded approval and then turned to leave.

"To your adventure, Hagen," Tarek said. "Don't be such a stranger next time."

Hagen gave a mock salute and strode into the night, not looking back. Fucking Libyans.

The next morning, he was airborne again, having spent the better part of the night working the rolled Semtex into the tubular frame he'd installed for just such purposes in the Hartmann two-suiter. Checking his watch, he ordered black coffee from the pretty Egyptian stewardess. With any luck, he figured, he'd be in Harare by midafternoon.

Then he would see about the best way of slipping into Fado.

ELEVEN

Sometimes, Gub thought, the little man rolled tape whenever the hell he felt like it. Sitting at Teresa's handsome ebony table on one of the six matching ladderback chairs, his long face shimmering up at him blackly, Gub studied the six-pack-shaped water stain for so long he finally felt himself slipping into it, reels spinning back in there behind his eyes, images of Teresa gleaming in the dark wood, marrying with a long shot of him and Mireles as kids on a beach, now a tight one of Betty swimming far out in the ocean, her chestnut hair streaming behind her like the wake of a big powerboat, Gub skiing behind it, a little man far away, his hair flying in the sun. The images flickered and blurred, a slow dissolve, and Teresa's face swam up towards him again, the planes of her cheeks framing dark eyes that radiated promise, the lustrous hair in curls tight to her head, the way she always wore it. Even on the little man's musty old tapes, Gub mused, she was still far, far away.

"You know why it's so lonely being an atheist?" she had asked once, during a particularly inventive session in bed.

"Why?" he'd heard himself gasp, ever the straight man.

"Because there's no one to talk to at times like this."

It was vintage Teresa, Gub thought, gently mocking, laughing somewhere far away inside herself, the company there more amusing than anything available outside. With Teresa, Gub thought, it was a habit of mind, arrived at consciously, implemented unfailingly. With himself, the little man rolled tape and there was a kind of slippage of gears, then crazy-quilt images swimming in and out of focus, Teresa's funeral, his grandfather's ruined house on the river, Mireles naked in the hole, bloodied and filthy, the Swiss machine gun in his arms on full rock and roll, bodies splitting like melons. The music was deafening, a real Götterdämmerung. Definitely nothing conscious or ordered about it. Just pure randomness, or at least mainly.

The stick snapping against the kitchen window sounded like a pistol shot, and Gub shoulder-rolled to the floor, taking one of the ebony chairs with him, lying flat-out behind it. After a small eternity of silence, he crawled beneath the expensive table and finally peered over it. "Jesus Christ, Matthias," he shouted, "can't you knock like normal people?"

Matthias gave him one of what Betty called his Mr. Serious looks, jutting his chin out and beetling his eyebrows. Then he ruined the effect entirely, pressing his lips to the glass and making a long farting noise.

"Come around the front," Gub said, laughing. "It's open."

From across the living room, Gub noticed a mess of what looked like fresh insect bites on the boy's lower legs and a few bent blades of dead grass in his hair. Other than that, he thought, Matthias didn't look too much the worse for wear since he'd seen him twenty-four hours earlier.

"How about some coffee and breakfast?" he asked, then remembered the two heads in the refrigerator. "Maybe just coffee, huh, since I'm in a rush?"

Matthias ignored the offer, grabbing Gub by the hand and aiming with his pointed stick out the front door.

"Okay," Gub said reluctantly, "I'll play." Giving the damaged table a final look, he followed Matthias around the side of the building where he usually parked the Toyota. Next to the air conditioner he had installed himself, cutting a neat rectangular hole in the cheap green clapboard, Matthias pulled back an armful of the big hydrangea bush, directing Gub's attention with the pointed stick again.

Gub inspected the little campsite behind the bush carefully. Matthias had probably moved his stuff from wherever it was he kept it some time the day before, but already he had things well in order. Three layers of cardboard covered the flattened earth between the base of the bush and the cinder-block foundation. A dirty blanket and a ragged sheet of heavy plastic were rolled bedroll-style and stowed against the foundation of the apartment house. Three shirts and two pairs of shorts were folded neatly in a plastic milk crate that had been turned on its side and covered by a board. On top of the board were what Gub guessed were Matthias's treasures: a red and green plastic whistle, a can opener on a filthy piece of string and a sharp, single-blade fishing knife. Gub noticed that the overhang from the roof of the apartment would keep the worst of the wind and rain off Matthias; the thick hydrangea would probably do most of the rest. Gub looked at the boy closely. "It's a helluva good setup, Matthias. A helluva good job."

Matthias let the hydrangea slide back, and Gub noticed you could barely see the little campsite from just a few yards away. He was going to compliment Matthias on the fact, but the boy was already marching around the house, gesturing impatiently with the stick for him to follow.

"Okay," he said, "okay."

When he rounded the corner near the TV-satellite dish, Matthias was waiting under the bedroom window, using the stick, Gub thought, like a professor illuminating a particularly tricky point of geometry. Snapping the stick back, Matthias rapped the windowpane with the newly replaced glazing.

It really did sound like a pistol shot, Gub thought, small caliber, probably a .22. Gub moved closer and examined the fresh glazing carefully for a full minute. "You see who did this?" he asked finally.

In the windowpanes smudged by the oil in the glazing putty, Matthias's reflection nodded its head up and down.

"How many men?"

Matthias held up one finger, then waved the stick ambiguously out towards the road.

Gub couldn't make much of that, but the one finger was good enough for now. He'd ask Betty for translation help later on. "Matthias," he asked, "did you see the man go? Did you see where he went?"

Again the reflection nodded yes, the boy resting both hands over the end of the stick.

"In a car?"

The small head bobbed in affirmation once again.

Gub was ecstatic. "Let's get your stuff, Matthias. It's about time I had myself a proper partner."

It took no more than a couple of minutes to shuffle Matthias's few belongings into the apartment, Matthias insisting they hold on to the cardboard. Probably a fallback, Gub thought, in case things don't work out. They were arranging his stuff in the bottom drawer of the bedroom's second dresser when the phone on the night table rang, Gub grabbing it on the first ring.

"Detective Gub?"

He recognized the singsong lilt of Dr. Pran immediately. "What is it, Doc?"

"Another head. The night watch found it about one o'clock in the O.R."

"Jesus, in the operating room?"

"That's correct, Detective. About one, I was told."

"Christ, anyone see anything?"

"I don't think so, but you will have to ask for yourself, I'm already late. If you want to see it, I left the head in the refrigerator with the others."

Gub was going to ask Dr. Pran something else when the tiny Christmas-bulb light next to the phone winked, indicating he had another call. They didn't have call-waiting in Fado; Gub had gotten the idea from the States and jury-rigged the light himself. "Okay, thanks, Doc, I'll see you later."

Depressing the two clear plastic buttons in the phone's cradle, Gub switched to the second call, rewarded by the rasp of Fado's chief of police. Carlos was already in full cry. "Two fucking heads again, Gub. The fucking Justice Palace, of all places. Same shit as Calamidades. Fucking heads like pumpkins, like the city's a fucking pumpkin patch for severed heads."

Gub let him play with the notion for a few seconds, motioning for Matthias to bring him a pen and paper, grunting every so often for the benefit of Carlos, let the boss know he was paying attention, taking the shit seriously.

"We gotta put a stop to this bullshit, Gub, it's getting out of hand. The president is asking for copies of our reports. The president wants to know what the department's doing about it, what we've got planned."

Gub smiled at the pronouns. "You remind him he's the one

virtually wiped out the department, Chief?" When he wanted to stick the needle in good, Gub addressed Carlos by his official title. They both knew how ridiculous it was.

"That's not the point, and you know it. Gub, we've got to do something to stop this, try and figure who's behind it."

"Tell me about the heads at Justice," Gub interrupted.

"Well, there's the two. One in the chief magistrate's chambers, right square in the middle of his desk, on another neat little square of waxed paper. The judge isn't in this week, so he don't know about it yet. The other's in the big courtroom, sitting right up there in the witness box."

"Who found 'em?"

"Night watch, the old guy who's always around there, you know, he sleeps in the place and cleans up. I forget his name, Oliver or Amos or something. Anyway, the old guy ran and told the bailiff chief, who lives just near here, and the bailiff chief phoned me up a couple of minutes ago."

"Okay, Chief," Gub rang off, "I'll be in touch."

Three more heads last night, plus the fourth in his refrigerator. Plus the four from the night before. Plus who knew how many more somewhere else? These guys don't fuck around, Gub thought. Dialing the department's answering machine, he left a message for Ellis to meet him at the Justice Palace as soon as possible. Then he dialed Betty, got no answer, tried Save the Children and left a message for her on the machine there. If she could help him get something useful out of Matthias, he might have a shot at finding the midnight messengers who seemed intent on littering the city with neatly barbered severed heads.

He thought about the next call for a minute or two, realized he didn't know the office number in New York and went to the kitchen to get his tattered leather address book from the junk drawer. It was late afternoon in New York, but he dialed the number anyway. "Mary Pat, is that you?" Gub spoke with Mireles's secretary maybe twice a year, but he made a point of chatting all secretaries up. They exchanged news about the weather for a couple of minutes before Mireles got on the line.

"To what do I owe this rare honor?"

Gub got right to the point. "I need to tap your vast network of information resources."

Mireles grabbed a pen and paper. "Got a name?"

"You remember one Viktor Alleja?"

"Guy you did that big investigation on, the South African?"

"Well, actually, he's Portuguese, but he worked for the Directorate something like forever."

"Yeah, after your case, I looked him up in our computer. We had a little something on him that went nowhere. A tax thing, I think, had to do with alleged charity foundation run by a guy out of Baton Rouge, one of these wingers sworn and bound to root out commies wherever they are."

"Freedom Fighters, right?"

"Yeah, the guy was a legitimate businessman, had a big insurance outfit down there. But he was also involved with this Viktor Alleja collecting donations for the bandits for this Freedom Fighters group. Only there was some question about whether Freedom Fighters was actually sending the money to the bandits, skimming some of it or maybe even all. I don't remember the details, but I know nothing ever came of it."

"Too bad. You wouldn't have any way of checking on this Viktor Alleja now, would you?"

"I can make a few calls. What is it he's up to?"

"I'm not sure. Nothing maybe. The situation's kind of been going back and forth here lately, but the army's been doing better, and they got a new guy over at Calamidades who seems to be making things happen. So things were starting to look up a little, until a couple of days ago, and all of a sudden these severed heads start showing up all over downtown."

"Whose heads?" Mireles was still taking notes.

"Don't know, Tom. They're not locals. The bandits must be killing the people outside Fado and bringing the heads in. The thing about it is the placement, the locations. They got into Calamidades the night before last, the hospital last night and the Justice Palace. One of these assholes even broke into my place last night and left one here."

"You okay?"

"Fortunately, or maybe unfortunately, I wasn't home. But the thing is this isn't the typically sloppy bandit SOP."

"It's professional."

"Exactly. And that's why I think Viktor Alleja may be back in the picture somehow."

"I'll check around and get back to you as soon as I can, Gub. How're things otherwise?"

"You mean except for the heads, the situation and life generally?"
"Yeah."

"They're fucking beautiful, Tom. You wouldn't believe it."

"You're right, Gub, I wouldn't. I'll call you."

Gub rang off and went out to the living room to check on Matthias. He was looking at a Tom and Jerry cartoon on the TV, so Gub didn't interrupt, heading back to the bedroom and the big walk-in closet next to the bed where he kept the Chief's Special Mireles had left him, the Browning double-barrel with the sawed-off stock and the Swiss-made SIG-10 machine gun he hadn't fired in maybe six or seven years.

On his hands and knees, he found the six shoe boxes of ammo he kept stored way in the back of the closet, down on the floor. He emptied the first of the boxes onto the bed and was sliding the hollow-points into the chamber of the handgun when he noticed Matthias eyeing him speculatively. "Improving my hand, Matthias," he said. "I just hate it when the other guy's holding all the face cards."

Matthias went back to Tom and Jerry.

He would have to disassemble and oil the SIG-10, but he had cleaned the Chief's Special and the shotgun recently. Stowing the ammunition in a zippered canvas bag with the guns, he showered and changed into khakis, loafers and a clean white oxford button-down. Matthias, suddenly tired of the TV, decided to mimic him, scrubbing his face and changing into the Shell attendant's shirt and a clean pair of shorts. It was just 8 A.M.

Back in the Toyota, Gub strapped Matthias into the passenger seat, the boy already pawing through the box of cassettes. "We got Bob Marley in there already."

Matthias smiled as he jammed the On button, then turned up the volume. The Wailers were shucking into "I Shot the Sheriff," which Gub, contemplating the small arsenal in the canvas bag behind his seat, didn't think was a real good omen. He pushed the scan button, Matthias notched the volume up again, and as they skittered between a purple and orange Tap-tap and a prehistoric donkey cart on Vladimir Lenin, "Swing Low, Sweet Chariot" was sailing out the Land Cruiser's windows, Gub saving on the A.C. and wondering whether the second tune was a more dire portent than the first. Braking the Toyota near the main entrance of the Justice Palace, he figured he'd have a pretty good idea before the day was out.

Before he even had a chance to lock the Toyota, Erasmus Wilding was shuffling out of the high marble pile that had been christened grandly some four decades earlier as the Palace of Justice. Gub thought it was a rococo nightmare; it reminded him of the wedding-cake building next to the White House he'd seen on vacation a few years back. Since the government had no money for maintenance anymore, Gub noticed, the veined marble was going all to hell, dark blotches of brown and green mildew like liver spots on an old lady's hands.

There wasn't much Erasmus Wilding could have done about it, even if he were a much younger man. Gub guessed he was somewhere between sixty and eighty, but with the unlined gray-brown face and the erect and steady gait, he was sort of inclined to fix it on the low side.

"How you doin', Erasmus?" Gub couldn't imagine how Carlos had gotten "Oliver" or "Amos" from "Erasmus," but then Carlos was lousy with names.

"Just fine, Detective. Kinda spooked by these heads here, but just fine, considering."

Gub had seen Erasmus Wilding around the Justice Palace for maybe a dozen years or more. He swept up, used to serve as a combination bailiff/usher when they still had big trials in Fado and had even sat in one time as an alternate juror in one of the capital's first and only bribery trials after the revolution. "How did they get in, Erasmus?"

"I didn't see 'em come in, Detective. I did see 'em go, though, and if I was having trouble sleeping like I do most nights, I probably would've heard 'em coming and going in there, and I would've thought to give you a call. My room's just downstairs, and there ain't a creak in this old place I don't hear usually. Only last night, for some reason, I had some pretty good sleep."

With Matthias in tow, Erasmus Wilding escorted Gub around to the west side of the building, where he had found the basement window that had been forced. Gub noticed that whoever had done it hadn't bothered to replace the damage. Someone had kicked in the base of the window frame, breaking the catch inside. On the way out, they'd just left it ajar, shards of busted window frame in the dry grass. Inside, Gub and Wilding, Matthias in the lead, trekked down the long marble hall, their footsteps echoing hollowly. At the door of the chief magistrate's chambers, Gub asked Matthias to wait, then asked Wilding if he had anything he could use to cover the head. The detective figured Matthias must have already seen the head of Vladimir Lenin, and maybe even a whole lot worse in his short life. No need to expose him to any more grisly stuff, though, he figured. With the brown bag Wilding gave him, Gub quickly collected the head off the chief magistrate's gleaming mahogany desk. Nice to see someone still trying to keep up standards, he thought. The head was that of yet another male, dark-skinned, the eyebrows shaved. Just like every other one so far. The second head in the central courtroom also fit the bill, Gub thought, remembering when they used to have real trials in the place, Gub and Mireles testifying yes-sir and no-sir to appreciative jurors, everything ordered and proper. The place wasn't even used for ceremonial purposes now, Gub thought, placing the second head in the bag next to the first, there being too few occasions for ceremony in Fado anymore.

With Matthias once again in tow, clacking his pointed stick down the echoing marble corridor out to the Justice Palace's still-imposing front stairs, Erasmus Wilding told Gub the rest of what he knew.

"After I heard the noises, I come up the basement stairs to the front hallway, near the clerk's office?"

Gub nodded, holding the brown bag gingerly and wondering whether it would leak. "Could you see them get away, or what they were wearing?"

"Well, you know, it was dark, and my eyes ain't good like they was, so I just saw a little, just a shadow really. I may be wrong, Detective, but you keep talking about *them*; I only saw the one guy, and he kept to the shadows pretty good when he went out towards the road there. After about a minute I heard a car start up and move away, and I couldn't sleep much after that."

"Just one guy?" Gub asked.

"That's right, Detective," Erasmus Wilding said. "Just the one."

Gub turned as the department's battered brown Nissan Stanza careened into the empty parking lot, Ellis at the wheel, a bleary-eyed Anna-Marie in the passenger seat beside him and none too pleased about it. "Skinny-assed suckup," he heard, as Ellis clambered up the stairs three at a time.

"I had to wake her up and almost dress her myself," Ellis was saying, "but I thought you'd need her for the report. Also, Little Meyer called, or I would have been here sooner, but I couldn't get him off the phone."

"What's he want?" Gub asked. For as long as he could remember,

Wilhelm Kleinemaier had run the Ready-Stop Market just off Vladimir Lenin near the Grand Salon du Thé. A proper Swiss, he would never have dreamed of calling Gub at home, even after all these years. No matter what the calamity, he'd prefer to wait, deriving some strange inner satisfaction from knowing he had gone through the proper channels. The Ready-Stop was the best of Fado's three modern markets, and Herr Kleinemaier enjoyed a certain distinction in the capital as a result. That everyone called him Little Meyer, translating somewhat liberally from the German, was the furthest thing from a slight.

"He's got a head in the meat department," Ellis said. "He can't figure out how they got in, and that's what's really bothering him. He wants to know if you could come by right away. I told him I'd ask you. He opens at nine, by the way."

Gub tallied again. That made five heads last night: the one Dr. Pran called in from the hospital, the two from the Justice Palace, the one at Little Meyer's Ready-Stop and the one sitting in his refrigerator next to Vladimir Lenin. Nine altogether, counting the four from the night before. "Do me a favor, Ellis," Gub said. "Take Her Majesty there inside with Mr. Wilding. You know Erasmus, don't you?"

Ellis nodded yes, shooting Anna-Marie a look.

"Get a full statement from him and have Her Majesty tape it. I'll want a transcription by one, so tell her to move it. Then take her to see Little Meyer and do the same thing there. I'll get over there now, then I'm going to the hospital. I also have to do something with these heads," Gub said, shifting the weight of the bag from one arm to the other, "before it gets any hotter."

"What about after Little Meyer?"

"Stick by the phone," Gub said, grabbing Matthias by the hand and bidding Erasmus Wilding goodbye. "I'll be in touch."

It was just ten minutes back across town to the Ready-Stop, and the first thing Gub did when he got there was to ask Little Meyer if he could stow the two heads in one of the butcher department's two iceboxes. The big Swiss grunted what sounded like a yes, and it took Gub less than five minutes after that to discover the scrape marks on the hinges of the three-by-two swing window over the air-conditioning unit in the back of the store. Whoever had done it had simply removed the two hinges with burglar tools, probably just a hammer, sharp chisel and screwdriver. Then they had reached an arm inside, popped the snap-catch that fastened the window from the bottom on the inside and lifted the whole thing out. For someone who knew what they were doing, Gub figured, it couldn't have taken more than five minutes. Leaving, the man or men who delivered the head—Gub never had had any illusions that this was woman's work—had pushed the snap-catch back into the slotted window molding where it wouldn't work anymore but at least didn't call attention to itself. Then they had refastened the two top hinges from the outside and left.

Little Meyer, Swiss to the bone, was impressed with the workmanship. "Very clever," he told Gub. "Now, what shall I do about the head they left?"

"I'll take it," Gub said.

Little Meyer seemed surprised. "What are you going to do with it, Detective?"

"I've got a pretty good collection going. This'll make a really great addition."

Collecting Matthias from the soda aisle, Gub got him a bottle of Sprite, and when Little Meyer waved away payment, he asked the groceryman if he'd answer a few questions when Ellis and Anna-Marie came around later on. Little Meyer said no problem, and Gub mused that, what with the accounts of Erasmus Wilding and Wilhelm Kleinemaier, this would be one hell of a report, typo-wise. He could hear Anna-Marie's swearing already. The grocer had given him a cardboard box for the three heads, and he stowed it in the back of the Land Cruiser.

Heading to his last stop, Our Lady of Fatima and the newest head in Dr. Pran's increasingly crowded refrigerator, Gub wondered what he'd do when they ran out of space there. Maybe rent some more, he thought, although he wasn't exactly sure there was any money in the department's budget for that.

TWELVE

~~~~~~

On the final approach of the UTA DC-9 to Fado's Prince Henry the Navigator International Airport, Hagen was sure he heard small-arms fire somewhere beyond the edge of the runway, but the plane bumped down gently and without incident, the French pilot wedging it expertly in front of the shuttered terminal building between an ancient Soviet Ilyushin and a much newer Boeing 707 with Japanese markings. Hagen pegged the latter for yet another of the aid planes from Tokyo that could be seen all over the continent. Skinny soldiers in filthy uniforms guarded both planes, and Hagen noticed they were carrying Chinese-made AK-47s, the newer ones.

On the short flight from Harare to Fado, he had worried briefly about using César Ochoa's purloined passport yet again, but this far south, Hagen figured, airport security was lax, and besides, his turnaround in Tripoli had been so quick that Spanish police might still be puzzling over the identity of the body he'd left in the locked maintenance closet of the Barcelona train station. Either way, it was a pretty safe bet, certainly safer than hanging around Tripoli or Harare and trying to boost a new passport there. Having cleared the perfunctory customs and immigration checks inside the half-darkened terminal building, one of only eleven passengers on

119

the flight from Harare, Hagen congratulated himself on his good judgment.

Finally, he was in Fado.

Hagen didn't expect there would be any cabs at the airport, and he wasn't disappointed. Surveying his options, he avoided three reasonably new four-wheel drives, their chauffeurs leaning against fenders, letting the engines idle. Embassy or aid-organization cars, Hagen figured. A middle-aged black man tinkering with the air-cooled engine in the rear of a gray VW van looked more like what Hagen was looking for. The man seemed to be waiting for someone, but the terminal behind Hagen was emptying out fast, and the man fiddling with the engine didn't seem to have much interest in the stragglers.

"Excuse me, sir," Hagen asked. "Are you waiting for someone, or could I pay you to drive me into town?"

The man looked up from the shallow engine well in back of the van, a small grease smudge on the bridge of his nose. "Where at?" he asked, ignoring the first part of Hagen's question.

"It's in town, but this is the first time I've been in Fado, so I don't know exactly where," Hagen lied. "I have a map and directions, though."

The man got up stiffly, examining the city map of Fado that Viktor Alleja had marked for Hagen. "The coast road," he said, scratching his head and examining Hagen's drip-dry navy blazer and the heavy brogues with the gum-rubber soles. "It's way on the other side of town, you know?"

"I'll pay," Hagen said. "You name the price."

"Twenty-five dollars," the man said. "But only if we go now. It'll be dark soon, and only fools stay out in this town after dark."

"Deal," Hagen said. He never did figure out who the man was waiting for, and the man never did tell him.

From the middle seat in the gray van, Hagen surveyed the city carefully, the squatters' camps that rimmed the road in from the airport on either side, the small homes and low apartment buildings on narrow streets closer to the center of Fado and finally the business district that seemed to be defined by two broad boulevards, Avenida Vladimir Lenin and Avenida 21 July. The man in the van took the latter, claiming it was faster, and before too long, they were turning onto the coast road, Hagen consulting the map every few minutes. From Viktor Alleja's description, he recognized the big chalet with the wild vegetation out front as they passed it, then asked the man in the van to drop him about a mile and a half beyond it, at the junction of Avenida de la Revolución. "I'll walk from here," he said, handing the man a twenty and a five. "Thanks."

The man in the van looked at Hagen quizzically for maybe a second, shrugged his shoulders, then depressed the clutch and ground the VW into first gear, the pressure plate complaining. Then he made a tight U-turn and headed back down the coast road, south towards the center of Fado. When he was nearly out of sight, an oblong gray blip on the wide black highway, Hagen started walking in the same direction, hefting the Hartmann two-suiter easily and keeping to the narrow dirt track that paralleled the coast road. Viktor Alleja had marked the coast road on Hagen's map but not the house he was going to. Viktor Alleja had told Hagen he couldn't miss it once he got there, and, as usual, he was right. Fucking jungle of a front lawn, Hagen thought, walking past the big chalet nonchalantly, conspicuous with his suitcase and looking for a gap in the traffic before ducking into the thick papyrus at the south end of the property.

From the far side of the house, he could hear the beach noise of crashing waves and crying seabirds. There was still plenty of light left, but the shadows were long, and it wouldn't last. Between the shadows and the dense papyrus, the approach to the big chalet was easy. The basement door was another story entirely, however. Hagen picked the top lock with no problem, using the flexible five-inch stiletto he wore strapped to the inside of his right calf. The big Schlage dead bolt had him stymied, though, and he finally had to give up on the basement door. Moving north around the beach side of the house, keeping close to the foundation, Hagen tried several basement windows covered with wrought-iron latticework, each without success. A bit further on, a dozen wood steps led to a large, comfortable deck with French doors that gave onto what Hagen figured was probably the kitchen. Crossing the deck quickly from the stairs to the doors, Hagen found the doors were locked, but, thankfully, the dead bolt was not. Using the stiletto again, Hagen made quick work of the French doors, stepping into the big center-island kitchen and setting the Hartmann two-suiter gently on the black and white tile floor, the stiletto in his palm, flat to his thigh. The place was dead quiet, Hagen noticed.

Maybe too quiet.

Letting his eyes roam slowly around the kitchen, Hagen noticed the dirty plate and a coffee cup sitting next to the sink. There were three empty bottles of Pilsen Urquell on top of the kitchen trash in the lined plastic pail under the counter next to the stove. Hagen noticed the bottles had no trace of moisture on them, however; whoever had finished them had done so some time before. Working his way west into the house away from the French doors and the deck, Hagen peered into the living room that looked like no one lived in it. Nice big leather sectionals framed a conversation area around a freestanding chrome and brass fireplace of the type that had been popular in the fifties and sixties in expensive German country homes. Hagen figured the furniture for Roche-Bobois. Very nice indeed.

Stepping past the open doorway, he sensed more than felt a quick movement of air behind him and was already pirouetting, the stiletto in his right hand, blade flat to the floor, when he felt, then saw a muscular arm sliding around his throat. Bringing his left elbow back, Hagen aimed for the rib cage of the man behind him, but the man knew the move and the one that followed it, stepping back a half-step so Hagen's elbow merely glanced off his chest, Hagen's foot missing those of the man behind him entirely, his gum-rubber sole finding only Congoleum tile instead of fragile toe bones. With the stiletto, Hagen punched the man once in the left thigh, air exploding from his lungs. The second time, the arm around his neck loosened slightly, and Hagen slipped free, pirouetting again, the blade carving a wicked arc in front of him.

"Easy now, Sturua."

"Who the fuck are you?" The Romanian, who had a good fifty pounds on Hagen, was gripping his bloody thigh with his left hand and brandishing a heavy wooden paper-towel dispenser with his right. "Use a knife on me? Come on, motherfucker!"

"Shut up!" Hagen threw the stiletto on the counter of the kitchen's center island and went to the phone on the far wall, Sturua watching him intently. Punching the number he had memorized into the Touch-Tone wall phone, Hagen waited till the call went through, then tossed the receiver to Sturua.

"Nicholas, how nice!"

"What the fuck is this, Viktor?" Sturua couldn't believe his ears. Massaging his thigh, the blood already dribbling out of his shoe, forming a small puddle around it on the black and white tiles. "What is this shit, Viktor?"

"I thought you could use a little help, that's all, Nicholas. You know Otto Hagen, I'm sure, don't you? Formerly of the Stasi?"

Sturua looked up at Hagen, who smiled.

"Goddammit, I thought we had a deal, Viktor."

"We do." Viktor Alleja's voice seemed weak and far away. "But I also have a deal with Hagen, and now, unless you have any objections, we all have a deal together. I told you time was short, and between you and Hagen now, you should be able to get things done very quickly."

Sturua paused for several long seconds, thinking as he examined the slight German with the sleepy blue eyes. "Makes perfect sense, Viktor," he said finally, winking at Hagen, who was busy rinsing his knife under the kitchen faucet. "We'll talk things over and get back to you in a bit."

"I thought you'd see the wisdom of this, Nicholas. You and Hagen have a chat, and I'll be waiting for your call."

Sturua tossed the receiver back to Hagen, who caught it easily in his right hand and toweled the blood off it with the dishcloth he was using to dry the stiletto.

"You owe me for the pants, asshole."

Hagen smiled again. "If we weren't going to be partners, I would have cut your fucking leg off, Sturua. What kind of place is this anyway?"

Sturua relaxed a bit. "It belongs to a fucking medicine man, if you can believe that. Some friend of Viktor's."

"No kidding. Old Viktor moves in strange circles."

"How much is he paying you?"

"I never discuss money, Sturua. But money isn't the issue, is it? I mean, even you wouldn't have taken this crummy job six months ago."

"You got the same rap from Viktor."

"Yeah, but you have to admit it, he's got a point."

"Sure, he's got a point, that's why I'm here. I just don't like deals where I don't know what's going on, assholes like you waltzing in on me out of the blue like that."

Hagen nodded, kneeling to put the stiletto into the leather holder strapped to his calf, a point of pride or something, Sturua thought, turning his back on him.

"I don't need you, Hagen. The truth of the matter is this deal is a piece of shit, and it isn't nearly enough of a piece of shit for the two of us. So that's first thing we got to talk about."

"What're the others?"

"Well, there are a couple of others. We got this medicine man, whom I have never met but who seems to have some kind of piece of the action that Viktor has never bothered to explain. That's one. Then we got this hard case named Afonso, he's also got some kind of deal with Viktor, which I don't know about either. Afonso's the guy arranges for the heads I've been putting all over town, and he is dumber than whaleshit, let me tell you. A scary motherfucker. You want a beer or anything, by the way, long as we're talking business?"

"You don't have any vodka, do you?"

"Over the refrigerator, in the cabinet there. Glasses are over the stove." Sturua pulled one of the three high cane-backed chairs out from the center island, grabbed a dishcloth from the drawer of clean ones next to the tall cupboard, folded it twice in a neat square and set it on the chair cushion to protect it from his bloody trousers. "Why don't you get me a beer while you're up, huh? It's in the refrigerator, in the rack on the bottom."

Having poured the vodka into a tumbler with a few ice cubes, Hagen opened the refrigerator to get the bottle of beer. "Pretty fancy beer cooler," he said to Sturua. "The food doesn't look too bad either."

"It's the medicine man. Man likes to live well."

"What's the deal with the heads?" Hagen asked, watching the light die on the ocean outside, a faint pink, as he climbed into the cane-backed chair next to Sturua.

"Afonso or one of his guys drops the heads off at night. They get them from somewhere outside the city, I don't know. Then he and I go deliver them around downtown. You pick the right spots, you get people talking, that's the idea. That's how we talked about it, Viktor and me, in Lisbon. So far we've done ten, five the first night, five last night. Got the city in an uproar, Afonso's people say."

"Why is that?"

"They got the whole country here fucked up with this civil war. The 'situation,' they call it, according to Viktor and Afonso. But so far, the other side, the bandits, they've never been able to work much trouble inside of Fado. That's mainly Afonso's fault, I think, but that's not the point. The point is the government keeps hanging on, collecting aid money and keeping the airport and the port open. As long as they can do that, the bandits don't stand a chance. And as long as the government's still here, Viktor Alleja stays in Lisbon and can't play the big power broker for whoever his friends are. And you and I are stuck working for chump change."

"The heads working?" Hagen got up to pour himself another.

"Get me another beer if you don't mind, Hagen, my fucking thigh's killing me. Yeah, I think they're working pretty good. Afonso had this idea to shave the eyebrows off and trim the hair nice and neat. Kind of a signature, he says. But the main thing is where we've been putting them. We left a couple in the emergency-relief place, Calamidades. And another two in the main courts building, and a few in some other different places around town. I even snuck into the police detective's place last night and left one in his refrigerator. The fucking guy had another head already in there, can you believe it?"

"Sounds good," Hagen said. "What's next?"

"You come all the way down here just to applaud or what, Hagen? What do you mean, what's next? Viktor Alleja send you down here to take lessons from a real pro, or are you planning to actually bring something to this little party?"

Hagen got down slowly from the cane-backed chair and retrieved the Hartmann from where he'd dropped it near the French doors. "Oh, I brought a little something, Sturua, don't you worry." Unfolding the well-worn suitcase on the white countertop, he removed the tubular frame, dismantling it quickly. Unstopping the chrome cap from one leg of the frame, Hagen turned it upside down and shook it gently, a long putty-like thing snaking out of it. "Semtex, Sturua, you ever hear of it? It's a helluva lot of fun."

"The Czech stuff, yeah, I've heard of it."

"It's bad. Real bad. What do you say, maybe we try some of it out tonight?"

"I think you might be all right after all, Hagen. But this still don't change the fact you owe me for a new pair of pants."

THIRTEEN

─────────────────────

"THERE'S not much to tell, Gub, really."

After she got his message at Save the Children, Betty scrapped the weekly training class for the orphanage's nurse-minders. They were all local women, and Betty thought they did a fabulous job. Part of the program funded by the U.S. State Department, however, required rudimentary medical and psychological training so that the orphanage eventually could be turned over to local people, and Betty had to run the once-a-week training sessions to certify them. She liked the idea of local control, just as she was continually embarrassed by the weekly classes. The nurse-minders had all raised broods of their own children and had skills and intuitions Betty could never begin to teach; to the contrary, she found the sessions taught her more than she could ever teach the staff. Anyway, it was a relief to find an excuse to cancel the session, and Betty had raced home to shower and change before going to Gub's flat for dinner. She had remembered to bring her crayons and drawing paper, and she worked with Matthias and the Crayolas while Gub cooked.

Gub thought she looked especially cool and beautiful in her lapis madras shorts, huarache sandals and a sleeveless tennis shirt. But he had to concentrate on dinner. He was fixing another of his favorite dishes, *penne alla puttanesca,* and he wanted to get it right. The story was that the dish had originated as a throw-together, a "whore's pasta," made late at night for the working girls with whatever was left in the kitchen. Done right, however, it was a tricky dish to pull off. It called for black olives, capers and anchovies in a simple tomato sauce. It sounded simple, but Gub knew any one of the ingredients was strong enough to tip the sauce out of balance, and he had a tendency to go heavy on all three.

He stirred and tasted the sauce as the penne came to a boil. It was his favorite pasta. Small and ridged, it held just about any sauce well.

"So there wasn't just the one guy, but three?" Gub had the salad already done, and he added a pinch more salt to the sauce before pulling the pasta off the range, shutting the gas and pouring the penne into the colander in the sink to drain.

"Right. Matthias says the first two guys were here for a long time after it got dark, looking in the windows, and evidently chattering like jaybirds."

"That's good. What else?" He dried his hands on a dishcloth and wandered over to the ebony table where Betty and Matthias were working. He had covered the water stain with a tablecloth earlier in the afternoon, after delivering the two heads in his refrigerator to Dr. Pran's office at the hospital.

Betty concentrated on the boy's drawings. "Matthias could see all three of them from his little camp next to the house."

"He had a good view, with the Toyota out of the way."

"After the third guy got here, it looks like the other two stayed away from the house, out near the street, but close to the hedgerow back from the curb. We did a couple of drawings on that, but I'm not real sure what Matthias is trying to say."

"Lookouts," Gub interrupted. "The guys in the road."

"Yeah, but why did they move away from the house right away? Anyway, Matthias watched the one guy go in your bedroom window and then waited till he came out. The other two guys left in a car right after that, and Matthias waited probably just a few minutes until he got out to follow him. I can't tell. The crayons and the paper aren't real helpful when it comes to time. God, I wish I could get him to talk."

"Well, that's damn good. Good lad, Matthias."

"Don't encourage him, Gub. He could've gotten killed messing around with these people."

Gub winked at the boy over Betty's bronzed shoulder.

"The problem we have is the car," Betty said, ignoring Gub and focusing once again on the three drawings in front of her. "Matthias is certain it was blue, but he only got a look at it from the back, so it's hard to say how big it was or what kind."

Gub looked at the drawings more closely. Betty had drawn three generic-type cars with a fat blue Crayola. There was a four-wheel drive with big tires, a standard sedan with four doors and, just to lay out all the options, a low-slung sports car.

"Was it fast, Matthias," Betty asked, "like a racing car?"

The boy shook his head no.

"Like my Toyota?" Gub asked, suddenly remembering the penne in the sink.

"Matthias says it wasn't like the Land Cruiser either."

Gub poured the penne into a large bowl, then added some of the sauce, making sure each piece of pasta got some.

Betty gathered up the crayons and drawing paper. "Do you have cheese?"

"On the counter, already grated. So, a blue sedan-type car of some kind, and the two lookouts: that's more than we knew this morning. Great job, guys."

Betty carried the crayons and paper into the living room, then placed the salad in the wooden bowl in the center of the table while Gub ladled the pasta into three shallow bowls and added more of the sauce on top and carried them to the table. Matthias climbed onto the ladderback chair at the head of the table, and Gub and Betty joined him, one on each side. "Just a regular little family," she said. "Shall we say grace?"

They each had seconds, and Betty was nearly finished when Gub finally broached several subjects he had been wondering about for most of the afternoon, how he'd bring them up. "Would you mind keeping Matthias for tonight at your place? I don't think it's a good idea for him to stay here, and I'm going to be going out anyway."

"By yourself?"

"I'm taking Ellis with me," Gub said, looking at his watch, flicking the last bit of salad off his plate with his forefinger. "I'm supposed to pick him up in about an hour."

"Great. Why not take Anna-Marie and her typewriter, too? You guys will make a heck of a team." It was the same flash of anger she had shown in the Save the Children office. "Who do you think you're kidding, Gub? I mean what is this, some kind of ego thing? You're just one guy. Ellis can't help you, and you know it."

"Ellis will be fine. He's bright, and he wants to learn. Now, if you would just listen for a minute, you can hear me out, and then you decide what you want to do. Your call, okay?" His tone was low and measured, and Gub was amazed to find he wasn't forcing it this time, summoning it up like he used to. Mireles called it his "closer" voice, and Gub had used it to great effect on a number of occasions, though none lately, persuading killers to confess, juries to convict and, once, even a jumper on the cathedral to climb back down and talk about things. Betty sat back down at the table quietly, the dirty dinner dishes still in her hands, Matthias looking back and forth from Gub to Betty and back to Gub again.

"I'm not the one kidding myself, Betty, if that's what you think. And maybe this has more than a little to do with ego than I would happily admit. We could dig out your old Psych 101 text, have a field day, right? But that's not the point. You go on about the kids here, Matthias, Fernando and Philippe. What is it you think will happen to them, and to everyone else trying to help them, if the bandits finally take over the city? Sure, no question, I'd rather be home, forgetting about the heads and the guy who broke into my place last night and all the other shit we never talk about. The situation? What a joke! The situation is this, if you want to know: for the longest time, when it was just farmers, herders and little people in little villages getting murdered and dismembered far from downtown, none of us ever really cared. Well, now we got heads showing up every morning all over Fado, and the situation is that someone has to do something about it if this place is going to make it. It's not what I would call high moral ground, responding only when it's you that's threatened. But that's where we are. It isn't even a place particularly worth dying for, this place, but it is time for some choices. And besides, what are the alternatives? So you chalk it up to my ego, to whatever. Fine. And maybe even right. But lately I find it kind of hard to sleep, or even to make love to someone I care about, when what I should be doing is my job."

"You're finished?" Betty was still holding three bowls rimed with tomato sauce, her elbows resting on the edge of the table. Matthias was staring at Gub.

"I think so, yeah."

"You didn't leave anything out, none of the stuff about honor and loyalty and finishing your plate because of all the hungry people tonight around the world?"

"I don't think so, no. Besides, I always clean my plate."

"That was the longest I think you ever talked."

Gub said nothing.

"What do you want me to do with Matthias?"

"You want to take him?"

"I can't leave him, can I? Besides, the boy needs a bath and some ointment for those legs. I've got to tell you, though, Gub, I don't like it, this goddamn hero stuff."

"There are a couple of other things."

"Oh, God, what else?"

"First, I want to switch cars. They know mine, and it'll be useless if I'm in it. We can leave the Toyota somewhere near your place, and I'll drop you and Matthias off. If I have time, I'll even try to look at your air-conditioning and see if I can see what's wrong."

"Do me a favor and don't worry about the A.C., okay?"

Matthias got up and went into the living room. TV sounds emanated a few seconds later, and Betty carried the dirty dishes to the sink. She started rinsing them under the faucet when Gub got up from the table and went into the bedroom.

He was back in an instant. "Just leave that stuff, okay?" Gub heaved the zippered canvas satchel onto the ebony table. "The other thing we've got to talk about is a little good old-fashioned protection."

"Jesus!"

"You've seen guns before, Betty. Weren't your father and brothers big hunters up there in those fabled Michigan woods?"

"Yeah, but that thing, I never saw anything like it."

Gub handled the Browning double-barrel easily. He had fitted the end of the sawed-off stock with a thick piece of black India rubber, which he had fused to the wood using an acetylene torch, shaving off the excess and smoothing the edges with a small disk sander and running a thin bead of clear epoxy around the whole thing to seal the joint. He handed the weapon to Betty.

"Pretty light, isn't it?"

"That's only part of the beauty of it," Gub said. "But it packs a hell of a punch. Anyone comes at you, you have that thing, you can just cut him in half."

"Great. I just cut him in half, huh?"

"Right."

"You want me to take this home?"

"I want you to take that home."

Betty Abell cradled the Browning on her left hip and arched her eyebrows. "Gee, I never had an offer like that before."

AT midmorning, it was already over ninety degrees in Plumtree's little cemetery, and even under the protection of the great arching boughs of the ancient baobab that shielded the burial place, Padre Francisco had felt the heavy purple funeral vestments dragging him down. For the second day in a row, he had had to preside over a mass funeral. He had heard gunfire at the edge of Plumtree the night before, and just after dawn one of Fonseca's sons had banged on his sliding glass doors with the news: a farmer at the edge of the village just this side of the 1A highway that ran north from the edge of Fado past the village had found five bodies. Like the five from the day before, all had been decapitated, all were males. Fonseca's son said two were from outside the village but worked at the cashew plant. The other three were small ranchers from outside Plumtree who had volunteered to spend a few nights a week on Plumtree's ad hoc security patrol. It didn't take a coroner to tell the five had been jumped by someone with far superior firepower. The torsos were riddled with bullet holes. With their bolt-action rifles, the five men hadn't stood a chance.

Padre Francisco could understand a shoot-out between the bandits and the village security force. What he couldn't come to terms with was the mutilation. Why decapitate the men?

He had made a stab at it, but felt he had come up short again. He had read from Ecclesiastes, and then I Corinthians:

So when this corruptible shall have put on incorruption, and this mortal shall have put on immortality, then shall be brought to pass the saying that is written, Death is swallowed up in victory. O Death, where is thy sting?

But there was sting aplenty for the grieving people of Plumtree, and for all their faith, jumbled together as it was with the vestiges of strong animist beliefs, Padre Francisco was convinced they blamed the grisly murders not on any supernatural force, but on the bandits who had tormented them now for years.

Tongue-tied, he had been unable to say much that was meaningful on that score. The burials completed, he had trudged back up to his small house alone, perspiring under his habit.

Dozing on his patio after lunch, Padre Francisco felt he had to do something. It took him the better part of the afternoon to figure out how to do it. Now he needed a messenger.

In the confessional on Saturday afternoons, Padre Francisco admonished, forgave and assigned Hail Marys and Our Fathers to the wayward. But he also took notes. On a small unlined pad, his precise hand recorded life's little infidelities as they manifested themselves in his little village, recording in detail only those he found entertaining; even so, his notes extended to well over one hundred pages.

Waiting on his patio, the twilight rent by the dead khaya's garish limbs, the priest knew it was wrong, but it did supplement his reading and bird-watching nicely, a little something to fill the long, empty days. It was precisely because the priest was such an inveterate snoop that when he decided to contact the authorities in Fado, he knew exactly who to send.

The sun was still high in the sky when he sent his cleaning lady to invite Fonseca for a drink that night.

In her monthly confession before Christmas, Fonseca's wife had asked forgiveness for her gossiping, for swearing at her husband when he rolled on top of her one night after consuming several bottles of port with his brother. The brother was really the problem, Rosa Fonseca said. Younger and wilder than her husband, Guy, Arturo Fonseca didn't keep up his half of the farm their father had left them, and the family was barely making ends meet. Arturo was involved in the war against the bandits, was always running off in the night, and now he had gotten Guy involved in the village's defense committee, spending two nights a week with his father's shotgun and a thermos of coffee, patroling the perimeter of the old truck route that ran in and out of the village, west to east towards Highway 1A. "Be patient, my sister," Padre Francisco had comforted the hydrant-shaped Rosa. "These are trying times." He had given her fifty Hail Marys and sent her on her way, consigning the information immediately afterwards to his trusty notepad.

Consulting the pad as he returned to the patio beneath the branches of the twisted roundwood, Padre Francisco wasn't so sure he had done the right thing. Doubtful of how things might turn out, the priest was already on his second Campari and soda, though Guy Fonseca had not yet arrived.

Fonseca was a small-time trader, mostly in skins and meats for the capital. Because travel was so risky with the bandits controlling sections of the highway to Fado, however, the trade had fallen off badly in the past few months, and Padre Francisco, trying to be fair, and watching as the sturdy, bowlegged figure of his neighbor finally approached around the rim of the hill, wondered whether that wasn't at least part of the reason for the Fonseca family's current economic travails.

"Padre Francisco, thank you for the kind offer of a visit."

"It has been too long, Guy," the priest said, rising. "Neighbors. Much too long. What will you drink?"

"The situation, the holidays, work and family. Ach, you know how it is, Padre. If you have port, that would be fine, but anything. Really."

The priest bustled in the kitchen, the unlabeled bottle of Porto already on the counter, patting his pocket to check for the fifth or sixth time for the note he had sealed that afternoon with old-fashioned sealing wax of the kind his father had used decades before. Returning with the glass and the bottle, the priest poured a full measure, Fonseca making small talk about the weather, which had continued hot, and the bandits, who had been spotted by the village security men twice in the past three nights. The priest nodded, sipping the Campari, his third, and making his own small contributions whenever Fonseca paused for drink or air. As Fonseca embarked on what promised to be a long disquisition on the fortunes of the cashew plant, Padre Francisco filled his neighbor's glass again, wondering how to make the request.

The bandits, Fonseca was saying, would surely try again, any day now, he thought. The bandits, the priest echoed, tired and unsure of himself, seeing his opening at last. "There have been bandits even on our own property the last few days, Guy," Padre Francisco said. "I have seen them myself."

Fonseca was about to fulminate some more about bandits, but Padre Francisco, fueled by the Campari, cut him off awkwardly, coming quickly to his point. "Guy, do you know anyone who can get a message for me to someone in Fado?"

Fonseca tried without success to conceal his surprise. "I thought the Campari came in by the water, Padre, that the supply was okay."

The priest colored, but in the dark under the roundwood, his neighbor couldn't possibly have noticed. Everyone in the village knew Padre Francisco paid one of several local smugglers who supplied villages along the coast north of Fado, working on consignment, cash in advance. "It's not the Campari, Guy. It's a message I must get to the proper person in Fado, to the chief of the police, I think it must go."

"Ahhhh." Fonseca's exhalation betrayed nothing.

"It would be good not to look at the note," the priest said, pulling it from his pocket awkwardly. "And whoever delivers it in Fado, he does not need to look at it, I think. I have sealed it; it is simply a private communication. But I think that it could perhaps help the village and put an end to these murders. To get rid of the bandits."

If Fonseca was smirking in the darkness, Padre Francisco couldn't see it. "I don't want to know what it is, Padre Francisco. But I think I can get your letter to Fado if it is truly as important as you say."

"You would be doing God's work, Guy."

"It is not me, Padre. It is my brother. He has gone twice to Fado now and back, but I think I would like to have him go again one time. Between you and me, he has been hanging around Rosa a lot lately, and I am afraid even of what I am thinking."

"I see," said the priest, stopping himself before he could reach for his little pad. "Then a trip to Fado would be helpful?"

"Very helpful," Guy Fonseca said, draining his glass and rising unsteadily.

Padre Francisco removed the envelope from his habit and rose also, handing the envelope to his guest. "He will be careful, I hope?"

"If he is not more careful around my wife, Padre," Guy Fonseca said, "the road to Fado will seem like child's play, believe me."

"Peace be with you, Guy."

"And with you, Padre. The letter will go tomorrow, first thing."

THE first thing Mireles did was to access the big Raytheon computer terminal behind his desk. The Bureau had all sorts of computer systems, and they were always trying out new ones, in so-called "test bed" sites in one or another of the bigger field offices. They had separate data bases, and even whole separate systems, for organized crime, narcotics, securities crimes, terrorism (domestic and foreign) and counterintelligence. Mireles was known as something of a queue shark in the Bureau, but with all his clearances, reviewing files from the FBI's other divisions was hardly improper. Once or twice, when his log-on turned up in some strange corner of the computer network on the monthly security report, someone raised an eyebrow. Just curious, Mireles would reply. Just trying to stay abreast of things.

With a few keystrokes, Mireles was out of the FCI data base and into CID, the criminal investigative division. He punched in Viktor Alleja's name, last name first, and hoped for the best, since he had forgotten to ask Gub for a DOB, the birth date that queued all the Bureau's computerized files. The file was listed "Inactive," and Mireles had to queue-switch one more time to access it. A quick review showed it was pretty much as he had remembered it. The case had been worked from New Orleans, where an assistant U.S. attorney had shown enough interest in the findings of a Special Agent Warren Hedges to present information to an already-sitting grand jury. The case, as Agent Hedges reported to the grand jury, according to the file on Mireles's screen, involved a foundation called Freedom Fighters that was registered with the IRS as a 5(c)3 organization, charitable in purpose, and therefore tax-exempt. According to a confidential informant working with Agent Hedges, Freedom Fighters solicited money from a vast computer data base provided by a Mr. Robert Gautier, a Baton Rouge businessman prominent in conservative circles in Louisiana and Washington, D.C. Gautier owned a network of more than twenty small but highly profitable insurance, investment and tax-counseling firms across the South, from the Florida Panhandle to Baton Rouge, then north to Little Rock. "Odds-Beaters," the companies were called.

According to Agent Hedges's C.I., a former employee fired from the Odds-Beaters office in Fort Walton Beach, Florida, who was drifting through New Orleans, the companies were soliciting heavily for the Freedom Fighters organization, which also just happened to be located in Odds-Beaters' corporate headquarters in Baton Rouge. The company had collected over $200,000 for Freedom Fighters, the C.I. testified, most of it after a series of speeches and luncheons laid on by Gautier for a man named Viktor Alleja, who was described as Freedom Fighters' "man on the front lines" in the fight against the government in Fado. Agent Hedges's C.I. had chauffeured Viktor Alleja for the Panhandle part of the tour: Apalachicola, Fort Walton Beach, Panama City and Dauphin Island. The C.I. recalled that Viktor Alleja wore a heavy wool suit, despite the humidity and the ninety-degree weather. Besides the dubious eleemosynary intentions

of Freedom Fighters, Agent Hedges's C.I. also testified briefly as to
the speaking ability of Viktor Alleja. "Damn lousy" was one of the
descriptions taken down by the federal courthouse reporter. Also
boring. The C.I. did allow as how Viktor Alleja nevertheless had a
certain presence before a group. The C.I. also swore, but could not
prove, that Viktor Alleja was a minority partner in Freedom Fighters.
He further testified that of the $200,000 raised by Gautier and Viktor
Alleja, less than $20,000 had gone to actual freedom fighters in or
around Fado.

Incredibly, Mireles thought, reading the final section of the file,
neither Agent Hedges nor the young AUSA in New Orleans had
thought to include any mention in the record of the bandits and their
documented record of atrocities since the situation had begun. A
professional point, but Mireles thought it would have swayed the
grand jury. As it was, Agent Hedges and his C.I. could carry the case
only so far. By the time the IRS consented to an audit of Freedom
Fighters' books, it appeared that Gautier had already transferred
funds in small amounts from his offices across the South. And since
they had been raising the money primarily from Odds-Beaters' cli-
ents anyway, it was impossible to show conclusively that a fraud had
been perpetrated. Agent Hedges noted in his final report that the
evidence might have warranted prosecution under what some older
Bureau agents still referred to, quaintly, Mireles thought, as "com-
mingling of funds." But the grand jury's term finally expired, and the
New Orleans AUSA was unwilling to start over again before a new
grand jury with such a technical case.

Mireles made a printout of the file, then dialed Langley.

After he had first joined the FBI, Mireles had come to the attention
of the Africa Division of the Central Intelligence Agency. About the
only people besides his wife who were interested in his prior life in
Fado were the Africa specialists at the CIA, and Herb Cohen, in
Mireles's judgment, was far and away the best of the lot. On his two
brief swings through Washington during his time with the Bureau,
Cohen had made a point of seeking Mireles out and bouncing all
sorts of theories, questions and scenarios off him. Mireles resented it
at first, preferring to forget the old days, and pleaded that he hadn't
kept up with events. Cohen insisted gently, however, and Mireles
found he was such a nice guy, his interest so genuine, that the two
had become good friends.

Mireles figured if anyone in the Agency knew what had become of

Viktor Alleja, Cohen would. He had seen some scary moments while working for the Agency's Directorate of Operations out there and made some amazing contacts. Back at the D.O., with its calming views of the Virginia woods just outside Washington, he continued to handle large sections of the Africa account.

Cohen's secretary put the call through right away, and Mireles made a bit of small talk before getting to the point.

"Viktor Alleja, funny you should mention him." Cohen was a chain-smoker, and Mireles could hear him wheezing between sentences. "He's been quiet for quite a while, but we had something new on him just the other day. Seems he's in Lisbon, and he's been seeing some rather interesting characters, according to this information."

"How good is this stuff, Herb?"

The CIA man took another scratchy breath. "Well, you know Lisbon. The movies always make it out like Casablanca was the big den of spies, when really it was always Lisbon. Still is, in many respects. Lot of retired guys there, too, but they keep their eyes open. So when a guy like Viktor Alleja comes through, even though he's not familiar to a lot of the European players, it doesn't take long for word to travel. Turns out he's got a place in the Alfama, rented. A checking and savings account at the Credit Suisse branch in the Rua Augusta, and that's about it. One of our guys in the embassy paid a little money for a couple of reports. Obviously, I don't know the source. The station was just collecting string, you know."

"Doing its job."

"Right. Anyway, so there's nothing new except now we got a current address on a guy we used to be pretty interested in."

"But what?"

"But this: all of a sudden he's getting visitors. We don't have a confirmed on any of them, but one guy already looks interesting. In fact, I understand your people here have been doing some checking on it, too. Not that they'd tell us, of course."

Mireles knew Cohen's oblique way of asking favors. "If I hear even a whisper, I'll let you know, I promise. So who's the guy?"

"Well, like I say, it's not confirmed, but as I understand it, we've had some talks just in the last day with the BND guy in the embassy here."

"What do the Germans have to do with this?" Thanks to his job, Mireles had his own contacts in the German intelligence agency.

"They've been going through all the Stasi stuff, reams of it, I'm told. Unbelievable. And they're coming up with plenty. Some you see in the newspapers, about how all these high East German officials were also working as informers. But the BND thinks they're onto an important Stasi network inside the Federal Republic, and the ID our people in Lisbon got on this guy spotted with Viktor Alleja is evidently pretty damn close to that of a guy the Germans would dearly love to have."

"What's he done?" Mireles was scribbling fast.

"If it's the same guy, plenty. Our folks in the CTC got a lot on him." The counterterrorism center was a clearinghouse for all the American intelligence agencies. "The guy was based in Frankfurt, but he traveled plenty. Even taught for a while at Qaddafi's famous frogman school. Did logistics and operations stuff for Baader-Meinhof, then the Red Army Faction, apparently funded directly by Stasi. We think he was involved in the hit on the La Belle disco. And the Germans think they can tie him up with the hit on that DeutscheBank director and with a couple of other things they've never worked out. Most recently—again, if this is the same guy—the Brits and the Germans have got him linked up with that IRA bombing of the Quebec Barracks."

"The British Army garrison, the one at Osnabrück?"

"Right. The thinking is, if he helped do that one, he's helped do them all."

"This guy got a name?"

"Hagen, Otto Hagen. The BND's checking on this Lisbon business now. We passed it along, of course. A matter of professional courtesy. But already they turned him up in the area. Interpol picked up an American in Barcelona, a doper. He was moving hashish out of Morocco for the swells in Ibiza. The kid had a passport that links up with one of Hagen's in the Stasi records. The records indicate he had at least three passports, by the way. The other two are still unaccounted for. Spanish cops also got a dead businessman from Colombia that could figure in this, but the Germans are interested in the American for now. The kid is scared shitless, and the BND guys are apparently really working on him, laying the Stasi killer rap on him and like that. They're frantic, but I'll give you odds the kid don't know shit."

"Why are the Germans in such a sweat?"

"If this guy is really Hagen, it looks like he had been living under the Germans' noses for years. They tumbled his place in Frankfurt, near the zoo. Landlady says he's been one of her best tenants. Quiet, polite, always paid on time. And he was living there seven years. Seven fucking years."

"Kind of embarrassing. So what's the guessing on what he's doing with Viktor Alleja?"

"Nobody knows. You got any ideas?"

"Well, you know what's been going on in Fado the last few days."

"Yeah, we've had reports. You think that's Hagen?"

"Man needs work, a place to go."

Herb Cohen wheezed loudly. "I'll make some calls, but let's stay in touch, huh?"

"You bet." Mireles rang off, wondering. The fucking Stasi in Fado? Sometimes, he thought, what goes around comes around.

FOURTEEN

IT was nearly 8 P.M. when they left Gub's Toyota. Gub parked it at the broken curb, just over half a block from Betty's apartment, the rust and the ugly mustard-yellow paint job seeming to run together in the thin moonlight as the three of them walked away. Before he left the apartment, Gub had Betty demonstrate one final time how to use the Browning, waiting until the target was close enough to do some real damage, then squeezing one trigger at a time so that she could get off two shots instead of one monster blast that just might miss. Drawing the heavy curtains across the dirty glass doors, Betty double-checked the locks before setting Matthias's bed up on the couch.

Gub listened from the outside hallway as she secured the lower lock on the apartment's front door, drew the chain, then fastened the dead bolt. He didn't really think she was in any danger, but he had no idea how much surveillance the people distributing these heads had been doing. Just about everyone in Fado knew where he lived, so the fact they had found him was no big deal, but someone had known specifically that he was not in when they had broken in and left the head in his refrigerator.

Anyway, Gub mused, having dropped Ellis at the Works Ministry, his whole countersurveillance scheme could be a waste of time, although Ellis had certainly dressed for the occasion. Gub thought he must have picked up the idea for the black trousers and black turtleneck from *Mission: Impossible,* or maybe *Man from U.N.C.L.E.* They were playing the reruns again on one of the cable channels he got on the satellite dish. Too bad they didn't have those tiny two-way transmitters that fit into a wristwatch, Gub thought. Instead, he had given Ellis a bulky Radio Shack hand-held job that had a range of maybe two miles. It wasn't great, Gub thought, but it was good enough for their purposes. Because Ellis had never fired a gun, Gub figured it was probably unwise to leave him with one. He instructed him to confront no one at the Works Ministry, just to call him quickly on the radio.

Parking Betty's British Land-Rover with the broken A.C. and the Save the Children logo on the back window, Gub wondered if he shouldn't have left Ellis with some kind of weapon, even an unloaded gun. But he was close enough by, he figured, if anything happened, just over a mile away, near the executive offices of the president's staff. If Ellis called, he could get to the Works Ministry in a couple of minutes, max.

Gub had had no trouble choosing the surveillance locations. Whoever was delivering the severed heads had already hit Calamidades and the Justice Palace. Of course, they could decide to deliver some more severed heads to both places, but Gub didn't see the percentage in that. Of the other potential government targets, there was the Works Ministry, the presidential staff's executive offices, the presidential palace and Prince Henry the Navigator Airport, which everyone called Henry International. The army had a good presence at the airport, so Gub had ruled that out. And the small but competent presidential guard had been garrisoned on the palace grounds ever since the situation had begun, making it a difficult target, at best. That left the Works Ministry, which was unguarded even though it housed a dozen heavy army trucks awaiting spare parts and repairs in a locked yard behind the two-story administration building, and the presidential staff's offices, which Gub figured was the most symbolic of the unguarded targets. There was also the Okavango, of course, the government-owned hotel, and a few other candidates. But with only himself and Ellis, Gub figured the two locations he'd picked made the most sense.

Starting out, he had felt confident. But it was nearly midnight, and Gub had heard and seen nothing. Ellis had checked in every thirty minutes, as ordered, the last time at exactly 11:30. Nothing, he had reported; visibility tolerable in the light of a quarter-moon. Once or twice, Gub had heard a car engine cough and the hiss of tires moving slowly across asphalt, but they had faded away, the gauzy silence descending on the city once more, split by the bark of a dog every now and then.

From the western end of the marble porch that ran the length of the president's executive office building, Gub could survey the ruined gardens that ran down to the street, Avenida de la Revolución, where he had left the Land-Rover in a thick stand of bushes. In his jeans and navy tennis shirt, Gub was sure, he was more or less invisible in the shadows of the marble columns, the Chief's Special in Mireles's old leather holster under his right arm, the SIG-10 fastened on his left side by an ingenious metal clip that fit onto most any belt. Leave it to the Swiss, Gub thought.

He was about to make another circuit of the building, keeping to the thick boxwood and hydrangea bushes that ringed the foundation of the Justice Palace, when the Radio Shack transmitter he had placed on the marble railing exploded. A short cry, then a long burst from an automatic and finally, as Gub vaulted into the street, digging for the keys of the Land-Rover in the front pocket of his jeans, Ellis moaning.

Gub fishtailed the powerful Land-Rover down Avenida de la Revolución towards the Works Ministry, looking for cars down each side street but seeing nothing. He was within a block of the two-story administration building when he heard the roar, then saw the flash, a fireball lighting the night sky. "Oh, God," he swore, "the fucking embassy district."

Gub jammed the accelerator to the floor, willing even more speed from the big four-wheel drive for the last half a block. Brakes screaming, he jumped from the vehicle about one hundred yards from the front of the administration building, where more ruined gardens blocked the way, racing the rest of the distance on foot. From twenty yards away, even in the shadows where Ellis lay, legs splayed across the marble floor, Gub could see there was no hope. The automatic had caught him full in the face, a long burst, Gub figured. A handsome young man, his features were unrecognizable now. "Help me improve my skills," Gub swore, recalling Ellis's constant request. "Fucking waste."

Running back to the Land-Rover, Gub jammed it into gear, hitting eighty-five on the way back up Avenida de la Revolución, the big engine screaming as orange flames colored the sky over the newer residences and apartments in the new embassy district. From the look of it, Gub figured, it couldn't be a big fire, but who the hell knew? It took him nearly seven minutes to race the five miles from the Works Ministry, and Gub swore when he saw the small knot of people gathered just down the street from Betty's flat.

He was out of the Land-Rover almost before it stopped, junior and mid-level diplomats in robes and slippers mingling with a few of the neighborhood's night watchmen, the crowd of maybe twenty people giving way as Gub strode towards the burning hulk of his Toyota. The heat was intense over the gas tanks; he had installed a reserve years before in the rear of the jeep. Gub didn't give a shit about the car, it was a ten-year-old wreck. What surprised him, as he tried to get closer, was not the deflated and melting tires or the acrid chemical smell of burning hydraulic and brake fluid from the engine well. The real surprise, he recalled long after, was the body burning merrily away on the ground next to the Toyota's driver's-side door.

Gub looked at the body a long time, watching it burn, knowing there was nothing to be done, the little man in his head getting it all on tape. A busy night for the little man, Gub thought, Ellis's ruined face flickering in the dying flames, Betty with the Browning sawed-off crouched behind locked doors.

"Gub!"

It was Betty's voice, but at first he thought it was the little man playing tricks on him, pulling a stunt with the audio. The little fucker.

"Gub!" She had the Browning dangling at her side and Matthias, drowsy and confused, hard by the hand, nearly sailing behind her. "Jesus, are you all right?"

Gub fought the images in the flames, shaking as he embraced Betty and Matthias in a big bear hug, the knot of onlookers watching.

"We heard the explosion, but we were afraid to come out. Then I thought it might be you, so I got the gun and Matthias and we ran down here. What the hell happened?"

Gub listened absently, disengaging finally to look at Betty, tears streaming down her face. "A bomb, I think," he said finally. "What I can't figure is who the guy on the ground is."

Betty took a quick look over Gub's shoulder, small flames still licking at the torso in the gutter.

When he saw the shoulders start to go, dry sobs coming from deep inside her, Gub held her tightly, Matthias looking up at the tall man and the pretty woman in his arms, then at the dead man burning near the jeep, then back at the man and the sobbing woman with the strange gun still hanging at her side. As usual, the boy didn't say a word, his pointed stick making lazy figure eights in the dirt.

Gub wasn't sure how long they stood there like that, several minutes maybe. Finally, he pulled away and looked at Betty. "Let's get home." He took the Browning from her right hand, flicked the safety on and grabbed Matthias by the hand. Before he left, he asked two of the night watchmen to keep everyone there so he could ask a few questions when he got back.

Outside Betty's apartment, he listened for the second time that night as she did the lower lock, fastened the chain and slipped the dead bolt. "Don't open the door until you hear my voice and I say the secret word."

"What's the secret word?" Her voice sounded drained and empty from the other side of the wooden door.

"Fast break," Gub said, turning and jogging back down the hallway and down the four flights of stairs to the street.

The two gas tanks still burned in the rear of the Toyota, but the fires were out in the rest of the truck, as well as on the dead man in the street. Grabbing a pad of paper from the backseat of Betty's Land-Rover, Gub identified himself for the few who didn't know him and began interviewing rapidly, dismissing those immediately who had questions but no answers. Within minutes, Gub sorted through the knot of people, finally dismissing them all but one, the night watch for the apartment building across the street. It was owned by a British company, Gub knew, but most of the flats had been let to members of the U.S. mission, which had thoughtfully agreed to pay the salary of the watchman, whose name, Gub learned, was Ernest Tyson, age fifty-nine.

Mr. Tyson told Gub he had heard a couple of cars on the road during the early evening hours. He had noted the mustard-yellow Toyota Land Cruiser outside the apartment building and done as he was instructed, reporting it to the marine guards at the embassy building downtown, and to the regional security officer, whom he had located at dinner at the ambassador's residence on the coast road. For some reason, Mr. Allsworth, the DCM who had the penthouse suite on the fourth and top floor of the apartment building, was not at the dinner, and when Ernest Tyson learned he was at home, he phoned up to the penthouse to let him know about the suspicious Toyota. Mr. Tyson told Gub that Mr. Allsworth had told him to call back the RSO and the marine guard downtown and inform them that he would look into the matter of the mustard-colored Toyota, and if there was any problem that he would call them back.

Gub was writing furiously. "Then what?"

"Well, Mr. Allsworth, he came downstairs after a while, and he had a drink with him, it smelled like Scotch."

"What'd he do?"

"He went on out into the street, and he looked down toward the coast road a good while. Then he looked back down the other way, towards the big apartment place in the next block. I was watching from my post right over there by the entryway, so I could see him good."

"Then what?"

"So he turned and raised his glass to me, toasting like. Then he went over to look at the jeep. He walked around the front end, and then the back. And when he tried the driver's door, that's when the damn thing blew. I ran over to see to Mr. Allsworth right away, but he was burning and maybe already dead. There was fire all around the jeep, even the road was burning with gas, and I couldn't get to him to pull him clear."

"What'd you do next, Mr. Tyson?" Gub asked, turning abruptly as two dark blue Chevrolet sedans wheeled into the road.

"Well, I called these gentlemen from my post and told 'em what happened to Mr. Allsworth."

Gub knew the RSO, Glenn Burnie, and the marine with him, Sergeant Britt Hills. He decided to spare them the loquaciousness of Mr. Ernest Tyson, and the two men listened intently as Gub spoke, nodding their heads.

"Any ideas who did it?" Burnie, the embassy's regional security officer, asked Gub. Normally, RSOs were not based in backwaters like Fado, but since the situation had gotten worse, Burnie had been dividing his time between Harare and Fado.

"Same guys who've been spreading severed heads all over town. You got any different ideas?"

"Nope," Burnie said, "I expect that's about right. A shame about the DCM, though. They were going to be moving him out next month, back to Washington."

"Is that right?"

"Yep. Between us, he'd been hitting the sauce pretty good lately, and the ambassador, she couldn't control him. They weren't even on speaking terms, except for the embassy business they had to get done. That's why Allsworth was home with his bottle and not at the ambassador's place tonight."

Gub promised he'd leave that out of his report the next morning. He thought he ought to go back to check on Betty and Matthias, but first he had to take care of Ellis. Leaving Mr. Tyson and his American bosses to take care of their own, Gub drove back to the Works Ministry, and it took him fifteen minutes of hard work to carry Ellis's body to the Land-Rover and get it stowed away in back. By the time he reached the hospital, it was nearly 4:30, and by the time the two night orderlies got Ellis tagged and documented in the morgue, it was nearly six.

IN New York, it was nearly 7 P.M. before Mireles locked his office door and headed for the elevator, but he wasn't going straight home.

After getting off with Cohen, he had called Bernd Koehler at the embassy in midtown and asked if he had time for a drink. Mireles liked the BND man and most but not all of his colleagues. They had plenty of reason to like him. Not two years before, another BND man, an attaché at the embassy in Washington, had been in a hotel on Forty-fourth Street when New York City vice-squad detectives had broken down the door and found him naked, tied to the bed, with two huge transvestites standing over him with whips. The man had been unharmed, however, and his story had had way too many holes in it. The attaché's first call, foolishly or not, had been to the German mission at the United Nations, and the BND man there, unsure what to do, had called Mireles to ask for advice.

Mireles knew plenty of New York's finest. Several hundred were on permanent assignment to the FBI field office on lower Broadway, and plenty more rotated through the place. Mireles had simply made a few calls, and someone had encouraged the vice-squad guys to back off. There wasn't much of a case there anyway, but the New York tabloids would have had a field day with it if it had come out. The compromised BND man had been quickly spirited out of the country, and on one of his two visits to BND headquarters in Pullach, near Munich, senior BND officials had made it clear to Mireles how much they appreciated his "understanding of the sensitivity of the matter."

Mireles merely saw it as an opportunity to call in a favor later. Hence the call to Bernd Koehler.

They met in the bar of the Parker Meridien Hotel on West Fifty-sixth Street. There was parking close by, and it was convenient. Mireles could jump on the Fifty-ninth Street bridge afterwards and take Queens Boulevard to the expressway.

Koehler had a dinner at 8:15 so the meeting was quick, but Mireles got the reaction he was looking for. At the mention of Otto Hagen's name, Bernd Koehler, correct in a dark suit and tie, spit some of his gin gimlet back into his glass.

"You know where he is?"

Mireles was bluffing. "I said I think I know, Bernd. I have some leads, one lead actually, but it's a good one."

Koehler was silent, dabbing at his pouchy lips with a napkin. "He is important. And dangerous."

"I know, Bernd. But what I need is anything you can give me on him. Anything at all, but especially what your people know now, or think they know, about Lisbon. I think I can help."

"I'll have to make some calls. Where can I reach you later?"

Mireles wrote his home number on the back of his business card, and they both rose to leave.

As he crossed the Fifty-ninth Street bridge on the upper level in the big Bureau-owned Ford, Mireles admired the skyline, the slim profile of the U.N. building off to the right, the angular Citicorp building scraping the black sky behind him.

Suddenly, he thought, his life was spinning out of control.

His wife, as usual, had been right. The conversation with Amy the night before had brought into the open something he knew but somehow could never admit: that the life he had built in the States, for all its worth and satisfaction, was still a fragile thing erected on an old foundation never properly razed and then rebuilt. The flight from Fado, the two years of self-imposed silence in Providence—he had never really dealt with them, let alone the events that had caused him to flee in the first place. Then Amy had come along, a gift, he still thought of her, from a blessedly prodigal providence. And then the twins. And all of a sudden, it seemed, he didn't need to confront the past at all; the future was what counted.

After Miami, his stock soaring in the Bureau, Mireles had buried

himself in the job, the heavy accent slipping away almost unnoticed.
And then there he was one day, as if by magic, driving home in the
LTD Crown Victoria, a pretty wife, two great kids, a nice house and a
closetful of Brooks Brothers suits, the boxy three-button models that
the Judge and some of the senior Bureau guys favored. Amazing.

And now he was working like a zombie. And now Gub was in real
danger, perhaps at the hands of a Stasi killer. It all had an odd,
dreamlike quality.

Yet for almost as long as he could remember now, it had not
seemed like a dream, none of it. Mireles had made it all his own, this
new life in America and its strange trappings. The so-called peace
dividend, how that had been chewed up by the S&L mess, and then
the whole thing with Iraq, the end of history, what the world after the
Cold War was going to look like. Mireles read the newspapers, talked
with the guys at the office about it all. It mattered. Or seemed to. It
all had to do with where the country was heading. And it was his
country now.

Escaping the stop-and-go congestion of Queens Boulevard for the
steady sluggish pace of the Long Island Expressway, Mireles remembered the first time he had felt as if he had truly left his life in Fado
behind, when he had felt for certain that he had a new place to call
home. Before that, Amy and the kids had kept him on an even keel,
and so, God knew, did the job. But by himself in the car, or nights
when he couldn't sleep, memories of the old life, nearly thirty years
of it, seeped in like moisture from walls in a damp basement. It had
gotten better with time, and then the one day at Fenway, a gray fall
afternoon—they didn't have fall in Fado—he had felt the old life slip
away for good. He and Mike Marshall had been at the ballpark
together, as they always were, in Mike's box along the first-base line.
Mireles had still been learning the game, but he had a pretty good fix
on it, and his father-in-law was a patient teacher.

Mireles remembered it like it was yesterday, the last game of the
'83 season, a meaningless contest between the Red Sox and the last-
place Indians. But it was also the last game Carl Yastrzemski would
ever play as a professional, and Yaz, Mireles had decided years before,
sitting up nights in the lonely bungalow in Green Hill, Yaz was his
kind of hero. It wasn't the homers Mireles loved so much, though
they had made his throat ache, or the rifle-shot doubles caroming off
walls; it was the rally-ending throws, the way he worked every at-bat
like it was life or death, right then and there at the plate. There,
Mireles thought, that was a pro, the way to live a life.

Yaz got his first and only hit that day, a weak opposite-field chop-per past the third baseman, and Mireles rose and cheered with the Fenway multitudes. The rest of the day, he remembered, braking hard to avoid an Allied Van Lines truck in front of him, was like an epiphany. The Sox took it 3–1, but what Mireles remembered was the end, Yaz standing with a microphone in the first-base coaching box, maybe forty yards from their seats. He and Mike could see his face clear as day, Yaz waving, his cap raised high, saluting the left-field fans out towards the Monster, then the bleacher rats, and finally the fans behind the home-team dugout, his neighbors, the people he'd watched dozens of ball games with. After that, the players had come out, Jim Rice and the others, hugging him, taking turns, and finally, a piece of white paper in his hand, Yastrzemski had tried to say something. "Thank you very much," was all he managed. Then he took a few steps out onto the diamond, his head down, and Mireles could see the tears on his cheeks. And then he realized he was crying too, big tears rolling down his own face in the damp fall air. It was getting dark when the fans summoned Yaz back for the last time, and Mireles was sobbing deeply then, gulping air as Yastrzem-ski lapped the old ball yard once, Mireles unsure whether he was crying for Yaz or himself or both. Either way, it was like a kind of baptism, he had thought at the time and afterwards, the true begin-ning of his life as an American.

And now, it seemed, maybe it was and maybe it wasn't. All he knew for sure was that he needed to deal with his life differently. To be more attentive to his wife, to the girls. To be less obsessive. And perhaps, if friendship meant anything and Gub really was in trouble, to put all that at risk. It was a matter of principle, Mireles thought, turning the LTD onto Glen Cove Road and home. Yaz would have understood.

FIFTEEN

The twins were still awake when Mireles pulled into the driveway and hit the Up button on the garage-door opener. Two nights in a row, he thought, a record.

Amy was wearing jeans and one of his old oxford shirts, her favorite uniform around the house. When Mireles walked in, she was at the kitchen table, paperwork from school and her briefcase open in front of her. She gave him an abstracted "Hi" and went back to a personnel-evaluation form. Mireles dropped his briefcase near the refrigerator and kneaded her shoulders before kneeling next to her chair and smothering her with a kiss.

"Mr. Romance. You stopped for a drink?"

"I had to meet someone, but I've been thinking about you all day."

"Liar." She got up and kissed him back.

"Would you believe most of the day?"

"Most of the day I'd settle for."

Mireles could see she was tired. Amy worked long hours, too, and the job was every bit as demanding as his, he thought, probably more so given the emotional strain of dealing with difficult kids and the burdens they caused their families. Still, Amy found plenty of time for the twins, the house and her spouse. All she was really asking of him, Mireles thought, was that he do the same. He vowed he'd try.

"Seriously, Ame, I thought about what you said last night, and you're right, as usual." He glanced at his watch. "Let me get the girls off to bed, and then we can talk, okay?"

Amy Mireles blew her husband a kiss and went back to her paperwork.

The Simpsons had just ended when Mireles walked into the den to turn off the TV, and the twins went tractably, Kate's turn this time to ask about their plans for the weekend. Mireles started to answer when he heard the phone in his office ring. "Right back, girls, don't forget the teeth."

Bernd Koehler said he had broken away from dinner but had to get back shortly. "I have relayed our conversation to Pullach. We have a team in Lisbon and another in Barcelona. The BKA is also involved." The BKA was the German federal police, the equivalent of the FBI in the U.S., and Mireles had a lot of respect for them. "Klaus Bauer will be calling you from Pullach shortly. But what you really want, I think, will come tomorrow. A scrambled fax to us, and I will have it couriered to your office immediately."

"What's in the fax, Bernd?"

"The Sicherungsgruppe has prepared a very preliminary report on Hagen, everything we know up until now."

Mireles cocked an eyebrow. The S.G. was the BKA's security group. It was based in Bonn and handled counterterrorism cases and intelligence-related police matters. It wasn't often anyone outside the Federal Republic saw their work product, especially a raw report like this. "Good work, Bernd."

"I'm not sure how helpful they are prepared to be, frankly. It took a lot to get it out of them, pressure from the very top. We are all terribly concerned about this Hagen matter—it was ordered that the S.G. provide the report. Finally, and I just heard this from Pullach, Interpol has traced the passport of the Colombian killed in the Barcelona train station."

"And?"

"It was used by a man on a TAP flight from Lisbon to Rome with a connection to Malta. We're checking with Valletta now to see if they have any leads."

"Libya," Mireles said. "We'll never trace him there."

"It will be difficult, Tom, but the BND has some ways there. We can try. I've got to go, but I'll have the fax delivered to you first thing tomorrow. Then we must talk."

Mireles thanked Bernd Koehler, hung up and went back to the

twins' room to tuck them in. He gave each a long kiss. Glancing into the kitchen, he saw Amy still poring over her papers; whether it was a studied concentration designed to send a message, he couldn't say. He had been a good investigator but he was just plain dumb when it came to picking up clues like that. He ducked back into his office and made another call.

Mike Marshall picked it up immediately. "Sweet Christ, Tom, if it isn't the shining light of our own Federal Bureau of Investigation!" Mireles thought he could feel the blarney oozing through the phone, and he laughed out loud. Everyone should have such a good father-in-law.

"You sound good, Mike. Everything okay?"

"Yeah, fine. I don't see my beautiful granddaughters nearly enough. That's an ass-breaker for an old man. But you'll be sure to invite him to the college graduation?"

"You're at the top of the list, Mike."

"It's a great solace, that."

"I'm taking a couple of weeks in July, Mike, but maybe we can come for a few days even sooner. You have your fill of the twins and see if you're still up for July and the graduation."

"I'll be up for both and for any other time. You know there's plenty of room in the old place."

"We'll be there, Mike," Mireles said, changing the subject. "Listen, I need to ask you something."

"Shoot."

Mike Marshall handled transitions better than just about anyone he had ever known, Mireles thought. "I talked with an old friend out in Fado today, and he needs a bit of a hand, and I'm thinking of going out there."

There was a distinct silence at the other end of the line.

"I'm not asking your permission or anything, Mike, and I haven't told Amy yet, but I wanted to see what you thought."

"This is Gub?"

Mireles and his father-in-law had talked about things in Fado, usually in the car on the way to the ballpark. "Yeah, things there are going to hell in a hurry, and he's in a bit of a jam."

"How serious is it?" The old man had a way of cutting to the quick of things.

"Pretty serious, Mike. Maybe dangerous even."

"But you've got to go."

"A friend needs help, what can I say?"

"Then you should do it. And don't worry about Amy. Her mother raised her well and smart, right up till she died, God rest her soul. And I did the best I could after. She's a smart gal, Tom, she'll understand."

Mireles let his breath go. "Thanks, Mike. You don't know how much that means."

They made some more small talk about the disaster that was the New England Patriots, and Mireles finally rang off before he headed back into the kitchen.

Amy had cleared away her papers and was grilling him a ham and cheese on rye. She would have fixed him whatever, but her husband went for sandwiches after work, and that was fine with her. "Who were you on with there?"

"The Germans," Mireles lied, then backtracked immediately. "I also gave your dad a call."

"You did?" Amy Mireles turned to look at him, still as slender as the day he had married her, despite the twins.

Mireles worried that she was working too hard. "Yeah, I told you, I really have done some thinking about what you said last night."

"Well, how is he?"

"He's good, but he'd love for us to come up and bring the girls. I think he's lonely up there."

"He never did get over my mother." Amy brought the toasted sandwich to the table, and Mireles was rising to get a couple of beers from the garage when the phone in his office rang again.

"Shit," Mireles said, running to get it.

Amy Mireles took the sandwich from the table and shoved it in the microwave that was suspended from the bottom of the cabinet to the left of the sink.

In the office, Klaus Bauer came to the point quickly. "We cannot prove it yet, Mireles. We had indications before about Hagen's travels since November, but nothing very good."

This was the P.R. call, Mireles thought. The one from the brass ensuring a sister service that they had not really screwed up after all. Mireles wondered whether Bauer had called anyone in Washington, and bet that he had. He made a mental note to make some calls of his own tomorrow.

"We are convinced now that he has gone to Libya, perhaps to stay," Bauer was saying. "We are trying to check on that now, but it is rather difficult, as you can imagine."

The Libya theory made sense on the face of it. No one would get

Otto Hagen if he stayed there. But it didn't square with the admittedly sketchy evidence on the meet with Viktor Alleja, and with Gub's reports from Fado. Mireles kept those thoughts to himself for the moment. "I look forward to reading the report Bernd mentioned, and of course, I will copy your people immediately on anything we might come up with." Mireles thanked the German for his help, hung up and went back to the kitchen.

"Now what?" Amy punched the microwave timer for thirty seconds.

"That was the Germans. I forgot to tell you, I talked to Gub yesterday. He called and asked me to check on a guy."

"How is old Gub?"

"He's good. He said to say hello."

"He's a dear. How're things going?"

"It's tough, what with the situation there. But the interesting thing is, the guy he asked me to check on turns out to be involved with a German, a guy from the Stasi that all sorts of people, mainly the Germans, are interested in. From what Gub says and the stuff I was able to pry loose today, it looks like this guy is being paid to run a kind of terror campaign right into Fado, and Gub, naturally, is right in the middle of it."

"Oh, no." Mireles could see his wife was genuinely distressed. She really liked Gub.

"I know the Bureau's going to be interested in this guy for a lot of things, probably including some of the bombings of U.S. troop trains in Germany that have never been solved. But it looks like he may be involved in a lot of things. Anyway, my bet is that he's in Fado, running this terrorism campaign."

"I didn't hear anything about it on TV or see anything in the papers."

"They never cover it. It's too far away, too unimportant."

"What can you do, Tom? This is terrible." Amy pulled the sandwich out of the microwave.

"I thought about it on the way home, and I just don't know. In a strange way, this jibes with some of what you said last night, but maybe that's just me looking for an excuse."

"Is that why you called Mike?"

"I guess. But it was great to hear his voice."

"And what does he say?"

"Go. If that's what I think I have to do."

Amy Mireles put her half-finished beer on the kitchen table and stared at her husband. "Have you lost your mind, Tom? We haven't seen you for weeks on end, the twins and I, and now you're going to go halfway around the world to help a friend you can barely find time to call once or twice a year? With a professional killer there to boot?"

"I know, it sounds crazy, I know it does. But all morning, I sat through this long goddamn security meeting, and I kept thinking about it, how I've let the job block out my family and my friends and the things that matter."

"And this is all because I said you're working too hard?"

"It's that and a lot of things, but it's mainly that I've used you and the kids and the job as a kind of shield from my old life. When I talked to Gub, some of it came flooding back, like it does when he comes to see us. But when I talked to the Germans tonight, I just realized he needs help."

"So when are you leaving?" In her wrinkled shirt and jeans, Amy Mireles rose and walked around behind her husband's chair, cradling his handsome head in her arms. She thought of the morning he had been shot in Miami, how she had been both scared and angry.

"You think I really am crazy?"

"I'm thinking, first, that I should keep my big mouth shut, and second, that if this is something you feel you really have to do, then you should do it. But goddammit, Tom Mireles, you better be really, really careful."

Mireles sighed. His eyes closed, he could feel his wife's breasts through the rough cotton shirt. "I don't want to go, you know that?"

Amy Mireles nodded.

"But I think it will make a difference somehow."

Amy Mireles squeezed her husband tighter.

Mireles looked at his watch. "It's early there, but I guess I better call Gub and tell him I'm coming, huh?"

His wife nodded. "Give him my love."

IT was a little past seven, a weak sun spinning the wave tops a frothy pink beyond the big windows of the *curandeiro*'s study. Inside, the splendor of the morning was lost on Hagen and Sturua, however; they were drunk.

"Never," Hagen said, "in thirteen years with the Stasi was it this easy. Just do it, and that's it. No after-action reports, no review boards, none of that stuff. Even Bucharest couldn't have had forms like the Friedrichstrasse. Agent payments, travel vouchers, equipment expenses—unbelievable! And everything seconded to the KGB in triplicate."

"Ceaușescu just told Moscow to shove it up its ass. That was one thing the old man should get credit for. We fucked the KGB every chance we got, especially under Brezhnev and after. But they were crazy, the Ceaușescus. It was like an asylum of lunatics, calls in the middle of the night, pick up this cousin, cover up this fiasco. Rapes we didn't worry about with the boys; who would be crazy enough to file a complaint? But the women, Nadia and some of the others, you heard about that stuff?"

"Just rumors," Hagen said, emptying the last of the Polish vodka into his glass, spilling a little on the medicine man's polished floor.

"I got a call one night, from Ceaușescu himself. 'We have a problem,' he says. 'Fix it.' So I go out to the address this colonel gives me, a big apartment in the Strasse Turda, fucking freezing out in the middle of February, and I have to walk, because naturally there are no cabs, and my own car is in the Securitate basement, locked for the night. Nearly two miles."

"This was Nadia?"

"Yeah, and one of the cousins, much younger. Nice. So anyway, I find the apartment. I almost never even go to this part of Bucharest, but I find the apartment, I climb the stairs to the sixth floor. There was no trouble knowing where the party was with the music, real loud rock and roll, heavy metal, and I pick the lock and open the door, and there are the two Ceaușescus, blondes, Nadia and the other one, buck naked except for these fucking G-strings."

"Jesus."

"These broads are on something, I don't know what, because they don't even look at me when I come through the door. So I take a few seconds to see what's going on, check things out. There's cognac around, good French stuff. And cocaine. It must have been really pure, because, like I say, these broads are wired. And they got these three guys—three of them—handcuffed and naked. I still have no idea how they got there. Anyway, there's the one guy on the couch, he's clearly dead, a fat guy, maybe forty, blood bubbling out of his mouth, I can't figure from what, strangled maybe. The other two, one guy laid out on the floor and the other hanging by his wrists from a rope tied to a hook in the ceiling—they don't look so good either.

And this is the great part—the young broad, not Nadia, she's trying to do the guy on the hook."

"Come on!"

"I swear it. And still these fucking Valkyries aren't paying the slightest attention. I figure something extra's called for, so I pull out this Walther I carry, you know the one, the new PPK? A scary piece of equipment. And still I can't get them to wake up. I go nuts. First I start breaking bottles and yelling, dumping the cocaine on the floor."

"That worked, I bet."

"They started to focus a little, yeah. Then I slap the big one, Nadia, on the ass, tell her and her cousin to get some fucking clothes on."

"What'd they do?"

"They start coming on to me, man! And the younger one, she's something, a great ass, built. I start thinking, hey, this isn't so bad. Then I think, first the dead guy, who knows what they're into, these two. Then the old man. Certain trouble for yours truly if they're not out of here by morning or sooner. But these broads don't get the message, fooling with their G-strings, rubbing their tits against each other." Sturua paused to savor the scene, spilling some more Johnnie Walker into his glass. "Hey, how about that spook last night?"

"You gonna end it, just like that?" Hagen was in the medicine man's Barcalounger, studying the ceiling. "That's a lousy deal, you know, Sturua. You start a story with two blondes in G-strings, then you go and change the subject in the middle."

"Sorry. Well, anyway, I tell the broads the old man sent me. Somehow he heard about what was going on, the guy had eyes and ears everywhere. I emphasize the 'old man' and wave the Walther and my Securitate badge a little more, and finally they start to come around. They're a little woozy, but all of a sudden they're scrambling for their clothes, and when they're dressed, in sweaters and all, they look like a couple of schoolgirls, or at least the young one did. She was something. So I finally get a car to come from downtown, it's almost dawn. And I got the girls out of there. We got a team of techs in the next day to clean the place up, but the three guys, or at least the two who were still breathing, they're offed, and no one ever said boo. That's the kind of shit we got in Bucharest, at least sometimes. You guys got all the fabled Prussian efficiency; we had the truly weird shit in Bucharest."

"Yeah, but we had the Libyans and the longhairs," Hagen said, "the Baader-Meinhof assholes."

There was a long silence. Sturua finally broke it. "What about last night, though? This could work, don't you think?"

Hagen was irritable. "The head count's a loser, Sturua. The Semtex is definitely the way to go. We got the detective's truck with just a few ounces of the stuff, and look, all of a sudden we got diplomats in the street. In their fucking pajamas. How many cables do you think are being drafted right this minute about the 'deteriorating political-violence situation' in Fado? These diplomat assholes, they kill me. They got the hardship-post money, but they always have to let everyone know how dangerous it is, how they put their lives on the line every day for flag and country. But that's the kind of thing. The cables. Maybe they remove a few more dependents from the embassies. That's what brings this fucking place to its knees."

"What about the spook?" Sturua was still running over the events of the past eight hours.

"I guess he was working with the cop."

"I wish we would've grabbed the radio."

"Yeah, we fucked up."

"Well, you whacked him good with the AK."

"Yeah, but if we're staying, I want some Uzis. That Chinese stuff, I don't like it."

"We can ask Viktor, we have to call in anyway." Sturua sipped on his drink, taking his time. "You want to tell me what your deal is with Viktor, I don't mind."

Hagen contemplated the ceiling, the morning light off the ocean painting slo-mo pastels through the floor-to-ceiling windows. "Sure, Sturua. We did fifteen K for the first couple of weeks, with an option to re-up for another."

"Fifteen, huh?"

"That's it." The pinks and blues looked nice on the white ceiling.

"I knew I was being fucked."

"Yeah, but you were fucked already. You're lucky you're alive and working."

"I wouldn't have lasted too long in Bucharest, but I've known Viktor a long time. Longer than you, I bet."

"We met in '75, in Lisbon, right after the revolution." Hagen remembered how the other bloc services had made fun of the Romanians. Pederasts and perverts, they'd called them. "Stasi was helping out with a couple of things there in Portugal, and Viktor was kind of the intermediary, he knew both sides and brought them together. We kept in touch since."

"It's still a lousy deal."

"Take it up with the man, see what he says."

"You think this deal is for real, that he can put a new government in here, make us ministers or something?"

"If there's anyplace you could pull off a stunt like that today, and I'm not so sure there is, it's gotta be here. Viktor's got some heavy money behind him, and he just might do it. If it works, great; if not, it's still very decent money, and it's a hell of a long way from Europe, which is right where I want to be just about now."

"I'm going to talk to Viktor."

"Sturua, you do what you have to do."

"I'd like to mention the fifteen K, see what he says."

"You do that, Sturua," Hagen said, propelling himself awkwardly out of the leather recliner. "You can even let me know what he says if you want. Right now, though, I'm going to bed. I've got to have some sleep."

HIS jeans and tennis shirt were filthy, and his hair was caked with blood from hefting Ellis over his shoulder fireman-style. Gub was trying to decide whether he wanted a shower, a drink or some coffee when the phone in the bedroom rang. It was 10 P.M. in New York, 6 A.M. Fado time, and Gub caught the phone on the second ring, just before the answering machine cut in.

Mireles said hello.

"You picked a hell of a time to call."

"Yeah, and you sound terrible."

"I need a drink is all."

"You got time for a story, or you want me to call back?"

"I'll tell you what, hold on. It's been ages since I heard a good story." It took two tumblers of Cardhu, no ice, about twenty minutes, and Gub listened carefully to Mireles's account of Viktor Alleja in Lisbon and the sketchy business about Otto Hagen. "So you think he's here?"

"I couldn't prove it, Gub. But it makes sense, doesn't it?"

Gub had to concede that it did. Especially since the bombings last night. He filled Mireles in on the events of the past twenty hours.

Mireles, compulsive about notes, was at the desk in his office off the den, scribbling, as Gub told about Ellis, the bombings downtown and the murder of the American DCM, Emerson Allsworth. Mireles started at that. "The Bureau has an interest here now, Gub," he interrupted. "The DCM isn't anything I could lay claim on, but the Bureau has a legal claim on the inquiry, since he's a U.S. official. I can't do much there, but the Hagen case falls right square in my line. I've already talked about it with Amy, and if you don't mind, I'm going to come out."

"Old times, Tom?" Gub was tired, the salty smell of Ellis's blood filling his nostrils. "I just asked you to check on someone."

"I'm serious, Gub. It's something I want to do. But I also got a case there now." All the marbles, Mireles thought; there they were, after fifteen years, right out on the table.

"Well, I think you're fucking crazy."

"Yeah, and I say I'm coming."

Gub drained the last of the warm Scotch and rubbed his eyes. "Look, Tom, I appreciate the sentiment, but whether this guy Hagen is here or not, the last thing I need is to get involved in some complicated FBI op. I mean, if you're going to come all this way so you can read this asshole his Miranda rights, let's forget it right now. You know what this place is like, and it's gotten a whole lot worse since you left."

"This is nothing to do with the Bureau, Gub." Mireles was studying his hands. "This is purely personal. I owe you one, remember? I owe you one big-time."

Gub lay back on the bed. This was going to be interesting.

"I'll call you tonight, your time, and let you know my plans." Mireles rang off and wondered if he was, in fact, crazy.

THE next day at work was weird. Bernd Koehler's messenger was waiting for him in the twenty-eighth-floor lobby, at security. Mireles had to sign for the Sicherungsgruppe report in three places, and the messenger then demanded his FBI badge and wrote down the number on a long form with a lot of other writing on it. If this was ever going to leak, Mireles figured, the Germans would have a real short list of suspects.

The report ran to sixteen single-spaced typed pages, much of it devoted to the background Mireles had already heard from Herb Cohen and Bernd Koehler. The new stuff had to do with the contents of Hagen's apartment in the Sandweg Strasse, all pretty routine stuff. A long statement from the American kid in Barcelona. He had given a positive ID on Hagen, and there was a Spanish police artist's rendition of the made-over Hagen. Gone was the shaggy, collar-length hair and the light brown moustache. Hagen was clean-shaven now, the brown hair an even, quarter-inch crew cut. The kid said he had paid $2,000 for the Stasi passport and agreed to cooperate in any way with a subsequent investigation. Meanwhile the cops had him on the hashish-importation charge. There was a lengthy police report on the murder of César Ochoa, which shed very little light on anything. In Rome, the immigration and customs inspectors had a record of the Ochoa passport being stamped en route to Malta, but that was it.

Mireles read the report twice to make sure he hadn't missed anything. Then he ran up the two flights to McMahon's office, and he suddenly felt light-headed. No matter what happened in Fado, Mireles was sure, it would finish the foundation work he should have done years ago.

McMahon was a confederate of Fox's, Mireles's rabbi, but the New York SAC had a special fondness of his own for Mireles. He had lobbied hard, as had Fox in Washington, for Mireles to get the foreign-counterintelligence job, and he had never had reason to regret it. Indeed, McMahon had suggested that Mireles anchor the writing of the report for the attorney general, since so much of what the A.G. wanted on the East Bloc spy services since the collapse of communism would inevitably come from the New York office. It was a big coup for an A-SAC, writing a report for the attorney general, but no one in New York or Washington doubted Mireles was up to the job.

McMahon had someone with him when Mireles got to his office, and he had to wait a couple of minutes before the Irishman with the shock of white hair ushered him into the corner suite. There was a big desk and three brown government-issue couches.

Mireles came quickly to the point, requesting a week's leave, citing family reasons; Gub, after all, was damn close to family. In the fourteen hours since he had talked with Gub, Mireles decided he would tell only a couple of people besides Amy where he was going and why. When he explained to McMahon that he was returning to Fado to help an old friend, Mireles couldn't help noticing how the twinkling blue eyes narrowed for a fraction of a second. It was as if the Bureau had erased that part of his life altogether, Mireles thought—just as he had tried to do himself. McMahon assented, of course, Mireles assuring him the quick trip would not interfere with the report for the attorney general and that Wasick, an acknowledged pro, would run things in his absence.

"Take good care, Tom," McMahon said in dismissal. "And hurry back."

Running back down to his office, Mireles dwelled for an instant on the funny look in his boss's eye. It's what you get, he thought, stepping out of one life and back into another. At his desk, Mireles made three quick calls, the first to Fox, the second to Herb Cohen at the Agency and the last to Gene Lamonica at Quantico. No one was in, so Mireles left messages.

Glancing at his watch, he took the elevator down twenty flights to the Bureau's credit union to make a withdrawal. Mireles figured he would need maybe $4,000 in cash. If he took half from the credit union and half from his and Amy's joint account at the Dime Savings Bank, it wouldn't be so bad. He'd put the plane ticket on his American Express and worry about that later. Which reminded him, he still had to make plane reservations for tomorrow before leaving the office.

A bitter wind was blowing tiny whirlwinds of trash between the cabs and car-service Lincolns as he left the bank on Broadway and hurried back to the office. In the thirty minutes he'd been gone, Mary Pat, his secretary, told him he had had callbacks from Fox, Cohen and Lamonica. Dropping into the swivel chair behind his cluttered desk, Mireles thought it sounded like one of those cheesy walk-up law firms near the courthouse in Boston. He called Fox first. He couldn't see Jack Fox's eyes, but he could feel the odd silence when he told him he was going back to Fado.

"What in God's name for?" the older man asked.

"An old friend. He needs a hand with something. But it could be something we're interested in, too. They got this wave of terrorism that just started in the capital there?"

"I saw something on it, yeah." Fox seemed distracted.

"I did some checking, and the Germans think it could be a Stasi guy, pretty big. I also heard they might have checked with us to see what we have. The Germans, that is."

Fox didn't bite. Either he didn't know or he wasn't saying.

"Anyway, what they think is this guy was involved with the Libyans, with La Belle, maybe with the IRA and the U.S. troop-train bombings." Mireles was reading from the Sicherungsgruppe report but decided not to mention the fact.

"And he's supposed to be in Fado now?"

"It's unclear. Interpol has him as far as a Rome to Valletta flight, and the Germans are convinced, for obvious reasons, that he probably went on to Libya. Whether he somehow got to Fado from there, that's still anyone's guess."

"But you think he's there."

"I wouldn't stake my life on it, but yeah."

"And what are you going to do with this bad hombre if you happen to run into him out there?"

Mireles noted thankfully that he was not being ordered not to go. "If he's who we think he is, and I happen to see him while I'm there, I'll cable home for instructions. Between us, the Spanish and the BND, maybe we can get a warrant for him."

"I'm not wild about this, and I think you can tell, Tom."

Mireles thought it was past time to back away from the Hagen business. "You're right, of course. Look, I'm going to go out there for a few days to help out a friend with some things. And if anything interesting happens while I'm there and I can be useful in some way, the first thing I'll do is phone you, okay?"

Fox grunted on the other end of the line. "You've been working hard, Tom. And God knows you could use the time off. I just hope you'll get some rest out there and not get involved in any wild-ass stuff. Just recharge the batteries, huh?"

"That's the idea. You'll see, I'll come back a new man."

Fox's voice sounded strange. "Just come back the same old Mireles, okay?"

Mireles thanked him, rang off, then dialed Cohen at Langley. They spoke briefly, agreeing to meet the next morning in the Agency lobby.

Last on his list of callbacks, Gene Lamonica picked up on the third ring. A Vietnam vet and, his admirers in the Bureau swore, one of the best halfbacks ever produced by Joe Paterno and Penn State's Nittany Lions, Eugene Lamonica was a senior weapons instructor at the FBI Academy in Quantico, Virginia. Mireles and Lamonica had met in the weight room shortly after Fox had brought him up to the Academy from Miami after the shooting on Calle Ocho. Thankfully, not too many Bureau personnel have ever taken a bullet, and those who have inhabit a kind of special aura. Between clean-and-jerks, Lamonica had questioned Mireles at length about the details of the meeting with the Cubans in Little Havana, pointing out things he might have done differently, things he should have looked for. They had stayed in touch over the years.

"What do you mean, hypothetically, Tom?" Lamonica hadn't been a great street agent for nothing; he had a sixth sense for bullshit.

"Just indulge me a minute, Gene, okay?" Mireles wasn't so sure the call was a good idea, but he would rather have made it than go off unprepared. That was the way he was. "I'm talking about a very small number of guns, something that would travel, but the whole range of firepower, small-caliber to heavy-duty automatic."

"You going into the crack business, that's it."

"Gene, I'm serious. What would you recommend?"

"Well, it depends on a lot of things, but generally, if you want reasonably cheap, I'd stay away from all the European stuff, the Belgian, Swiss and German—the exchange rate alone will kill you, with the dollar what it is. Ditto the Israeli stuff, though the Uzi is a class weapon. Go with the good old USA, I say. In the sidearms, you can't beat the Smith & Wesson. For long shooting irons, Browning and Remington. Of course, I'm a Made in America kind of guy, but that's all quality merchandise. You want something truly nasty, though this doesn't strike me as your style, Tom, there's a neat little .22-caliber called a Qual-A-Trac. Comes with a silencer that even works. That's pretty much it. Lots of people pretend it's a complicated business, but the gun stuff is pretty straightforward."

The phone cradled against his shoulder, Mireles was writing carefully on a yellow legal pad. "That's great, Gene, that's real helpful."

"I don't suppose you're going to tell me what it's about?"

"It's kind of up in the air at the moment, Gene, I swear. But I'd be grateful if you wouldn't mention it around. I'll give you a fill in a few days, how's that?"

"You're the boss. Just remember, keep your head down."

Before he left the office, Mireles booked his plane reservations himself: Pan Am from Dulles International outside Washington, to Orly in Paris, and from there on UTA, the French carrier, to Harare. Mireles was betting that Cohen would know who he could talk to there about a few discreet purchases. It might be personal and it might be business, but Mireles figured he wasn't going to go back to Fado after all these years without a little protection. He intended to come back in one piece, after all.

FOR once, Mireles got out of the office before six. After briefing Wasick on what they had going and promising to check in daily, he had given Mary Pat the rest of the week off. The last thing he did before leaving the office was to ring Gub. There was no answer, so he left a message on the machine. He'd be arriving in Fado the day after tomorrow. As he rode down in the elevator, the trip still didn't seem quite real.

Even on the Northern State, the traffic at high rush hour was unreal, and it took him more than ninety minutes to get home. Coming up the drive, he could see the dining room lights on. That was unusual. So was the black dress Amy was wearing as she stirred something on the kitchen range. Surprise!

Mireles gave his wife a kiss, and then an admiring look as he held her by the shoulders. "I'm canceling my tickets."

"Not after all the fuss we've gone to, you're not."

Mireles looked around. The candles were lit in the dining room. He wasn't much of an eater, but whatever was cooking smelled wonderful. He wrinkled his nose.

"Rack of lamb," Amy said.

"Where are the girls?" But even as he said it, the twins, in matching pinafores, were carrying two small boxes into the kitchen. Angels, he thought, bearing gifts.

"For you, Daddy."

While Amy bustled with some last-minute things at the range, Mireles opened one box, then the next. The first contained a small travel kit, and Mireles kissed both girls on the forehead. The second contained an unusual travel alarm clock.

"It has two clocks," Alison said.

"So you can know what time it is there," Kate added, "and here at home, too."

Mireles thought he was going to cry. Instead, he kissed the twins again. "I'm sorry about this weekend, kids, but this just came up. As soon as I get home, though, how about we drive up and see Grandpa on the Cape?" The girls loved the big house on the water, and their grandfather spoiled them rotten.

"Yay, Grandpa's!" The twins were getting big. It was a cliché, Mireles knew, but fuck it: before he knew it, they'd be grown and gone. When he got back from Fado, he swore, he would do whatever it took to slow down the process.

While Amy hustled the girls to the table, Mireles went to wash up. He couldn't even remember the last weeknight they had all sat down for dinner together. Months, it must have been.

Dinner was delicious, but what Mireles remembered long after was the way the house smelled so homey, the roasting lamb perfuming the whole place. Way different than grabbing a quick sandwich at the kitchen counter long after the twins were in bed. Something else to change, he thought.

Mireles cleaned up afterwards, while Amy got the girls ready for bed. He came in to kiss them good night and thank them again for the gifts. In their bedroom, Amy had already packed for him, and she doused the light as he slid into bed beside her. They made love for a long time, slowly and more tenderly than he could remember. "I love you," he said. But Amy Mireles, her fine red hair scattered across her eyes, was already breathing deeply, a smile playing across her lips. Mireles rolled over gently, so as not to wake her. And it seemed like just a few minutes later when the alarm near his head saluted the dawn.

OUTSIDE the Marine Air Terminal at La Guardia, Mireles gave Amy a long kiss while the twins giggled, then he gave each of them a hug. "Make sure to help your mother," he said. "And do what she says."

"Bring us something back," Alison said, as Amy hustled them back into the car.

Lowering the electric window on the passenger's-side door as she pulled away, Mireles saw his wife mouthing the words "Be careful!"

The Pan Am shuttle was crowded, as usual, but with the one carry-on, Mireles was out of National Airport in no time and in a cab for the fifteen-minute drive to Langley. The Federal Protective Service cops who provide security at the two main entrances to the CIA's sprawling campus examined his FBI badge with interest and finally scratched his name off the day's visitor list. Paying the cabbie in front of the seven-story headquarters building, Mireles was struck once again by the bizarre lines of the place, a kind of star-crossed hybrid that somehow mixed up the simplicity of Bauhaus with some of the more unfortunate notions of the Benito Mussolini School of Architecture.

Cohen was in the marble lobby, waiting. And after Mireles got his V-badge from the nice blue-haired ladies at the security desk whom Mireles always imagined as packing small but lethal derringer-type pistols, they rode up in the key-lock elevator off the left side of the lobby that was reserved for the Director of Central Intelligence and a few other super-grades, members of the Senior Intelligence Service.

Cohen let Mireles out on the sixth floor, where some remodeling was under way, furniture and paintings with a distinct sixtyish feel giving way to newer, more comfortable couches and muted color schemes.

"I don't know about the Hagen business, but I'm going back to Fado for a few days, anyway. I was hoping your guys could tell me what's going on."

"Well, it's not good, you know that." Cohen lit a Merit, and Mireles noticed there were already a half dozen in the green-glass ashtray.

"I was also hoping to get a look at some of your marvelous maps, and maybe even copy a few to take with me."

"No problem. You didn't hear anything more about Hagen and our friend in Lisbon, I take it."

"The Germans are all over the case. They've got a team in Lisbon and another in Barcelona. Hagen or someone who looks very much like him offed a Colombian businessman in the Barcelona train station, and they traced the guy's passport as far as Malta, where the trail disappears."

"But you think he's in Fado."

It was the second time in as many days the question had been put to him as an assertion. "I don't know, Herb. I'm going to see an old friend, and I'm not going to look for trouble. If this guy is there, though, my bosses know I'm going to call in for instructions." Mireles figured he ought to stick to that line. It was simple and it was the truth. As far as it went.

Cohen got a metal pot full of steaming coffee from the executive dining room and left Mireles in his oblong office with the nice wide windows. Before long he was back with two long reports out of Africa Division, and then he vanished again to see about maps.

It took Mireles the better part of an hour to get through the two reports, each of them packed with dreadful economic data and some closely reasoned analyses of the political situation, which mainly concluded that nothing good had happened since he had left. Mireles had no idea how the bandits had bankrupted the place, and that except for Fado itself, the bandits controlled most of the rest of the country. Actually, as the analysts pointed out, "control" was not the right word; the bandits were not a political force and had no interest in controlling territory. By attacking, pillaging and murdering, they simply made vast stretches of the country uninhabitable, natives by the thousands fleeing to Fado or across borders to safer havens.

Cohen had marked the satellite-generated topo maps with dates and brief descriptions of documented bandit activity. "Of course, there are plenty we are sure we don't know about," he said. "But you know better than I how difficult it is to get hard intelligence in that part of the world."

Mireles thanked him for the maps and the reports. "I've got one more rather ticklish question, Herb, and I'd be grateful if this could remain just between us."

Cohen gave him the fisheye.

"I'm not sure just how long I'm going to be in Fado, but I'm a bit concerned about security."

"The countryside's a mess, but you know that. The trouble in the last few days, in Fado itself, that's new. But the embassy and our other buildings there are all secure. You shouldn't have any problem."

Mireles paused; this was difficult. "I'm going back on my U.S. passport, Herb, but I'm not going back for the Bureau or any part of the government, and I aim to steer clear of the embassy. An old friend of mine is a cop there, and it sounds like he's going to need a little help."

Cohen raised an eyebrow.

Mireles persisted. "It's just something I've got to do, Herb, and what I was wondering is if you knew someone in Harare who could fit me out with some protection."

"Guns."

"Right," Mireles said. "And vests and arrange to get them to me quickly in Fado. It's nothing to do with the U.S."

Cohen tugged at his ear. He had served with the D.O., the Agency's Directorate of Operations, all over, including two years in Harare. The arms trade in that part of the world was pretty much wide open, and small arms were available to anyone willing to pay cash; the only real problem was shipping and delivery, and Mireles was betting Cohen knew someone who could lick that one. From a lower desk drawer, Cohen pulled out a locked metal canister about the size of a shoe box. Inside, it contained neatly printed blue index cards. It was organized alphabetically, but Mireles couldn't see whether it was by name or subject. "Write this down, Tom. I'll need the card back."

Mireles copied the name quickly into the address book in his leather Day-Timer, entering it under "H," for Harare. Then he handed back the card. "This guy's good, huh?"

"None better," Cohen said. "But you didn't get it here."

They rode down in the DCI's key-lock elevator in silence. In the cavernous lobby, under the gaze of Wild Bill Donovan, the founder of the old OSS, the CIA's predecessor, Mireles and Cohen shook hands hastily. The Virginia cabbie at the curb was cleared only for a five-minute pickup.

"Let me know if you learn anything, will you?"

Mireles nodded and headed through the big glass doors to the waiting cab, which whisked him to Dulles International, thirty minutes away. Three hours after that, he was sound asleep, the Pan Am jumbo jet clearing Nantucket en route to Paris, the first leg of the long journey home.

SIXTEEN

WHEN he saw the white thread from the doorjamb sitting in the middle of the hemp-weave mat on the front porch, Gub wondered whether he could have been that clumsy on his way out or whether Matthias might have done it sometime after he left. Then he asked himself, not for the first time, why he didn't just get a real security system and avoid this shit once and for all. It was just after 2 A.M., and he had spent the past two hours prowling the streets and gardens along Avenida de la Revolución on foot. Setting out a few minutes after midnight, Matthias asleep on the living room couch, Gub figured that the odds of him running into the crazed head merchants who had now taken to blowing up cars were real low on a stakeout; better to keep moving around the most likely targets. His luck had been lousy, however, continuing his streak, and now the thread on the doorjamb was out of place. Pulling the Chief's Special from his shoulder holster and rechecking the safety on the SIG-10 on his belt, Gub wondered anxiously where Matthias was, whether he was inside, and if not, who was.

After he had gotten off the phone with Mireles that morning, Gub had gotten cleaned up, then gone around to the neat little bungalow behind the Lisboa that Ellis shared with Claire, his sixteen-year-old

170

wife of less than a year. When they had heard the young woman's cries of grief though the thin walls, neighbor ladies had come running, and Gub had made his exit as graciously as possible. Next he'd gone to the department to brief Carlos on Ellis and the ruined Toyota. And then he'd gone home to catch a few hours' sleep, rising just after noon to make a circuit of downtown and the embassy district in the Save the Children Land-Rover with the broken air-conditioning. He had seen nothing, and stopped finally at the fish guy's place near the port and picked up a fresh pompano, a fat red snapper, some mussels and some prawns. There was nothing else he could do until much later that night, and Gub figured he might as well get a good dinner in the meantime. Specifically, what he had in mind was a bouillabaisse, and he had spent the tail end of the afternoon absorbed in the cooking of it, julienning the leeks, careful to use the white parts only, mincing the garlic and chopping up the fish, mixing the whole business in the big black stockpot, another of Teresa's expensive wedding presents. Betty had come by just after seven in the clunky Save the Children passenger van, and she, Gub and Matthias had dined silently on the fish soup, which, Gub conceded, was not one of his better efforts. He had left the pot simmering on the range, unsure whether to throw the whole business out or try to salvage it somehow the next day.

Gub had sent Betty home with the Browning, he and Matthias settling in for an evening of television, Matthias making car noises every time the tube showed Crockett in the red Ferrari Testarossa gunning the $175,000 engine. Gub liked *Miami Vice*, a has-been American police show that was still regular prime-time fare in much of the rest of the world, but the fancy cars and the two detectives' dippy clothes were a bit much.

Gub was still standing on the front porch, playing the evening back in his head, fretting over the crummy bouillabaisse and the misplaced white thread when a fist in his kidneys interrupted his musings, fishy-tasting air whooshing from his lungs. The thing that hurt most, Gub thought, cursing as he fell into the rhododendron under the kitchen window, was how careless he had been. A black boot at the end of a frighteningly thick leg swung at his chin as Gub floundered in the bush. The boot caught him just above the right ear, and the drumming in his head began seconds later, tom-toms in both temples. The boot swung again, rhododendron bushes cracking, and Gub fumbled for the Chief's Special. Where the fuck was it? This time the boot caught him in the gut, and Gub tasted fish soup in his throat. Sucking air, he grabbed the thick leg attached to the boot, hugging it to his chest like a lover. The man was amazingly strong. Failing to see what his other options might be, Gub bowed his head over the muscular calf, the tom-toms in a crescendo as he sank his teeth into the khaki fabric, biting down as hard as he could on the flesh beneath. Garlic filled his mouth and nostrils. Somewhere high above him, Gub heard a curse as the man struggled to pull free. Gub bit down hard again, and the man screamed this time, as Gub used the split second to roll clear of the rhododendron.

On all fours, he scrambled for the Chief's Special against the cinder-block foundation, but the black boot swung one more time, missing his head by inches, but catching him in the left shoulder. A sharp blade of pain stabbed across his back and up into his neck. Gub went down on his right elbow, rolled and came up in a crouch, protecting his damaged shoulder. The black man—Gub could see his face finally—was shorter than Gub, maybe six feet, but he was heavier by maybe fifteen or twenty pounds, and in far better shape. The man feinted with a right, the fingers extended in a kind of karate chop. Gub moved counterclockwise and came in high with a right, trying to take advantage of his reach. The blow glanced off the man's head, and Gub's knuckles began to ache. The man brought his elbow down hard on Gub's extended arm as Gub rabbit-punched him twice in the face with his left hand. Unfazed, the man had Gub's right arm in a lock and brought his knee up into his midsection as Gub raked an elbow into the man's windpipe. He was sucking air, and his head was pounding. The man used his knee again. This time it was below the belt, and it brought Gub to his knees. He was panting, out of gas, and the black man knew it. When he looked up, the man was pointing an ugly little snub-nosed revolver at him. Ridiculous, Gub thought, in every circumstance but the present.

"Cheap shit, Mr. Po-lice. They teach you that at the academy, to bite like a girl?"

Gub struggled to a sitting position, bells joining the tom-toms in his head and going like high mass. He tried to catch his breath.

"I should put you away right here, man."

"The kicking, though, that's okay, huh?"

"Jujitsu, my man. The real thing." Waving the revolver, the big man with the bush jacket and no shirt collected the Chief's Special from where it lay against the foundation of the apartment house. "Now the machine gun, Mr. Po-lice, handle first."

How stupid could he be! He had forgotten about the SIG-10 clipped to his belt. Disgustedly, Gub snapped off the catch and gave it over.

"Inside now, through the front door."

The bells were still pealing as Afonso ordered Gub into one of the ladderback chairs near the ebony table, the machine gun and the Chief's Special way out of reach on the end table next to the couch in the living room.

"What you got to drink here, Mr. Po-lice? Anything decent, which I doubt?"

"Next to the refrigerator," Gub said. "Beer in the icebox, which I wouldn't mind, as long as you're up."

"You won't be needing no beer, man. You been fucking up my plans big-time, and I don't like people fuck up my plans."

"The heads?"

"Fucking-A right. Got a job to do, leaving heads nice and easy around town, and you go around cleaning 'em up after me?"

"It's just something about litter, I don't know. I never could stand it."

"Funny man." Afonso spilled three fingers of Cardhu into a water glass and waved the little revolver in Gub's direction.

Gub was catching his breath now, the bells beginning to fade.

"Who's paying for the heads? If you don't mind my asking."

Afonso left the bottle of Cardhu on the range next to the simmering stockpot, ignoring him. "This is fine Scotch, Mr. Po-lice. A single-malt, I like that, shows real class."

"I wouldn't mind sharing a dram with you. You know, just friends like?"

Afonso downed the rest of the Cardhu and poured another couple of fingers. "Who pays me is a secret between the man pays me and me."

The pistol shot surprised Gub, then he saw Matthias at the window, and Afonso dove for the floor, the expensive Scotch flying. He moved quickly for a big man, Gub noticed, skittering crabwise towards the kitchen. Gub dove headlong from his sitting position and caught Afonso by the seat of his pants, letting all his weight fall on him, driving him into the floor. The man's arms were still free, though, and Afonso used his hands behind him to good effect, reaching for Gub's face, raking the fingernails of his right hand across Gub's right eye. Blinded for the moment, Gub struggled for a better purchase on the big man's behind. Some fight, he thought.

Gub didn't know where the little revolver had disappeared to, so when Afonso reached for something beneath a cupboard, Gub loosened his grip around the man's waist and hammered down hard on the man's forearm just above the elbow. Afonso grunted, and Gub hit him again as he tried to get up, the big man crawling towards the cabinets beneath the gas range. Gub wheezed as he got up, cursing the extra weight on him, blood in his right eye. Taking a page from the big man's book, Gub tried a kick and caught the man with his leather work boots square in the tailbone, sending him face-first into the cupboard beneath the range. In two quick strides, Gub was over him, reaching for the stockpot.

The bouillabaisse hadn't been particularly good, not nearly gelatinous enough. Before he'd gone out, Gub had put it back on the range to see if it would reduce and come up a little thicker. More like stew, the way he liked it. Afonso turned and was lying on his back, grabbing Gub by the knees and using his powerful arms to bring him down, reduce his leverage. Sinking, Gub grabbed a handle of the stockpot with his left hand and pulled it slowly off the gas burner, closer to the front edge of the range. The son of a bitch was heavy, nearly four gallons of hot fish soup. Gub wondered what it weighed.

"What you doing, Mr. Po-lice?" The big man was trying to lever himself up as he pulled Gub down.

"Just checking on this bouillabaisse. You like fish soup?" With a final tug, Gub edged the stockpot off the range, propelling himself backwards quickly as he did so.

"Fucking-A!"

The steaming broth hit Afonso first, scalding him, then the pot bounced off his head, and he howled, releasing his grip on Gub's legs as he clawed at his eyes. The smell of garlic was everywhere, as Gub jumped clear, a piece of pompano flapping in the black man's lap. Blinded, Afonso flailed for Gub's legs with his right arm, rubbing at his eyes with his left, Gub stepped neatly inside the big forearm.

"Son of a bitch, I got you now."

But Afonso didn't get it at all, and Gub stepped into the kick, putting all his weight behind it, his right knee mashing Afonso's head into the cheap cabinetry. The second time, Gub heard the cupboard splinter, and after the third, Afonso slid all the way down onto the floor, blood trickling from his right ear, his neck at what looked to Gub like an awfully uncomfortable angle. The big man's expensive bush jacket was lousy with fish parts and steaming bouillabaisse. Gub didn't think the Chinaman on Vladimir Lenin would be able to do much about it, though.

He was still looking for Afonso's ugly little revolver when Matthias marched into the kitchen from the living room, his sharpened stick and the Chief's Special in his right hand, the Swiss machine gun in his left. "That's the ticket, Matthias," Gub breathed, grabbing for the little revolver under the refrigerator, "let's have us some real guns."

Stepping carefully around Afonso, the boy handed the Smith & Wesson and the machine gun to Gub.

"Good job, Matthias. That stick is really something on the window like that."

The boy looked up at the detective, his lips working. "Piece of cake, Tubbs."

It sounded like a long, reticulated croak. Afonso was beginning to stir, so Gub shoved the barrel of the Chief's Special just in front of his nose, wanting it to be the first thing he saw when he came to. Then he turned back to the boy. Gub still couldn't believe it. "What did you say, Matthias?" Trying to make it no big deal.

"Piece of cake, Tubbs." Matthias looked around, twirling his sharpened stick and smiling.

It still sounded like a long croak to Gub, but he could definitely make out the words: Sonny Crockett to his partner, Tubbs, after some particularly nifty piece of police work. "That's just what I thought you said, Matthias."

Afonso came to slowly, then closed his eyes when he saw the muzzle of the big handgun two inches from his nose. "First the biting, now this fish shit."

"Some people just don't know how to fight fair."

"Let's us talk this over, now, Mr. Po-lice."

Gub was suddenly very tired. He pressed the muzzle of the Chief's Special under Afonso's nostrils. "Roll over, asshole."

Afonso thought about it for a second and rolled onto his stomach. Gub had Matthias get the clothesline from the backyard, and within minutes, he had Afonso trussed up nicely on the kitchen floor littered with fish parts.

Question time.

"I told you, man, that's all I know." It wasn't the easiest thing, trying to understand Afonso as he talked into the old linoleum and new fish broth, but Gub got most of what he needed. Afonso said that two of his men delivered the heads to the *curandeiro*'s chalet on the coast road each night from up in Plumtree, the first sizable village on the old 1A highway north of Fado.

Why Plumtree? Gub asked.

Afonso told him about the little security force the village had put together recently. The bandits didn't like that, the people taking the initiative that way, especially so close to the capital. The bandits had overrun Plumtree two or three times during the course of the situation. This time, they wanted to send the village a lesson it wouldn't forget. Besides, Afonso said, they needed the heads to deliver around the city. That was the plan, he was told. And since the man living in the medicine man's house didn't know his way around Fado, Afonso was supposed to act as his guide. Afonso insisted that the new man was in charge, however. His tone indicated he didn't think much of the arrangement.

Gub asked about the man in the *curandeiro*'s house.

Afonso said his name was Strew-a. Something like that, he said. Gub couldn't tell if that was the man's name or Afonso mumbling into the slimy linoleum. Afonso said he thought the man's orders came from the *curandeiro*, but he wasn't sure. Anyway, Mr. Achebe paid him well, and it was none of his affair. He was just following orders.

The Nuremberg defense. Gub had seen all sorts of assholes try it.

Afonso said a second man had shown up at the medicine man's place sometime in the past couple of days, a small guy with a crew cut. When he told Afonso they were going to hold off on delivering any more heads for a while, that's when Afonso decided to come pay a call on Gub.

Gub was digesting the information while Matthias sipped a glass of apple juice at the ebony table when three huge explosions lit the sky outside his apartment, one right after another. Gub thought they were simultaneous or damn close to it, coming from different directions. Matthias fell out of his chair, sending the apple juice clattering to the floor. Afonso rolled quickly in the fish broth but Gub was on him, pressing the Chief's Special into the back of the big man's neck.

"What the fuck, man?"

"You tell me, Afonso. Those your buddies out there blowing things up?"

"I swear to God, I didn't hear nothing about any explosives. My job was just the heads."

Gub waited, watching the sky outside the windows turn a bright Halloween orange. It was no car bomb, that was for sure. "Just the heads, huh? No bombs?" Gub jammed the muzzle of the big handgun harder into Afonso's bulging neck.

"Not my thing, man. I don't fuck with that stuff, I swear."

Gub checked the knots on the big man's wrists. "See you in a while, pal." Then he grabbed the machine gun and turned to Matthias, who had just poured himself another glass of juice. "Come on, Sonny, it looks like these assholes are blowing up the city."

MIRELES was tired when he got to Harare. It was nearly 6 P.M., and he had left Dulles more than twenty-four hours earlier, his only rest what he could grab in one of the impossible plastic chairs during the seven-hour layover in Orly. Clearing customs in Harare with his virgin U.S. passport, Mireles went immediately to one of the booths that lined the gleaming concourse to the main terminal, rain slapping against the big plate-glass windows. Mireles had made sure to get coins for the phone from the Deak-Perera office near the Dulles departure lounge, changing a twenty-dollar bill so he'd have some pocket money. He dialed the number he had copied from Herb Cohen's little index card.

"Mr. Tuck?"

The man answered after five rings. "Who's calling, please?"

"A friend from the States," Mireles said. "I was told you might still have some carnations?" He felt like a fool, remembering his days back in Boston, the mob guys thinking how clever they were, using the word "suits" for drugs years and years after the Bureau had broken the ridiculously simple code. Government lawyers had even used the code word in open court, figuring the mopes had come up with something new. They never did. Cohen's blue index card said that "carnations" was the all-clear signal for Mr. Flower Tuck.

"It's late in the season," Flower Tuck said. "But yes, we still have some carnations."

Mireles explained that he had just arrived from Paris and was on his way out the next morning. If the carnations were available and fresh, he could pay for them, cash immediately, but maybe Mr. Tuck could meet him out at the airport. Herb Cohen had told him that Flower Tuck liked the airport, its anonymity. Flower Tuck said he could be at the airport in thirty minutes.

The two men met in an empty lounge off the main concourse, and Mireles recognized Flower Tuck immediately from Cohen's shorthand description. A bluff Brit with a web of broken veins in his wide nose, he still looked fit, a muscular six-footer. Flower Tuck was wearing a red and blue rep tie and a starched white button-down shirt over light gray slacks; the blue blazer completed the uniform. Mireles pegged Flower Tuck at somewhere between forty-five and fifty-five and guessed he'd probably seen some of the Rhodesian unpleasantness. "Thanks for coming, Mr. Tuck," he said, rising from his table near the far window.

Flower Tuck wasted few words.

A pro, Mireles thought.

There were a few probing questions, but not many. Tuck raised an eyebrow when he heard the weapons were to go to Fado, but there was no indication that that was a problem. Mireles had memorized his wish list, based on the conversation with Gene Lamonica, but Tuck shook his head no. "Can do you as many used but very clean M-16s as you want, right away, with plenty of ammo. Anything else, my friend, that'll be taking some time."

Mireles figured he had overprepared for the trip back to Fado and underestimated its problems. He told Flower Tuck he would take two of the M-16s and a large quantity of ammo.

Flower Tuck nodded briskly. "Done."

"And what about vests?" Fondling the small travel clock the twins had given him, the one with the two faces on it, Mireles wanted to make the odds as long in his favor as he could.

"Kevlar," Flower Tuck said. "No problem." He pulled out a Sanyo pocket calculator and did some quick figuring. With shipping to Fado, the bill came to just under $2,500, more than Mireles had planned on. Flower Tuck must have seen the look on his face. "Of course, that includes delivery to Fado. You give me an address, and it will all be there within twenty-four hours."

Mireles was impressed. Some of the markup had to be for friendly customs inspectors along the way. Flower Tuck certainly knew his business. Mireles paid the Brit in cash, and he counted it carefully, twice. He didn't offer a receipt, and Mireles didn't ask, figuring the arms dealer knew a useful connection would be blown if he didn't deliver.

Their business done, the two men rose from the table by the window, their beers untouched.

"A pleasure," Flower Tuck said, offering his hand. Then he turned

and trudged back down the empty concourse, patting the inside
pocket of his blue blazer while Mireles went to find yet another
uncomfortable plastic seat to wait for the flight that would carry
him on the last leg to Fado.

GUB headed for the largest of the three fires first, passing a tan
Mitsubishi behind his flat that he figured must have belonged to
Afonso.

It took him nearly fifteen minutes to reach Avenida de la Revolución, and by then he could see flames leaping out the lower windows
of the presidential staff's executive offices where he had wasted
hours in the useless stakeout the night before. Gub didn't even stop,
heading back up the boulevard as tongues of orange flame licked the
night sky over the embassy district, an eerie reprise from the night
before. He made it there in just over six minutes, shaving nearly a
full minute off his time from the previous night, the Save the Children Land-Rover whining in protest. Two blocks from Betty's place,
Gub could see the fire was in the same block but not her building.

Thank God, he thought.

The apartment buildings were a matched set, six-story structures
with outside hallways leading to each of the units. Gub parked the
Land-Rover and grabbed Matthias, hoisting him over his shoulder.
Ignoring the crowds milling in the street, he ran the four flights up to
Betty's apartment.

"Who is it?"

The voice behind the door was edged with fear and fatigue. "It's
me. And Matthias."

"What's the password?"

"What password?"

"You told me not to open the goddamn door unless I get the
password."

Gub racked his brain. "Fast break, goddammit, I forgot." The door
opened, and they embraced, the Browning banging against his leg as
it hung from her right hand.

"Gub, what the hell is going on? You're a mess."

"They bombed the place next door, I think, but it looks like your
building's okay. Can you take Matthias? I've got some things to do,
but I'll be back as soon as I can."

"Sure, but look at you, you're filthy and bloody."

"Never mind," Gub said, breathing hard from the run up the stairs.

"I'll be back soon. Keep the door locked. And, oh, yeah, before I forget, Matthias talked."

As he ran back towards the stairwell, Gub saw Betty and Matthias standing in the doorway looking at each other uncertainly, shadows from the flames next door playing across their faces. It took him nearly eight minutes to reach the last fire, and Gub felt his stomach knot when he got to the Lisboa. The place was in flames. "Fully involved," as the firefighters say, and volunteers from the Fado fire department and some neighbors stood helplessly by, the heat too intense even to approach the old hotel. Gub thought it looked like the bomb must have blown the gas main, judging from the strange color of the flames. He searched for nearly twenty minutes for Tony Sebastião in the crowd and on the hotel grounds, but he couldn't find him anywhere. There was no way Tony wouldn't be there if he were still alive, Gub thought. Sick and angry, he got back in the Land-Rover once more, accelerating up the coast road.

The *curandeiro*'s big chalet looked silent and empty in the thin moonlight. Shifting the Land-Rover into four-wheel drive, Gub drove it across the medicine man's expensive papyrus plantings and parked it on the beach side. He checked the ground-floor windows, but it looked like there was nobody home. Using the Chief's Special, he shot the dead bolt off the basement door and went in, going up the one flight of stairs quickly. On the main floor he glanced in the kitchen and the big living room with the expensive leather sectionals. In the study that ran the length of the house, Gub detected the odor of good cigars. He walked the length of the room, looking out the big windows towards the beach, checking the Land-Rover out in the sand. Then he turned to check the upstairs bedrooms.

That's when he saw the pair of feet protruding from the leather Barcalounger in the corner.

He was getting real careless.

The chair was all the way in the down position, and Gub raised the Chief's Special and approached it slowly. With his left foot, he pressed hard on the chair's front panel, bringing it perpendicular to the floor and raising it almost to the sitting position. The fish smell hit Gub first, then he saw the blood puddled in the bottom of the chair from the round hole in the left side of the big man's chest. It couldn't have been much more than an hour since he had left him trussed with clothesline on his filthy kitchen floor.

"Afonso," Gub said, "what the fuck are you doing here?"

SEVENTEEN

〜〜〜〜〜〜〜〜〜〜〜〜〜〜〜〜〜〜〜〜〜〜〜〜

THE UTA DC-9 slipped down through the last layer of ragged cirrus clouds, and Mireles felt his stomach go liquid. It wasn't the flight or the long trip, he thought, or even the flutes of black smoke that flew up to meet him from over the downtown area of Fado. What it was, was coming home.

A long time, Mireles thought.

On the ground, striding across the broken tarmac into the shuttered terminal, Mireles wondered idly why the government had never changed the name of the airport. They had renamed every street and alley, but for some reason they had decided to stick with Prince Henry the Navigator. Henry International. As the efficient young man at the customs desk went through his one carry-on, Mireles could see Gub beyond the row of metal fences, the blond head bobbing above the small knot of other waiting heads. Dismissed at last by the inspector, Mireles was maybe a dozen yards from Gub when he made out the ugly purple welt on the right side of his face and the unmistakable puffiness behind the dark glasses.

"What the hell happened to you?"

"Carelessness."

"Well, you wear it well."

"Welcome back."

"I saw the smoke from the plane."

Gub took Mireles's American Tourister and stowed it in the back
of the Save the Children Land-Rover. "It happened last night. I know
it's bad form to welcome an old friend with bad news after a long
journey, but I thought you'd want to know: Tony Sebastião is dead."

"Christ, I'm sorry."

"Someone wired a charge to the Lisboa's gas main, it looks like."
Gub was all efficiency, wheeling the Land-Rover out of the airport
drop-off and into traffic as he spoke. "By the time I got there, the
place was gone, there was nothing anyone could do. I've been around
to Tony's place, and there's been no one there in a couple of days. I
figure he must have been living at the hotel, trying to keep an eye on
things. They've begun pulling some bodies out of the wreckage, but
they're unrecognizable. Anyway, Tony would have called by now."

Mireles said nothing. At one time, Tony Sebastião and Tom Mireles had been best friends. A year older than Gub, they had been the
hotshots, the guys who dated first, did just about everything first.
Gub's size had made him an equal partner after a while, and the
three had remained fast friends right up until Mireles had left the
country. After that, Gub had stayed in touch with Mireles, seeing
him and the family in the States on his annual vacation. Tony
somehow had never forgiven Mireles for leaving, however. Maybe
Tony understood, Gub didn't know. But he certainly never forgave,
and Tony Sebastião had done nothing to stay in touch. Since Mireles
had been such a mess for so long, and afterwards so preoccupied with
his job, the lines between Tony Sebastião and Tom Mireles had fallen
down completely. Because of that, Gub wasn't sure how Mireles was
taking the news. Mireles offered no clue, staring out the Land-
Rover's open window at the rows of squatters' shacks steaming in the
morning heat.

"I've got to see about some kind of service," Gub said, breaking the
silence. "I don't know what the deal was with the hotel, if the
government had a share or what. Anyway, Tony had no family, so
someone's got to look into it."

"That was last night, the fire?"

"Yeah." Gub turned off the airport road onto Avenida 21 July.
"Whoever got the Lisboa also took out an apartment house in the
new embassy district. Fortunately, the charge didn't take out the gas
line, and the place took a while to burn. I don't know about casu-

alties yet, but a lot of people got out. The last place they got was the executive offices of the president's staff. It doesn't look like there were any casualties there, but the building and everything inside are gone."

"That wouldn't have anything to do with the shiner and the belt you took on the side of the head, though?"

Gub pulled the Land-Rover into the space alongside his apartment and grabbed Mireles's bag. "I thought we'd stop here. The department's kind of depressing these days, and most of the calls I get, I get at home."

"You never moved."

"Too much trouble, and Teresa really had the place fixed up nice." Gub let Mireles in the front door. "I've let it go since then, of course. Anyway, for what it's worth, welcome home."

The fish smell hit them both as they walked in the door.

"Bouillabaisse," Gub said, opening a window in the living room and removing the sunglasses. Mireles could see both eyes were worse than he thought, the right much worse than the left, three gashes brown with dried blood along the nose. "It wasn't one of my better efforts. They say you really have to have the kind of fish, the kind they have in the Mediterranean, I forget the name of it, to get the consistency right."

Mireles watched Gub, saying nothing.

"It worked out okay, though, because the guy who was kicking the shit out of me, he got the bouillabaisse on the head, and, well, it's a long story."

"You're okay, though?"

"Fine, a little bleary. I'm sorry about the smell, though. I scrubbed the floor pretty good this morning and rinsed it. But we better get some more windows opened."

Mireles started working on the front windows in the living room. "What happened to the guy?"

"Dead," Gub said from the kitchen. "But not because of the bouillabaisse. It wasn't that bad. It was the damndest thing. I had him tied up with some clothesline, it was all I had, and when I heard the explosions, I left him here. It was maybe ninety minutes, max. The guy was one of the ones involved in leaving the heads around the city, and I prodded him some with your old Chief's Special. I got a name from him, too, for what it's worth. But it didn't sound like this guy Hagen."

Mireles started to say something, then stopped.

"The man's name is Strew-a. No first name. And this guy Afonso says he's working out of this big chalet on the coast road. So after I leave the Lisboa, I drive up there, it's not even two miles. It looks like there's no one there, so I let myself in the basement. I was so pissed I shot the lock off the door and went in. I was going to wait for whoever it was to come home, but in the study, I find my friend with the fish soup. Shot through the chest."

"He undid the knots."

"What else? He was a strong fucker, but I thought I had him tied up pretty good. He must have slipped them somehow and driven back to this medicine man's place, I don't know why, to alert this guy Strew-a. He said there's also a second guy there, who just got there.

"Any name?"

"I don't think Afonso knew it. But he said the new guy decided they'd lay off the heads for a while."

"Description?" Mireles had Otto Hagen on the brain.

"Not much. Short guy with a crew cut."

Maybe, maybe not, Mireles thought. "What about this medicine man, what's the deal with him?"

"Afonso says he was paying him for the heads, which the bandits were getting from up in Plumtree. Evidently, they've been killing a bunch of people up there and cutting off their heads. Afonso said he and this guy Strew-a delivered them around the city. That that was the plan."

"And Strew-a or the other guy offed Afonso?"

"You gotta figure. When he gets back to the medicine man's place with the fish soup all over him, they ask him some questions, he gives some answers, and they decide he's a fuckup. It could have been Strew-a, the new guy or the medicine man."

"When did the new guy get here?"

Gub checked his watch. "Afonso said sometime in the past two days."

"And that's when the bombings started."

"Right. There were the three last night. And my jeep the night before that."

"The Toyota?"

"Yeah. I left it on the street and was using a friend's car. They must have wired a charge to the gas tanks and rigged the thing to blow when the driver's door opened. Unfortunately, the DCM, this guy

Allsworth, tried the door after a security guard alerted him. Heart attack, I think they're listing now as the cause of death. But the body was burning when I got there, so you can pretty much take your pick."

The phone in the bedroom rang, and Gub ran to get it.

Mireles walked to one of the open living room windows, feeling the warm breeze against his face.

In the darkened bedroom, Gub listened for just over a minute, hung up and came back into the living room. "My boss. He sounds like he may have something. Maybe even something useful, which would be a change."

Mireles turned from the open window, the light slanting across his dark head. "Listen, Gub, I told you I didn't come all this way to run leads on a dead diplomat, or even to check out this guy Hagen. The Bureau knows I'm here, and I'll have to call in if we run across Hagen. I've got to do that. But the main reason I'm here is because I owe you, because you're a friend and because mainly for a long time I have not thought a lot about trying to give something back. That's the way Amy puts it, who by the way sends her love. And besides, there's no way I could explain the M-16s, the ammo and the Kevlar vests I picked up on the way out here."

Gub looked at Mireles, amazement spreading across his face. "Mr. By-the-Book brought some M-16s?" It was the kind of thing Gub would have done maybe, but not Tom Mireles, at least the Mireles he thought he knew.

"They'll be here this afternoon," Mireles said. "Unless I got played for a real fool, which I don't think I did."

"Fucking amazing." Gub laughed though his eyes hurt like hell. "They're hot, no doubt, too. No, I don't imagine the Bureau would understand about the M-16s."

Mireles was laughing now, too. "Probably best not to mention it, then, huh?"

"That would be my guess, yeah." Gub put his sunglasses back on. "Let's get out of here, this fish smell is making me sick. We should go see Carlos. He's got a letter from a priest up in Plumtree. Sounds weird, but it could be a lead."

NEARLY twelve hours later, sitting on the sun porch of the old hotel and watching the waves breaking on the reef a half mile out,

Nicholas Sturua was still trying to decide whether he had done the right thing. He swallowed some more beer.

Everything was so confusing.

After he had shot Afonso, Sturua had thought seriously about shooting Hagen. He figured the German probably had most of Viktor Alleja's $15,000 on him somewhere. And with what was left of his own $5,000 and the money he had taken from the safe in Bucharest, it would make a nice little stash to start fresh somewhere. The problem with that, though, was the same one he had had back in Bucharest: where to go, what to do? For the whole of his life in Romania, even before he had joined the Securitate, Sturua had never had to think strategically. Life was whatever the state happened to allow, and that was pretty much that. Sturua was smart enough to know he had to think strategically now, and he didn't want to make any mistakes. Waxing Hagen would get him some quick cash, but if the two of them stayed together and made Viktor Alleja's game plan work, there was a long-term solution somewhere in there. At least he hoped there was. Anyway, by that time Hagen was already on the phone to Viktor, and Sturua was hoping they already had a plan.

Hagen had been big on using the Semtex, but Sturua wasn't so sure about it now. Get a few more of these diplomat assholes out in the street, he had said, maybe take a few of them out with a charge on their place, that would get the cables whirring back to Europe and the U.S. That's why they had hit the apartment building in the new embassy district, Hagen's idea. The presidential staff's executive offices had been an easy call that they had both agreed on. It was official, and with no guards, it was a soft target to boot. The Lisboa had been a toss-up. Sturua had argued that the place represented stability; blowing it up would send a powerful message. Hagen had finally agreed, but only after he was convinced there were several foreign-service and aid-agency employees living there.

Sturua had listened as Hagen reported the bombings to Viktor Alleja. Softening him up for the bad news: Afonso and the fact that the medicine man's place was clearly blown. He went over the conversation again.

"He's pretty mad." Hagen had held the cream-colored receiver at arm's length, and Sturua had heard the stream of invective from the far side of the medicine man's study.

"Tell him we're in a hurry, we can discuss it later."

"He says the operation is off."

"Bullshit."

"Maybe, but that's what he says."

"Look, tell him if we have a place to go, we can keep the bombings up, and in another few days he can send in his Salvation Front guy on a white horse. Tell him that's the way they did it in Bucharest."

Hagen had motioned for Sturua to shut up, and he had wondered again whether he should shoot him. "Yes, Viktor, that's right." Hagen had gestured for paper and pencil, and Sturua had handed him a calendar and a Bic Fine Point from the desk.

"Okay, give it to me again, right." Hagen had scribbled quickly for nearly a minute, directions.

Then they had begun loading food, guns, ammo, liquor and all of the beer from the icebox into the blue Yugo. Sturua had driven while Hagen navigated. It was on the way to the old hotel that Sturua learned of the last piece in Viktor Alleja's puzzle.

Hagen had said that Viktor was steamed about his shooting Afonso, even if he had spilled his guts to the detective. But what really bothered him was shooting him in the medicine man's house.

Sturua told Hagen he couldn't understand it. "What, is he worried about the carpets or something?"

"No," Hagen had said, "he's worried because the medicine man is the man Viktor is fixing to put in the presidential palace when we're all done."

Which made Sturua glad, at least for the time being, that he hadn't shot Hagen. Still, it was confusing. In the warm sun, the bottle of Heineken cool against his stomach, Sturua tried to decide whether it made sense, Viktor putting a medicine man up for president. It seemed crazy, he thought, but it just might work. Hell, he had heard of crazier schemes.

EIGHTEEN

Gub could see that Mireles was disgusted by Carlos. They met in his office at the department, and Gub saw the look of shock that crossed Mireles's face at the rows of empty desks in the bullpen area. The streaky light through the dirty windows high up on the wall gave the place a kind of ghostly look.

Carlos had already started drinking, but Gub was used to that by now. What he was not used to was a bona fide useful bit of information from his boss. While Gub studied the letter from Padre Francisco, Mireles and Carlos contemplated each other across the cluttered desk. When Mireles had occupied the office, years before, the place had been immaculate. Gub had almost forgotten. But he had no time for reminiscences now.

The priest had addressed the letter, "To the Chief of the Police, Fado." Carlos said that a young man in his twenties had delivered it to the department that morning. The priest wrote in an elegant, cursive hand, describing the radio device, which he clearly did not understand, but which he claimed to have taken from a bandit. He described the one conversation he had heard, with the reference to "detective," which he also did not understand. And he described the two mass funerals over which he had presided, ten of the men from in or around Plumtree shot and then beheaded in the past week. Gub read the final paragraph aloud. "In the name of God and what is right, I appeal for any help you can provide for the people of our village. The little security force we have is no match for the bandits with their weapons, and something must be done. If the radio device I have in my possession can be of some help, I offer it to you or the appropriate authorities in the government. But even if it is not, on behalf of this small and besieged place, I ask for your help." The priest had signed it, "Yours in Christ, Francisco Russi, OFM."

"What do you think?" Carlos was obviously pleased with himself.

"We've got to check it, obviously. The medicine man's place is blown, and if Calamidades can lay on a few people to keep an eye on it, this is our best bet for the moment." Privately, Gub had some misgivings about the letter. Teresa had told him years ago about the strange priest in Plumtree, but he didn't feel the need to share the story with Carlos just now.

"The 1A highway is dangerous. With all the bandit roadblocks, Calamidades and the army have only been traveling it in convoys."

"There's no time for that now, Carlos." Gub worried about the road north himself. It was just over twenty miles to Plumtree, but the bandits owned the road. "If we leave within the hour, we'll have plenty of daylight to get there and back. We'll just have to take our chances."

Mireles watched the interplay between Carlos and Gub. More than ever, he didn't understand how Gub had stayed in Fado all these years.

Gub asked Carlos if he could take the priest's letter with him and pocketed it. The three of them made a bit of small talk before Gub and Mireles took their leave. Over his shoulder, Gub could see Carlos reaching into the lower left-hand drawer of the desk. Gub knew that's where he kept the beer, which is all he ever drank. He just couldn't understand how he drank it warm.

"So how bad is the 1A these days?" Mireles thought it was pointless to bring up the depressing state of affairs at the department. Some things were better left unsaid.

Gub had gone on one of the Calamidades-organized convoys more than a year before, a bumper-to-bumper death run in ten-ton lorries through the pitch-dark. There had been one roadblock and some shooting, but the convoy had gotten through. It was one of the scariest things Gub had ever done, and he had not been on the 1A since. "Hairy, Tom. It could be hairy. But then again we could be lucky. Let's pray for luck."

On the way back to his flat, he gassed the Save the Children Land-Rover at the British Petroleum station and bought two new jerricans, filling them as well. The conversation with Mireles was still sticking and bumping along. Like it always did at first, Gub thought, neither one saying exactly what he was thinking. Maybe that's why they had been friends for so long. Gub couldn't tell, for instance, how hard Tony Sebastião's death had hit Mireles, if at all; they had simply talked around it, talked of other things, until they eventually got to the nub.

They were nearly back at the apartment, Gub driving, when Mireles struck it. "I don't see how you've done it all this time, Gub, especially after Teresa died."

"What was I supposed to do?"

"I told you, you could have come to the States." Mireles was studying one of the multicolored topo maps Herb Cohen had given him at Langley.

Gub concentrated on the road. "I don't know. I'm seeing this woman. It's more serious than anything since Teresa, but this place isn't as bad as you think. I mean, I have no idea where things will go. She works with these orphans at Save the Children. She really loves the kids, you can see it, and maybe if we ever did get together, we'd just stay here." He braked the Land-Rover in front of his flat and was climbing out when he saw the thin man in tan shorts and a green windbreaker who was sitting on his front porch.

What now?

The man had a wooden crate with him. Stenciled on the side was "Drilling eqpt." Gub had never seen the man before, and he offered no name. He asked only that Mireles sign an eight-by-eleven onion-skin receipt and waited around just long enough for Mireles to pry open the crate and check the two machine guns inside.

Gub whistled as the thin man walked away. Someone had taken great pains to recondition them, right down to the new paint on the black stocks and muzzles. The Kevlar vests were in a plastic bag, and the ammunition was in boxes at the bottom of the crate.

"I had no idea what I was getting into," Mireles said, checking both weapons. "But my friend at Langley said this guy was good. Turns out he was better than I expected."

"I didn't know you mixed it up with the CIA."

"Since I took the job in New York, it's pretty much all the time, keeping up with the security people there and the counterintelligence people. They're a good group, smart and honest. You'd like them."

"That where you got the maps?"

"A guy in Africa Division. He marked what they had from the most recent bandit attacks around the city. Looks like there's been plenty of activity up near this priest's place."

"There's a big cashew-shelling plant there, I don't know if you remember it. The bandits have hit it. A couple of times, I think." Gub looked more closely at Mireles, still studying the map like the A student he once had been. It was crazy, he thought, Mireles coming all this way, and with guns. He started to say something, then stopped. "If we're going, we better move it."

Mireles already had the gray Kevlar vest on over a red tennis shirt and a pair of khakis. Carefully, he folded the map, leaving the page showing the area just north of Fado on the outside. Then he shoved it in his back pocket.

It took them less than ten minutes to load the Land-Rover, and Mireles was stowing the two bedrolls between the crate for the M-16s and Gub's zippered canvas bag with the other guns in it when the Dodge van with the Save the Children emblem on the windshield pulled in behind. The driver climbed out, a slender brunette in a loose chambray shirt, jeans and cowboy boots. The passenger door opened, and a small black boy in shorts bounded out with a stick. Mireles introduced himself, and the three of them turned as Gub came trotting across the small lawn.

"Those eyes don't look a hell of a lot better than last night, Gub." Betty's color was high, like she'd been exercising hard. "Did you get some ointment for those cuts?"

"Not yet." Gub gave Betty a quick kiss on the cheek and ran a hand through Matthias's tangled hair. "You all have met, I take it?"

"You bet." Mireles watched with interest, unsure how the kid fit into the scheme of things. "I told him about the eyes, too, but he doesn't listen."

Betty eyed the back of the Land-Rover. "Going somewhere?"

Gub explained quickly about the priest and the murders in Plumtree. "I'll have to settle up with Save the Children on the jeep. I'm going to need it a few more days, if it's okay."

"Gub!"

Mireles recognized the tone of voice. He thought it was probably universally recognizable. Then he stared at his shoes, evidently finding something interesting there.

Gub saw Betty's cheeks coloring. "If there's anything to this, it could be important, Betty."

"And how do you plan to get from here to there, just drive?"

"Right up 1A. The road's been clear for the past couple of weeks."

"That's because there have been no convoys." Save the Children had two small planes to supply programs in the interior and up the coast, the few they were still running. The pilots gave Betty a fill on bandit activity that was based on whatever they saw from the air and whatever they heard from other pilots and people in the villages they serviced.

"Maybe, but this is too important to pass up. Besides, Tom got us some nice protective vests, so we'll be safe."

Betty looked from Gub to Mireles and back to Gub. "When will you be back?"

"Tonight, I hope. I'll call."

"You better." She stood on her toes, gave Gub a long kiss, then turned without a word, grabbing Matthias by the hand, and strode back to the Save the Children Dodge.

Mireles watched the long legs in the tight jeans flashing in the sun, turned to Gub and smiled. "Lucky man."

Gub thought that that was true. "Let's get going so we can get back, huh?"

Before they left, he took care to leave a couple of windows on either side of the flat open, to get the stale air moving. Then he grabbed a cracked leather case he had hauled out from under the bed. Turning the key in the front door and adjusting the white thread on the doorjamb, he lugged the case towards the jeep.

Mireles was studying another of Herb Cohen's maps, leaning against the back fender. "What the hell is that?"

"Remember when we were kids, my grandfather's elephant gun?"

"Seems like a hundred years ago. Does it still work?"

"I take it out every few months to look at it and give it a cleaning, but I haven't fired it in years. I thought I'd bring it along, see if we can try it out if we have time."

Mireles scowled. "Just how much trouble are you expecting?"

"None maybe." He wedged the big gun in its cracked case between the two jerricans of gas. "To tell you the truth, I'm more worried about the 1A than whoever blew up the Lisboa."

Mireles buckled himself in on the passenger's side after lowering the rear window. Gub did the same on his side, hoping the breeze would compensate some for the lack of air-conditioning. It was just after 2 P.M., the hottest part of the afternoon, though, so it was a vain hope. A few minutes later, even with the breeze off the ocean as he turned onto the coast road, Gub could already feel the oxford shirt beneath his Kevlar vest sticking to his back.

"I'm surprised you've still got the old man's gun." Mireles was looking out towards the ocean, and Gub could barely hear him over the rush of the wind.

"It's about the only thing that survived the fire. There were pots and pans and things like that, but this was the only thing I really wanted."

The wind rushed through the open windows, and Gub sweated while the little man rolled tape. His grandfather had died in 1963, and Gub's father, the eldest and the only boy, had inherited the big house on the river and some 450 acres surrounding it. In the thirty-two years since he had left Lisbon with his bewildered family, Humberto Gub, Sr., had done well for himself, buying piece after piece of choice property, financing the purchases with the money he had made on everything from the breeding services of his bulls to the paperwork he handled for the Europeans who streamed into the countryside around him. After all those years, Humberto Gub, Sr., had still hated the law, but if he could do it in his spare time to make it pay the way for his increasingly ambitious schemes, he forced himself to do it, late at night, after working hours in the field. Unfortunately, Humberto Gub, Jr., was not similarly inclined. He hated the hard work of the fields and loved the law. Though he had no degree, he took on more and more of the legal work that came his father's way. After the old man died, of a massive heart attack in bed, after an erratic but ultimately robust seventy-three years, Humberto Gub, Jr., paid even less attention to the crops and animals, leaving it to the hired men. Gub's mother passed on a year after that, but she had been dead to her family for a long time before, wasting year in and year out with something the doctors called myelomalacia, a poorly understood softening of the brain tissue brought on, they thought, by a parasitic infection. A few years after that, less than half the Gub family's plantation was under cultivation, and when the revolution came, the whole thing was expropriated by the new government. Gub was at school in Cape Town when it happened, the beneficiary of his father's abiding faith in education. He was hurrying back when Mireles, a year ahead of him at the university, came to tell him of the fire. The belief was that Humberto Gub, Jr., had set it, immolating himself and the rambling farmhouse so that all the new government got was the tangled land around it. The tape flickered, a long shot of a gutted farmhouse, a young man in city clothes ambling through it, lost in the foreground.

"I wish I'd known him, your grandfather." Mireles's voice broke his reverie.

"You would have liked him. He was kind of a student of history. Kind of like you in that way, though my father used to say he got a lot of stuff wrong."

"It's easy to do." Mireles saw the long look in Gub's eyes. He remembered it from when they were kids, then cops together. He changed the subject. "In the States now, for instance, everyone is talking about this argument, about how history has ended?"

Gub shook his head, indicating he hadn't heard about it, keeping his eye out for the turnoff to 1A.

Mireles pulled out the CIA map and studied it. "Looks like we're actually going northwest when we get on it."

"Yeah, it bends inland, sort of following the edge of the first line of dunes, if you remember."

Mireles put the map away. "Anyway, it's this debate that with the collapse of communism in Eastern Europe and the unraveling of the Soviet system all around Gorbachev, the great Cold War collision is ended and the West supposedly has won."

"What's the prize?"

"Well, they get into all sorts of debates about it. About the new role of the military, the budget deficit."

"The war with Iraq."

"Exactly. But the point they make—and I don't buy it, especially from where I sit, seeing all these East Bloc intelligence guys still running around—is that in terms of the conflict of ideas, market-oriented democracies versus the communist totalitarian structure, the commies have lost."

"Can't argue with that." Gub made the left turn north onto 1A. The highway was empty.

"It's a Hegelian argument." Mireles, too, was scanning the road ahead. "The problem with it is it doesn't begin to address things like Iraq or even the situation here."

"It's kind of useless, you mean." Gub pressed the accelerator all the way to the floor. If they hit one of the bandits' roadblocks at a curve, he wanted to be going fast. Real fast. The speedometer inched to 85 mph, which was about top-end, Gub figured, turning his head towards Mireles. "You might want to pull out one of your new shooting irons before we reach these curves up ahead. Better leave the safety off, too."

"It's not exactly useless." Mireles unbuckled the seat belt and reached around behind him for one of the M-16s, grabbing three clips of ammunition while he was at it. "You know something *I* ought to know?" he asked, buckling himself back in. "The road ahead looks clear as day."

"That's the way it always looks. But if there's trouble, it'll be a few miles ahead, where the road bends and the tree line comes up close on your side."

"Great."

"There's probably nothing to worry about. It can't hurt to be ready, though." Waves of heat shimmered off the cracked asphalt. "So this end-of-history stuff is hot?"

"It's interesting, I'd say." Mireles jammed an ammo clip in the machine gun and snapped the safety off, sighting out his window at an imaginary target. "But it's theory mainly, and what it fails to do is explain things like why you and me are riding down the highway with a bunch of guns on our way to see a priest about some bandits' radio gizmo."

"One thing I forgot to tell you about the priest?"

"What's that?"

"Well, technically, he's dead. Teresa told me about this guy years ago. Officially, the Vatican listed him as dead after he got shot up in one of the early raids on Plumtree. But he's been living up here for something like forever."

Mireles took aim at another imaginary target out the window. "Interesting," he said over the roar of the wind. "This ought to be real interesting."

NINETEEN

By the time they reached Padre Francisco's place, Gub and Mireles had both sweat clear through their shirts. There had been no bandit roadblocks, but the burned husks of trucks and four-wheel drives on either side of the 1A confirmed what Gub knew well enough: they had been lucky.

Off the highway, the Land-Rover dipped and fell down the broken two-lane road to Plumtree. Gub had had to ask directions in the village, but after that they had found Padre Francisco's place with no problem. The priest was waiting for them.

Gub made introductions, showing the priest his letter by way of bona fides. Then they followed the old man through the small, dark house, Gub pulling the Kevlar vest off as he went, Mireles behind him. The radio contraption was already laid out on a table on the back patio.

"I didn't know if it was important," the priest said, gesturing for them to sit, "but we have had bandits right in the village several times in the past weeks, one even on my hill out in the back. After the killings and then the radio, I thought I would send a letter and see if someone could help us. They are good people here, I can tell you." The priest paused for breath, then asked Mireles and Gub if they would like something to drink.

They requested water, and the priest returned an instant later with two tall glasses.

"May I ask how you got the radio, Father?" Gub wanted to make sure right off the bat that this wasn't some kind of setup. And he didn't want to waste time.

The priest seemed to be expecting the question. "I stole it, Detective. That is the correct title, isn't it, the right way to address you?"

"That's fine, Father." Gub took a long drink of water and felt it clear down in his gullet as it washed away the dust. "And did you steal it actually from a bandit in the area?"

"Yes." The priest parceled his words carefully. "From the one who was on my hill."

While Padre Francisco told the rest of his tale about the bandit on the hill and how he had become angry at the man and at the repeated shelling of the cashew factory, Mireles began fiddling with the radio device, setting the little conelike thing out on the grass and running the wire from the end of it back to the patio, inserting the plug into one of the jacks in the back. Gub was handy—he could wire a lamp or tune a car—but he knew virtually nothing about electronics and was content to let Mireles play with the thing while he and the priest made small talk. The old man seemed like the genuine item.

"All these years and all our efforts," the priest was saying, "undone by a group of murderers. Mutineers."

"It was a brave thing to do," Gub said. "How is your leg now?"

Padre Francisco rubbed the swollen area above his right knee where the bandit had struck him with his rifle. "It's sore as hell, if you want to know."

Gub thought that he was going to like this priest.

The radio on the metal table crackled feebly as Mireles played with it. "The batteries are solar, and they're a little weak," he said, interrupting. "But I think they're coming back. It must have been in the dark for quite a while, huh, Father?"

"Since I found it, I've kept it hidden. Except the one time I tried to turn it on and heard the talking." He reached into his brown habit and pulled out a page he'd torn from his unlined notepad, handing it to Mireles. "This is the number I had it on when I heard the conversation about the detective," he said, nodding in Gub's direction.

Gub looked at it over Mireles's shoulder. It meant nothing to him.

Mireles explained. "I've never seen one exactly like this, but the Bureau uses a system that's not too much different. What it looks like is a basic radiotelephone with a satellite uplink. With the

satellite, it can be used to call just about anywhere; without it, my
guess is it functions basically as a shortwave radio. The one the
Bureau has comes with a scrambler, and we use it on straight car-to-
car transmissions. It's a relatively new system. This thing has the
solar-powered batteries, which are good for a few weeks to a few
months, obviously depending on the weather." Mireles spun the big
dial slowly, Gub and the priest listening as the static chaff grew
louder, then fainter. The batteries were definitely giving more juice
to the thing as they gained power in the afternoon sun. Mireles
dialed up the number on Padre Francisco's pad, and they were all
amazed to hear a voice, faint but still quite clear.

Gub nearly jumped out of his seat, but it was Padre Francisco who
picked up on the reference to the beach. The Magellan was an
abandoned hotel beach club nearly ten miles south of Plumtree, at
the far north end of Fado where the coast road dead-ended at Costa
do Sol.

Gub thought the voice sounded familiar, but he couldn't place it.
When the second voice came through, though, it came booming out
of the little speaker, and Gub had no trouble identifying the deep
baritone.

"I'll take care of it," Paul Achebe said. "And be back to you."

"The medicine man," Gub mouthed to Mireles.

"And something about that old hotel," the priest whispered. "I
remember it from years ago."

The three of them hovered over the radiotelephone, willing it to
say more. That was it, though; they had caught just the last fragment
of conversation. Still, it was something. Afonso had said that the
medicine man was paying the people orchestrating the deliveries of
the severed heads, and maybe the bombings. Perhaps Paul Achebe
had been talking to them. Clearly, something was going on at the
Magellan. The place was supposed to have been razed when construction of the big new hotel had begun right behind it, but then
things had ground to a halt suddenly, the rebar and most of the
concrete decking laid for most of the twenty-three floors, and after
that there had been no money to bulldoze the Magellan. Gub hadn't
seen the place in years, but he remembered it well enough. He and
Mireles and Tony had all taken dates there one time when they were
seniors at St. Francis Xavier.

"I guess I know our next step." Mireles was still trying to coax
something more out of the radiotelephone.

"Yeah. But we've got to hurry." Already, he saw, the dead tree on the hill was casting a long shadow on the brown grass.

Mireles was not quite ready to give up on the radiophone, however. "We could still learn something from this thing, Gub. And there's this: do we really want to go in there in the dark? It's your show, but it might be better to get there right at dawn. That way at least we could see where we're going. And in the meantime, we'll be able to use this thing."

Padre Francisco interjected. "You're welcome here." His hands fluttered like delicate birds. "I have food and things. It's no problem."

Gub wasn't wild about the delay, but he had to concede, as usual, that Mireles had a point. If there was something going on at the Magellan tonight, they would miss it, that was for sure. On the other hand, going into the old hotel in the dark was plainly risky. And they did have the radio, a wonderful edge. If they missed whatever was happening at the Magellan, the radiophone would help them pick up the trail again easily. Besides, he had not even had time yet to question the priest about the murders in Plumtree. "Okay. We'll take you up on your offer, Father, if you don't mind. We leave right at dawn, though."

Gub went to get the bedrolls from the Land-Rover, and the priest set out a plate of sausage and cheese and uncorked a bottle of Burgundy he had been saving for a reason he couldn't remember anymore; he didn't even like the stuff. Mireles continued to fiddle with the radio, but as the light died he picked up less and less, the last thing a snatch of conversation between a container ship out on the ocean and a shipping agent, evidently somewhere to the north. An easy silence settled on the patio as the three of them watched the green dial and waited for the radio to say something more.

But when the dial dimmed perceptibly, Gub leaned over and flicked the power switch. "Save it for another day."

"Tomorrow," Mireles agreed.

The priest mixed his second Campari and soda, and Gub poured another glass of wine. Mireles declined, rolling his bedroll out on the slate patio. Within minutes, he was snoring softly, and the priest and the detective stared up at the sky, ink black against the blacker limbs of the dead khaya. Neither man spoke for a while, and Gub thought it was mighty peaceful.

The priest finally broke the silence. "Will you be able to help these people here, Detective? The last few days have been terrible for them."

"If you could tell me what you know about the murders, Father, it might be helpful. You may not know it, but the heads from the men killed here have been used in what I would call a campaign of terrorism in Fado."

The priest set the Campari and soda on the metal table in front of him. "What do you mean?"

"In the past few days, someone has been placing the heads in strategic locations around the city. In the offices of Calamidades, at the Justice Palace. They even broke into my apartment and left one there."

"Was that what I was hearing on the radio that night?"

Gub nodded and sipped some more of the Burgundy.

"Goddammit, that's barbaric."

"The point, I think, is to terrify the capital and to put the government even more on the defensive and hope that somehow it will fall. At least that's my theory."

"What about Plumtree?"

Gub admired the priest's persistence. "I can't provide security here, if that's what you mean, Father. I have just myself. I had another deputy, but he was killed two nights ago. And Mireles here isn't even a police officer. He's an old friend, here to help."

"So the killings will continue." Padre Francisco still hadn't touched his drink.

"The best hope we've got, Father, is to find the people talking on this radio, the ones behind the killings. If we can somehow cut off the bandits' support, identify and stop whoever is providing them with guns and money, that's when the killing will stop." Gub took another sip of wine. It wasn't a very satisfactory answer, he knew, but it was the only one he had.

THE sun had set on the other side of the hotel, away from the ocean, so there hadn't been much of a light show on the water, and for some reason it seemed later than it actually was. The sun porch was only good till midafternoon, it turned out, when the building behind him blocked off the rays. Still, it had felt good, Sturua thought, the sun beating down on his legs and chest. He just worried now whether the medicine man would show up. This would be their second night in the place, and there was no sign of him. "What do you think is keeping him?"

"Who?" Hagen had mended one of the hotel's woven hammocks and was lying in it, sipping from a plastic cup filled with ice and vodka.

"The medicine man. Viktor said he'd be in touch."

"It hasn't even been a day yet, Sturua. Ease up."

"I don't want to stay in this dump forever, that's all. You see all the rats in this place? I fucking hate rats."

"It can't be any worse than Bucharest."

The man was too smug for his own good. Sturua got up to fetch another beer from the cooler under Hagen's jury-rigged hammock. There was no percentage in making the point at the moment, he thought, but soon. "I just hope this fucking medicine man shows. I didn't come all this way to work on my tan."

THEY were up early the next morning, the Land-Rover packed and ready well before dawn.

The priest had insisted on coming along, and Gub had finally run out of reasons why he shouldn't. The Magellan was an enormous, rambling old place, he remembered that much; another pair of eyes certainly couldn't hurt. Sitting in the backseat of the Land-Rover as Gub accelerated through the first of the curves on the way back down the 1A, the first rays of dawn peeking through the trees to his left, Padre Francisco confirmed his judgment: a pair of small Ernst Leitz binoculars dangled from his skinny neck on a frayed leather band. Mireles had one of the M-16s out in the seat beside him as Gub shot the jeep into the second curve, depressing the accelerator and scanning the road ahead for any sign of a bandit roadblock. Nothing. Maybe, he thought, eyeing the SATCOM radio on the backseat next to the priest, his luck really was changing.

"You're going to kill us all before any bandits do, you know?" Mireles had on a fresh tennis shirt beneath the Kevlar vest and the same pair of khakis from the day before.

Gub wore a white oxford button-down and faded jeans. "It's been a long time since I've been on this fucking road, I forgot just how much it scares me. It scares the shit out of me, if you want to know." Gub checked the rearview mirror. "Sorry, Father."

The priest waved his hand in benediction. Earlier, he had refused

Gub's offer of the second Kevlar vest. He had been dead once, he said; there was no danger.

Gub thought about it once again, as the third and last of the tight curves came and went without incident. He had decided the night before it wasn't worth trying to argue with the priest. Scanning both sides of the road, Gub eased up on the accelerator just a little, wondering again about the old man. A stubborn bastard, that was sure. Nearly ten minutes later, the 1A dead-ended into the cutoff to the coast road, and Gub followed it east, breathing easier as he approached familiar turf, turning north along the ocean finally and running over his plan a final time. He had discussed it with Mireles as they were folding their bedrolls an hour before, but Mireles had said he didn't remember the Magellan at all.

Your show, he had said. Friend.

After he locked the Land-Rover, the three of them left it in the lee of a high dune and started walking. It was far enough away from the old hotel that engine noise wouldn't have bothered anyone there. Gub had the Chief's Special in the shoulder holster, one of the M-16s, his grandfather's elephant gun in its cracked leather case and the SATCOM radiophone. He felt perfectly ridiculous. Mireles had the other M-16 and Gub's Swiss machine gun clipped to his belt, while Padre Francisco brought up the rear with his Leitz glasses and his trusty three-iron.

"Quite a team." Gub paused to let the others catch up with him, looking back at Mireles and the priest and then down at the Magellan. A blotchy pink concrete structure with a cracked barrel-tile roof, it sprawled along the ocean for maybe two hundred yards. The rusting plumbing fixtures in the courtyard and the curtains that blew like ragged pennants from the second-story windows testified to its abandonment. It had had a succession of owners, Gub recalled, but it was too far from the center of the capital, and after the revolution, when the situation had started getting worse, the last proprietor of the place had just given up and walked away. Gub was surprised that squatters hadn't taken over the place. Probably too dangerous, too far out of the way. Even for them.

"You'd need an easy three dozen agents to secure the place right." Mireles had zippered his Kevlar vest and was examining the windows one by one for signs of life.

"Well, we've only got three." Gub checked his own vest and nodded at Mireles. "It looks empty from here, but let's just take it slow."

Mireles winked and moved off to the right, cradling the M-16 and using a tangled hedgerow for cover.

Gub led the priest downhill to his left. There was an old car park on the far side of the littered courtyard that afforded a long view of both floors along the front of the hotel. The priest would stay there, Gub decided, their eyes and ears to the west. He and Mireles would have to worry about the beach side of the Magellan themselves. "You see anything, Father, just yell."

"Don't worry about me, I've got my golf club."

Sturua and Hagen had taken two adjacent rooms at the south end of the Magellan, up on the second floor. Each boasted a king-size Sealy Posturepedic encased in carved blond-wood frames bolted to the wall. The only problem was, the mattresses were blooming with mold. Hagen had laid blankets from a ransacked chambermaid's closet on top of his mattress and claimed to have slept blissfully. Sturua, complaining of the smell and the small brown rats that patrolled the hotel in squads, slept sitting up in a wing chair, his feet propped on a drawer pulled out from a sagging cedar bureau.

A fitful sleeper even in good times, Sturua felt more than heard the approach of Gub, Mireles and Padre Francisco. Checking for rats first, he set both feet tentatively on the floor, then grabbed his AK-47 from the top of the bureau and sidled to the open window, spying Mireles immediately as he made his way down the tangled hedgerow. The dove-gray Kevlar vest shone dully in the early light. "Shit," Sturua said. "Professionals."

Ducking below the window, he crept quickly into Hagen's room. The Stasi man was sleeping pole-straight on top of a half dozen covers on the bed, his AK-47 next to him, just within reach of his right hand. Sturua merely tapped him on the shoulder, and Hagen's blue eyes opened abruptly, his forefinger already curling around the trigger of the ugly Chinese assault rifle. Sturua noted that the safety was off. "Visitors," he said, nodding to the open window.

Hagen moved fast, from bed to the window in a single, fluid motion, his khaki trousers and blue work shirt barely rumpled after a night's sleep. "How many?"

"Just one that I saw," Sturua said. "But he was wearing a vest and had a weapon. He ain't hunting ducks."

"There's got to be more. I'm going to move." Away from the window, Hagen was jamming extra ammo clips into the back pockets of his trousers. "I don't know what the fuck's going on, but if this is some kind of joke by Viktor or this fucking medicine man, someone isn't going to like the punch line, and it ain't going to be me."

Sturua watched, fuming. But before he could say anything, Hagen was out the door, bolting back up the corridor towards the broad landing at the top of the staircase from the Magellan's once-ornate lobby, now littered with spent condoms and broken furniture. "Asshole," Sturua said. Back in his own room, he grabbed extra ammo clips from a nylon bag he had hung from a doorknob and took up position at the window, scouring the broken hedgerow for any sign of the man in the bulletproof vest. Seeing none, he scanned the lip of the broad bowl in which the Magellan squatted like an obscene old toad. Nothing.

MIRELES was just off the littered courtyard, flattened against the chalky pink concrete of the hotel, roughly midway between the front entrance and the south end of the building. Using a slender bottlebrush tree for cover, he was scanning the car park for signs of the priest when he heard footsteps above him, someone running. Mireles checked the zipper of his vest again and fondled the twins' travel clock in the pocket of his khakis. What the fuck was he doing here?

From the car park, he caught a glimpse of flashing metal and cringed. Hearing no shot, he peered through the leaves of the bottlebrush. It was the priest. Mireles wondered how he could see so well, then he remembered the binoculars. With his golf club, Padre Francisco seemed to be signaling something, but Mireles couldn't figure out what. He watched closely, and the priest aimed the three-iron like a rifle and pointed above him, to his left. Mireles turned just in time to see the outline of a muscular man with an assault rifle, and he dove to his right. A long burst followed a fraction of a second later, spattering the wall above him, but Mireles was already scrambling on all fours to get further away from the man with the gun and cut down his angle. He breathed chalky pink dust and rubbed his eyes. The man running and the man with the gun, Mireles thought. That made two, at least. He was willing to bet one of them was Hagen.

GUB was halfway through a window on the north end of the first floor when he heard the automatic. Tumbling into what looked like the hotel's breakfast room, he pulled the cracked leather bag with the big gun and the SATCOM phone behind him. Then he scrambled to one of the big front windows. The automatic fire had definitely come from the front, but there had been no return. Gub didn't want to think about that just yet. In the car park, Padre Francisco was aiming his three-iron at the second floor. He was looking south and obviously didn't see Gub.

Upstairs, Gub thought. He grabbed the leather case with the elephant gun in it and stashed the SATCOM phone behind a pile of broken chairs, covering it with what might once have been a tablecloth, now shreds of moldy, blackened fabric.

He had to find Mireles. He didn't intend for his friend to come all this way back to Fado just to get himself shot. But that meant traversing the hotel from north to south. And if Padre Francisco was right, getting upstairs. Gub had no idea how many they might be up against. Except for the single burst of gunfire, he had heard and seen nothing yet. What he needed was a diversion, he thought. Mireles would have to take care of himself for just a little bit longer.

Avoiding the broad hallway that ran the length of the first floor from the breakfast room to the hotel's main lobby, Gub used connecting doors from one room to the next. In the main dining room, someone had started a small fire in a corner. A straggler trying to cook something or keep warm, Gub thought. The flocked wallpaper was bubbled and black with smoke, and more broken furniture lay scattered in piles. Gub paused to listen. Still nothing. There was a sitting room between the dining room and a small door he hoped would lead to the main lobby. Once there, he thought, he could see about getting up to the second floor. The silence was driving him nuts.

Time for the diversion. Gub set the M-16 carefully on a still-serviceable settee and unzipped the cracked leather case. His father might not have approved, but Humberto Gub, Sr., would have doubtless been happy to see the old gun put to good use. It had an enormous mahogany stock and an iron barrel nearly three feet long. Gub had brought along only six of the huge antique rounds, and he slid one of them carefully into the chamber. He had cleaned and oiled the gun religiously, and despite what he had told Mireles, he was pretty confident it would work. He crept to a casement window behind the settee and looked out. The panes had all been shattered years before. Through the mullions of the topmost frame, however, he could see Padre Francisco gesturing with the three-iron. He was still pointing to the far south end of the hotel and upstairs.

Coming. Gub levered the rifle on the sill of the window, aimed at nothing whatsoever and pulled the trigger. The noise was deafening, and it rolled through the old hotel like a wave. He forgot about the leather case, grabbed the M-16 from the settee and was already moving towards the small door on the other side of the sitting room when he heard running footsteps above him. Coming, he thought again. I'm coming to get you, you motherfuckers.

FOR a split second, Hagen thought it must have been a bomb, then he rejected that, fumbling in the pocket of his blue work shirt for cigarettes. Finding none, he swore. A gun, he thought, but what kind of gun? Shit, it sounded like artillery.

Falling back into his Stasi training without thinking, Hagen had taken up position on the far side of the second-floor landing. Wide stairs in three flights led up from the lobby. Like the first floor, the second was trashed, condoms and rat shit all around. Hagen had picked the spot, a doorway onto a narrow veranda on the northeast side of the landing, for three reasons. It gave him an unobstructed view of anyone trying to get up the stairs; the west side of the landing was piled high with a tangle of bedroom furniture and crumbled packing boxes. Avoiding that, he had also left himself the widest field of fire. And, in the unlikely event he needed it, the veranda allowed him an escape. It was a long way to the sun porch below, but Hagen had scouted it, and there was a heavy bronze leader from the rain gutters on the roof. He would be able to use that to climb down. Below him, he heard a door open and a floorboard groan.

Hagen checked the safety on the AK-47 and smiled. It looked like he wouldn't need to worry about scampering down a drainpipe after all.

MIRELES also heard the noise of the floorboards and slid quickly behind the old concierge's desk, checking the M-16 as he flattened himself against the wall to the left of the pocket door behind the desk. He had to stifle a sneeze from the chalky dust still in his nose, but when Gub stepped through the door, sliding it back into its recess in the wall behind him, Mireles simply tapped him on the shoulder and grinned.

Gub sucked in his breath, then let it out slowly.

Mireles motioned him back inside, then slid the pocket door closed behind them.

"You okay?"

"Except for the dust in my lungs. A near miss, but I know where one of them is. In the last bedroom on the west side. Big guy. The priest spotted him. Maybe saved my life. I also heard someone running up there, so that makes at least two. After the guy on the end took a whack at me, I crawled along the building and ducked in the front door. So I figure we got the one on the end and another one somewhere else up there."

"Get the one we know about?"

"That's the rule, right?" Mireles looked down at the elephant gun and sneezed.

"There another way up?"

"Has to be. The place is too big for just the one center stairway."

"Then let's stay on this floor till we find some back stairs and go up that way." Gub hefted the elephant gun and reached for another round from the plastic pouch on his belt.

"You hit anything with that thing yet, or you just having fun?"

"This, my friend, is our secret weapon. Not only does it concentrate the mind wonderfully; it provides one hell of a good diversion. As I shall now demonstrate."

Mireles stepped back out into the main lobby first, careful not to kick any of the debris littering the floor. The sun was full up now, and the creamy yellow light magnified from the ocean outside bathed the hotel's blotched walls. The place almost looked nice. Gub followed Mireles, nodding towards the hallway off the lobby to the south side. Then he shouldered the big gun and aimed straight above him, at the last big unbroken pane of the skylight overhead, nearly three stories above him. The blast seemed to convulse the old hotel, the falling glass like chimes behind a timpani.

FUCKING-A, Hagen thought. His ears were ringing, and there were spikes of glass in his crew cut. He trained the barrel of the Chinese assault rifle on the crest of the stairs. That was the drill, right, soften up the enemy with heavy stuff, then charge? Hagen checked the sight again, barely breathing.

But nobody came.

GUB and Mireles were almost halfway down the long first-floor hallway to the far south end of the Magellan when Gub motioned for a left turn. The kitchen was back on the southeast side of the hotel, on the beach side, and Gub figured there had to be stairs from there to the second floor. How else to provide for room service?

The kitchen was gutted, like the rest of the Magellan, equipment like ovens and iceboxes either sold off or stolen. The smell of rat shit was overpowering.

Gub spied the stairs, behind a set of swinging double doors, and he motioned for Mireles to follow. The stairs groaned under his weight, and once, turning on a narrow landing before ascending the last flight, he banged the elephant gun against a wall. Gub looked back, grimacing.

"Fuck it," Mireles mouthed. "Let's go."

The stairs gave onto a narrow alcove that led to a short hallway that led to the wide center corridor that divided the Magellan's second floor down the middle. Gub waited for Mireles to catch up, and they walked the rest of the way to the end of the hallway together, Gub facing south, his M-16 in his arms, Mireles walking backwards, watching for any action behind them.

It was madness, Mireles thought. The instructors at Quantico would have bounced them for such sloppy procedure. But then, he thought, this ain't Quantico. They reached the end of the hallway, perspiring and exhausted. "This is it," Mireles said, gesturing at the peeling oak door.

Sure enough, Gub thought. The last one on the right.

WHEN the second blast roared up from the floor below him, Sturua had banged his right hand reaching for the AK-47 on the bureau beside him. What the hell was that thing? He had never heard anything like it.

In an undershirt and the boxer shorts he had worn to sunbathe in the day before, Sturua wondered again whether he should leave the room or stick it out. If he knew where Hagen was, they could figure something out, outsmart these guys, whoever they were. But as usual, Hagen was into his own thing. The room was a better bet, Sturua thought. There was no means of escape besides the window, but that wasn't an option. The Magellan had been built on a grand scale, and though it was only the second story, Sturua figured it was a good forty to forty-five feet to the ground. No way. He'd stick with the room. If anyone was going to get him, they would have to come through that door, and with the AK on full automatic, Sturua figured they'd be dead before they even reached the bed. No, he'd stick with the room all right. Let Hagen do his thing, he thought; in fact, to hell with Hagen.

"READY?" Sweat was stinging the welts around his eyes as Gub pulled a new round from the pouch on his belt. He chambered it quickly, and Mireles stood a few feet off to his right, his M-16 ready. Gub aimed squarely at the center of the closed door, bracing his back against the opposite wall of the corridor.

"Hey, Gub?" Mireles was grinning.

Gub glanced over. His eyes burned.

"This is something else Hegel never figured on."

Gub smiled. "You know what," he said, squeezing the trigger of his grandfather's elephant gun. "Fuck Hegel."

In the closed end of the corridor, the third explosion sounded even louder than the first two, Gub thought, tucking the gun to his chest and rolling sideways to the floor. The door above him exploded inwards, and Mireles followed it with a short burst from his M-16, turning immediately to see if anyone was coming from the other end of the hallway. Nothing. Gub scrambled to his feet next to the gaping doorway, his ears ringing, the taste of cordite on his tongue. Mireles joined him on the other side of the place where the peeling oak door had been just seconds before.

"Anyone home?" Gub didn't know what else to say.

"Ah, shit." The voice sounded more angry than scared.

"Sounds like he's pissed off." Mireles was still watching the north end of the hallway.

"I knew this was a fucked-up deal from the beginning."

"Yeah," Gub agreed. "I would say pissed off. Definitely pissed off." He rubbed the sweat from his face with the back of his hand and called into the room through the empty doorway. "The gun first, safety off. Kick it into the hall. Then crawl out on your hands and knees. Backwards. And slow."

The AK-47 slid out first. Then Nicholas Sturua's feet came out, socks with no shoes, followed by thick legs, in jockey shorts with big red hearts on them.

Gub stood over the man while Mireles covered him with the M-16. "How many more of you assholes?"

"Just one." The man seemed defeated, but still angry.

"A German?" Mireles would have bet plenty on it. He held the M-16 on the man while Gub stripped tattered curtains from a window.

"German, yeah."

Mireles smiled. "Name of Otto Hagen?"

Gub came back into the corridor and pulled the man's hands behind him, knotting the cord twice. He said nothing.

"Hagen, yeah. You know him or something?"

Gub interrupted, lifting Sturua roughly to his feet and checking the knots on his wrists. "No, but we will soon."

Nicholas Sturua shrugged his shoulders. "I were you, I wouldn't waste my time."

"No, huh?" Gub seemed genuinely interested.

"Hagen's an asshole. A slimeball."

Gub was still studying Sturua when Mireles screamed. From the corner of his eye, he saw the man in the dark shirt at the far end of the hall. And he heard the burst a split second later, as he was driving the Romanian and Mireles in a running bear hug through the splintered doorway.

The gunman had fired from much too far away, however, well beyond the range of the Chinese assault rifle. Gub guessed he was probably a little jumpy. Like me, he thought, listening as the automatic finally fell silent. It would take him maybe five seconds to reload; who knew how much longer before he poked his head out to try again? On the floor, Gub reached into the hallway and grabbed the elephant gun.

Then, inspired, he crawled across the hall into the alcove opposite Sturua's door. From there, he could see that Mireles was already on his feet, the M-16 trained on Sturua. With his forefinger, Gub made a circling motion to Mireles.

Then he disappeared.

OTTO Hagen had a problem, and he knew it.

A professional terrorist, he had always had the element of surprise on his side. A bomb in a car, a sniper setup: that was easy stuff, and Hagen had always prided himself on the fact that he had never made too much of what he did. Terrorism, as he often said, was not brain surgery.

Too bad he couldn't have confided the epigram to someone, he thought; he liked the sound of it.

But Hagen was out of his element. Instead of having the element of surprise on his side, he had been the one surprised. And now if he were to get out of this place alive, he would have to wage the equivalent of a pitched battle, he on the one side, the two guys who had grabbed Sturua on the other. He had a long, dark corridor to traverse. That was bad enough, Hagen thought. But they also had that fucking gun. Whatever it was.

Think! He had fired the first burst way too early. But the one guy, the smaller one, had seen him and yelled. The next time he would have to be smarter. They weren't going anywhere, after all. And he had plenty of ammunition.

He had used the burst from the AK to one good advantage anyway. While the two guys with Sturua were ducking for cover, he had run forwards another twenty yards before ducking into room 212. It was one of the cheap rooms that didn't front on the beach. But Hagen didn't care about the water view; that's why he and Sturua had stayed on the west side of the hotel. For better surveillance. Only then they had been surprised.

Shoving another clip into the AK, Hagen surveyed the room. Another dump. A moldy mattress, shit on the floor. He checked the window. The Magellan sat at the lowest point of a natural declivity. It had once been dune, Hagen imagined. But soil had eventually replaced sand, and then weeds, shrubs and finally trees had begun to sprout. It had probably taken centuries. And now Hagen was stuck here. He didn't like the proposition.

But how to get it back on terms he was familiar with, comfortable with? Hagen scanned the lip of the big bowl and saw no one. If it was truly him against the two at the end of the corridor—forget Sturua, he had never had any use for the Romanian anyway—he should be able to make something out of his circumstances. But what?

The corridor outside was a loser. With two against one, and whatever that fucking gun they had to boot, he needed a different approach. Hagen checked the lip of the bowl again. Still nothing. Then he studied the window casing more closely. The Magellan had been built in the early days, when architects and city planners from Europe happily made the long journey, but only because of the fat commissions. Whoever had designed the Magellan, in the days before air-conditioning, had specified thick mortar walls. The window

casings were deeply recessed, to help shut out the heat, especially on
the upper floors. Hagen took another careful check of the tangled
gardens, running his eyes over every bit of ground to the top of the
bowl. It was nearly 8 A.M., and the bright sun promised a beautiful
day. If only he could figure out how to survive it.

Carefully, he leaned out the window. The deep window casings
provided easy footholds. But the windows were spaced about ten feet
apart or so, two to a room. Hagen was in 212. But Sturua was in 222.
That made five rooms between them, ten windows in all. But how to
get from room to room on the outside of the building? Besides its
thick walls, the Magellan had been handsomely designed. It wasn't
Hagen's taste, but the place was meant to convey a sense of opulence,
and the architect had done that, not just by the festive pink paint
that had been mixed into the cement as it was being poured, but by
the wedding-cake white trim in the eaves and above the first-floor
windows.

Hagen studied more closely. The first-floor windows were high
and formal, capped by carved marble crowns. By using the tops of the
marble crowns and stepping up an easy four feet to the second-floor
window casings, Hagen figured he could make his way to room 222
with some difficulty but not much. He would have to hope that parts
of the old hotel didn't give way beneath him. But he preferred those
odds to the long odds of the dark corridor.

Surprise, Hagen thought. His trusty ally.

GUB moved slowly, keeping each foot at the far edges of the kitchen
stairs. There were probably one-by-twos under the edges, he thought,
and they would give and groan less than the middle of the stairs,
which had sung their arrival a few minutes before.

Sweating, the perspiration stinging the cuts around his eyes, Gub
finally made it down to the kitchen. The smell seemed even more
overpowering than before, and he made his way quickly to the front
of the hotel.

His options were simple. He could take the main stairs from the
ruined lobby in front of the old concierge's desk. Or he could go back
to the north end of the hotel and look for another, less obvious set of
stairs like the one he and Mireles had found on their way to the
Romanian's room.

Hugging the walls in the lobby, he studied the tiny shards of broken glass from the skylight above. The bright sunlight made them shine like flecks of gold. He looked up and saw that the blast from his grandfather's gun had taken out what was left of the entire skylight, a huge hole at the top of the Magellan.

Gub ducked back inside the pocket door where he had met Mireles. It seemed like hours ago. Padre Francisco! Gub cursed himself for not thinking straight.

From the topmost pane of the casement window where he had fired the second blast from the elephant gun, Gub could see the Franciscan clearly. The old man was gesturing frantically with his three-iron. Upstairs, he was indicating.

Gub knew what was up there, but what could the priest be seeing from the car park? He couldn't tell if the priest knew he was watching him or not, but Gub had no doubt Padre Francisco saw something. He decided to see what it was.

STEPPING gingerly onto the first of the marble cornices and testing it, Hagen told himself: "Go with what you know." He knew surprise, and that was what he was betting on. The AK-47 strapped over his shoulder with a piece of cord, his stiletto strapped to the calf of his leg, Hagen figured that with luck he could be outside Sturua's room inside of ten minutes.

It was risky, but it did have the element of surprise. And the odds were a hell of a lot better than taking his chances in that hallway. He was convinced of that.

GUB poked his head out the front door of the Magellan, and Padre Francisco spotted him immediately. Gub thought he was going to sail into orbit the way he was gesticulating with the three-iron, but he followed the priest's point. It was off to his left and up.

"Hagen," he said to himself. Even from there, he could see that the man fit the description Mireles had given him from the Germans' Sicherungsgruppe file.

Gub checked his grandfather's gun and reached for another round from the pouch on his belt. He had just three left. He loaded one and strode out into the courtyard, stepping around a cracked, footed tub and two splintered porcelain toilet bowls.

Hagen heard the noise Gub's feet made on the gravel immediately, and he turned awkwardly, suspended like a cat, on a window casing in the room next to Sturua's.

Gub raised the rifle and called to Mireles. Hagen tried to grab for his AK-47, but Gub waved the elephant gun at him and he stopped. "Right there, Hagen. Just a minute, now."

At the sound of his name, Hagen stared at Gub more closely.

Gub yelled up for Mireles again, and this time his head appeared at the edge of the window. "It's okay, Tom. Take a look out, and I think you will see our friend Otto Hagen. Formerly of the Stasi. Now thinks he's some kind of Spiderman or something."

Mireles pushed the broken window open wider and stared at the ex-Stasi man for several seconds. "Mr. Hagen, I'm with the FBI, and you are in more trouble than I can possibly describe to you in these circumstances."

From the ground, Gub watched curiously. It was a good beginning, but this wasn't how he had envisioned things playing out. He didn't know what he had had in mind. He did know this wasn't it, however.

Mireles talked while Gub watched. "We've got lots of things to talk about, Hagen. The Libyans and the La Belle disco. The American troop-train bombings." He was thinking fast. "We got poor Mr. César Ochoa in Barcelona, and then the American diplomat, the one who was killed when Detective Gub's jeep blew up."

Hagen was crouching on the window casing, mute.

Mireles started to continue, but then Gub saw his face go red, and he fell from the window.

Sturua!

Hagen used the moment to grab the AK-47, and Padre Francisco yelled from across the courtyard.

Gub already saw it, though. He had just the one shot with the elephant gun, and he wanted to make it count. "Don't do it, Hagen. There'll be nothing left but little pieces."

Hagen got the Chinese rifle around in front of him.

"Big mistake, man. Big, big mistake."

The Stasi man lifted the AK-47 to his hip, calmly.

In these circumstances, Gub didn't like calm. "Little, itty-bitty pieces, Hagen. Think about it."

The Stasi man lurched.

Gub simply reacted. He squeezed the trigger softly, and then took a breath. The window casing above him was red with bright blood, shards of wood and bits of glass exploding around it. There was a piece of what looked like blue work shirt floating in an updraft near the rain gutter in the sunshine, but Gub was already vaulting the wide stairs up from the lobby and racing to the room at the end of the corridor, swearing.

On the second floor, he looked quickly into the room where Hagen was. The face and most of the head were gone, along with a considerable portion of the upper body. Itty-bitty pieces. Gub had warned him. He had also aimed high, he thought, running to the end of the hall towards Mireles.

He was still a few yards away from Sturua's door when he heard Mireles's voice. Thank God, he thought. Then he stood in the splintered doorway, amazed.

"Asshole head-butted me." Mireles was in a fighter's crouch. The Romanian was far bigger than Mireles. But Mireles had been a weight lifter for as long as Gub had known him. For a guy five ten, he was amazingly strong. And quick.

On the far side of the room, Sturua had a dark welt under one eye, and his nose was pushed to one side.

Mireles stared at Gub, an unspoken question.

"Hagen's dead."

"Serves him right. Another asshole."

Gub hadn't seen Mireles like this in years. He smiled.

"Our friend here slipped out of your knots, and now he's got to decide whether he wants to go with or without a fight."

"Looks like he's already been in a fight."

"He hasn't seen anything yet. Our friend says he's from the Securitate. This place is lousy with old commies."

Gub could see that Sturua was fighting more out of anger and frustration than anything else. And he was not a good fighter, even under far better circumstances. Gub had left the elephant gun on the grass outside, but he still had the M-16. Somehow, though, as the Romanian closed with Mireles, he didn't think he would need it.

Sturua moved slowly, bearlike. Despite his longer reach, he was no match. The Romanian closed to within four feet of Mireles, and the smaller man rabbit-punched him twice around the eyes. Next Sturua went for a roundhouse left, but Mireles ducked under it and came up fast, landing a lightning-quick series of combinations on the bigger man's rib cage and belly before he stepped back. Stung, Sturua lunged with his left again. Mireles was much too fast and thorough. It was almost as if they had practiced the move together. Except that with the Romanian off balance after the left, Mireles planted both feet carefully, and then threw every one of his 155 pounds into an evil right-handed uppercut.

Gub felt the blow in his shoes.

The Romanian fell into the rat shit he had worked so hard to avoid the past couple of days, and as Mireles stepped over him, they both saw Sturua's eyes roll back in his head.

Gub was impressed. "You haven't lost much."

Mireles laughed, wiping his mouth with the back of his hand. "And you tie lousy knots."

By the time they got Sturua outside, it was a gorgeous morning. Padre Francisco had collected Gub's elephant gun from the beaten grass near the courtyard of the Magellan. Then he had insisted on administering last rites to Hagen, even though he was already dead. After that they adjourned to the sun porch, while Gub decided whether to ask Nicholas Sturua his questions right away or help himself to something from the cooler he had discovered near the ragged hammock Hagen had mended two days earlier. Since Sturua was still groggy, but more because the three of them were famished, Gub, Mireles and Padre Francisco decided it made more sense to eat first, especially once they saw what Sturua and Hagen had pilfered from the medicine man's icebox. There were the boiled lobsters and the beer. They would do nicely, Gub thought. For starters anyway.

These guys have pretty good taste, Mireles said. For commies.

TWENTY

GUB left Mireles watching Sturua on the Magellan's sun porch while he and the priest kept a lookout from a second-floor room for the medicine man. The cold beer had tasted good after the morning's exertions. Padre Francisco had even split his with Sturua, pouring half a bottle of Beck's down the grateful Romanian's throat. Gub decided to hold off on the lobsters, however, after it became clear Sturua really didn't know what the game plan was. He had insisted that he hadn't spoken directly to Viktor Alleja; Hagen had. Sturua knew only that they were supposed to come to the Magellan and wait for the medicine man there. He would set them up with a new place to operate from.

Padre Francisco poked him in the shoulder with his three-iron. "Two men." The priest handed him the Leitz glasses.

Using the ragged curtain for cover, Gub held the binoculars to his damaged eyes. The large man in the black tunic with the cane he recognized immediately: Paul Achebe. The smaller man was the Brit, Archie, the medicine man's factotum. They were still maybe a thousand yards away, picking their way carefully down the washed-out gravel drive towards the cracked courtyard with the plumbing fixtures. No way to get a vehicle down here, Gub thought. He snapped off the safety on the M-16 and rechecked the ammo clip. He had already instructed Padre Francisco how to pat someone down. They went over it again, quickly. Then Gub and the priest went downstairs to wait.

Achebe and Archie were crossing the last stretch of courtyard before the Magellan's sagging entryway when Gub stepped into the doorway. "If you've got a weapon on you, Paul, put it down on the ground and kick it away. The same for your friend."

The priest stepped out from behind Gub to watch.

"Detective Gub!"

The look of surprise on the big man's face was gratifying. The medicine man had been operating right under his nose all this time, sheltering and paying Sturua and Hagen.

"No, we are not armed."

Gub didn't believe the big man, and the little Brit was twitchy. "I'm going to keep this thing trained right on your big belly, Paul. It's a machine gun, so if you make a move I don't like, or your friend does, it will take about a half a second to kill the both of you. Understood?"

The two men nodded.

"Next, I'm going to ask my friend Padre Francisco here to frisk you. Don't try anything with the Padre either. He's been killed once, and it doesn't bother him. I'll shoot regardless."

The two men looked at each other, and the big man shrugged his shoulders as Padre Francisco shuffled across the courtyard in his brown robes. It took him a minute to run his hands over the two men, checking their waistbands, trouser legs and under the armpits. He gestured to Gub with both hands: nothing.

Gub couldn't believe the men were unarmed. With the M-16 on Achebe and Archie, he walked out from the hotel doorway and circled the medicine man and the Brit slowly, checking for telltale bulges. Amazing, he thought, finally satisfied. "Let's go inside."

They walked slowly through the Magellan's double front doors into the filthy lobby, a carpet of shattered glass crunching under their shoes. Out back on the sun porch, Mireles was already standing, his M-16 resting easily in his arms. Sturua sat morosely, evidently lost in thought on one of the three usable chairs he and Hagen had found in the hotel's dining room the night before.

"Company." Gub made introductions to Mireles, gesturing the medicine man and the Brit into the remaining two chairs. "I think you want to keep an eye on Archie. He didn't like our little welcome out front, I don't think." Gub had seen the type many times before, the milky blue eyes in the sun-battered face. There were old RAF guys just like Archie all over the continent, barnstorming the bush, pretending times hadn't changed.

While Mireles kept his gun on them, Gub got more cord and bound the hands of the new arrivals. "In the interest of time, Paul, maybe I'll fill you in on things. If you don't mind."

"Please." The big man was placid, relaxed, even with his hands tied behind him.

"This is Mr. Nicholas Sturua. From Bucharest, I believe. He's the fellow who shot Afonso in your sitting room."

Sturua looked up briefly, and Paul Achebe regarded him with interest.

"Mr. Otto Hagen, Mr. Sturua's associate, is dead. Unfortunately, I had to shoot him."

Sturua straightened again, his eyes clouded. "I tell you, I wouldn't worry about that asshole. He's the guy who waxed your buddy, the young guy at the presidential palace. And he's the guy who's been blowing all the shit up the last few days."

Gub filed that away and continued. "So there has been a considerable amount of unpleasantness, Paul. And if I understand things right, you have played no small part in it, lending these gentlemen your house and paying them to distribute the severed heads around the city. And to conduct these bombings. Now what I want to know is why, and specifically what Viktor Alleja has to do with it. You remember Viktor, of course."

Paul Achebe breathed a deep sigh. "Detective Gub," he began, "you have known me for several years, and in that time, I believe, I have not acquired a reputation as a violent man."

Gub recalled the story of the highwayman with the broken limbs, but he kept his face blank.

"You may not know this, but I knew your wife, Teresa. Perhaps even better than you did. In any case, from her I learned a great deal about you, about your integrity. So I hope you will believe me when you hear what I have to say."

Gub locked on the big man's pink eyes. If he was trying to bait him, it wouldn't work.

"I met Viktor Alleja many years ago, when I was still working in the mines in Johannesburg. The dormitories the miners lived in were very political, but I wasn't interested, then or now. What I was interested in was money. Then as now. And Viktor paid me regular sums to inform on the troublemakers in the dormitories. I'm not ashamed of that. After I came to Fado, we renewed our acquaintance, but I was not as interested as before. I had money by then, and I was enjoying my work with the people in the squatters' camps, and there was very little he could do for me with his pretentious hotel project. It was that way for a long time. Until you came to arrest him, in fact. He had heard about it—I don't know from whom, that is the truth—and he came to me for help. I hid him in my house for one day, and he gave me a withdrawal slip for his company's construction account. I took everything out, $187,000. Then I took $25,000 for myself. That was my fee. Viktor didn't like it, but I thought it was fair, considering his predicament. Besides, it included Archie flying him out of the country on my plane."

So that's how Viktor Alleja had escaped.

"I heard almost nothing from Viktor Alleja for most of the past two years. Until recently. In Johannesburg, I knew Viktor Alleja as a serious man, not one for wild schemes. Practical. In Fado, however, he was changed. Bitter over what had happened to him in the Directorate there. But also with wild ideas about money. The hotel project he talked about constantly. And his big house, that small man living all alone in the mansion off Avenida 21 July. You remember it? It was pretentiousness, foolishness. In any case, when he reestablished contact—he was living in Lisbon then—his ideas were even more wild. He spoke of toppling the government. And you will enjoy this, I think: he spoke of installing me as the new president."

The medicine man paused, but nobody laughed.

"So I encouraged him. I didn't believe he was serious, but I knew he was paying Afonso. I was the conduit. And he was raising money from different places. Johannesburg, Lisbon and the States. When Viktor asked me to make my house available for two of his associates, I still didn't believe him. Of course I charged him for the place, and for stocking it with food and liquor. But it all seemed unreal. A dream."

Gub could see how the poor people in Fado's slums were lulled by the man. He didn't believe Paul Achebe for an instant, and he looked up, and Mireles shot him the fisheye under a cocked eyebrow. Another skeptic. Still, the man was captivating. It wasn't his size or whatever skill he had as a *curandeiro* that wowed the people; it was his presence, his solidity.

"So," the medicine man concluded, "that is the story. I didn't see anything wrong with putting the heads around the city. 'Operation Head Count.' Do you know that's what Viktor called it? Wild, but not so wild. And it might have worked. Truthfully, I don't believe there is any hope for this government, and perhaps what comes after will be better."

"Except that the heads came from living human beings, sir. People with families and loved ones." Padre Francisco had said nothing since Paul Achebe and Archie arrived. "You see nothing wrong in simply killing people in order to use their heads as symbols of terror?" The priest was white-faced.

The medicine man looked at the priest, confused, as if seeing him for the first time. "These are brutal times, Father, in a difficult place. I never paid much attention to what Afonso and his bandits were doing in the countryside, but I knew from my people in the camps. With all due respect, Father, violence is as much a part of this place as the air and the water."

"What about the bombings?" Gub rubbed his eyes.

"The bombings came as a great sorrow to me." The medicine man turned his gaze from the priest to the detective. "Especially the Lisboa. That was not in the plan. Viktor Alleja said nothing about it to me."

Gub blinked. The big man was lying, that was clear. But what was strange was the utter lack of remorse. He didn't even seem to understand the premise of Padre Francisco's question, that there could be something wrong and inhuman with killing people merely to use their heads as a terrorist's totems. Under his tunic, Paul Achebe made the muscles in his shoulders ripple, and Mireles trained the M-16 on his midsection.

"It is not an especially pleasant tale, but there it is." The medicine man stopped flexing his muscles and stared at Gub. "So where does this leave us, Detective?"

While the big man was talking, Gub had settled on the beginnings of a plan. Paul Achebe had plenty to pay for, but Viktor Alleja had more. If he managed things right, perhaps he could use the one to get the other. He had a question first, however, and it mattered. "How did you know Teresa?"

Paul Achebe sighed again.

Mireles and Sturua seemed captivated by the big man. Padre Francisco had already turned away from the group, however, while Gub waited intently for the answer. Only Archie seemed profoundly bored, scratching his crotch.

"A dalliance, Detective. She was at one of her projects up the coast. It was right after she got her pilot's license. I happened to be working there that day. High winds made it unsafe to fly, so we sheltered our planes and stayed in the village. It was nothing, a few months. Then the two of you were married. A sorrow to me, but we kept in touch, just every so often. Your wife was a very beautiful woman. You were lucky."

It was the second time in as many days he had been told how lucky he was. Somehow, he didn't feel lucky. Gub felt a surge of emotion, then forced himself to shake it off. Not now, he thought. Instead, he looked the medicine man squarely in the face, locking on his pink eyes. "What I would like you to do, Paul, is make a phone call."

The big man looked up at him with interest.

Mireles kept his M-16 on the medicine man, watching Gub. It was his op. But Mireles wasn't sure what he had in mind.

Gub asked Padre Francisco to fetch the radiophone from where he had hidden it, behind the pile of broken furniture in the Magellan's breakfast room. "I want you to call Viktor, tell him things are going according to plan. Tell him you have taken me hostage, and that it's time for him to return and direct the last phase of Operation Head Count. You can send Archie to pick him up wherever he wants, but you stay here until this is over."

"And then what, Detective?"

"And then we see." There was plenty he could charge the medicine man with. But the prize was Viktor Alleja. Gub was sure the old arrest warrant for him was still good. But he hadn't worked that part of the plan out yet.

A smile spread across Paul Achebe's face. He smelled a deal, a way out. "Where's the phone?"

The priest was already shuffling through the broken French doors onto the sun porch with the radiophone in its nylon backpack. Mireles rested his assault rifle on the low stone wall of the sun porch and began laying out the small cone dish and cable while Gub kept his M-16 on Sturua, the *curandeiro* and his pilot. When Mireles turned the thing on, it crackled to life. In the bright morning sun, the light playing off the waves, it took just a few seconds for it to crank up. When Mireles signaled that it was ready, Gub covered him, and Mireles untied the medicine man and gave him the handset. The big man studied it for an instant before punching the numbers in.

Gub and Mireles watched silently. The medicine man knew the number by heart.

Viktor Alleja answered on the second ring.

"Success," the big man said.

"What the hell does that mean? Where are Hagen and Sturua?"

They couldn't hear terribly well, but the tone came through the SATCOM phone clear enough. Gub thought that Viktor Alleja sounded tense, overwrought.

In his chair near the radiophone, Sturua pulled a face, and Gub waved the M-16 at him.

"Here, with me, Viktor. The bombings have been going splendidly. And they have captured the detective, the one who was interfering with the heads."

"Excellent, Paul, that's excellent."

"Things are beginning to go our way. Fado was a very soft target, as you said. But now I think it is time for you to begin supervising things directly, as we discussed."

There was the briefest of pauses, Mireles, Gub and Sturua waiting for the reply as the medicine man cradled the handset, relaxed. There was no trace of emotion this time in the voice that came across on the receiver. "You will send Archie for me?"

"It will cost, but naturally, Viktor."

"Screw the cost. Do you want to be president or not?"

Paul Achebe pulled a face at Gub, smirked, and spoke into the receiver again. "Yes, yes, I'll have him meet you. In fact I shall come myself."

The medicine man was a very good actor, Gub thought, but he had no intentions of letting Paul Achebe out of his sight. He listened some more as Viktor Alleja dictated the plans for a rendezvous the next day, Paul Achebe interjecting a "Very good, Viktor" every now and then.

At first, Gub thought it was a trap, the medicine man's offer to meet Viktor Alleja in person. The more he thought about it, however, the more he saw it as an opportunity. With the big man still on the phone, he began revising his original plan. Mireles could take Sturua back to Fado with the priest and have Carlos send someone for Hagen's body. And he would go with the medicine man and the pilot to meet Viktor. That way he could keep an eye on both of them instead of letting them split up. He would still have to decide what to do about Viktor Alleja, but that would take some thinking.

Paul Achebe finally rang off, and he went over the details of the plans dictated by Viktor Alleja. When he was done, Gub announced his plan. Padre Francisco looked at Gub uncertainly, but Mireles seemed to know what he had in mind. He nodded briefly to Gub, and Sturua shrugged. The priest toyed with his Ernst Leitz glasses but said nothing. Mireles reassembled the SATCOM phone while Gub held the M-16 on Sturua, the medicine man and Archie. Within five minutes, Gub in the rear, the group was moving back out through the Magellan's ruined lobby.

Gub ordered the medicine man, Archie and Sturua to walk up the washed-out gravel drive ahead of them. Mireles had his M-16 cradled in his arms while Gub wrestled with his grandfather's elephant gun and the other assault rifle. Padre Francisco followed with the SAT-COM phone and his three-iron. It took nearly ten minutes to reach the medicine man's Lincoln Town Car. The Save the Children Land-Rover was another ten minutes on foot, and Gub planned to leave the blue Yugo Sturua and Hagen had driven to the Magellan two nights before.

Mireles worried about Gub handling the big man and the pilot by himself. Gub was determined, however, and they said their goodbyes hurriedly.

Gub stowed the SATCOM radio and elephant gun in its cracked leather case in the Lincoln's enormous trunk. He kept the M-16 with him as he climbed in the backseat, the Chief's Special in the shoulder holster bunching up his dirty white oxford. Archie was already in the driver's seat, and the medicine man in the passenger's seat beside him. Gub pressed the button for the power window, and it slid down silently. "So you'll talk to Carlos, and I'll see you in a couple of days."

"No sweat." His play, Mireles thought, again.

"Thanks, Tom." Gub waved to Padre Francisco. "You're a brave man, Father. I owe you both."

The priest swung the three-iron and gave Paul Achebe a bleak look. "The pleasure was mine, Detective. Watch these bastards. And don't hesitate to shoot them if they give you any trouble. They deserve far worse."

Gub unholstered the Chief's Special and signaled Archie to go. Paul Achebe gave the priest another mystified look, and Gub saluted as the Lincoln moved off slowly. Through the dirty back window, he saw Mireles wave the M-16 at Sturua while the priest took another swing with the three-iron. The Lincoln lurched onto the narrow road to the coast highway, a big dust cloud in its wake. Out the narrow back window of the sedan, Gub watched as Mireles, the priest and the Romanian got smaller in the swirling air. Then they were gone altogether.

In the back of the Lincoln, Gub had plenty of time to think, and they were nearly to the medicine man's chalet when he settled on the last phase of his plan.

Two Calamidades guards were sitting on the wide front porch of Paul Achebe's chalet, and they bolted to attention when Archie wheeled the Lincoln into the drive. A fish eagle screamed from somewhere in the papyrus as Gub climbed out of the car and waved to the guards. They recognized him immediately. Presumably, the two men had removed Afonso's body from the leather Barcalounger in Paul Achebe's study and secured the place, as Carlos had promised. Archie came around the front of the car to get the door for the medicine man, and Gub covered them both with the M-16. Paul Achebe uncoiled himself from the padded seat, and Gub remarked again to himself at the man's size. He hoped like hell he wouldn't have to tangle with him.

"Home, sweet home, Paul." The Calamidades guards approached from the front porch, and Gub instructed them to open the place up. They would be staying overnight, and the big man and the little Brit would be placed under constant guard. Gub couldn't remember the names of the two Calamidades men, but they were brisk and efficient, unloading the elephant gun and the SATCOM radio from the trunk of the Lincoln and frog-marching Archie ahead of them towards the house. Gub lagged behind with the medicine man, reviewing his plan once more for holes. There was plenty he didn't like about it, mainly the part about letting Paul Achebe skate free so easily. But the medicine man was right about one thing, Gub thought: these were brutal times in a difficult place. Work with what you got.

The fish eagle screamed again, further off this time in the papyrus, and the big man eyed Gub speculatively. He had said nothing since they had gotten in the car near the Magellan.

Gub cradled the M-16. "This is the proposition, Paul, and I'm only going to state it once, and you don't have much choice about it at the end."

The medicine man was standing near a tuft of papyrus, prodding it with his cane. "Why is that, Detective?"

"Because if you don't accept it, Paul, I'm going to use that fucking elephant gun the boys just brought into the house, and I'm going to blow you and your little friend Archie from here to kingdom come."

The medicine man poked at the papyrus some more. "I see."

"The proposition is this: I want you to make one more phone call. I want you to tell Afonso's people up near Plumtree what happened to him. I want you to tell them the truth. I want you to tell them that the man who shot Afonso through the head was hired and paid by Viktor Alleja."

The medicine man interrupted. "Those people won't give a good goddamn, Detective. Most of them despised Afonso. They were scared shitless of him, many of them."

"Tell them anyway. But I also want you to tell them about Viktor. About all the money he's been spooning off all these years. My friend Padre Francisco says the bandits are filthy and half starved. Maybe they'd be interested in knowing about Viktor Alleja's big house in Fado, about his digs in Lisbon. I bet they're nice. I remember how he liked to eat. I bet the bandits would be interested in knowing how he used the money he raised for the bandits to eat in a bunch of fancy restaurants."

"That, I'm not so sure about."

"Then make it up." Having come to his decision, Gub thought there was no point in debating niceties.

The medicine man smiled. "Make them mad, you mean?"

"That's right. Tell them how he sold them out, stealing their money, then hiring these so-called pros from Europe."

"Then what?"

"Arrange a meeting. After we pick up Viktor tomorrow, he ought to have a chance to visit the field, see his brave shock troops out in the bush. He'd like that, don't you think?"

The medicine man stopped stabbing at the papyrus and looked up. "What's in it for me?"

"Depends on how things turn out, Paul. Me, I intend to come on back to Fado on the plane. You and Viktor go to your meeting with the bandits. You set up the place. Afterwards, you can have Archie come back and pick you up."

Paul Achebe smiled. "But not Viktor."

Gub gestured with the M-16 towards the front porch. "Well, like I say, Paul, that just depends. Now let's us go and make that call, okay?"

Paul Achebe strolled up the slate walk that wound its way through the mounded papyrus. On the front porch, he turned to say something, but Gub gestured with the M-16 again and he changed his mind. Inside, the two Calamidades guards had handcuffed Archie and set him on a couch in the medicine man's study. Gub asked one of them to unpack the SATCOM radio, and handed the M-16 to the other while he set it up, remembering how Mireles had done it. He ran the cable over to the window, opened it, and hooked it up to the little cone dish, which he placed on the ledge outside. Waves crashed in the distance.

Gub turned back to the medicine man and reclaimed his M-16 from the Calamidades man, flicking the safety off and double-checking the ammunition clip. "So?"

"Put it away, will you?" The big man was already sitting down next to Archie on the couch and leafing through a small address book he had pulled from the breast pocket of his tunic. Finding the number he wanted, he punched it into the SATCOM set and waited a long time before someone answered.

Gub listened as Paul Achebe explained about Afonso, Viktor Alleja and the money. The man was good, Gub conceded once again. A born persuader.

The big man arranged the details of the meeting for the following afternoon, repeated them slowly for the man on the other end. Then he rang off, set the handset back in its cradle, looked up at Gub and smiled. "Done, Detective. Satisfied?"

Gub instructed the shorter of the two Calamidades guards to handcuff the medicine man, and after he did, Gub snapped the M-16's safety back on. "Why so easy, Paul?"

"I'm a businessman, Detective. It's what I do, evaluate options and make decisions based on them."

Gub was tired and his eyes ached. "Just what options are you talking about, Paul?"

The medicine man smiled wide. "Precisely my point, Detective. Precisely."

GUB couldn't say much that was good about Paul Achebe, but the big man did have style. Flying north the next afternoon at twelve thousand feet in the medicine man's customized Cessna, Gub sipped from a glass of warm Laphroaig with a single ice cube. Across the dinette table, installed where the Cessna's standard seat configuration used to be, the medicine man sipped from a flute of champagne. Gub didn't catch the label.

"So you're sure about this, Detective, are you?"

Gub had run it all through his head the night before. After removing their handcuffs to let Paul Achebe and Archie eat, the Calamidades guards had put the cuffs back on, and Gub had given the M-16 to the shorter one while he stretched out on the floor to rest.

He would have loved to ask the medicine man what he and Teresa had talked about, what they had done together. She had never even mentioned the medicine man to Gub, another part of her secret life. That was the problem, Gub thought, the real reason things wouldn't have worked out: Teresa really hadn't needed him, or probably anyone else, for that matter. For that reason, Gub felt it better not to ask.

More history, he thought. Who needs it?

Instead, he focused on the plan. He wasn't especially proud of it, but he had to take into account some tough facts. Work with what you got. As much as he might like to put Viktor Alleja on trial on the old charges, and stack a host of new ones on top, the country was just too screwed up to pull off that kind of exercise. Ditto with Paul Achebe. With their money and connections, Viktor Alleja and Paul Achebe could come up with 101 ways to wire a trial.

Besides, the key was Viktor Alleja, not the medicine man. Viktor Alleja had skated free twice before, Gub thought; third time pays for all. And that's where the medicine man came in.

He stared across the dinette at the big man, the Chief's Special on the table in front of him. "I'm sure, Paul. But you don't deliver, and you'll see me behind you every waking hour. You'll see me in your fucking dreams, pal."

The medicine man, resplendent in a white tunic, raised his flute of champagne and smiled.

Gub sipped his Scotch and worried, and thirty minutes later Archie banked the little Cessna gently over a hard clay pan, and Gub could see a Mercedes truck shimmering in the shade of a sturdy acacia. Viktor Alleja was waiting.

Two minutes later, the plane bumped down, and Archie taxied up close to the acacia, but not too close. Gub had given him instructions earlier.

The medicine man climbed out of his seat and pressed the wrinkles from his tunic with his hands. "I'll go meet him."

Gub grabbed the Chief's Special and aimed it at the big man's stomach. "And I'll be right here."

Out the window a minute later, he could see Paul Achebe bending awkwardly to embrace the shorter man in the starched shirt and the dark suit. Greetings and congratulations. Five minutes more, and Archie and the truck driver were humping expensive Gurkha luggage into the nose of the Cessna while Viktor Alleja and the medicine man chatted amiably. The big man really was quite an actor.

The luggage stowed, Archie climbed in first.

Then Viktor Alleja got in behind him.

Gub was standing in the center aisle next to the dinette. He aimed the Chief's Special at the center of the shorter man's starched Bijan shirt, focusing on the diamond pin that kept the handsome burgundy tie in place.

Viktor Alleja turned on his small legs, his face the color of beets. But Paul Achebe was right behind him, all 270 pounds of him. The shorter man looked from the medicine man to the detective and back again, and then Gub said, "Welcome home, Viktor." Then they all had a seat around the little dinette table.

Archie wound the engines and rolled the plane down the brown pan. The Cessna cleared the top of the acacia, and Gub saw gulls off in the distance. The plane's little engines thrummed like bumblebees.

Paul Achebe had said it would be only seventy minutes' flying time to the drop-off near Plumtree, and Gub stared out the window as the tumbled landscape flew below. He kept the Chief's Special on the table in front of him, but according to the terms of the deal, Viktor Alleja was the medicine man's charge now. The two sat side by side on the other side of the dinette table, and Gub thought it was just as well there was no conversation.

When Archie eased the Cessna down in a field of flattened grass just over an hour later, Viktor Alleja's eyes darted from Gub to the medicine man and back to Gub again.

Gub turned the question over in his mind a final time, and still he came up with the same answer. Outside, he saw a mud-spattered Mitsubishi four-wheel drive and six ragged men leaning against it. One had a large knife. The medicine man got up first, but Gub made no move to do so. "Viktor, I'm afraid this is where you and me part company."

The small man's ruddy color deepened perceptibly, right to the line of the salt-and-pepper crew cut. "The problem with you, Gub, is you don't understand. You never did understand."

Gub put the Chief's Special back in its holster and sighed. "Well that may be, Viktor. And maybe you could even fill me in on some of these things it is I don't understand. But it looks like you're keeping folks waiting out in the heat there, and me, I've really got a plane to get, back to Fado."

The medicine man gave Viktor Alleja a tug on his dark Aquascutum, and Gub studied the flattened grass out the window, the little man in his head rolling tape of pastoral scenes, birds flying, a swan on a lake. The next thing Gub knew, Archie was winding the engines again, and when the Cessna dipped its wings over the empty field below, Gub could still make out a tall man in white, a short man in a dark suit and six skinny guys hovering around a muddy jeep. He figured it was probably just a few minutes' flying time back to Fado.

If they were lucky, he'd be there in time for dinner.

TWENTY-ONE

~~~~~~~~~~~~~~~~~~~~~~~~~~~~~~~~

ANNA-MARIE's report was a model of clarity, if not absolute veracity. It included the sworn statement of Nicholas Sturua, wherein the former Securitate man confessed to the distribution of ten severed heads within the jurisdiction of the Fado Capital District Constabulary. Gub had had to dispatch a Calamidades man to the international-arrivals lounge at Henry International to find the only head he had been unable to account for. The young inspector finally located it in a maintenance closet, and a cleaning lady confessed to having hid it; she had been afraid to tell anyone about it for fear of losing her job.

Sturua had also confessed to the shooting of Afonso, and assisting Hagen with the bombings of the presidential staff's executive offices, the apartment complex in the new embassy district and the Hotel Lisboa. Anna-Marie's report documented a total of eleven deaths in the three bombings, including that of Eduardo Antonio Sebastião, the Lisboa's proprietor.

Sturua swore under oath that both he and Hagen had been paid by one Viktor Alleja. His statement ran to sixty-three double-spaced pages, and Carlos examined it intently for typos.

Amazingly, there were none.

In addition to the lengthy Sturua statement, Gub's earliest reports to the Justice Ministry and the president on the activities of Viktor Alleja and Costa do Sol Ltd. were included to supplement the record, as was an annotated copy of the Amnesty International report implicating "business interests" in Fado in the support for the bandits. The original arrest warrant for Viktor Alleja was appended to the file, and Gub noted that it was, in fact, still valid.

There was also a statement from Thomas Mireles, formerly of Fado, now of Locust Valley, New York. A duly authorized representative of the United States Federal Bureau of Investigation, coincidentally in Fado on personal business, Mireles testified briefly before a court reporter that the Bureau would be providing copies of its own reports on Viktor Alleja's fund-raising activities in America, as well as any other relevant documents from sister law-enforcement and intelligence agencies. Should the authorities in Fado decide to extradite Nicholas Sturua to the authorities in Bucharest, Mr. Mireles said, he was authorized by the U.S. Justice Department to assist with the transfer of Nicholas Sturua from Fado to Romania. Nowhere in the Mireles statement was it mentioned that Sturua's return to Bucharest meant almost certain death. And neither was there a statement from the authorities in Fado as to the Romanian's likely fate should he remain in Fado; in both instances, the odds of his survival were embarrassingly low.

Carlos had spared no expense in completing the official record. He had even authorized a special supplemental to the department's budget in order to pay Dr. Pran for an official coroner's report on Otto Hagen. That, too, had been added into the record, along with Dr. Pran's official invoice. For $650, Dr. Pran had concluded that the cause of death was massive trauma due to gunshot wound of the upper chest cavity and respiratory tract. It described the collateral but massive damage to Hagen's face and head, but made no mention of an elephant gun. Father Francisco Russi, of the village of Plumtree, also gave a sworn statement, notwithstanding the fact that other records available to the authorities in Fado listed him as deceased. The priest testified that he had witnessed the entire series of events up to and including the shooting of Mr. Otto Hagen by Detective Humberto Gub III. The detective had tried to avoid using force on Mr. Hagen, the priest's statement said, but when Mr. Hagen had attempted to fire his automatic weapon at the detective, the detective had fired with his own weapon.

Finally, there was a long statement from Detective Gub himself relating most but not all of the events between the discovery of the first head on Avenida Vladimir Lenin and the gun battle at the defunct Magellan Hotel and Beach Club at the north end of the Fado Capital District.

The documents were all signed, witnessed and duplicated within thirty-six hours after Gub's return to Fado on the medicine man's modified Cessna. But the record was not yet complete. When they left the department, Gub still needed one more piece for that.

FROM the smell of it, Gub thought, the batch of bouillabaisse on the stove promised to be far better than the last. The odor of garlic suffused the place.

While Matthias played with Save the Children's Crayolas and drawing paper, Betty dabbed at the cuts around Gub's eye, and Gub winced, reaching for his glass of Chardonnay. "Never mind that now." Betty Abell was an impatient and determined nurse. "Let's get this done before it gets infected."

Gub obeyed, winking at Matthias and admiring Betty's tanned legs as she sat on the edge of the ebony table. She was wearing camp shorts and a baggy white oxford she had grabbed earlier from the side of his bed. Gub winced again, then smiled.

In the bedroom, he could hear Mireles, still on with Amy. Gub had spoken with her earlier. They had had a fine time, he had said, and he was looking forward to seeing them in a few months. He would be bringing a friend with him. Yeah, Tom had met her, but, no, it wasn't serious, he lied; not yet.

After he'd gone off to check on the bouillabaisse, Mireles had gotten back on the phone, telling the twins how much he missed them and peppering them with questions about school.

Amy had listened in on the extension. "It sounds like a new you," she said, after the twins got off.

"New and improved, I swear it." He couldn't wait to get home, but it was up in the air whether he would have to go to Bucharest. A lot depended on how much he would put in his report for the attorney general about Hagen and Sturua; a lot would have to be left out. Mireles was explaining when Gub's jury-rigged call-waiting system began to blink. Mireles said he would call back. Then he switched to the other line, spoke for a second with Carlos and summoned Gub from the kitchen.

Carlos came to the point directly. "You're not going to believe this, Gub, but we got another fucking head."

Gub blinked. His eyes stung. "Describe."

"It's right here on my desk in the department. I came in this afternoon, and there it was, just sitting here. I'm looking at the fucking thing now, and there's not even any fucking waxed paper under it. Oh, Christ, what a mess!"

"Chief." Gub waited while Carlos collected himself. He looked up at Betty and Mireles, watching him from the bedroom doorway, silhouetted by the brighter light from the kitchen and dining room. "Describe it now. Slowly."

Carlos reached for another warm beer from the bottom drawer of his desk and took a long pull. "Okay. White guy, maybe mid to late fifties. Heavyset, he must have been. Deep coloring in the face, even now, those little webbed veins near the surface."

"Hair?"

Carlos took another gulp of beer and burped. "Fucking eyebrows gone, just like the others. But the hair, they didn't shave it. It's just real short."

"What color?" God, the man was dense.

"Salt-and-pepper." Carlos sounded suspicious. "You know about this thing already or what, Gub?"

"Hell no." Gub tried to inject a mixture of incredulity and indignation into his voice and did a halfway good job of it.

"Well, what the fuck should we do?"

"You found it, Chief. Better write us up a report."

"You're not going to come in?"

"I was just fixing to have some dinner, Carlos." He winked at Betty and Mireles. Viktor Alleja, the final piece.

"But I don't know the first fucking thing about this."

Gub smiled. "You'll do fine, Chief."

Carlos felt impotent. "What do I do with the head?"

Gub told him he should deliver it to Dr. Pran, but only after he had examined it long enough to describe it accurately in his report.

On the other end of the line, Carlos burped.

Gub lifted his nose to smell the bouillabaisse. It was going to be good. He listened to the silence on the other end of the line, then he wished Carlos luck and hung up.

In the kitchen, he kissed Betty tenderly on the lips and shook hands with Mireles. He stirred the stockpot brimming with dense broth and tasted some from a ladle. At the ebony table, Matthias was still drawing. The picture showed eleven heads sitting in a row. The boy was just finishing off the last one, and Gub swore it had salt-and-pepper hair.

The boy had grass in his own hair, and he looked up at Gub and smiled.

"Piece of cake, Gub?"

Gub nodded and winked back.

"Piece of cake, Matthias. Piece of cake."

broth and tasted some from a ladle. At the ebony table, Matthias was still drawing. The picture showed eleven heads sitting in a row. The boy was just finishing off the last one, and Gub swore it had salt-and-pepper hair.

The boy had grass in his own hair, and he looked up at Gub and smiled.

"Piece of cake, Gub?"

Gub nodded and winked back.

"Piece of cake, Matthias. Piece of cake."